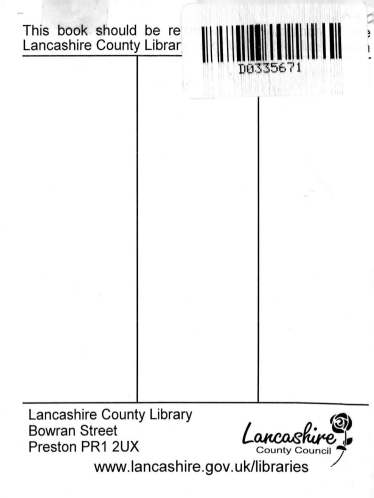

'I reckon it's you,' said Jana, turning round and flashing Kaz a cheeky smile.

'Me?'

'Yeah,' said Jana, teasingly. 'You came back and rescued me and Dora from Quil in 1645. Very heroic, that was. Just like you to do it again, this time in disguise.'

Kaz laughed. 'Maybe, who knows.'

'Seriously, though, do you trust her?' asked Jana.

Kaz was surprised by the question. 'Of course,' he replied. 'Don't you?'

'She freaks me out, Kaz,' said Jana. 'The girl we knew was so sweet. Sure, she was really, really screwed up and capable of mass murder – which of us isn't? – but ninja superhero? Really?'

'You said she was badass,' said Kaz.

'Oh, she's badass all right.'

'And she did save our lives.'

'Yes, I know that, but . . . oh, I dunno,' Jana sighed. 'She's just too different. It's not right. I think she's way more damaged than she lets on. And God knows what stuff Garcia filled her head with. I still can't believe she not only tracked him down, but persuaded him to train her.'

'He was a big deal, huh?' asked Kaz.

'The biggest,' said Jana emphatically. 'He was legendary. Anything unexplained, the press would say it was him. Never identified, never caught. If Dora knows all his secrets, just think of the book she could write. Maybe I can persuade her to tell me it all.'

'Good luck with that,' laughed Kaz. 'She's *so* talkative.'

'Hmmm,' said Jana.

'So what are we going to do, Jana?' asked Kaz after a few moments' silence.

'Do?'

'Next,' said Kaz. 'What are we going to do next? I say we get out of here, set up home in whatever time period we like, forget about Quil, Mars, her war, all of it. It's not our problem.'

Jana shook her head. 'We can't just run away, Kaz,' she said, audibly disappointed at his suggestion.

'Why not?' he asked. 'If Dora's telling the truth and this is all about human rights for mining clones in the distant future, then it's not our fight. We're not clones, and we're not the people oppressing the clones. We were just in the wrong place at the wrong time and we attracted the attention of a homicidal psychopath, that's all. None of us have a personal stake in this.'

Kaz noticed Jana's face register a brief expression of distress, as if he'd said something painful, but before he could question it the moment had passed.

'But don't you want answers?' asked Jana, exasperated. 'Don't you want to know how it is we can travel in time? Or why? Don't you want to find out what we're supposed to have done to Quil on Mars, and how she ended up in 1640 with us at the top of her hit list?'

Kaz shrugged. 'Not really,' he admitted. 'I mean, look what happened when we went looking for Quil. You were stabbed, Dora's brother was stabbed, I lost half my teeth and Dora's so messed up she's turned herself into the Terminator. It's a miracle none of us are dead. Why would we go looking for a rematch?'

'So you just want to run away and hide?' said Jana, her voice scathing.

'Yes, I do,' said Kaz. 'Why not? Quil is like the nutter at

32

a party, you just have to ignore them and eventually they go away and stop bothering you.'

Jana tutted. 'That's pathetic, Kaz,' she said. 'I thought you were the hero type. I thought you were all about the action and adventure.'

Kaz looked down at Jana in the wheelchair, her weakened frame and sunken cheeks, and he thought 'Action and adventure nearly got you killed'. He could have told her that all he really wanted to do was keep her safe, but she wouldn't thank him for the sentiment.

'There's a difference between going on an adventure and trying to get yourself killed,' he said firmly. 'I prefer sharp metal objects to stay outside my body, thanks.'

'I never thought you were a coward, Kaz,' said Jana spitefully.

That hurt, so Kaz bit his tongue, knowing there was nothing he could say that wouldn't escalate the argument.

Ten minutes later, as he pushed the wheelchair towards the hospital again, Jana broke the silence.

'Sorry,' she said quietly. 'I didn't mean that. I know you're not a coward. I just want answers. I want to understand what's going on. And hey, if Quil turns out to be too much of a problem, Dora can just jump back in time and put a bullet in her head.' She turned and looked up at Kaz, smiling sheepishly.

He laughed, relaxing again.

'I wish it were that simple,' he said ruefully.

'As soon as I'm fit enough, I'm going with Dora,' said Jana. 'She and I have agreed we're going to do what Steve suggested. I'd really like it if you came with us, Kaz. I know I can count on you.'

'Of course,' said Kaz, smiling.

What he'd come to realise was that all she'd had to do was ask; he'd follow her to the end of time, if she wanted. But he wasn't going to tell her that.

Not yet, anyway.

Date - Unknown / Location - Unknown

Kaz, Dora and Jana burned into being holding hands in a circle with their backs to each other, facing outwards. The configuration had been Dora's suggestion – she argued that it would allow them to assess their environment more quickly and could save their lives if they materialised on a battlefield, a motorway or somewhere similarly dangerous.

In fact they materialised in darkness, lit moments later when a single fluorescent strip light flickered to life.

'Boring,' said Jana, and Kaz had to agree.

Following Steve's advice, they had joined hands and he and Dora had steered them from Kinshasa as far into the future as they could. Not knowing what to expect, he was disappointed to see that they had arrived in a small window-less room with filing cabinets around the wall and nothing else to recommend it.

'This is a filing cupboard,' said Kaz, incredulously. 'Who uses paper files in the future?'

'Someone with dirty secrets who doesn't want to risk being hacked,' said Dora, drawing her sword.

'And this is where Steve thinks we're supposed to be, is it?' said Jana. 'In this exciting cupboard.'

'Did you feel it, Kaz?' asked Dora.

'If you mean something pulling us here, yes,' he said.

'It was like we were diverted in transit,' agreed Dora. 'Some kind of force, like it was a magnet and we were . . .'

'A fridge?' offered Jana, her voice dripping with sarcasm.

'It was weird, though,' said Kaz. 'Didn't you feel it, Jana?'

'I wasn't steering, was I?' she shot back petulantly, obviously annoyed that her powers were still the most undeveloped.

Jana turned and began trying to open the nearest filing cabinet. 'Locked,' she said after punching and kicking the metal cabinet a few times.

'We could just open the door,' said Dora, reaching for the handle.

But it was locked too.

'Terrific,' said Jana, achieving maximum snark.

'Um, yeah,' said Kaz. 'So do we kick it down or take off again?'

'And go where?' asked Jana. 'This is the only direction we have, so we might as well see it through. Kick the door down, Kaz.'

'Why do I get door-kicking duty?' he protested.

'Because you've got the strongest legs, of course,' she snapped back.

Dora glared at Jana and unleashed a powerful kick at the door, which budged not a millimetre.

'See,' said Jana, folding her arms triumphantly and cocking her head at Kaz.

'You know, there comes a point, Jana, when even my patience with your attitude starts to run out,' he said through gritted teeth.

Before she could fire back a rejoinder, there was the sound of a key in the door and it swung inwards to reveal a tall, chubby Asian man in a brown wool cardigan, jeans and slippers.

He stared at them for a moment in surprise.

'Oh,' he said. 'You've arrived. Finally. What did you land in here for?'

'Um . . .' said Kaz.

'Where are we?' asked Dora, sword raised.

'Shouldn't you be asking when are we?' said the man, his eyes twinkling with amusement.

'You were expecting us?' asked Jana.

'Of course,' said the man. 'A little sooner, really. I was beginning to worry you'd got lost. I put the kettle on when the temporal arrival alarm went off. Come along.'

With that, he turned and walked away down the nondescript windowless corridor.

Kaz, Dora and Jana exchanged puzzled glances, shrugged as one and filed out after him.

'I think you can probably sheathe the sword, Dora,' said Kaz as they followed the man.

She did not.

Kaz patted his ribs, reassured by the gun nestling in his shoulder holster; Dora had insisted they all be armed before they left Kinshasa.

'Are we underground?' asked Jana as they walked.

'No windows, slight smell of damp. Think so,' said Kaz.

The corridor ended in a pair of swing doors through which their unassuming receptionist had passed. Dora led the way, pushing through, sword at the ready. Kaz followed and found himself at the bottom of a stairwell. Their host's footsteps echoed down from above, rattling on the metal staircase as he ascended. The trio followed him up and out through the doors at the top of the stairs, emerging into a familiar chamber – stone-flagged floor, brick walls and barrel-vaulted ceiling.

'Oh crap,' said Kaz, feeling his stomach sink as he recognised the undercroft of Sweetclover Hall.

'Didn't we just leave here?' said Jana. 'And wasn't it about to explode?'

Kaz surveyed the undercroft in astonishment. It had once been an open space but it was now subdivided by glass walls that broke it up into rooms. He saw one with a conference table and chairs, another with ranks of desks, each boasting a plush ergonomic office chair but no computers or screens that he could make out; yet another held a tower of technical equipment that looked like some kind of server farm. But all of this high-tech stuff paled into insignificance when held against the thing that floated at the centre of the chamber.

A coruscating curtain of light stretched across the ceiling. It reminded him of the aurora borealis. Suspended within this sheet of energy, pushing downwards into the chamber from above, stretching it inwards like a bowling ball on a trampoline, was a huge rock. Surrounding the rock was an explosion, solid and unchanging, like a sculpture of flame. Debris blossomed out from it in all directions, and Kaz could see past it into the wreckage of the room above.

There was a missile in the act of exploding hanging directly above their heads, frozen at the moment of impact, caught in the curtain of energy like a fly in a web.

'What the hell is that?' he asked.

'I call it the timebomb,' said their host, peering out through the conference-room door and beckoning them to join him. When they stayed rooted to the spot he walked out and stood directly beneath the explosion.

'That doesn't tell us much,' said Jana curtly.

'It is a very unusual asteroid,' he explained. 'Converted into a weapon and fired at this building. When it impacts – and it will impact when I eventually switch off the quantum generator – it will shatter time and begin the chain of events that brought you here.'

Kaz wanted to reach out and stop Jana as she walked away from him and stood beside the man, looking up at the explosion in wonder, but he knew better than to try.

'How are we not dead?' she asked.

'We are encased within a quantum bubble,' said their host with a theatrical flourish and huge, proud grin.

Kaz waited for him to elaborate. He didn't.

'Which is . . .' Dora prompted.

'A very clever thing that you would not understand,' said the man.

'Try us,' said Jana, caustically.

'Well,' he said. 'Essentially I have generated a field of indeterminability around us, holding us in an artificial super-position and freezing time. Within the bubble, time moves forward for us, while it seems to us that the world outside is frozen. In actual fact it is more accurate to say that we are outside the flow of time entirely, in our own little pocket. Safe from the explosion. The plan was to switch on the bubble before the bomb was launched. As you can see, our timetable slipped somewhat.'

'What happens if your quantum bubble, er, bursts?' asked Kaz.

'We will be atomised,' said the man, matter of fact. 'But we are getting ahead of ourselves, literally. Please, join me and I shall explain as much as I am able.'

He returned to the room with the conference table and

seated himself at the head of it, waiting for them. Dora, Kaz and Jana exchanged glances and, seeing little choice, filed in and took seats at the table.

'Good,' said their host, pushing mugs across the table towards them. 'Cappuccino for me. Green tea for you, Dora. Black coffee for you, Jana. Turkish coffee for you, Kaz. That is right, yes?'

'Yes, thank you,' said Jana, eyeing her mug suspiciously.

'You have us at a disadvantage, sir,' said Dora, who had lain her sword on the table beside her, well within reach.

'Apologies, my name is Yasunori Kairos,' he said. 'I am a professor of quantum physics at MIT in the mid-twenty-second century. I am here to help.'

'But how—' began Kaz.

'If you will forgive me,' interrupted Kairos, 'I will be unable to answer many of your questions at this time. It would be better, I think, if you just let me tell you everything I can.'

Jana nudged Kaz. 'OK, so he's definitely Steve,' she said. Kaz knew what she meant – their mysterious, disguised rescuer had played exactly the same game, withholding information, apologising that he couldn't tell them anything useful.

It was really, really annoying.

Kairos took a breath and braced himself, as if he was about to deliver an important speech, or a notification of death.

'My reasons will become clear, so I beg patience,' he said. 'I know who you are, what you can do and why you have come here and, as I said, I have been waiting for you. I cannot yet tell you how I know the things I do, or why I was waiting here for you, but it will all become apparent in time.'

'We've been here before, in the 1640s,' said Dora. 'This is Sweetclover Hall, right?'

Kairos nodded. 'I understand that was its original name, yes,' he said. 'In this time period it is nameless. It does not officially exist. The only reference you will find to it in any documentation is as Site 2A. It is a top-secret government facility for the processing of political prisoners.'

'This house used to belong to a woman named Quil,' said Kaz, studying Kairos's face and seeing a definite reaction to the name. 'I see you know her.'

'I know *of* her,' said Kairos. 'Outside of this bubble it is 8.22 a.m. on the seventh of April 2158, and hers is a name that everybody knows. I am not working with or for her, if that is what is concerning you. Although she is the reason I am here.'

Kaz noted that Kairos looked at Dora as he said this, and wondered if the professor was one of the secrets she was keeping from him and Jana.

'I need to explain to you about time,' said Kairos. 'It's important that you understand how it works.'

'I want to know how it can work for us,' said Jana pointedly.

'Then listen closely,' replied Kairos.

Most people punctuate their words with pauses – ums and ahs and y'knows denoting the moments when their brains stick for a second while searching for a thought or phrase. Professor Yasunori Kairos was not most people. As he launched into lecture mode, words poured from him in an uncontrollable torrent, tumbling and crashing over Kaz and his friends as if Kairos's mouth were racing to keep up with his brain, but the effort left him permanently breathless and harassed. His only concession to delay was his habit of beginning every burst of explanation with 'Well . . .' as if to give his brain time to take a run-up.

41

'Well,' he started. 'Time follows rules, like any physical effect or state, but the rules it follows are those of quantum rather than Newtonian physics. Time is part of the quantum structure of the universe. As such, of course, its laws all relate to the observation of its passing. You are familiar with Schrödinger's Cat?'

Kaz shook his head and then stopped, embarrassed, when he found both Dora and Jana looking at him as if he were stupid.

'What?' he asked defensively.

'Seriously?' said Jana. 'What did they teach you in school in the twenty-first century?'

'I moved around a lot,' said Kaz grumpily. 'My education was a bit of a mess.'

Kairos gestured theatrically as he spoke, as if the enthusiasm he contained needed to find physical expression. He cleared his throat.

'Let me explain, then,' he said kindly. 'A subatomic particle exists in both positive and negative states until it is observed, upon which it fixes in either positive or negative. The act of looking at a subatomic particle forces it to, in effect, *choose* whether it is negative or positive. When it is both, when it is unobserved, it is what we call a superposition of both states, a quantum effect – both positive and negative at once until the superposition collapses upon observation.

'So if you were to put a cat in a box – and I don't envy anyone trying this experiment in reality because, and I can only speak from experience, my cat scratches the blue blazes out of me when I try to put it in the carrier to take it to the vet – and in the box you put a subatomic particle and a machine that measures whether the particle is negative or positive and is set to release cyanide and kill the cat upon

42

that measurement being made, then close the box, the cat exists in a superposition. It is both alive and dead at the same time, until you open the box and observe it, upon which you either have to deal with a really, really angry cat or you find a dead moggy and then, shortly thereafter, are dead yourself, gasping for breath as you realise that opening boxes full of cyanide gas without some sort of breathing apparatus is a stupid mistake and why oh why didn't you think of this before but you were so excited by your experiment that you totally forgot to order a gas mask.'

Kairos stopped to giggle at his little joke.

'And this is relevant to us how?' asked Kaz, impatient with being talked at.

Kairos sighed. 'I can see I shall have to break this down for you,' he said. 'Well, because time is quantum, it is a product of perception. Hours, minutes, seconds – these are human creations that have no objective reality. Animals do not measure time in days or weeks, they have no conception of past or future, they live in a constant now. And so did our distant ancestors, our animal forebears on the African plains. Because time is quantum, and because it was unobserved, we have no idea what kind of superposition it adopted.

'How did time behave before we became conscious of its passing? Did it flow backwards? Did it skip randomly from one moment to next week and then back to yesterday? Did it flow sideways in some fashion? We can never know. All we can know is that one day a neuron sparked in an ape brain, the ape stepped out of the endless now and thought "I'll do it later." At that instant, time was observed, the superposition collapsed and it began to flow in a linear fashion. One moment began to follow another in a nice, orderly procession. It relates, quite neatly, to the Quantum Zeno Effect—'

'This is all very interesting,' interrupted Dora before the professor's explanation could go off on another tangent. 'But it is theoretical, Professor. How does this relate to time travel?'

'As I explained,' he said, rising from his chair and beginning to pace up and down, 'it all comes down to observation. You are probably familiar with the idea of the grandfather paradox.'

'Assume I'm not,' said Kaz, folding his arms.

'Well. It is the question of what would happen if you travelled back in time and killed your grandfather before he fathered children,' explained Kairos. 'If you were to do this, then one of your parents would never be born, which means you couldn't exist, and so couldn't have travelled back in time to kill him. This is a paradox. An impossibility. So, what would happen if you were to try this? There have been many theories.'

Kaz didn't think he'd ever listened so carefully to an abstruse scientific explanation in his life.

'First,' said Kairos, 'there is the theory that the killer would, by killing his or her grandfather, create an alternate timeline parallel to their original one. They would not be born in this new timeline but that wouldn't matter. If they were then to travel back into the future, they would travel forward along the new branch of time that their actions had created, unable to return to the branch whence they sprang. They would have, so to speak, jumped a time track. No paradox.

'Second, there is Novikov's self-consistency principle, which holds that the killing is literally impossible and every attempt to kill the grandfather would be foiled in some way, by chance. In this model, time is a self-correcting system, almost intelligent.

'Thirdly, there is the possibility that a paradox would be

44

created and that the entire fabric of space and time would unravel, like pulling on a dangling thread from a woolly jumper. The end of everything. Of the universe itself. Boom. This applies to any attempt to change recorded history. Killing Hitler, preventing the assassination of JFK, grounding the planes on 9/11. Any attempt to change the established flow of history would result in one of those three outcomes.

'We could test these hypotheses, establish for certain which of these three models is the correct one. But such an experiment would be wholly reckless for, in the worst case scenario . . . well, as I said, boom.'

He fell silent and Kaz, Jana and Dora sat there mulling over his words.

'So basically, you're telling us to be really, really careful,' said Jana.

'Time travel is the most horrendously dangerous thing,' said Kairos, nodding. 'Without meaning to, any one of you could accidentally destroy *everything*. But!' He shouted this word triumphantly, making Kaz jump involuntarily. 'According to my calculations there is a loophole! Time is, as I said, quantum. Its behaviour is governed by the observer. Let me pick an example.' He pointed at Kaz.

'Kaz,' he said gently, 'I believe your mother died as the result of a car bomb explosion.'

Kaz nodded mutely, both uncomfortable and kind of angry at where Kairos's monologue was heading.

'Well,' he continued, 'if you were to travel back in time and stop the bomb going off, you would know you were changing history, and thus would create a paradox. You would observe the change, time would be forced to react and so, possibly, boom. But, you could change the outcome of events if those events still conformed to your memories.'

45

'I don't . . .' began Kaz.

'Did you ever see her body?' asked Kairos.

That was too much for Kaz. He stood up angrily. 'Who the hell do you think you are?' he shouted, and then felt the electric tingle of Jana's hand on his arm.

'Think about it, Kaz,' she said calmly. 'Did you see your mother's body?'

'No,' he said shortly, addressing Jana rather than Kairos. 'It was a closed casket funeral. She was . . . very close to the bomb.'

Jana continued. 'So what I think he's saying – correct me if I'm wrong, Professor – is that since you never saw her body, it would be possible for you to go back in time and ensure that she survived the explosion. As long as your younger self still experiences that day exactly as you remember it.'

'That is correct,' said Kairos. 'Intervention in one's own personal history is possible, but extraordinarily risky because one remembers what happened. Intervention in a period of history about which the time traveller knows nothing, on the other hand, can be achieved with little or no risk at all.'

'You think,' said Dora.

'Yes, I think,' affirmed the professor.

Kaz's anger was not subsiding. 'My mother's murder is not just some story you can use to explain a damn theory,' he said. 'It's a real thing, that really happened. To me.'

Kairos looked uncomfortable. 'I am sorry,' he said. 'I meant no disrespect. I was just trying to use an example that you would understand.'

'How the hell do you know so much about me, anyway?' spat Kaz.

'Um, I'm under strict instructions not to tell you,' said Kairos apologetically.

SECOND LIVES

Scott K. Andrews

HODDER

First published in Great Britain in 2016 by Hodder & Stoughton
An imprint of Hodder & Stoughton
An Hachette UK company

First published in paperback in 2017

1

Copyright © Scott K. Andrews 2016

The right of Scott K. Andrews to be identified as the Author
of the Work has been asserted by him in accordance with the
Copyright, Designs and Patents Act 1988.

A CIP catalogue record for this title is available from the British Library

ISBN 978 1 444 75211 3

Typeset by Palimpsest Book Production Ltd, Falkirk, Stirlingshire
Printed and bound by Clays Ltd, St Ives plc

Hodder & Stoughton policy is to use papers that are natural, renewable
and recyclable products and made from wood grown in sustainable
forests. The logging and manufacturing processes are expected to conform
to the environmental regulations of the country of origin.

Hodder & Stoughton Ltd
Carmelite House
50 Victoria Embankment
London
EC4Y 0DZ

www.hodder.co.uk

This one's for Thomas, whose good humour and
kindness are an inspiration to me every day.

Prologue: Cornwall, England, 7 April 2158, 8:21 A.M. - 1 min to timebomb impact

The woman who called herself Quil stood on a ridge with oak trees behind her, looking down into a shallow dell. The morning air was cool and crisp, the sky was blue and the pollen-rich air was alive with insects and birdsong. Below her, within an ornate garden hidden behind tall hedges and ancient brick walls, a familiar building stood, swathed in ivy.

Sweetclover Hall.

Quil knew there were guards within and without, pressure pads, laser grids, cameras and traps surrounding the place, but they were skilfully hidden. From her vantage point she could have been looking at any old English pile, home to some blue-blood descendants of a once-powerful family. But she knew the truth – this discreet, sheltered building was one of the most secure holding facilities in existence at this point in time. Behind its walls interrogations were being conducted, pressure brought to bear on political dissidents, terrorists, activists – whichever undesirable sector of society was currently designated enemy combatants. Fully authorised, fully deniable,

1

officially non-existent, Sweetclover Hall was the place people went to when they disappeared.

The men and women who ran the facility sat smugly in the house, safe in their control centres and meeting rooms, watching the inmates on CCTV, feeling powerful and in control, the unassailable enforcers of the powers that be, ruling absolutely the forgotten and misplaced human flotsam that washed up in their cells.

Somewhere in the house, Quil knew that her younger self was sitting in a nondescript little room talking to a nondescript little man, beginning a battle of wits she knew she would lose.

Quil looked up into the sky, raising her hand to shield her eyes from the rising sun. She squinted, searching the heavens for a sign.

There, high in the stratosphere, a flash of light heralded the arrival of a new star in the sky. It hung there silently, growing larger at a leisurely pace until suddenly it seemed to elongate into a ribbon of flame, arcing down from space trailing fire and smoke, screaming towards the ground. The sonic boom hit her just as the star fell to Earth, knocking her off her feet and making her head ring.

The missile detonated in the heart of the ancient building, the very structure of time itself shattered in a billion places, and the dark secrets hidden beneath Sweetclover Hall came spilling out into the light of a frightened world.

Quil sat up, smiling.

All was as it should be.

MIT, America East,
24 May 2158, 3:35 P.M. –
14 days to timebomb impact

Professor Yasunori Kairos did not like giving lectures.

Today he was attempting to explain imaginary time, and the blank looks of all the students in the front row of the lecture hall were making his temples throb. They had understood the linear directionality of real time within specific light cones, but once he had stepped beyond that and tried to explain the mathematical possibilities of imaginary time, he had seen their eyes glaze over. When the bell rang to signal the end of the lecture he breathed a sigh of relief, sat down and rested his head against the surface of his desk, closing his eyes and picturing equations to calm himself as the students filed out gossiping.

When silence had finally fallen, Kairos opened his eyes and sat up, only to find himself staring across at three students, two young women and a young man, sitting in the front row.

'Oh, hello,' said Kairos, somewhat discomfited. 'Can I help you?'

One of the young women, the white one dressed entirely

3

in black, smiled softly. 'I hope so,' she said. 'My name is Dora Predennick, and I want to show you something, if I may.'

The young woman rose from her chair, walked up to Kairos's desk and held out her hand. Kairos regarded it suspiciously, but she leaned forward and grabbed his hand in hers before he could react. He was immediately overcome with the strangest feeling. His hand tingled, as if with pins and needles, and red sparks flew from it. Alarmed, he tried to pull his hand back but the woman's grip was too strong for him. The feeling that had begun in his hand flashed quickly up his arm and then across his chest. He briefly wondered if he was having a heart attack, and became certain of it when his vision began to blur and darken. The tingling soon engulfed his whole body, his head felt tight and painful and he felt his feet leave the ground as if he were floating weightless – a sensation he had experienced once before, on the outward journey to Mars, and which he had not enjoyed at all.

He cried out, but could not hear himself do so. He felt the deepest, most profound sense of panic. Had she drugged him, perhaps? Some kind of chemical patch on her hand? Was he being murdered or kidnapped?

Then, as suddenly as it had begun, the sensation began to abate, he felt solid ground beneath his feet and his vision began to clear. But this didn't make sense at all. He was outside. He squinted in the bright sunlight that warmed his skin. He could smell grass and flowers.

He felt Dora unclasp his hand and his legs gave way beneath him. He crumpled to the ground and cried out in alarm.

'Don't worry, Professor,' he heard Dora say, from somewhere above him. 'You'll be fine. It kind of messes with your head the first time.'

4

His eyes adjusted to the light and he looked around him. Trees, shrubs, a wide plain ahead of him. Blue sky, hot sun. The air smelled and tasted like nothing he'd ever known, and the sounds of the birds were alien but soothing.

'Where,' he stammered, 'where am I? What . . . what happened?'

'Calm down, Prof, you're hyperventilating,' said Dora.

He nodded and took control of his breathing. There was a soft trumpeting sound close by, animal rather than instrumental. Kairos sat stock-still, feeling a primitive fear deep in his belly.

'What was that?' he whispered.

Dora leaned over him smiling, and whispered, 'Look behind you and see.'

Gulping, Kairos turned his head and looked up into the eyes of a woolly mammoth, which was staring down at him curiously, its trunk swaying like the pendulum of a long-case clock. He held its gaze for a moment, then turned back to Dora.

'Welcome to history, Prof,' she said, smiling broadly. 'Now, can we talk about quantum effects in interaction with large amounts of temporally unstable materials?'

Part One

Parental intervention

New York, America East, 8 June 2141 – 17 years to timebomb impact

Kazic Cecka sat on the black rubber seal of an old skyscraper roof, the concrete lip at the edge digging into his back. It was hot and silent up here, high above the bustle of the city streets yet beneath the opaque gaze of the buildings that towered over him. They were totally unlike the skyscrapers of his day, the solid, blocky type like the one he was sitting atop. These taller buildings curved and twined around on themselves like huge silver tree trunks corkscrewing out of the ground, reaching high up where the air was thin.

Kaz knew that he was in New York in the year 2141. He knew this because Jana, the young woman who lay unconscious beside him in a pool of her own blood, had brought them here by accident as they fled 1645. Focusing on the point of her departure, she had jumped into time and materialised herself and Kaz at the very time and place she had originally left on her first trip, when she had flung herself off the roof to escape a group of men intent on killing her.

9

These men now lay before Kaz in various pieces, their blood mingling with Jana's. There really was a *lot* of blood.

Standing in the middle of the spreading puddle was Dora, the young woman who'd spilled most of it.

'Take my hand,' said Dora, sheathing her dripping sword with one hand while reaching out to Kaz with the other.

Kaz looked up at her in amazement. The Dora he knew was a fourteen-year-old girl from a seventeenth-century English village – curious and capable but young, unworldly and, the last time he'd seen her, deeply traumatised by her experiences. She had pulled away from Jana and him as they'd joined hands to jump into time. He had no idea where and when she had been whisked off to, but the Dora who stood before him, who had appeared in the nick of time and saved Jana and Kaz by cutting down their attackers with ruthless efficiency, bore little resemblance to the girl he'd known.

'We need to get her to a hospital,' said Kaz, leaning over towards Jana, who lay face down taking short, shallow breaths.

'I've taken care of it,' said Dora briskly. 'Let's get out of here; this is one place we really shouldn't linger.'

Kaz reached out and took Dora's right hand, while she grabbed Jana with her left. He felt the world around them shift, his stomach felt hollow and his vision swam, and then they were in a lavish reception area – large glass doors, fancy desk, sofas.

The instant they had solidified, the internal doors slid open and a man and two women in clean white medical coats ran out, wheeling a stretcher and a trolley laden with instruments of all sorts.

'Come on,' said Dora as the doctors lifted Jana on to a stretcher on the count of three. 'We should get out of their way and let them work.'

'Yeah,' said Kaz, knowing she was right but unwilling to leave Jana without a friendly face while she was in such bad shape. 'Where and when are we?'

'Kinshasa, 2120. Trust me, this is the best clinic there is,' said Dora, placing a reassuring hand on his shoulder. 'She's going to be fine.'

Reluctantly, Kaz allowed himself to be led away. One of the attackers in New York had kicked Kaz square in the mouth, and now he tongued his teeth to find two missing and one split in two. 'I think I'm going to need some painkillers and a dentist myself,' he said as Dora led him out of the room into a pastel-coloured corridor lined with expensive-looking prints of African tribal designs.

'No problem,' said Dora, leading him three rooms down and pushing the door open to reveal a fully equipped dentist's surgery and a tall blonde woman standing by the big chair waiting for him.

'I hate dentists,' moaned Kaz through his bruise-swollen lips, hovering on the threshold.

'I shan't take it personally, sir,' said the dentist with a wolfish smile. 'If you'll please take a seat.'

Kaz turned to Dora. 'Fill me in while I'm being tortured by the scary lady with the nasty drill?'

Dora nodded, followed Kaz inside and perched on a table by the door.

The dentist's chair was deeply upholstered leather, and Kaz relaxed into it gratefully; he was bruised all over and dog-tired.

The dentist handed him a glass of pink mouthwash and he swooshed, gargled and spat the foul medicinal stuff, expecting pain but surprised to find it made his mouth feel pleasantly numb.

'Wass tha?' he said, his tongue feeling like a lump of useless meat.

'Dentistry has improved a bit since your time,' said Dora.

'Wa yeer agai'?' asked Kaz, frustrated by his now useless mouth. 'Oh fa fu sa.'

Kaz was a bit annoyed that Dora didn't even crack a smile at his discomfort, which he was playing up for laughs. But then, he mused, he didn't really know this older version of Dora at all, although there was perhaps a line to be drawn between the girl who had snatched Jana's gun and dispatched a group of Roundhead soldiers in 1645, and the black-clad warrior who sat opposite him now.

'We're in Kinshasa. The year is 2120,' replied Dora patiently. 'This hospital is very private, very discreet and very expensive. The staff have all signed non-disclosure agreements and we have this entire wing, and all its staff and resources, at our disposal for as long as we need them.'

Kaz tried to incline his head by way of mute question, but the dentist firmly pushed it back, pulled open his mouth and shoved some kind of buzzing implement inside it. He grunted in annoyance.

'Lottery win,' explained Dora, finally cracking a smile. 'Lotteries are a time traveller's best friend.'

Kaz grunted his appreciation – anything to distract him from the sounds emerging from his mouth. Oh God, did something just go *scrunch*?

'I knew I'd need a place where everybody could be looked after,' said Dora, 'and this clinic is ideal.'

'Everboy?' asked Kaz as the dentist swapped tools and grabbed a pair of pliers. He felt a tugging in his jaw and something in his mouth went *pop* and then *crunch* and then a kind of slurping scrapey noise that made him want to vomit.

'It's been a long time, for me, since that day in Pendarn,' said Dora, hesitantly. Kaz could tell she didn't want to explain in much detail and was picking and choosing what to reveal.

Kaz remembered seeing Dora's mother, father and brother lying in a heap on the floor of the house's undercroft. Her mother had been unconscious, her brother looked like he'd been run through with a sword and her father, Thomas, had been cradling them both as the computer screen in front of him had counted down to the moment when a bomb would detonate and demolish the building around them. Dora had screamed as he and Jana had dragged her away into time, forcing her to abandon her family to their fate.

'One by one, I've scooped everyone up and brought them here,' said Dora. 'My family, Mountfort, you and Jana, that kid Simon from 2014. Oh, and Steve too.'

Despite the importance of what she was telling him, Kaz was distracted by Dora's speech patterns. The girl he had known spoke seventeenth-century English with a rich Cornish burr. This older Dora spoke with a different accent – hints of Australian and maybe Spanish, he thought – and her vocabulary and phrasing were what he, a product of the twenty-first century, would have considered modern.

Her speech patterns weren't the only thing that had changed – now she dressed like a ninja and moved with a lethal mix of martial arts readiness and cat burglar stealth. She was as graceful as she had been gawky, as controlled as she had been skittish. She was a different person altogether. He wondered what could possibly have happened to her since they'd last met. It had been only minutes for him but for her it had been, he guessed, at least four years. She had been fourteen when they first met, three years younger than him. Now he reckoned she was one year older. She was slightly taller than she had been, although she would still have been short by twenty-first-century standards. She was stronger and leaner; her figure had filled out and lost its puppy fat.

His attention shifted when he caught a glimpse of something big and red emerging from his mouth between the pliers' jaws. He tried to sit up, but the dentist pushed him back down again, brandishing a scalpel.

'I'm going to leave you to get your mouth fixed up,' said Dora. 'We'll talk later.'

Now the dentist was holding a clean white tooth between pliers and looked to be about to bang it into his gums with a little silver hammer. He was pretty sure that wasn't how these things were supposed to be done even in his own time, let alone in the future, but he couldn't voice his protest, not least because his head rang with every hammer blow.

Dora's face hovered into view over the dentist's shoulder. She grimaced as she looked into his mouth, which was hardly reassuring.

She surprised him again, this time by leaning forward and planting a kiss on his cheek, which earned her a glare from the dentist.

'See you in a bit,' said Dora.

'Right, now for the hard part,' muttered the dentist, reaching for what looked like a tiny chainsaw.

Kinshasa, Democratic Republic of Congo, 7 May 2120 – 38 years to timebomb impact

Kaz sat beside the hospital bed waiting for Jana to wake, trying to think what he would say when she did. Speaking was a bit difficult for him at the moment – he had developed a slight lisp as a result of his new teeth.

He dismissed 'Morning' or 'Hi' as too flippant, briefly considered 'Well, hello sleepyhead' before reminding himself he wasn't a middle-aged character in a bad sitcom, plus he should probably avoid sibilants, and was mulling 'Welcome to the future!' when she opened her eyes, blinked and said 'Hi' in a sleepy voice.

'Hi,' he said softly, smiling.

It had been a week since Dora had brought them to the clinic, and the doctor had kept them updated on Jana's progress throughout. The knife Quil had plunged into Jana's chest had just missed her heart, but it had collapsed a lung and done serious internal damage, all of which had now been repaired. She had regained consciousness on the fourth day, although she'd been groggy and confused, and now, after a few days of mostly sleeping, she had sent a message via a nurse that she wanted to see Kaz and Dora for 'a proper talk'.

The beige room was small but private, boasting a single bed ringed by all sorts of monitors and instruments, a small desk and a couple of chairs.

'Help me up,' said Jana, bending feebly at the waist; her dressings and deep bruising made it hard for her to sit up under her own steam. Kaz held her hand and pulled her into a sitting position, ignoring the red halo that flashed around their fingers as the temporal energy they both possessed interacted. He then bent forward and plumped the pillows behind her so she could lean back comfortably.

'Thanks,' said Jana. Her face was pale, her cheeks sunken, but there was a spark in her eyes that pledged the swift return of her old self.

'Sleep well?' asked Kaz.

Jana nodded, turning to look out of the window. The clouds were low and threatening above the green of the city park that began at the clinic's front door.

'Yeah, but I'm happy to wake up,' said Jana, turning back to Kaz. 'I mean, lucky to wake up. Very lucky.'

She glanced down at her hand and it took Kaz a moment to realise he was still holding it tightly; and it was still surrounded by an aurora of red. He blushed slightly and withdrew it.

'Where's Dora?' asked Jana.

'Right here,' said Dora, as she entered the room. In the week they had been in Kinshasa, Kaz had only once seen Dora wearing what he would have considered normal clothing – on one particularly hot day she'd worn a white cotton dress – but now she was back in black.

Dora was carrying a tray bearing a jug of iced tea, three

glasses and a plate of biscuits. She placed it on the desk, poured everyone a drink, then placed the plate on Jana's lap and pulled a chair up to the opposite side of the bed to Kaz.

'Has Mountfort gone?' he asked, referring to the Royalist spy they had met in 1645.

'Yes,' she said. 'He will never quite be the same man, of course. There is only so much even modern medicine can do for a body as broken as his was, but he is alive and back in his own time with a healthy coffer full of gold for his troubles. He told me he intends to spend the rest of his days in quiet contemplation of nature.'

Jana shook her head in amazement. 'I can't believe he made it,' she said. 'I mean, he was hanged, stabbed *and* shot.'

'He was touch and go,' agreed Dora. 'As were you, for a time.'

There was a brief, contemplative silence that went on just long enough to verge on awkwardness before Jana spoke again.

'So here we are,' she said. 'Safe and secure. The doctor says I've got a couple of weeks of recuperation left, at least, so I'm not going anywhere fast. Dora, was Mountfort the last? Those were the only people recovering here?'

It seemed to Kaz that this question was loaded somehow, as if Jana was trying to make it seem less casual than it was, but Dora didn't appear to pick up on it.

'Yes,' said Dora. 'Everyone I rescued and brought here has been returned to their rightful time and place.'

'So you've got no more errands to run?'

Dora shook her head.

'OK, good. Clean sheet,' said Jana firmly. 'You two can both jump through time solo now, can't you?'

Kaz nodded and so did Dora. 'After I touched Quil in the

undercroft in 1645, I was thrown sideways in time,' explained Kaz. 'It took me about six months before I was able to jump through time again. I could feel the power growing in me all the time, I just had to wait for it to reach the right strength.'

'It was the same for me,' said Dora. 'About six months after we were separated I also gained the ability to travel through time on my own. It took me many months of practice after that before I was able to steer myself accurately. I am impressed, Kaz, that you were able to return to Pendarn and aid in our escape from Quil so quickly after your power matured.'

Kaz shrugged. 'What can I say, I was highly motivated.'

This earned him a smile from Dora and a good-natured eye-roll from Jana.

'Unlike you two, it's still only a week or so since I first jumped through time,' said Jana. 'So for now I'm only going to be able to jump if I'm holding hands with one of you.'

Kaz could see how little Jana relished the idea of being reliant on somebody else but he thought it would do her good not to be completely in control for a change. He kept this slightly uncharitable thought to himself.

'Anyway, can we fill in the blanks, please,' said Jana. 'Let's start with you, Kaz.' She turned to him and he held out his hands as if to say 'Ask anything'.

'In Sweetclover Hall you touched Quil and off you went,' said Jana. 'I thought I was never going to see you again, so you can imagine my relief when you turned up with the cavalry. You say you were gone for six months, so where and when did you end up?'

Kaz barely knew where to start in recounting his adventures in history. 'It's a long story,' he said, 'but the short version is that I spent the time serving on a privateer on the Spanish Main in 1693.'

'You were a *pirate*?' said Jana, amazed and delighted.

'I was that,' agreed Kaz. 'And let me tell you, it wasn't nearly as exciting as the films. It was mostly deck swabbing, sail stitching, bad food, worse drink, unbelievable BO in the sleeping quarters and the singing. All the awful, awful singing. I don't care if I never hear another sea shanty in my life.'

'But you plundered ships,' said Jana. 'You wore a cutlass and carried pistols?'

'Once or twice,' said Kaz, smiling at Jana's uncharacteristic enthusiasm.

'And did you ever swing between ships on a big rope while they fired the cannons beneath you?'

Kaz found himself lying before he could stop – chances to impress her did not come along often and he wasn't going to let one pass.

'Only once,' he said. 'But it was *awesome*.'

'That is literally the best thing I have ever heard,' said Jana. 'Did you have a pirate name? Red-handed Kaz? Sealegs Cecka?'

Kaz laughed. 'No, Jana, I did not have a pirate name,' he said. 'I just kept my head down, tried to be the best crew member I could, and waited for my powers to develop enough for me to get the hell out of there.'

'I want to know every detail,' said Jana, folding her hands in her lap decisively and eagerly staring at him. Across the bed Kaz could see Dora looking less than thrilled at the direction the conversation was taking.

'Later, I promise,' said Kaz.

'Spoilsport.' Jana pouted.

'Dora, what about you?' asked Kaz. 'Where and when did you end up after 1645?'

'Auckland, 2063,' answered Dora.

Jana pursed her lips and breathed in sharply. 'Ouch,' she said.

'What?' asked Kaz.

'I learned about that period in history,' said Jana regarding Dora with concern. 'Not a good time to be in the Antipodes.'

'No,' agreed Dora. 'But I was fortunate, I found sanctuary in a shelter for orphaned refugees. They looked after me well.'

Dora did not elaborate, and after a pregnant pause Kaz asked, 'Is that it? If I had to guess, I'd say you're four years older than when we first met?'

Dora nodded. 'Approximately,' she agreed.

'But you said your ability to time travel solo kicked in after six months,' said Jana. 'So what happened to the other three and a half years? Did you stay in Auckland the whole time or did you travel?'

Dora fixed Jana with a steady, appraising gaze and Kaz could tell she was considering how much to reveal. 'I travelled,' she said eventually. 'With purpose.'

'You trained, didn't you?' said Kaz. 'You found someone to help turn you into a superhero.'

Dora rewarded his wisecrack with a tiny smile. 'Yes, that's exactly correct, Kaz. I found a sensei and learned the skills I felt would be necessary for me to rescue everybody. It took some years. You can thank me later.'

'Oh believe me, I've given thanks for you every moment since you skewered that thug on the rooftop,' said Kaz emphatically.

'So who did you find to train you to be a ninja?' asked Jana.

'I could tell you,' said Dora, deadpan. 'But I'd have to kill you.'

Jana did not smile and Kaz shifted awkwardly in his seat

as the two young women engaged in a staring contest. Eventually Dora smiled again and said, 'Garcia.'

The name meant nothing to Kaz but it obviously did to Jana, whose eyes widened as her mouth dropped open.

'No way,' she said, seemingly awestruck.

'Way,' said Dora.

Kaz waited for one of them to enlighten him and sighed dramatically when neither of them did. 'You know, I'm from 2014,' he said, 'and the only other time period I know well is the seventeenth century. I'm not like you two, I'm not from the future and I haven't been there much so . . .'

'Sorry Kaz,' said Dora.

'Yeah, sorry,' said Jana, turning to him. 'New Zealand in the 2060s was overrun with refugees from the Pacific Islands. As their homes sank beneath the water, they took to boats and tried to find somewhere willing to take them in. North America was in the middle of the second civil war, Chile had slipped into anarchy and Australia had started literally shooting migrant ships to pieces. New Zealand was the destination of choice for waterlogged refugees. But tensions were high and there was a lot of violence. I don't know why I'm the one explaining this, you were there Dora.'

'It was OK,' said Dora, shrugging. 'Watch the History Channel and you'd think it was constant urban warfare, but in reality it was a lot less dramatic. I only saw two race riots while I was there, and one of them was pretty tame.'

'Right. Wow,' said Kaz, processing the nuggets of future history that Jana had so casually dropped into his lap. Second civil war?! 'What about Garcia? Who was he?'

Jana whistled. 'He was a legend, a ghost,' she said. 'If you believe the stories, he was behind most of the unsolved political

21

mysteries of the twenty-first century. Supposedly he was the man who assassinated President Hurley . . .'

'Yes,' said Dora.

'Blew up the Kremlin . . .'

'Yes,' said Dora again.

'Hijacked the QE3 . . .'

'No,' said Dora. 'That was Tibetan special forces.'

'Kidnapped the pope and ransomed him . . .'

'Oh yes,' said Dora, smiling as if at a personal memory.

'Not to mention hacking the Chinese National Bank and wiping out most of the world's debt.'

'No,' said Dora, shaking her head and wearing her best poker face. 'That was me.'

Kaz genuinely couldn't tell whether she was joking or not. In that moment he found himself believing Dora capable of practically anything.

'And you hooked up with this guy when you were, what, fifteen, sixteen years old?' he asked.

Dora nodded. 'Think about it,' she said. 'For people like us, who can jump in and out of any time period at will, the most important skill is being able to move through the world invisibly. Who better to teach me that than a man many historians in this time period still don't think actually existed?'

Jana bit noisily into a biscuit and chewed slowly, staring at Dora with wide eyes. 'That,' she said after her last bite, 'is totally badass.'

'Yeah. Yeah, it is,' agreed Kaz, reaching for a biscuit.

They sat in silence for a while, munching their way through the biscuits, each lost in their own thoughts. Kaz was mostly trying to come to terms with the idea that the future was available to him. He had explored the past and accepted the idea that he could take a holiday in ancient Thebes, watch the Beatles play Hamburg or arrange to casually bump into Helen of Troy, but the opportunity presented by the future was dazzling, even if Dora and Jana did make it sound like a long series of wars and riots.

When the plate held only crumbs, he decided it was time to address the elephants in the room.

'There are two things I want to know,' he said. 'First, Dora, the other day you told me you rescued Steve from Io Scientific.'

Dora nodded. Although the person they knew as Steve had rescued them from captivity in 2014, risking his life to do so, he had remained in disguise the whole time, his (or her) identity concealed beneath something he called a chameleon shroud. He had told them some details about their future, so he was certainly someone they either knew or would come to know. It was even possible he was one of them, travelling back from the future.

'Did you see Steve without the disguise?' Jana asked, before Kaz could.

Dora nodded again, but said nothing.

'Well?' said Kaz impatiently. 'Who was he?'

Dora pulled an apologetic face. 'I can't tell you,' she said. 'Sorry. Steve made me swear to keep the secret.'

Both Kaz and Jana groaned in annoyance.

'You'll find out, I swear, when the time is right,' said Dora firmly. 'You just have to trust me.'

It was clear she was not going to budge on this.

'Fine,' said Jana with a distinct lack of good grace. 'Did he at least tell you anything else about our future? Anything that can help us? Anything at all?'

'He told me that when we are ready and want to find out about our powers and the responsibilities that come with them, we need to join hands and travel together as far into the future as we are able to go,' said Dora. 'If we do that, he said, we will arrive precisely where and when we are supposed to be.'

'That's it?' said Jana, disgusted.

Dora shrugged. 'That's all I could get out of him.'

'Ha! So Steve's a him!' said Kaz.

'Steve is,' agreed Dora, smugly. 'I never said the person beneath the mask was.'

Kaz gritted his teeth but was jarred out of his annoyance by the strange way his new dental work fitted together in his mouth. He grunted sullenly.

'What is the second thing?' asked Jana. It took Kaz a moment to realise she was addressing him. He looked at her blankly.

'You said there were two things you wanted to know,' she said slowly.

'Oh, yeah,' said Kaz, climbing back aboard his original train of thought. 'Dora, in your future travels, did you look into Quil? Do you have any information about her?'

'Some,' said Dora. 'The furthest forward I travelled was 2156.'

'That's fifteen years after my time,' said Jana. 'I don't think she was around in 2141 – at least, if she was I never heard of her.'

'She was around,' said Dora. 'She's a well-known and divisive political figure by 2156, but she didn't come to prominence till around 2150. And her life before then is a total mystery, so what she was doing and who she was when you were at school, I can't say.'

'So spill,' said Jana, leaning forward eagerly, wincing as she pulled at her wound. She leaned back again with a soft groan.

'Some of this won't be news to you, Jana,' said Dora, 'but Kaz needs to know some of the context. I certainly did.'

'Hit me,' said Kaz, excited at the prospect of getting some answers, however incomplete.

'Right,' said Dora, taking a deep breath. 'By 2156 mankind has left Earth. Not completely, it's still well populated, but people have colonised the solar system. Mars is being altered to make it more like Earth, but it is still early in the process. The people there live in huge domed cities. Further out, colonies have been established across the solar system, on moons and dwarf planets far out into space. The primary reason is to mine for minerals and other resources, which are shipped back to Earth and Mars. Ceres is particularly important, as they're breaking its surface ice into chunks and shooting it at Mars to create oceans.'

'Wow,' said Kaz, boggled by the scale of what Dora was describing.

'Out on the edges, where the mining concerns harvest asteroids and comets, the large companies began using specially created clones sometime in the 2120s,' Dora continued. 'These are humans, specially grown from an altered template to enhance their ability to live and work in deep space – they function better in zero gravity, cope well without sunlight, that sort of thing. They have very limited rights, though. By law, they are property of the corporations who created them. Their DNA is copyright and they don't get paid.'

'I know some of this,' said Jana. 'In my time there were rumours about exploitation out on the edge. The problem is that the mining companies have total control of their own stations, colonies and staff, and communications can be patchy that far out, so there was no proof. Eyewitness accounts would get out sometimes, but it was all hearsay. The basic thrust

25

was that the clones were slaves in all but name, but the governments on Earth didn't want to get involved.'

'Couldn't get involved,' corrected Dora. 'They don't have jurisdiction beyond the atmosphere.'

Jana shook her head firmly. 'So they say, but there was a legal challenge a couple of years before I left—'

'OK,' interrupted Kaz. 'I get it. Colonies, mining, clones, slavery. Moving on.'

Jana looked at him and he was surprised to see both disappointment and outrage on her face. 'Clones are people, Kaz,' she said angrily. 'They should have rights.'

Kaz held up his hands placatingly, taken aback; he hadn't thought of Jana as the crusading type. 'I didn't say they shouldn't,' he said. 'But what does this have to do with Quil?'

'Quil agrees with you, Jana,' said Dora. 'In 2150 a journalist on Mars published an exposé of conditions aboard the asteroid mining ships. Video, official documents, proof of inhumane treatment, terrible working conditions, summary executions. It caused a scandal, and all the journalist would reveal about the source of the material was her pseudonym.'

'Let me guess – Quil,' said Kaz.

Dora nodded. 'The corporations fought back,' she continued. 'Branded all the material fake, claimed it was the work of agitators and anarchists trying to destabilise the economy.'

'Nothing changes,' muttered Jana darkly.

'But Quil wasn't finished,' continued Dora. 'More material began to emerge, really detailed, lots of dates and times, names and places, all with her name on it.'

Kaz shook his head. 'Wait, so what you're saying is that Quil is a crusading human rights activist?' He tried to square this idea with the insane killer he had met in 1645 and it made his head ache.

Dora nodded. 'That's how she first appears,' she agreed. 'In 2153 she starts talking directly, releasing videos of herself giving speeches, trying to encourage people to protest, sign petitions, get Earth to intervene.'

'Ooh, what does she look like?' asked Jana eagerly.

'She wears a mask,' said Dora.

'But I thought she only wore that because she was so badly burned after her trip back through time?' said Jana, confused.

'So did I,' agreed Dora. 'But she wore one before as well. She says it's a representation of the faceless clones, a way of reclaiming individuality or something.'

'Huh,' said Kaz, nonplussed. 'So you don't know where she comes from, what her real name is or what she looks like.'

'No, sorry,' said Dora, unapologetically. 'She protected her anonymity very carefully in her own time. She was stirring things up, causing trouble, rocking the boat. She would have been a target. Best guess is she's one of the clones. It would explain why there's no record of her before 2050 – she was grown in a vat and then added to the work rota, just another faceless worker on a mining ship or colony somewhere far away from prying eyes.'

'Maybe it's not a question of her protecting her identity, but creating one,' suggested Jana. 'If she's a clone, then she has the same face, same body, same birthmarks even, as all the other female clones. They don't have names, only numbers. So by choosing a name and removing her face, she's created a persona that is uniquely hers. That would be a potent act of rebellion, if you think about it.'

'OK, so she's a clone on a crusade,' said Kaz impatiently. 'But so what? How does she get blown back in time? Why is she so angry at us? What's the war she mentioned?'

'All I know is that by 2156 she's leading an open rebellion,' said Dora. 'The clones in a number of the farthest colonies seized power, kicked out the corporations and declared independence. She's their figurehead, maybe even their actual leader, I don't know.'

'That must be her war, then,' said Jana.

'I guess,' said Kaz. 'And at some point after 2156 that war brings her to Mars, where she meets us—'

'If Quil's clone army reaches Mars, that's serious,' interrupted Jana. 'It means Earth is threatened.'

Kaz continued, 'On Mars something goes horribly wrong, we don't know what, and then some time after that she's blown back in time and lands in Sweetclover Hall in 1640.'

'That's about it,' agreed Jana. 'That's all we know.'

'So what do we do about it?' asked Dora.

Kaz looked at her and shrugged.

'Then to hell with you,' said Kaz, turning to Dora and Jana. 'I don't know about you, but I'm getting out of here. This whole thing stinks.'

He screwed his eyes shut and willed himself away from there, into the future, feeling the room fade away . . .

. . . only to find it fading right back again.

After a brief moment's disorientation, he realised he had somehow been prevented from jumping into time and was still standing in the conference room underneath Sweetclover Hall.

He drew his gun and pointed it at Kairos's head as Dora and Jana rose from their seats.

'I couldn't jump away, we're stuck here,' said Kaz. 'It's a trap!'

Kairos threw up his hands in alarm. 'No, no,' he shouted, 'you don't understand! Please don't shoot me!'

Dora's sword was at Kairos's throat before he finished speaking.

'Then explain,' she said curtly.

'The quantum bubble forms a barrier,' he said breathlessly. 'Travel into the future beyond this point is impossible.'

'Which would explain why Steve told us we just had to jump into the future,' said Jana, directing her comments at Kaz, trying to calm him down. He did not appreciate it.

'That is correct,' said Kairos, starting to nod and then thinking better of it as the sword's blade nicked his Adam's apple. 'Anyone who tries to travel beyond this point in time will find themselves pulled into the bubble. It is like, um, a temporal whirlpool.'

Kaz thought for a second, then said, 'Dora, jump back a day and then forward again. Let's see if he's telling the truth.'

Dora nodded and withdrew her sword. Kaz stepped

47

forward so his gun was pointed right between Kairos's eyes as Dora flared into nothingness and then, a moment later, reappeared.

'He's telling the truth,' she said.

Kaz lowered his gun slowly and Kairos let out a long sigh of relief.

'Thank you,' he said.

No sooner had Kaz holstered the gun then he felt a hard punch on his upper arm and turned to see Jana looking up at him furiously.

'Don't you dare run out on me,' she hissed. 'You promised.'

Kaz's anger began to subside and he nodded. 'I did, sorry,' he said. He turned back to Kairos. 'But I don't like this. What is it you want from us, Professor?'

Kairos, white as a sheet, drained his coffee and took a moment to compose himself.

'I want you to go to Mars,' he said. 'And prevent a terrible tragedy that occurred two days ago, on April fifth 2158. Thousands upon thousands of people died when—' he stopped himself.

'When what?' asked Jana.

'I can't tell you,' said the professor. 'It would be too dangerous for you to know exactly what happened.'

'Why?' asked Dora.

'Because if you know all the details, you'll be unable to stop it from happening without risking a paradox,' said the professor.

'You want us to . . .'

'Yes, Kaz,' said the professor. 'I want you to change history.'

An hour later, after Kairos had pitched his plan to them and they had asked him to leave them alone to consider, the three time travellers stood beneath the frozen explosion, staring up at it, each lost in their own thoughts.

Kaz couldn't stop obsessing over Kairos's first example of altering the past – was it really possible, he wondered, to save his mother from the car bomb that had killed her?

'Oh!' Jana exclaimed suddenly. 'I forgot!'

As Kaz and Dora turned to her in surprise, Jana hurried away to the farthest corner of the undercroft and began examining the wall. Kaz and Dora exchanged confused glances and walked over to join her.

'What did you forget?' asked Kaz.

'The cavern,' she said, still examining brickwork that, to Kaz's eyes, looked identical to the rest of the walls. 'There was an elevator here, in 1645. I took it down – really, a long way down – and there was a cavern. The one we arrived in after 2014.'

'The one with all the pods?' asked Kaz, remembering the huge cave lined with rows of glass cocoons holding frozen figures where they had stopped to gather their wits before jumping back to 1645.

'Yeah,' said Jana. 'It's directly underneath us. Or it was, back then. There were cold fusion generators running the suspended animation apparatus. It was an army. Quil's army.'

'You think they could still be down there?' asked Dora.

Jana stepped back from the wall, frustrated. 'I guess. There's no sign of the elevator shaft at all now. Must have been bricked up centuries ago. Probably nobody in this time period even knows they're down there.'

'If they are,' said Dora. 'They could have woken up and left years ago for all we know.'

Jana shook her head. 'No, they must still be down there,'

she said. 'This is the year of Quil's war and I think they're her ace in the hole.'

'Literally,' said Kaz.

'You think that's her plan?' said Dora, her detached mask dropping for a moment as she became excited by this new understanding. 'That she's working her way through history, heading back to this time period, gathering the things she needs to win her war?'

'Makes sense,' said Kaz. 'It's a good plan, if you think about it.'

Jana turned back to point at the timebomb that hung menacingly above them. 'There was a rock,' she said, her voice low with awe. 'A weird glowing rock right at the centre of the cavern.'

Kaz and Dora followed her gaze. 'You think . . .'

Jana nodded slowly. 'Maybe,' she said. 'When it detonates, the timebomb warhead might blow itself back through time. Maybe it even created the cavern sometime in . . . who knows how far back in time the explosion reaches?'

'Loops within loops,' said Dora. 'It's all connected, isn't it.'

That observation made Kaz uneasy. There was something about the way time worked that was making him feel trapped, as if no matter what he did he was just going through the motions, fulfilling some kind of plan. He didn't want to be time's puppet, especially when he couldn't be sure that Quil wasn't pulling the strings.

'I want to save my mum,' he blurted out, almost without thinking.

Jana and Dora turned to him, surprised at his outburst.

'What?' asked Jana.

'My mum,' he said again. 'If Kairos is right, if we can change history, then I want to save my mum.'

Dora whistled. 'Kaz, he used that as an example of how difficult it would be,' she said.

'Yeah, but possible,' he said firmly. 'If we were careful. If we planned it properly, meticulously.'

There was a long pause, and Kaz could tell they were trying to think of tactful ways to talk him out of it.

'What about Mars?' said Dora. 'Kairos said thousands of people died. If we can prevent that—'

'But Quil said she met us on Mars, remember?' said Kaz. 'She said it was our fault that everything went wrong. On her computer we saw photographs of ourselves in a war zone underneath a very different sky. It seems to me that Mars is absolutely the very last place we should ever go.'

'You don't need to tell me,' replied Jana patiently. 'I visited it, remember? Future me wasn't in very good shape at the time.'

'Steve told us what to do,' said Kaz angrily. 'Kairos is telling us what to do. Time itself is telling us what to do. And nobody is telling us why. I'm sick of it. I've been given this power, I didn't ask for it, but I've got it and I'm not going to let anybody else tell me what to do with it. If there is even a chance that I can save my mum, then I'm going to take it.'

'Even if you risk destroying the world?' said Dora, rising to anger herself.

'Yes!' said Kaz.

'You are being completely irresponsible,' said Dora, putting her hands on her hips and leaning towards him.

'Whoa there,' said Jana, stepping in between them. 'Time out.'

Kaz stepped back and walked away. Twenty minutes later Jana tracked him down to the cell-like room he had retreated to, and sat down on the hard bed next to him.

'I understand,' she said gently. 'I really do.'

Kaz grunted, non-committal. He did not feel like being generous or peaceable; neither did he feel like being reassured.

'I've talked to Dora, and to Kairos,' she continued, undeterred by his silence. 'I think we should jump back to Io Scientific 2014 and put a bullet in Quil's head. Dora thinks Kairos is right and we should go straight to Mars and try and prevent this mysterious disaster that set her against us in the first place.'

'I don't care about Quil,' said Kaz. 'I don't care about any of it.'

'No reason you should,' said Jana, her tone carefully neutral. 'Apart from the bit where she kidnapped, tortured and tried to kill you.'

Kaz sulked. He knew he was being childish, but he was too far gone to care.

'I proposed a compromise,' said Jana. 'Dora's in, if you are. Do you want to hear it?'

Kaz grunted again. 'S'pose so.'

'Dora and I will come with you to Beirut and help you save your mom – preferably without destroying the world,' she said drily. 'It can be like a rehearsal for Mars, testing whether we can really change history and get away with it.'

Kaz considered her words with mixed feelings. On one hand, the girls were willing to help him, and that increased the chances of success significantly. On the other . . .

'Saving my mum's life isn't a rehearsal for anything,' he said coldly, angry at the way the most important thing in his life was being relegated to some kind of dry run for a more important task.

'Of course,' said Jana, looking sheepish. 'Sorry.'

'It's OK,' said Kaz, easing off slightly. 'I know what you mean. Just remember this is my life we're messing with.'

'Understood. But if we help you and we manage to pull it off, then you have to come with us to Mars afterwards,' said Jana firmly. 'And if Mars doesn't work out, you and Dora are going to join me in putting Quil down in whatever time period we can get to her. Deal?'

Kaz didn't even have to think about it. 'Deal,' he said.

Jana nodded and stood to leave.

'Hey,' he said as she reached the door. 'Thank you.'

Jana looked back over her shoulder and smiled at him. 'Next stop: Beirut, 2010.'

Io Scientific, Cornwall, England, 2014 – 144 years to timebomb impact

The Rolls-Royce pulled up to the tall metal gates, gliding through a pall of smoke that whorled and spun in the car's wake, but the gates did not open.

Quil tutted impatiently in the back seat.

'Find out what is going on,' she barked as she turned round to peer out the back window. She identified the source of smoke easily – the wreckage of a motorbike lay by the side of the road. It was charred and twisted, no longer burning, but there were small fires in the foliage surrounding it and thin wisps of smoke still rose from the wreckage. She assumed it had crashed into a tree and the petrol tank had exploded on impact, but she was wary enough not to discount more sinister explanations.

Her chauffeur, a short, stocky man with blue facial tattoos and a shaved head, unclipped his seat belt and stepped outside, drawing a gun from a shoulder holster as he did so. He closed the door behind him, leaving Quil alone in the car, her only company the soft feline purr of the engine.

She rubbed her eyes, still slightly unaccustomed to feeling soft, supple skin where only recently there had been scars. Even in the future, when she had been much younger, she had habitually worn a mask, but it had become a necessity rather than a choice after she had been blown back in time and caught in an explosion during a brief stop aboard what she thought might have been an old-fashioned sailing ship. She and her husband, Henry Sweetclover, had recently travelled to 2076, where she had received the very best reconstructive surgery history had to offer. They had offered to make her look young, but by her reckoning she was nearing forty-five and felt she ought to look it, so there were lines and wrinkles where such things would naturally have occurred. She liked her new face; it was brand new yet it felt lived in, properly owned – but she was unaccustomed to having it uncovered.

Impatient, Quil wound down her window to demand answers from her chauffeur, who was in animated conversation with a security guard sitting in a little booth just inside the gate, who seemed unwilling to give them access to a large industrial complex that a sign identified as 'Io Scientific'. She leaned her head out, drew a breath to shout at them to hurry up but stopped dead as an explosion erupted from a series of windows in the top floor of the building, bright orange flame blossoming into the sky, showering glass and debris across the neatly kept lawn and the car park below.

Without hesitation, Quil climbed out of the car, drew her own weapon from her holster and pointed it at the security guard.

'I'm sorry, ma'am,' he stammered. 'But Mr Sweetclover gave strict instructions not to admit anybody. Anybody at all.'

'I am not anybody,' barked Quil.

'No ma'am, but, you see, somebody came in earlier, um,

disguised as Mr Sweetclover. Really, impossible to tell the difference it was,' said the guard, apologetic and afraid. 'And if someone could imitate him that well, then, how do I know you're, y'know, you?' He trailed off and winced, shrugging.

Quil considered his words as the sound of car alarms, tinkling glass and gunfire echoed towards her from the building on the other side of the fence she could not quite believe she was still on the wrong side of.

'Craig,' she said sweetly, stepping forward so the gun was just that bit closer to the guard's face. 'It is Craig, isn't it?'

The guard nodded fearfully.

'Craig, are you married?'

He nodded, even more afraid.

'Then you can return to your wife this evening in one of two conditions – unemployed or dead.' She cocked the gun for effect. 'You have three seconds to choose.'

Craig's shoulders slumped and he nodded once as he flicked the switch to open the gates. As soon as the gap was wide enough for her to slip through, Quil pushed past her chauffeur and ran as fast as she could towards the entrance. Had she looked back she'd have seen Craig shuffling dejectedly out the gates and walking off down the road into town, but her only thought was for her husband.

She realised just in time that the glass doors that would normally have slid open to admit her were going to stay firmly shut, and she skidded to a halt with her hand on the glass. The building was in lockdown.

There was no point shooting out the glass – she had specified it be bulletproof, a security precaution she now regretted. She could see no movement in the lobby, no one to let her in, so she ran round the side of the building to the fire escape, intending to climb up to the floor where the explosion had occurred and gain access through one of the blown-out windows, assuming the sprinklers had damped down the inferno. As she climbed she mentally filed through the likely causes of the explosion.

If the threat came from this time period, it was possible that another organisation or even a government was attempting to sabotage or steal their work – they were developing a number of revolutionary, top-secret projects that rivals around the world would certainly kill to obtain. On the other hand, if the threat was related to her past actions and future plans, then it could only be the three kids and their pathetic gaggle of allies causing trouble. Unless Earth's emergency government had developed time travel too and jumped back here to apprehend her. That thought chilled her blood, but she ran up the fire escape without pausing for breath, all the time thinking about Henry, praying that he hadn't been caught in the blast.

She reached the fire exit, which was hanging off its hinges, and ran straight inside. The air was thick with smoke and the floor was slick with water from the sprinklers, which were still dripping. She could see no flames but she hesitated for a second, stopped dead by an animal rush of fear as she flashed back to the explosion that had left her a charred wreck so many years before. She dismissed the vision as quickly as it had arrived and pushed on, blinking her tearful eyes to keep them clear, calling for her husband as she hurried deeper into the building. There was no more gunfire, so the only sound was the drip of water and the insistent whine of the fire alarm, which made her ears sting.

When she reached the corridor that ran the length of this wing of the building she saw the double doors of the central laboratory lying in her way, smashed and smouldering. She glanced right and saw that this had been the seat of the blast.

Looking left she saw a number of bodies littering the corridor, limbs at unnatural angles, pools of blood surrounding them. Again a rush of fear until she registered their uniforms – none of them were Henry, these were guards.

She ran past them and found a group of men round the next corner, coughing and checking each other for shrapnel wounds. One of them was her husband. She ran to him and flung her arms round him, startling him as she held him tight. After a moment's confusion, he returned her embrace.

Once her pulse had slowed, Quil disentangled herself and stepped back, slightly alarmed at the strength of feeling that had overtaken her. She mentally shook herself and resumed business.

'What happened?' she asked.

'It was the kids,' replied Henry. 'All three of them. We apprehended them at the Hall, as you said we would. We brought them back here, performed all the procedures we agreed.'

'Then . . .?' Quil wordlessly gestured towards the smouldering lab.

'They had assistance,' said Sweetclover. 'A fourth member of the party. A master of disguise. He infiltrated the building and affected their escape. You can see the result.'

'God dammit,' roared Quil, looking for something to kick or punch and finding only the guards within reach. She fetched the nearest one a hefty blow to the back of the head, which he seemed not to even notice, but it made her feel better.

'But you got Jana's chip?' she asked a moment later.

Sweetclover gestured towards the smouldering lab. 'It was in there,' he said. 'In the vault.'

With a wordless cry of rage, Quil turned and stalked into the wreckage. The vault door was open, the chip long gone. She worked hard to control her temper.

'What about the boy, Kaz. Was he interrogated?' she asked as she returned to her husband, who was looking abashed as he wiped blood off his face.

'He was.'

'Show me,' she said, and walked past him towards the stairs without hesitation, knowing he would follow.

They hurried down the stairs and wordlessly made their way to the room that contained the mind probe. Even as Quil pushed the door open she knew what she would find. Sure enough, the recording was gone and a guard lay dead on the floor.

She didn't have to say anything to communicate her disapproval. She hurried to the surgery with Sweetclover in tow and there, to her astonishment, found the doctor hunched over a microscope, apparently oblivious to the noise of the alarm and the sprinkler water that had drenched his white lab coat. He glanced up as they entered and when he saw who it was his face burst into the widest grin, excited and slightly manic.

'You have to come see this,' he said breathlessly. 'Dora's blood, it is exactly as you promised, it has the same properties as yours.' He indicated Quil. 'Which I thought was impossible.'

Quil harrumphed. This confirmed her hypothesis about the children – their ability to travel in time originated from the same source as hers. This wasn't really new intelligence though, not like the recording or the chip would have contained.

'Extract the mineral we need,' said Quil as she turned to leave. 'It will only be a trace amount, but it may be of use.'

She didn't wait to hear whether the doctor responded with enthusiasm, dismay or sycophancy. A few minutes later, back in her office, she poured Sweetclover a whiskey and they sat and considered their next move.

'Was this before they travelled to 1645?' she said, even though she knew the answer.

Sweetclover nodded. 'This was their first trip through time, yes.'

Quil shook her head mournfully. 'So that was our best chance to put a stop to all this, gone.' She looked up accusingly. 'How the hell did you let this happen, Hank?'

He shrugged. 'They had help, I told you,' he said. 'I don't know who it was, but he was well disguised and entirely duped the guards.'

'Another time traveller?'

'Yes. It could have been one of them, maybe Kaz, I don't know.'

'So now it's Mars, isn't it,' she said resignedly. 'They go on to Mars and screw everything up.'

'As far as we know.' He paused, and considered. 'There was one thing. I listened in on the boy's interrogation briefly.'

Quil leaned forward, interested. 'And?'

'He told a story about his mother's death. A bomb, it was. Somewhere called Beirut. Only a few years ago. Maybe we could use that?'

Quil threw her arms round his neck and kissed him hard. Now that was something she could work with.

Beirut, Lebanon, 18 March 2010, 11:41 P.M. - 30h 51m to car bomb detonation

The thunderstorm covered their arrival with uncanny accuracy, unleashing a simultaneous flash of lightning and sharp clap of thunder at the instant Dora, Kaz and Jana arrived. The commotion confused Jana for a moment; it was jarring enough jumping through time without being greeted by blinding light and deafening noise.

'Crap,' she muttered when her senses aligned properly and she was able to assess her surroundings.

The rain fell with brutal intent and the air had the tangy thunderstorm smell of scorched ozone. Despite the white electric light that had caused her to wince on arrival, it was night. There were no streetlights, so she blinked and tried to construct her surroundings from the after-image left by the lightning and the soft bleed of light from shuttered windows.

She and her friends were standing in the middle of an empty, narrow street next to a shabby old Volkswagen microbus. The walls on either side of them were three or four storeys high, with balconies that jutted out into the alleyway.

The walls were light but the whitewash on them was old and flaking, covered by a few desultory flyers that were even now in the process of coming unstuck in the face of the storm's onslaught. There was a narrow sidewalk lined with small bollards. Three scooters were piled up against the walls beneath a nearby balcony. A cat's cradle of phone lines tangled above them, spanning the alleyway.

Ahead of them was a dead end, the alley terminating in a three-storey house with shuttered windows and a doorway topped by a curving cupola-shaped window that rose to a point. Definitely Middle Eastern, which was a hopeful sign.

They'd been aiming for Beirut but they'd dressed for hot, dry weather, so Jana was soaked to the skin within a second of arrival.

She felt her wrist being pulled and allowed Kaz to drag her underneath a balcony, which provided scant cover.

'Is this it?' asked Dora.

'Think so,' said Kaz. 'Hang on a moment.'

Kaz, who was dressed in soggy shorts and a wet T-shirt, which clung to his scrawny boy's frame, hurried out into the downpour just as there was another lightning flash and thunderclap, again simultaneous, indicating that the heart of the storm was still directly overhead. Jana smiled as Kaz jolted in alarm. He made it to the open end of the alley without being struck down by the hand of God, and peered into the adjoining road, holding his hand above his eyes to shield them from the rain so he could see better. After a moment he turned and gestured for them to join him.

'I think I know where we are,' he said as they sheltered beneath a canvas awning that sagged threateningly, heavy with collected rain. 'If I'm right, it's only a short walk to United Nations House.'

When planning this trip they had considered approaching Kaz's parents at their home, but the possibility that Quil or her agents might be waiting for them had caused them to adopt a more circumspect approach. A better option would have been to catch his dad at the HQ of the UN mission in nearby Naqoura, where he spent most of each week, but the heavy military presence there made it unlikely that their arrival would go unnoticed. In the end they'd decided to seek out Kaz's mother at her workplace – she stayed in Beirut with Kaz and came to the UN building almost every day to collect documents, work contacts and get material for stories. The building was busy and large, well-protected and central. Even so, Jana was not happy.

Jana grabbed Kaz's arm as he made to walk away. 'Remember,' she said. 'Quil and Sweetclover could be waiting for us there.'

'And if they are, what better cover than a thunderstorm to help us sneak past them and into the building?' said Kaz reasonably.

'He's not wrong,' said Dora, whose light summer dress, which would have suited her beautifully four years ago, now looked incongruous pasted on to her lithe, muscular frame by the rain. Jana had preferred Dora when she spoke in seventeenth-century English; more recent colloquialisms sounded wrong coming from her mouth.

Kaz and Dora did not wait for Jana's approval, and they ran off into the downpour.

Jana rubbed her chest and winced as the scar from Quil's knife itched and throbbed. The doctor in Kinshasa had told her it was too soon to be putting herself under pressure, but after two weeks in bed she had gone totally stir crazy.

Jana sighed and ran after them, wondering exactly when

she'd lost the initiative in this trio. Another crash of thunder made her head throb and the rain lashed at her, as if trying to force her back to her proper time and place.

This street was wider, the buildings taller, but still the same crumbling balconies and jumble of wires strung overhead. There was no sidewalk, and cars lined both sides of the road close in to the walls, so the trio were forced to walk down the centre of the street where the rain – and possibly the lightning – could victimise them unhindered.

Jana saw a green dot flash at the limit of her peripheral vision, alerting her that there was new information on the interface chip that sat at the base of her skull. It had connected to a comms network and thereby to the system of global positioning satellites. A map appeared in front of her, a marker indicating her location. She used her eyes to toggle the map to the top right of her vision, where it retreated and became translucent but still readable, if she glanced up and left.

'Guys,' she said, catching up to them with some difficulty.

Kaz and Dora turned to her, Dora impassive, Kaz impatient. Jana held up a hand while she caught her breath, trying not to panic at how shallow her breathing was due to the now extreme discomfort her healing wound was causing her.

'I have GPS,' she gasped eventually. 'We're on Gemmayze Street. What address are we heading for, Kaz?'

'Riad Al Solh Square,' he said.

Jana thought the address and looked up and left to see a route clearly marked. She turned 180 degrees and began jogging back the way they'd come.

'This way,' she said archly over her shoulder. Although the pace was slower, they were now going in the right direction. Initiative regained.

Ten minutes later the worst of the storm had passed and

they were standing beneath an underpass staring across an ornamental garden towards a huge glass arch fronted by flagpoles. Between them and the entrance to UN House were circular patches of grass ringed with trees, an abstract stone sculpture and lots of open space.

'We can't approach this way,' said Dora, who had taken advantage of the momentary cover to strip her dress off and wring it out, standing in only her panties and bra. Remembering his reaction to her own nudity in Pendarn, Jana glanced across at Kaz and sure enough he was staring fixedly at his feet, his urgent drive to reach his parents momentarily overwhelmed by a mixture of embarrassment and hormones. But his reaction, endearing as it was, was far less interesting than what he was reacting to. Jana looked back at Dora, realised a moment too late that she was staring and blushed slightly when Dora caught her eye. She looked away.

Dora slipped her dress back on and led them in as round-about a way as she could towards the building's entrance, using trees and walls for cover, never venturing into the garden proper. As they moved, Jana finally set her eye-mods to night vision and scanned for signs of surveillance, but could see none. It seemed their instincts had been correct – if Quil and Sweetclover were lying in wait for them in this time period, they were probably watching Kaz's home.

They reached the front door, which was well-lit and guarded, and skirted around the side of the building. It only took a moment for Jana to bypass the keypad security on a service door at the rear, and they were inside. Jana toggled a switch on a small box attached to her belt and reminded the others to stay close – every person within a three-metre radius of her was now invisible to the security cameras.

'OK, Kaz, where now?' she asked.

Beirut, Lebanon, 19 March 2010, 8:12 A.M. – 26h 19m to car bomb detonation

Peyvand Golshiri felt every one of her forty-five years as she dragged herself out of bed. Her stomach rumbled and she rubbed her belly, feeling a pang at how soft and flabby it was beneath her aching fingers. She was not a young woman any more, and although she had only given birth once, it had taken a toll. Her husband claimed to like her with a bit of fat on her bones but that wasn't the point – he might not mind it, but she did. For the four hundredth time she vowed to go to the gym more often, and drink less wine.

She pulled on a shirt and walked barefoot to the kitchen, where she found Kaz already sitting at the kitchen table wolfing down cereal, his hair a thickety tangle, his eyes rimed with sleep. His cheeks were bed-warm red as he said good morning, inadvertently spitting Captain Crunch over the table.

Peyvand ruffled his hair affectionately but got her fingers stuck in its complex web of knots, forcing her to stop and untangle them as Kaz groaned in protest. He was fourteen,

66

which meant he was now, according to him, far too old for things like hair ruffles.

'Mum! Ow!'

Soggy Captain Crunch spattered on her thighs.

She really needed a coffee.

Kaz stopped squirming long enough for Peyvand to extricate herself and reach for the coffee maker. At this time of the morning she rarely functioned above the level of a trained chimpanzee and Kaz knew not to bother her until she'd had a good strong dose of caffeine. He kept his attention focused on the small portable TV on the counter, which was tuned to MTV Lebanon.

Peyvand started the coffee pot percolating and set about making breakfast, which, unlike her choice of beverage, was one of the Persian traditions she maintained. The taste of lavash bread with feta and jam transported her to the home of her childhood, the smells and the warmth of her mother's kitchen. Kaz hated feta, and pulled a face every time she tried to get him to eat some. She wondered if, when she was gone, he'd become as sentimental about her as she was about her own mother. When he was forty-five, would he eat lavash bread with jam and cheese, and think of her? She doubted it. He'd probably associate her with sugar-rich cereal and the smell of burning coffee.

She cursed and switched off the coffee pot, which was making an ugly gurgling noise as the reservoir burned dry.

She sighed and mumbled, 'This is going to be a long day.'

When her breakfast was prepared she sat beside Kaz and flicked through the day's news on her laptop. Rising tensions with Syria again, internecine conflict, infighting, religious intolerance. Same old same old. It got her down, this daily dose of gloom and misery. Not for the first time she questioned her profession, wondered whether journalism made a positive contribution to anything or whether it just kept people frightened and in their place. She had been mulling over a career change – well, not exactly a change, more a refocusing of her efforts away from interviews, breaking news and feature articles towards longer pieces, in-depth examinations of specific people and places, maybe even a book. She needed to choose a suitable topic, something original and surprising, something that hadn't been done to death.

She shook her head and drained her coffee cup. Maybe later. Today she had to drop Kaz off at school, hit the UN building to collect her pass, then head out to cover a UNIFIL project building a sports centre. Zbigniew was going to be there and she was looking forward to seeing him, even if it would only be for an hour or so. Maybe the brevity of their reunion would prevent them fighting.

She dragged Kaz away from the TV, hustling him to get ready as she flung a simple dress on, dragged a brush through her short hair and slapped a bit of colour on to her cheeks. She looked every bit the harassed mother, but there was nothing she could do about that, not without forty-five minutes alone time and a far better stocked bathroom.

She bustled Kaz out the door, locked it behind them, got down the stairs to the building's front door, went back up the stairs so Kaz could retrieve the books he'd forgotten, came down the stairs again, irritable and late, and finally emerged on to a muggy street thick with steamy mist as the morning sun burned away the remnants of the thunderstorm that had woken her in the middle of the night.

It was a short walk to Kaz's school and although she tried to kiss him goodbye, he wriggled from her grasp, embarrassed, and strolled through the gate without a backwards glance.

She stood for a moment, watching him run away from her, and felt a sentimental pang of loss, a small down payment on the way she'd feel when he finally ran away from her for good. Not long now, surely. He was a teenager, a taciturn jumble of acne, bad hair and sexual frustration that she could still not quite bring herself to stop thinking of as an unusually tall ten-year-old. How long before he packed his bags and took off in pursuit of whatever dream would possess him?

Blaming her maudlin musings on lack of sleep, she turned and hurried away.

The Beirut streets were noisy and crowded. Peyvand still felt drowsy, so she took a detour through a local street market that had a stall selling the most wonderful pastries. She exchanged pleasantries with the stall keeper, a thick matronly woman who always made jokes about how skinny Peyvand was and tried to force more sweets on her, and walked off with two boxes of treats. Ten minutes later, buoyed by the sugar hit from inhaling most of one box, she gave the other to one of the receptionists at the UN and was rewarded with a torrent of office gossip, the most salacious of which she filed away for future use; sweets and pastries weren't the only way of getting people to help her with stories.

Twenty minutes later she finally hit the small cupboard she laughingly called her office. She wasn't a UN official and had no official standing in the press, but her husband had pulled some strings, and she was useful for planting stories, so she was tolerated, even welcomed in some quarters. Nonetheless, the room was only a tiny bit wider than her desk, forcing her to sit with her back to the door, and it became oppressive on particularly hot days, so although she swung by daily she rarely stayed long. It was basically a glorified filing cabinet.

The desk was piled high with papers and notebooks, magazines, photographs, newspaper cuttings and printouts. Her laptop looked slightly forlorn sitting on a bed of *Time* and *Newsweek* in the middle of this towering monument to dead-tree journalism. Peyvand ignored it, instead rummaging out a battered Moleskine exercise book and grabbing a biro, the end of which had been bitten into a stippled mess of jagged peaks and troughs. She flicked through the book until she found the notes she had made last week; possible avenues of enquiry in her attempt to construct a profile of the new head of Lebanon's security services, a man whose public persona was well cultivated but whose private life remained opaque. She'd had a thought last night, as she was dropping off, and she bit the pen as she tried to excavate it from her memory – some connection she'd recalled and had decided to pursue.

She was beginning to get a sense of a memory bubbling up to the surface when she heard a voice behind her.

'Mrs Cecka?'

It was a girl's voice, young but confident, American. Surprised, Peyvand swung round in her chair.

'I don't go by my married name,' she said firmly. 'It's Ms Golshiri or Peyvand, I don't mind which.'

The girl smiled. Tall and skinny, about seventeen, she was dark-skinned but South Asian, not Arab. She was dressed simply in jeans and white shirt but looked dishevelled, as though she'd been soaked and had dried out crumpled. She needed a good ironing.

'Peyvand, then,' said the girl. 'You're a journalist, right?'

'Among other things.'

The girl stepped inside and closed the door. There was no other chair so she sat cross-legged on the floor with her back to the door, looking up at Peyvand.

'My name's Jana,' said the girl. 'I've got a story for you. The biggest story of your career. It's an exclusive, and it'll be a prize-winner.'

Peyvand considered her visitor for a second, feeling last night's elusive memory sliding away from her again. She sighed and put down her pen, taken aback by the girl's confidence, sceptical of her claim. She leaned back in her chair and folded her arms.

'How did you get in here?' she asked. 'You're someone's daughter right? Did Jerry in Press put you up to this?'

Jana smiled again. 'I'm nobody's daughter,' she said. 'And Jerry didn't put me up to anything. I have a story for you, that's all. But it's not something I can tell you. You'd never believe me. It's something I have to show you.'

Peyvand was immediately on her guard. If this girl was trying to lure her somewhere, this could be a kidnap attempt, albeit a very unusual one. It wouldn't be the first time a journalist had been targeted, and Peyvand's ties to the UN made her unique. When she had first begun travelling with Zbigniew she had been required to attend a training course on how to avoid being kidnapped, and how to behave if you were unable to. At the time she had thought it an overdramatic lesson in simple common sense. Now she tried very hard indeed to remember everything they had said, which was impossible because she hadn't really been paying attention.

She shook her head and said, 'I'm not going anywhere with you, young lady.'

The girl smiled. 'No, I can show you here, but I need to prepare you first. I have to tell you three things and ask you a question.'

'I'm listening,' said Peyvand cautiously.

'Your son, Kazic . . .'

Peyvand knew what was going to happen: the girl was going to pull out a mobile and show her live footage of Kaz. This *was* a kidnap attempt!

'. . . I know him,' said the girl. 'First, he wanted me to tell you that he still has the scar on his knee from when he fell off his scooter in the park in Guatemala. Second, that he hopes you're taking very good care of Bun Bun.' The girl smirked at this point but Peyvand barely noticed because she was fixed to the chair in horror. They must have snatched him the second her back was turned, from inside school. Her mind raced as she tried to think of a way to take control of the situation.

'Third,' the girl went on, 'he says he remembers the fight on Christmas Day and he thinks you were right and his dad was being a dick.'

'What have you done with my son?' asked Peyvand, drawing on all her reserves of self-control but unable to hide the slight tremor of fear in her voice.

The girl's slightly smug air evaporated. She looked uncertain, and something about her made Peyvand sure that uncertainty was not a common emotion for her.

'Nothing,' said the girl, seemingly anxious to reassure her. 'Honestly. I only have to ask you a question, and then everything will make sense, I promise.'

Peyvand nodded slowly, indicating that the girl should continue.

'The question is: can you explain Wyndham's law to me?'

Peyvand was very, very confused. It took a moment for her to recall a conversation she'd had with Kaz a week or so ago about a film he'd watched. It had been about time travel and Kaz had explained to her afterwards, in the patient way that a fourteen-year-old will explain things to a parent they secretly think is stupid, that time travel was impossible because of this law he'd read about on Wikipedia. She had only been half listening; if she paid full attention every time his enthusiasm caused him to explain something pointless in ridiculous detail, she'd have a head full of nothing but Halo hacks.

'Um, something about time travel being impossible because if it was there'd be people from the future all over the place,' said Peyvand.

Jana clapped her hands once and smiled again. 'Great,' she said brightly. 'Right, wait here a moment.'

The girl rose to her feet, opened the door and stepped outside. Peyvand sat, still scared, but now confused as well; this bizarre situation wasn't proceeding the way she'd feared it would.

A moment later a young man stepped into the doorway, also simply dressed in jeans and T-shirt. He was tall and skinny, the gangly, angular boniness of an older teenager. His hair was cut very short and he had the remains of a suntan. He stood there in the doorway, not saying anything, looking at Peyvand, and she looked back at him, her confusion growing. There was something familiar about him . . .

'Hi Mum,' said the stranger. And then Peyvand did something she prided herself on never, ever, ever doing – she screamed. It wasn't a full-throated I've-seen-a-monster-about-to-eat-me kind of scream, more a brief, strangled yelp of alarm.

The boy stepped hurriedly inside and closed the door behind him.

Peyvand was literally speechless. Her mouth moved but no words came out. Her thoughts were jumbled and chaotic, but within seconds she'd formed a hypothesis that Zbigniew had a child he'd never told her about and that little sod was playing a very, very nasty practical joke on her and oh my God, was her husband going to get it in the ear.

The young man was grinning so hard it looked a little painful.

'Mum, it's me, Kaz,' he said. 'Honestly. Look!' He pulled up his right jeans leg and showed her his knee, which had the exact scar her son had got two summers ago when he fell off his bike.

'Half the boys in the world have scars on their knees from falling off bikes,' hissed Peyvand, but her anger lacked conviction because her awareness that this was her son was strong and, try as she might, it was increasingly hard to ignore. It wasn't the face or the body language exactly, although they were both right; it was something else, something intangible. The smell of him, perhaps?

'OK, fair point,' said the boy, apparently taken aback by her anger. 'Jana told you the three things, yeah? The ones only I could know?'

'All that proves is that you've got my son,' said Peyvand, putting as much menace into her voice as she could.

'OK, right.' The boy looked momentarily lost for words. 'OK, um, ask me anything. Go on. Anything only Kaz would know.'

'Think I'm a dummy, do you?' said Peyvand, jumping to her feet. She grabbed the boy's head and peered into both his ears in turn, looking for earpieces. She was slightly taken aback when she didn't find any. And there was that subconscious tug again, even stronger when she touched the boy, the feeling that yes, this was her son; how could she ignore the evidence of her senses?

She stepped back and folded her arms. 'All right,' she said. 'Who was Kaz's best friend in Croatia?'

'Slobodan, whose hair was never combed,' said the boy, smiling.

'Where were we when I gave you the PS3 you nagged me about for a year?'

'Guatemala,' said Kaz. 'It was wrapped in red paper and had *Prince of Persia* preloaded, like I'd asked for.'

Peyvand stopped, unsure what to do. Her heart seemed to stop; her stomach twisted. It was impossible. This boy knew stuff he couldn't know, and her every instinct told her to hug him. She took a step backwards and felt the backs of her thighs press against the desktop.

'Je-egaretō bokhoram,' she told him.

'Jeegaré man-ee,' he replied, as her son always did.

'OK, I'll play along,' she said. 'So you're my son from, what . . .' she considered his appearance, 'four years in the future?'

The boy nodded. 'Yes,' he said.

'Right. And you've got a time machine parked outside?'

Kaz laughed and the sound of it tugged at her.

'It's very, very complicated,' he said. 'Really. I don't fully understand it myself yet. I can take you to someone who can explain it all to you. But first, we have to go and get Dad.'

Peyvand shook her head. 'I'm not going anywhere with you.' But her objection was half-hearted; the logical, reasonable part of her brain was giving up its objections one by one as the proximity of the boy overwhelmed her and her every cell felt the instinctive pull of maternal love.

'You can travel in time,' she said, in a last-ditch effort to apply logic. 'And you choose to show up on a muggy Thursday in Beirut. Why aren't you off saving JFK or killing Hitler or something? You really expect me to believe that you would choose to come freak me out in my office? And how did you get in here anyway? This is ridiculous.'

She sat back on the desk, knocking her laptop over and triggering a small avalanche of paper.

The boy knelt before her, reached up and took her hands in his. She looked down into his big brown eyes, so familiar but so different. Peyvand was taken aback to see tears welling in them.

'I came because there's something I need to do,' he said. 'Something I need your help with. And there isn't much time, so explanations will have to wait. You have to trust me.'

'Was that your girlfriend a moment ago?' asked Peyvand, surprising herself.

The boy laughed.

'No,' he said. 'No she's not.'

'Oh, are you gay?'

'Mum!'

And in that moment, with the embarrassed whine of a teenage boy forced to discuss sexuality with a parent, the last of her resistance crumbled and she finally felt certain that this was her son.

'Doesn't matter if you are,' she said, smiling. 'When you were four you went through a phase of dressing up as Cinderella. Your dad and I used to joke about it.'

'God, Mum, stop,' he said, but he was smiling again, relieved that she had finally accepted him.

Peyvand cupped his face in her hands and looked in wonder. 'My beautiful boy. How is this possible?'

He held her gaze for a moment, blinking back tears, then he reached up and gently removed her hands.

'Later,' he said. 'I know you must be full of questions but

it might be dangerous for us to stay here too long. We need to go and get Dad.'

Peyvand nodded. 'OK,' she said, rising to her feet.

As Kaz turned to go she grabbed the last pastry from the box on her desk and shoved it in her mouth before following him out the door. Today was going to require lots and lots of sugar.

'Wait,' she said as she hit the corridor. 'Dangerous how?'

Beirut, Lebanon, 19 March 2010, 11:40 A.M. - 22h 52m to car bomb detonation

Kaz's emotions were all over the place.

He was face to face with his mother for the first time in four years. The mother he had lost and mourned, whose violent death had defined his life for so long. As he'd prepared for the meeting he'd been unsure what he would say to her. Would he even be able to speak at all? He had thought it quite likely he'd burst into tears and bury his head in her chest, which, given that she wouldn't know who he was, was likely to earn him a knee in the groin and a right hook.

He had worked out the approach carefully. Letting Jana smooth the way, establish some facts before he showed his face. The idea had been to give him time to hear her voice first, to get used to the way it pulled at him, to choke back his tears before he tried to speak. But as he'd stood outside listening through her office door he hadn't felt like crying at all; he'd felt happy – overwhelmingly, heel-kickingly happy.

When he'd stepped inside to talk to her he'd found it hard to speak not because he was biting back sobs, but because he was grinning so hard his jaw kind of locked. And when she had finally embraced him, he'd felt a deeper contentment than he had ever known, something primal that he had been missing more deeply than he'd been able to acknowledge.

Once the reunion was over the questions had come flooding out of her. Had he done well at school? What happened to her and Zbigniew next? Had they overthrown the ayatollahs yet? He batted them all away, promising to tell her later, and tried to concentrate on his plan for approaching his father; he knew that was going to be a much trickier proposition.

'Mum, listen,' he said, interrupting a question about, of all things, what was going to happen on the final series of her favourite soap. 'I need you to talk to Dad first. You know what he's like; if I turn up claiming to be his son from the future, he'll have me arrested.'

'If you're lucky,' she replied.

'Yeah, so you need to talk to him,' said Kaz. 'Lure him away, get him alone and then prime him for me. Can you do that, do you think?'

'Of course,' she said, smiling. 'He's putty in my hands.'

Kaz knew that wasn't true, but her confidence made him smile regardless.

They reached the site of the newly constructed sports centre without incident. Dora became noticeably more twitchy once they stopped moving, and while Jana and Kaz sat on a patch of grass at the edge of a new playground that was part of the sports complex, she prowled the edges of it restlessly, on the lookout for threats.

A group of UNIFIL soldiers were gathered near the swings talking to a gaggle of journalists. About twenty young children, excited at being let out of school, were waiting to one side, ready to start playing so the press could get some photos of the new facility in action.

Kaz could see his dad, tall and straight in his uniform, schmoozing the press. He felt a pang of nerves as his mum touched his dad's arm. Dad looked round, surprised, and excused himself. They went off to talk in the shadow of a slide.

'How you holding up?' asked Jana, who sat beside Kaz, reclining on the cool lawn.

'I thought it couldn't get any weirder, but this is . . .' He trailed off, shaking his head.

'I bet,' she said. 'But good, yeah?'

He nodded. 'Oh yeah,' he agreed. 'I just worry it won't last. What if we can't save her? Or what if it's our intervention that gets her killed? There's too much uncertainty.'

'Which is kind of the point.'

'I know, I know. Still freaks me out.'

'Your mom's nice,' said Jana.

'She's great.'

'Must have been really bad, when she, y'know.'

'Yeah.'

There was a long pause, then Jana sighed. 'Blood from a stone,' she said, sighing for effect.

Kaz pulled his eyes away from his parents, who were locked in intense discussion, and smiled at Jana.

'Sorry,' he said. 'My brain's kind of overloaded.'

'I can imagine.' She reached out and squeezed his hand. He squeezed back. Sparks flickered in the air and they both pulled their hands away sharply.

'If we tried to have sex, we'd start a fire,' said Jana, laughing.

Kaz blushed.

'Yeah,' he said with a forced laugh, a moment too late.

The next pause was even more uncomfortable than the first. Kaz remembered that he was supposed to ask questions. His dad had once told him, during an awful, awkward, endless conversation about Kaz's non-existent love life, that women liked to talk about themselves, and advised him to ask lots of questions. He rummaged around in his head for a suitable topic.

'What about your parents?' he asked eventually. 'We've met Dora's, now you've both met mine. You never mention yours. What are they like?'

Judging by the sudden change in Jana's body language – the way her posture stiffened and her jaw hardened – Kaz had hit on exactly the wrong topic for small talk.

'Nothing special,' she replied curtly, staring fixedly into the middle distance.

'You said you were kind of rich?' said Kaz, inwardly cursing himself for not letting it go.

Jana grunted.

'Nothing,' said Dora, passing them on her circuit of the area.

'Then sit down for a minute,' said Kaz, relieved to have someone to interrupt the awkward.

'I should—'

'Oh sit down, Dora,' snapped Jana. 'Quil isn't here. She'd have made her move by now.'

Dora sat down between Jana and Kaz looking somewhat confused.

'Kaz,' Dora said after a moment. 'Long ago you told me your father was a soldier who made peace. I thought it strange at the time. Now I find that he does this by making playgrounds and it seems even stranger.'

'This isn't his project,' said Kaz. 'He's here to make up the numbers, do a bit of PR. Normally he's locked away in meetings, negotiating or training other soldiers to negotiate. But UNIFIL does a lot of different stuff to try and help communities recover after conflict. This kind of thing,' he indicated the playground, 'isn't unusual. It's better than having children play on bomb sites or partially cleared minefields. And it makes people feel good about the UN being here.'

Dora considered this and finally nodded. 'I suppose that makes sense,' she said. 'But I still think soldiers who build swing sets are kind of weird.'

They sat there in silence – Jana sulking, Dora puzzling, Kaz fretting – until Dora nudged Kaz with her elbow.

'Here they come,' she said.

Kaz looked up and saw his parents walking towards him. His mother had the look she always wore after an argument, a kind of strained half-calm grimace, while his dad looked furious, stomping slightly ahead of his wife as if itching for a fight.

Kaz took a deep breath and rose to his feet, steeling himself for a confrontation.

His dad walked right up to him, put his hands on his hips, stuck out his chin and chest and opened his mouth to speak. But then the strangest thing happened. He looked Kaz in the eye and in an instant all the aggression melted away. His mouth dropped open, his arms fell to his sides and he kind of deflated as he said softly, 'How?'

Peyvand stepped up beside him and slipped her arm through her husband's.

'See,' she said, not entirely managing to hide both her relief and a slight undercurrent of I-told-you-so.

'Hi, Dad,' said Kaz, shifting awkwardly on his feet, not

knowing whether to offer to shake hands, go for a hug, or slap his dad playfully on the arm. No not that last one, definitely not that. He opted for a limp sort of wave and immediately regretted it.

Colonel Zbigniew Cecka quickly regained control of himself. 'How?' he asked again, this time focused and direct.

'Long story, and we'll have plenty of time to tell it,' said Kaz. 'But first you both need to come with us. There's someone you need to meet, who will make it all a lot clearer.' He glanced around but nobody was looking in their direction: all cameras were pointing at a two-year-old girl who was giggling hysterically as two soldiers spun her on a roundabout.

Dora and Jana rose to their feet and they all joined hands in a circle. Then, with a flash of red, all five of them winked out of existence.

Quantum Bubble - Sweetclover Hall, Cornwall, England, 7 April 2158, 8:22 A.M.

Kaz had heard Kairos's long explanation of time travel already, but he endured it again as he sat between his parents in the undercroft conference room, holding his mother's hand and thinking about the awful conversation he was about to have.

'So,' said Kaz to his parents when Kairos had finished, 'you see the situation. We don't know for certain exactly how time travel into the past works, but we can't risk creating a paradox that could destroy everything, so we have to plan accordingly.'

'Plan for what?' asked Zbigniew, as always cutting to the heart of the matter. He really had no patience for shilly-shallying.

Kaz took a deep breath, let go of his mother's hand and leaned forward.

'The one question I haven't answered,' he said, 'is what happened to me in the years between that day in Beirut when we snatched you, and today.'

'Should we know?' asked Peyvand.

'I'm afraid you have to.' Another deep breath. 'Because, you see, we're going to have to try and change history – my history. Or, well, actually, not change it at all. Change yours.'

As he said this, he locked eyes with his mother and saw a sudden dawning of fear in her eyes.

'Mine?' she said with a nervous laugh.

'Yes,' said Kaz. 'And we can do it. We have a plan. So when I tell you what happened – happens – don't freak out. We have a plan, OK?'

Peyvand glanced at Zbigniew again but his gaze was set firmly on Kaz, who could see he was clenching his jaw. Kaz squeezed his mother's hand slightly harder.

'OK,' she said with a small nod.

'On March twentieth, the day after we snatched you to bring you here, we were all together in Beirut. We were walking to the cinema.' Kaz paused, momentarily unsure how to put into the words the terror of that day. 'As we passed that stall that does the pastries – you know the one – you broke away from me and Dad and told us to wait a moment while you got some sweets for the film. You walked back to the stall, you were only about ten, fifteen metres away from us. And then—' Kaz stopped, unable to continue. His mother sat silently, obviously terrified.

'Car bomb,' said Zbigniew after a few moments.

Kaz looked up at his father, held his gaze for a second, then nodded. He hated revisiting that day – it was a hard memory, one he had pushed down as deep as he was able, and he felt sick as he started to pull it all back up again.

'The head of national security service's convoy was the target,' he explained. 'The bomb went off as his convoy drove through the market. He was killed instantly. So were thirty-two other people. I remember – and this is important, because it's how

85

we're going to fix this – I remember being lifted off my feet, literally. I remember flying through the air. I think I blacked out for a minute or two. The next thing I remember is the smell of smoke. I couldn't see either of you. I got to my feet – I wasn't badly injured, no bones broken or anything, just lots of cuts and scrapes. I was lucky. I think I was crying. I went running through the smoke crying for you. I saw . . . horrible things. And then out of nowhere you, Dad, scooped me up and ran with me to the end of the road, out of the chaos. You were limping and held me with only one arm. And I was asking you where Mum was over and over, but you wouldn't answer me. Not until you'd checked me for wounds. Then you said "she's gone".'

Peyvand leaned forward and enfolded Kaz in a strong hug, making him well up despite his resolve not to cry.

'My poor darling,' she said, and Kaz realised that even though he had told her she was going to die, she was only concerned about the effect it had had on his younger self.

After a moment Kaz felt his father's hand on his shoulder.

'You said you had a plan,' said Zbigniew.

Peyvand released Kaz and he pulled out of the hug, although he regained his grip on his mother's hands and held on as if for dear life.

'Yes, we do,' said Kaz. 'It all hinges on one thing.'

Peyvand looked up at Kaz, who was still firmly focused on her even though he was taking to her husband.

'I never saw your body, Mum,' said Kaz, with an unwanted tremor in his voice. 'Not at the bomb site, not at the funeral. It was a closed casket. I only knew you were dead because Dad told me you were.'

'I don't understand,' said Peyvand. 'How does that . . .'

'It means we can save you, Mum,' said Kaz, smiling as

the tears finally rolled down his cheeks. 'We can go back in time and ensure that you survive the explosion. As long as my younger self still experiences that day exactly as I remember it.'

There was a long silence as his works sank in. Then Zbigniew spoke up.

'And all the days afterward,' he said.

Peyvand gasped at the implication and looked searchingly into Kaz's eyes.

Kaz nodded. 'Yes.'

'So what did happen between that day and this, for you?' she asked.

'We mourned you,' said Kaz. 'We buried a coffin.' Kaz turned to address his father. 'We returned to Poland. We fought a lot. I was, I don't know. Angry. Grieving. It was not a happy time. Eventually I ran away. Went to England to work. Met Dora and Jana, and the rest.'

Kaz saw an unexpected flicker of sadness in his father's eyes, but it was gone as quickly as it arrived.

'Your proposal,' said Zbigniew, 'if I understand you correctly, is that you and I work together to plan your mother's escape from the bomb. And then I will have to lie to your younger self for four years. Subject you to the loss of your mother, make you live through grief and pain, have you grow up without her, endure your anger and your rebellion and all the fights, knowing all the time that I was deceiving you.'

Kaz nodded.

'And me?' asked Peyvand. 'I couldn't see you, could I. Not for all those years.'

Kaz shook his head.

'Yes but no,' he said. 'I can bring you forward in time. For you, those four years could pass in an instant. It's only

Dad and my younger self who would have to travel in the slow lane.'

'Hey Zbig,' said Peyvand with a sad smile. 'You'd finally be older than me. Shame your parents aren't alive to see that.'

'Eh?' asked Kaz, who had only hazy memories of his paternal grandparents.

'They never approved of me,' explained Peyvand, rolling her eyes and smiling. 'A woman who was older than her husband was obviously a cradle-snatching harpy.'

'Oh yes, let's restart that old fight now,' muttered Zbigniew, smiling and rolling his eyes.

'I'm still not sure whether we'd be changing history by doing this or not,' admitted Kaz, anxious to deflect the argument. 'Maybe this is what always happened, maybe I'm only creating the circumstances for four years of misery. I don't know, and the professor doesn't either, not really.'

Peyvand glanced at Kairos, who shrugged.

'All I know for sure is that if we do this,' said Kaz, 'you won't be dead. There's one thing, though. I can't go with you. It will have to be Dora and Jana who manage things in Beirut.'

Peyvand opened her mouth to protest but Zbigniew spoke up first.

'Because if you were to come back to that day, and saw some detail that you realised was wrong, it might create a paradox,' he said. 'But Dora and Jana weren't there, so the new version of history they create only has to stick to the facts you give them.'

Kairos clapped his hands once. 'Yes, I see you understand,' he said. 'Very good.'

'So you agree?' asked Kaz, his face abeam with hope. 'You'll try it?'

His parents locked eyes and nodded at each other almost imperceptibly.

'Yes,' they said in unison.

Kaz felt a rush of emotion, but he couldn't have said for sure whether it was relief or terror. He reached out towards his father, then sat between his parents, holding their hands, crying in spite of himself.

Beirut, Lebanon, 19 March 2010 10:22 P.M. – 12h 10m to car bomb detonation

Peyvand did not sleep a wink the night before she died.

She had risen that morning expecting an ordinary day, the latest in a long line stretching back for years and stretching ahead much the same.

But now she knew that there were no more days stretching ahead of her. Tomorrow she would die, either literally or figuratively. And whatever became of her – spirited away to safety, or blown apart in the street – today had been her last day with Kaz. Her last day with her beautiful boy, the last day of the childhood she had shared with him. The very last day of the kind of motherhood she had found more fulfilling than she would have believed possible ten years ago.

Because it had not been an ordinary day, not by any measure, and she couldn't process it. Time travel, her boy transformed into a young man, a trip to the future, a lecture in quantum physics, a daring plan outlined and then unceremoniously transported back to her flat to prepare for the end of everything she knew. It was dizzying.

She drained her wine glass and reached for the bottle. Since she and Zbigniew had returned from the future, they'd been tense with each other, and young Kaz had picked up on it, becoming skittish and irritable. Not knowing the real reason for their nervousness, he had been expecting a fight and had set about making himself the centre of attention, diverting their anger his way. Peyvand wondered if he consciously decided to act as a lightning rod or whether it was instinctive, a character trait emerging in response to their rootless, unconventional life, one more way they were screwing him up, creating problems for the man he would grow into and the people who would share his life.

Throughout his childhood they'd travelled with Zbigniew's work, and she'd kept busy even while nursing – chasing stories, writing articles for magazines and newspapers, juggling her trade with her mothering. The novelty of each new assignment, each new country, had been thrilling to both of them; they'd been so pleased with themselves for showing Kaz the world, opening his eyes to new cultures and experiences, that they'd not really considered the downside. From what Kaz had told them about his future, she was concerned that the only lesson they had taught him was to move on when things got tough.

She looked across at Zbigniew, his brow furrowed, his face haunted. She felt a pang of pity for him, and the years of teenage rebellion he'd have to handle without her help.

'You'll be fine,' she said.

Zbigniew looked up. 'Not according to him,' he said. 'According to him, we'll spend the next four years fighting all the time until he runs away from home. I'm going to fail him. I'm *required* to fail him.'

'But he knows that now,' said Peyvand. 'He wasn't angry

with you when you met him, was he? He seemed happy to see you.'

Zbigniew nodded, conceding the point. 'But it's not much to look forward to, is it?' he said. 'Years of unhappiness, raising him in Poland. On my own. Boze moi, it's not a pretty picture.'

She knew that nothing she could say would puncture his melancholy, so she let silence fall again. He drained his glass and took himself off to bed without a word, leaving her alone with the wine bottle.

She was still sitting on the sofa two hours later, opening yet another bottle of wine as she listened to Zbigniew's soft snores emerging from the bedroom, when a figure appeared before her in a silent flare of red sparks . . .

92

Beirut, Lebanon, 20 March 2010 10:20 A.M. - 12 mins to car bomb detonation

'You're too different,' said Jana. She bit into a pastry and considered Dora. She recoiled slightly; her eye-mods were taking a moment to reset to normal magnification and her initial view of Dora consisted of one enormous nose pore. She resisted the urge to recommend a new exfoliation regime.

They were sitting on the roof of an apartment building overlooking the street market, bathed in mid-morning sun, repeatedly scanning the crowd, the rooftops, the traffic, the surrounding streets – looking for any hint of Quil, time travellers, anyone or anything that looked out of place.

'I am older,' Dora replied.

Jana shook her head, sprinkling flakes of pastry on her shirt. 'That's not what I meant and you know it.'

'Jana, we are in the middle of an operation,' snapped Dora. 'Can this wait until later?'

Jana shrugged and swallowed the last of her pastry. 'Whatever.'

'Let's go through it again,' said Dora.

'Seriously?' asked Jana. She already knew she didn't entirely trust this new Dora, but she was beginning to think she didn't like her much either. Far too bossy for her taste.

Dora's hard stare answered clearly. Jana shook her head wearily and began.

'In,' Jana checked her watch, 'seven minutes young Kaz – who is adorable by the way, did you see that hair! – will come round that corner with his parents. A minute later, as they pass the stall that sold me this delicious pastry that you refused to even try, Kaz's mom will stop to buy some goodies for the cinema. Kaz and his father will walk on. As soon as their backs are turned Kaz's mom will run to the far end of the street to a place of safety. Meanwhile a black sedan car carrying the head of the intelligence service will turn into the street from the opposite corner, moving past Kaz and his dad towards the pastry stall. When it draws level with the stall the nervous young man sitting in that blue Toyota down there, currently pretending to be on his mobile, will blow himself, his car, his target and half the market to bits. Kaz's mom will be safely away by this point, but Kaz and his dad will catch the shockwave of the blast and briefly be separated in the confusion. Eventually they will find each other and leave the area, heading to the hospital. Zbigniew will tell poor Kaz his mother is dead but in fact she'll rendezvous with us and we'll bring her back to the future.'

'Wild cards?' asked Dora.

Jana rolled her eyes. 'Immediately after the explosion me and Kaz, along with Steve, whoever he is, will appear in the midst of the wreckage during our attempt to escape from Sweetclover in 2014,' she said. 'But they quickly leave the area too, heading for a local cafe where they will eat some truly disgusting food before jumping back to Io Scientific.'

'And?'

'And at some point while all this is going on, you expect Quil and/or Sweetclover and/or their weird blue-tattoo fetish goons to intervene and try to snatch either version of Kaz, or maybe his mom or dad, or perhaps you or me, or older me and Steve. Basically, anyone she can get her hands on.'

Dora nodded.

'I still think you're being paranoid,' said Jana.

'Perhaps,' acknowledged Dora. 'But it's the perfect opportunity for her to make a move on us.'

'Assuming she even knows about any of this,' said Jana.

'Assuming she does.'

'We walked the area twice,' Jana pointed out. 'We saw no evidence of her.'

Dora paused, considering Jana for a moment. Jana did not like the calculating stare one bit. She couldn't read Dora any more, couldn't get a handle on her. It made her uncomfortable.

'Do I need to remind you, of all people, how resourceful and ruthless Quil is?' said Dora. 'We underestimated her once before and we all nearly died. You more nearly than any of us. Are you trying to convince me not to worry, or convince yourself that you're safe? Because someone who didn't know you better might mistake that for displaced cowardice.'

It took Jana a moment to gather her wits. As cold and hard as Dora now seemed, Jana hadn't expected such harsh judgement from her.

Before Jana could reply, Dora ploughed on. 'I don't blame you for being scared, because this is all about you,' she said. 'I don't know why, but that chip in your head is important to Quil. There's some connection between you and her that puts you right at the centre of this. I would suspect she was your future self, but she did try and stab you to death, so I don't think that's likely – not unless time travel is *way* more complicated than Kairos thinks. But whatever the reason, if Quil arrives here today, it's probably only because she thinks it's a way to get to you. It might have been better if you'd stayed behind and let me handle this myself.'

Jana clenched her jaw and took a deep breath, telling herself not to lose her temper.

'No, I'm good, thanks,' she said brusquely, staring down into the street and noticing Kaz's family coming round the corner. The conversation had become so uncomfortable for her, she was guiltily glad there was about to be distracting carnage. 'We're on.'

Jana was aware of Dora's body language changing as she became tense and alert, every inch a hunter. It freaked her out.

Down below, young Kaz was happily chatting away between his two parents. Zbigniew was stony-faced, looking straight ahead, focused and prepared. Peyvand looked as if she were on the verge of tears, but she forced a smile as she stopped and told her men that she was going to pop back and get some pastries for the film. Kaz smiled in return and then he and his father moved on down the street.

But Peyvand just stood there and watched them walk away.

'What the hell is she doing?' murmured Jana, alarmed by the black sedan nosing its way into the street. 'Move, for God's sake.' If Kaz turned round, he'd see her standing there and that's not what he remembered happening. The consequences of an error at this moment could be catastrophic.

Peyvand's face was a mix of terror and loss as she stared at the retreating backs of her husband and child, apparently frozen to the spot by the enormity of what was about to happen. Then she looked around her frantically, as if returning to reality, saw the black sedan approaching and opened her mouth. Jana realised with horror that she was about to try and warn the crowd about the bomb.

'Crap,' whispered Dora and then there was a flash of red sparks and she was gone.

Jana looked down at the market street, watching the scene play out, knowing there was nothing she could do.

Time seemed to slow for Jana as the car carrying the bomber's target pushed slowly through the crowd towards the Toyota, still parked opposite the pastry stall at which an old man was buying baklava for a young boy – his grandson perhaps – who stood looking up at the kind-faced old man in happy anticipation. Jana zoomed in on the bomber's face as he sat in the front seat of the innocuous small blue car. He was a young man, still a teenager, she guessed. His face was slick with sweat, his eyes open unnaturally wide, his lips moving silently. He saw the sedan approaching and in that instant he smiled widely. The beatific expression of rapture on the face of a boy who was about to kill scores of innocents froze Jana's blood.

A flash of movement drew Jana's eye away and she saw Kaz – her Kaz, the older one who was supposed to be sitting this day out in the quantum bubble – running through the crowd, pushing and shoving and barging his way past outraged families. Peyvand still stood, her back to him, rooted to the spot, her mouth open but no sound emerging. It occurred to Jana that maybe she was actually committing suicide. Is that what this was – not fear or combat panic but a death wish?

The black car drew level with the blue one . . .

The bomber opened his mouth wide and shouted something at the top of his lungs as he closed his eyes . . .

Kaz barrelled through the crowd, reaching out his hand, stretching towards Peyvand, trying to make fingertip contact . . .

And then the bomb exploded and the street became a maelstrom of fire, shrapnel and body parts.

It was the loudest noise Jana had ever heard. Even four storeys up and three buildings away, she was blown over by the blast, shocked by the physical impact of the shockwave. As she sprawled backwards she saw the engine block of the Toyota rising into the air, drawing level with her eyeline seemingly buoyed by a cushion of smoke and flame, then falling, as if in slow motion, back down into the confusion and death. She couldn't tell if the equally shocking silence that followed the detonation was real – a street of dying and injured people still too disorientated to cry out – or whether she was deafened and it was taking a few moments for her hearing to return.

After a long few seconds of surreal stillness, the screaming began.

Jana looked down into the street but was unable to see much. The smoke – thick, black, choking – masked everything. Some places glowed orange, as fires burned within the cloud. People ran out of the confusion at the far edges, some running headlong, screaming, some feeling their way cautiously, afraid of ploughing into debris or treading on a casualty. She stared for a few moments, at a loss what to do. Then, as the smoke began to clear – settling downwards, heads and pieces of market stalls emerging from the cloud as if rising from water – a red flash just at the periphery of the blast area drew her eyes.

Standing there, just about the only people fully upright and unscathed, were the earlier versions of Kaz, herself and their mysterious rescuer Steve, currently disguised as Sweetclover.

She watched as her younger self and Steve grabbed Kaz by the arms and pulled him away, in shock after his first-time jump and the memories of the blast that he was even now experiencing a few metres to his left, as a young boy. As her earlier self and her companions rounded the corner, she zoomed in on fourteen-year-old Kaz. He was standing, flapping his arms in nervous shock, crying for his parents. There was blood on his hands and he was coated in dust that caught in his tears and streaked his face. Before him were the remains of a man, disassembled by the explosion and dumped at Kaz's feet in pieces. Kaz was so desperate he didn't even seem aware of the horror that lay around him. Jana wanted more than anything to run down and comfort him, but she knew she couldn't. A moment later Zbigniew limped out of the smoke, scooped Kaz up with one arm and hurried out of the area, round the corner.

The smoke around the seat of the explosion had cleared enough for Jana to scan it. She had definitely seen Kaz – 'her' Kaz, the present-moment one from the quantum bubble – running towards his mother at the instant of the explosion. It was possible he'd made contact and spirited her away at the split second of detonation, but it was equally possible they'd both been blown to bits. The mess where they had been standing was impossible to decipher. Debris of market stalls and their wares, glass from the windows of the buildings, shutters, pieces of balconies and cars littered the street. And then there was the human wreckage, which turned her stomach. She'd thought the massacre in Pendarn was bad – and it had been, in the cold, calculated cruelty of the slaughter – but the violence of this devastation, the rending and tearing and dismembering of it, that was an order of magnitude more sickening to survey.

She forced herself to zoom in on the crawling wounded, the dying and the dead, the scattered body parts, hoping that she wouldn't find anything identifiably Kaz or Peyvand.

Oh, Kaz. She felt tears pricking her eyes, blurring her vision, making it hard for her to complete her careful quartering of the scene. She didn't think she could stand it if she lost him.

She felt a hand on her shoulder and spun in sudden panic to find a familiar figure standing over her, gun in hand.

'Stand up,' said Henry Sweetclover, 'and keep your hands where I can see them.'

Quantum Bubble - Sweetclover Hall, Cornwall, England, 7 April 2158, 8:22 A.M.

Kaz would be the first to admit that he had never been the most patient of people, but staying behind, twiddling his thumbs in the quantum bubble, deep beneath Sweetclover Hall in the distant future, while his friends tried to save his mother's life, was almost enough to drive him insane.

He stalked around the undercroft, restless, unable to settle. Every possible scenario played out in his mind. Stupid, ridiculous fears that some self-correcting property of time itself would find a way to prevent their meddling and ensure her death – his mum would trip and knock herself out and get blown up anyway; the bomb would go off earlier than he remembered; a freak piece of shrapnel would bounce off a building and ricochet into her, even though she was in the next street; the engine block would fly into the air and land on her like an anvil in an old Looney Tunes cartoon. No fear was too absurd, no possible outcome too horrible. He couldn't stop his mind racing. And that was even before he considered the variables Quil could add to the equation, if she turned up.

Maybe his mum would round the corner, make it to safety in time and run straight into the arms of Quil, who would use her to force his compliance; maybe she had people on the ground already, waiting for Jana and Dora, ready to swoop the moment the bomb went off.

He really, really hated sitting around waiting.

'You look like a polar bear.'

Kaz turned to see Kairos walking towards him.

Kaz stopped and cocked his head, confused. 'A polar bear?'

'They walk hundreds of miles in the wild,' said the professor. 'So when you cage them they go insane and walk in circles for ever, scratching off their fur.'

Kaz smiled in spite of his tension. 'I remind you of a mad, mangy polar bear in a cage.'

Kairos shrugged and smiled.

'When are you expecting them back?' asked Kaz.

Kairos shrugged again. 'The relationship between the flow of time within the bubble and the flow of time without makes it impossible for me to . . .'

'Forget I asked,' said Kaz with a weary smile of defeat.

He became aware that they were standing directly beneath the timebomb warhead. He looked up and shuddered. It hung there like a threat or a promise. The cloud of debris above and around it prevented him seeing into the house above, but he imagined Sweetclover Hall, ancient now, collapsing in on itself, funnelling tons of plaster, oak and stone down towards their heads. A sudden thought occurred to him.

'When we were in 1645,' he said, 'right here under the house, Quil set a bomb that was supposed to demolish the whole place, bury the evidence of her presence here. I suppose it didn't go off. Wonder why.'

Kairos shrugged. He hadn't been with them, how would he know?

Kaz shrugged too. 'I suppose Dora must have defused it.' He banished the thought.

Before he could formulate another one a shrill alarm began to sound, the door burst open and Dora ran into the room.

'Kaz, something's wrong,' she said breathlessly as Kairos switched the arrival alarm off with a key fob.

Kaz felt a rush of fear, all his stupid worries rising up again to taunt him. He stood rooted to the spot as Dora ran up to him.

'What happened?' asked Kairos, after apparently waiting for Kaz to ask and then realising he was dumbstruck.

'Everything was normal, no sign of a problem,' gasped Dora. 'But at the moment she was supposed to run, she just stood there.'

'Why would she—'

Dora interrupted. 'I zoomed in and there was something about the look on her face, the mix of confusion and fear,' she said. 'I recognised it. It was the exact same look my mother had when she was under the influence of the mind-writer in 1645. Quil must have got to her.'

'How do we save her?' asked Kaz bluntly.

Dora looked at him appraisingly, sizing him up; he could see she was considering what she could get away with saying next.

'I don't think we can, Kaz,' she said. 'I jumped away seconds before the bomb exploded and she was right next to it. I just can't see—'

But Kaz never heard the end of the sentence; he was already barrelling through time, hunting for the right exit point. Within seconds of his subjective time he was standing in the warm air of a Beirut street in the light of morning.

He blinked in the sudden sunlight; the transition from the quiet half-light of the undercroft into the sensory overload of the real world had left him momentarily startled. Impatient, angry at the delay his weakness was causing, he took a deep breath and focused as hard as he could on fighting through his disorientation. He needed to know where and when he was, exactly. He found himself staring into the eyes of a child. The little boy, about five Kaz guessed, was standing on the opposite side of the small side street on which Kaz had materialised. The boy's mouth and eyes were wide open in astonishment, trying to work out how the strange man had just appeared out of thin air.

Under normal circumstances Kaz would have winked at the boy, or held a conspiratorial finger to his lips, and walked off. But now he shouted, 'What street is this? What's the time?'

The boy only stared. Kaz hurried across the road, grabbed the boy by the shoulder and asked him again, this time in Arabic.

The boy's wide eyes began to tear up and Kaz realised he was scaring the child. He turned and ran. Time enough to feel guilty about his behaviour later. Right now, he didn't have the luxury of beating himself up for making a small boy cry.

He rounded a corner on to a larger street and got his bearings. The street was not busy; mid-morning traffic, some pedestrians walking along a row of shops, none of which he recognised. He stood there, looking for a clock on a wall or inside a shop; nothing. He was breathing so hard it took him a moment to realise that he was smelling something – food. He spun and stared through the window of the small cafe where he, Jana and Steve had sought refuge after the explosion.

He knew where he was. Kaz pushed himself, ran as fast

and as hard as he was able; ignored the stitch in his side, the shortness of breath, the pounding in his head. Round another corner and across the street, feeling the rush of wind as a truck passed him by, missing him by the tiniest of margins; he barely noticed. Weaving through traffic, horns blaring at him, faces leaning out of windows shaking fists and shouting; he couldn't have cared less. Another corner and now he was on a long side street. He kept going, tuning out the various pains and signals that his body kept sending to tell him he was pushing himself too hard. He raced across streets; more horns, more shouts, a cyclist sent wobbling into a wall. Still he ran.

One more corner and there, ahead of him, was the market. He pushed and shoved his way through the crowd. At one point he put his head down and charged through a knot of people standing enjoying a sales pitch from an oleaginous man with a table of knock-off perfume. And there, ahead of him, his mother. Standing with her back to him. And in the distance, seen over her shoulder, his dad and his younger self walking away. And to his left a big black car . . .

He was so close. He reached out his arm.

Shouted, 'Mum!'

She turned towards him, his fingertips brushing her blouse, and then . . .

. . . a pause. A hole in his memory. Black. Empty. Nothing.

Then the lap of surf on his feet, hot sand beneath his hands and the plaintive cry of seabirds, strangely muffled.

Kaz sat up on a deserted beach, his head ringing, his whole body vibrating as if someone had struck him like a huge gong. There was blood in his eyes, in his mouth, in his ears. His clothes were in tatters.

And he was alone.

Beirut, Lebanon, 20 March 2010 10:33 A.M. – 1 min after car bomb detonation

Sweetclover was older than Jana had last seen him, in 1645. This was the man who had imprisoned her in 2014, beginning the slide into middle age, greying at the temples. He was flanked on either side by intimidating men in black suits, standard-issue security goons with earpieces, dark glasses and very big guns.

After an initial rush of fear, Jana quickly regained her composure.

'Where's your blue tattoo gang?' she asked Sweetclover as she got to her feet. 'These guys aren't half as scary.'

'No reason to draw attention to ourselves,' he said. 'Ten seconds with the mind-writer and I have my own local protection detail.'

Jana nodded, feigning interest while considering her options. There were none.

She remembered Kaz asking her once, 'Who jumps off a skyscraper?' It was a good question. The last time she'd been trapped on a rooftop with no escape, it had seemed the obvious thing to do. She had known then – had pretty much always known – that the chip at the base of her skull would ensure her survival, in the only way that mattered. But when she had felt Quil's knife slide up between her ribs, Jana had confronted a fear she'd never before felt – fear of death, permanent and irreversible. There was no server backing her up in 1645; if she died off-grid, there was no coming back. She had been able to use that fear to leverage their escape from 1645, threatening to kill herself and destroy the chip to prevent Quil getting her hands on it, but she had been desperate, wounded, dying anyway. She had acted without thought.

During the long days recovering in the hospital in Kinshasa, Jana had tried not to think about her sudden and unexpected mortality, but it had preyed on her mind constantly. Her whole life had been lived within the protective cocoon of effective immortality, but that had been stripped away. Every day she spent in the past was a day on which she could die, for good and for ever. She was finding that less easy to come to terms with than she would like.

So as she stood facing hostile captors with no means of escape, she was humiliated and horrified to find that fear was rooting her to the spot, stopping her mouth and shortening her breath. She tried to tell herself that this was not who she was, but the reckless bravado that had characterised her life so far had deserted her and she was forced to face the question she had been avoiding since she first travelled in time – who was she without her backup, the safety net that made any action, no matter how reckless, acceptable?

'How did you find me?' she asked, playing for time.

Sweetclover scoffed and did not bother to answer. He was right: it had been a dumb question.

'So what now?' asked Jana. 'Back to Io Scientific?'

Sweetclover nodded and reached towards Jana with his left hand. Red sparks began to fly as their fingers nearly touched.

And then a larger flash of red obscured those sparks as Dora materialised six feet above Sweetclover's head.

Jana stepped back in surprise, almost tumbling backwards into the street but regaining her balance as Dora pirouetted in mid-air, her sword flashing in the light as she fell, graceful and controlled, and sliced Sweetclover's gun hand off at the wrist.

Jana was so focused on not falling off the roof, she missed the detail of Dora's attack, but by the time she had pulled herself back from the brink the two security guards were unconscious and Sweetclover was lying on the ground, clutching his wrist stump, mouth wide in a silent scream. Dora stood over him, sword pressed to his throat. She kicked Sweetclover's right hand, still clutching the gun, towards Jana.

Fighting back nausea, Jana leaned down and prised the warm, slack, bloody fingers away from the cold weapon. It was one of those nasty metal things from this time period. She snipped off the safety.

A loud buzzing behind her made Jana spin in alarm and she found herself confronted with a camera mounted beneath a small quadcopter. She smiled down the lens, hoping that Quil could see her as she raised her gun and shot the camera. The drone dropped into the street below, lost in amongst the smoke and wreckage.

'Run,' said Dora. 'I'll meet you at the rendezvous.'

On any other day Jana would have hated being ordered around, but right now she was kind of glad Dora was telling her what to do. Welcoming orders was a completely new experience for Jana, but she didn't question it.

So Jana ran past Dora and launched herself off the far edge of the roof.

She leapt into space, easily clearing the distance to the next roof but landing awkwardly; she felt her ankle twinge. No doubt Dora would have rolled to absorb the momentum and sprung to her feet gracefully.

She checked her chip and pulled up a map that hovered before her eyes as she limped down an outside staircase to ground level and ran on to a wide street lined with shops and cafes. It was eerily quiet apart from the sirens. An ambulance raced past her, wailing urgently.

She garnered no attention as she ran – everyone was either running towards the explosion to help, or cowering inside watching TV, waiting for the live coverage to start. There were sirens screaming from all directions as emergency vehicles converged on the area. Only a few streets away was the cafe where she had eaten that horrible kebab with Kaz and Steve. She knew it would be quiet there for at least half an hour. She ran to the door and peered cautiously inside, sighing with relief when she didn't see herself. She remembered that she and Steve had moved slowly, steering shocked Kaz in this direction gently. She had time, but not much.

Old Formica tables and hard plastic chairs sat drearily on top of faded lino. A couple of prints, sunwashed until they were basically green blurs, hung in gaudy frames on walls thick with old grease. The only occupants were a fat middle-aged man holding court with a group of friends at the serving counter, crowded around a TV.

She put the gun's safety back on and tucked it into her waistband, pulling her T-shirt down over it, then she pushed open the door.

The man behind the counter looked up as the little bell

tinkled to announce her arrival. Jana breathed in the spicy wild meat smell of the cafe, which brought back a rush of memory. She'd been so confused the last time she was here, trying to get a handle on what was happening to her, trying to get the measure of Kaz, responding to her situation as she always had, by trying to manipulate the people around her. She felt slightly ashamed of that now. Kaz had deserved better. That said, it was time to manipulate someone else.

'Hi,' she said to the cafe owner, trying not to focus on the single bead of sweat that was sliming its way down from the crown of his bald head towards his face. It was 50/50 whether his eyebrows would intercept it or whether it would splat into the salad on the counter beneath him. 'Gross,' she thought, 'that could be the salad he puts in my kebab. My younger self could be about to eat that exact bead of sweat.' Suppressing a shudder, she improvised a cover story.

'My twin sister,' she said, 'has got a date in this cafe any minute. My father disapproves of the guy she's seeing and has asked me to listen in. We think she's going to try and run away with him. Is there anywhere I can hide where I might be able to hear what they're saying but they can't see me?'

The cafe owner looked startled while his friends reacted variously, with laughter or serious nods of approval.

'Your twin sister?' asked the owner.

Jana nodded.

'Does she love this boy?'

'That's what I'm here to find out,' Jana said. 'And please, they'll be here any second.'

'I ran away with my wife,' said the cafe owner. 'Her father did not approve of me.' He stuck out his chest in a display of pride, his stomach straining against his shirt. 'But she loved me. I think maybe I should throw you out and give your sister and her boy a free meal. For love.'

Love is blind, thought Jana, amazed at how quickly her simple plan had gone south.

'He's no good,' she pleaded. 'Truly. He's a liar and a thief.'

'His father-in-law said the same thing about him,' said one of the cafe owner's friends. 'Of course, he was right.'

There was a chorus of laughter from the group at the counter.

'Look, please,' begged Jana, feeling humiliated to her very core. 'I'm only looking out for her.'

The cafe owner pursed his lips, unsure.

'Go on, let her hide in the cupboard,' urged one of the men, amused at the possibility of some drama happening in the cafe itself rather than on the TV screen.

The owner shrugged and led Jana to a small door in the back wall. 'You can hide in there. I don't think you'll be able to hear them, but you can watch through the keyhole.'

'Good enough, thank you,' said Jana.

'But afterwards, you buy some food, OK?'

Jana nodded. 'You bet,' she lied. 'Smells great!'

The owner opened the door to reveal a teeny little store-room lined with shelving heavy with jars and bottles. A thin window, rimed in ancient dirt, let in a gash of sickly light. There was barely enough room for her to stand inside, but she crammed herself in and he pushed the door closed.

Almost immediately she heard the bell on the door chime and leaned forward to peer through the keyhole, nervous although she couldn't say exactly why. She could just make out herself and Steve with Kaz in between them. They had their arms round him, pulling him inside. His eyes were vacant, his feet shuffling, in deep shock. They were all coated in dust and it was obvious they'd been near the explosion, so the men at the counter ran to help them, fussed and soothed, then began bombarding them with questions. Jana remembered this so vividly. It was surreal to be watching herself, as if she had stepped into her own memories.

She crouched there and watched as Kaz gradually returned to reality, as her younger self sized him up, took control, banished Steve outside and made a pact with Kaz. Jana remembered every thought she'd had at that moment. How she'd assessed Kaz as if he were some kind of experiment, trying to establish how easy he would be to control and manipulate. She had thought she was being clever but watching herself now, Jana was horrified at how blatant she seemed, how unsubtle. She saw every devious thought clearly on her dust-streaked face and couldn't believe Kaz wasn't seeing through her.

Wow, this was uncomfortable. Jana had never much worried about how she appeared to other people, but now, for the first time, she was confronted with herself at her worst, and was forced to the nasty conclusion that she didn't like herself much.

Kaz and her younger self rose and left and a moment later there was a knock at the storeroom door.

'They're gone,' said the cafe owner as he opened the door. He looked in at her, not bothering to hide his disgust. 'You saw?'

Jana nodded.

'You saw that they had been in the bombing,' he said, 'and you didn't come out and comfort your sister?'

'I—'

'Get out of my cafe.'

Jana nodded. She felt about as disgusted with herself as the cafe owner did, though for different reasons. She left without saying a word.

Beirut, Lebanon, 20 March 2010 10:36 A.M. – 3 mins after car bomb detonation

'You are not very good at this, are you?' said Dora, kneeling before Sweetclover and applying a field dressing to the wound where his hand used to be. He was quivering as shock set in and was unable to answer her. He just stared at the hand that lay before him on the rooftop.

'So you're a time traveller now too,' said Dora. 'How did that happen?'

Sweetclover's reverie continued, so Dora broke off from her ministrations to deliver a hard slap to his face. That got his attention and he looked up and met her gaze.

Dora greeted him with a smile. 'Long time no see, boss,' she said as she jabbed a hypodermic into his forearm and delivered a strong anaesthetic.

'Good as new,' she said, admiring the dressing.

'Not really,' said Sweetclover darkly, the words short and guttural, forced out through pain and shock.

'Give the drugs a moment to work, and you'll be fine,' said Dora, raising her sword again and pressing the tip of it against Sweetclover's breast. 'I can kill you before you have time to jump away, so let's talk for a moment, Henry.'

Sweetclover looked across at her and she saw his gaze clear as the pain subsided. After a moment he seemed to have partly regained his composure.

'Hello, Dora,' he said. 'It has been a long time for you, I think, since we last met.'

Dora nodded. 'Last time you met me, you gave me sandwiches and chocolate,' she said.

'And the last time you met me, I imagine, was in 1645, yes?' replied Sweetclover.

'I ask you again, how is it you are now able to travel in time, as I am?' said Dora.

'It is thanks to you, in fact,' said Sweetclover. 'Or your blood, to be precise.'

It took Dora a moment to realise what he was referring to, but when she did, she exclaimed, 'The blood sample you took!'

Sweetclover nodded. 'Quite so,' he said. 'We were able to extract enough of the active element that infuses your blood and transfer it into me.'

'Why did you need my blood?' asked Dora, suspecting a lie. 'If there is something inside me, something I have absorbed, that triggers my abilities, why not use your wife's?'

'Her blood is different in some regard. It was explained to me, but I confess I did not entirely comprehend the explanation,' said Sweetclover, his angry face belying the apology in his words.

'Quil sent you here for Jana.' It was not a question.

'She really does want that chip in her head very badly indeed,' said Sweetclover.

'Why?' asked Dora. When Sweetclover did not answer she

pressed the sword into his breast just far enough to draw a bead of blood through the white of his shirt.

'Why?' she asked again.

'A memory,' he said through gritted teeth. 'That is all I know. She wants access to Jana's memories. She has not told me why.'

Dora only believed half of his answer, but she was conscious that Sweetclover's reinforcements might be arriving any moment and she did not want to push her luck by extending the interrogation any longer than necessary.

'What did you do to Kaz's mother?' she said.

'Nothing,' said Sweetclover. 'However, my wife used the mind-writer on her. A simple instruction to stop moving at the crucial moment. She would have had no idea why she was unable to run.'

Dora grimaced at his callousness. 'But why?' she asked.

'To flush you out,' he replied. 'To distract you while we moved in on your position. And it worked.'

'At the cost of the life of an innocent woman,' said Dora, pushing the sword in a little bit further, feeling the slight release of tension as the skin parted around the sharp metal.

Sweetclover surprised Dora by responding with a sneer. 'If what my wife tells me of your actions on Mars is true,' he said contemptuously, 'you have far more innocent blood on your hands than I.'

'What has she told you?' asked Dora urgently. Kairos had revealed very little and Dora was not keen, despite all the professor's warnings about the danger of paradoxes, to journey to Mars without knowing what events they would be attempting to undo.

'Only that many people died, and it was your fault,' he said, regarding her closely. 'I try not to kill, Miss Predennick, unless absolutely necessary. I wonder whether you are as scrupulous?'

'My scruples are not the subject of this discussion,' said Dora coldly.

Sweetclover's tone softened as he said, 'You have changed so much since we last met. Did I do this to you? My attack upon you, my murder of Mountfort – is that what drove you to become . . . this warrior? If so, I owe you an apology. In 1645, back home, before I left . . . the way I acted was unforgivable. I became enraged and behaved in a manner most cruel. It shames me to recall my actions.'

Dora considered, not for the first time, the contrast between the furious younger man who had advanced towards her in 1645, his knife dripping with Mountfort's freshly spilt blood, and the older, more solicitous Sweetclover who had welcomed her to 2014. True, they seemed like different men in many ways, but she had always assumed that the violent killer was the real Sweetclover, and the gentle host merely a role he played to put her at ease so he could better manipulate a naive young girl. But as he looked up and met her gaze, looking for a response to his apology, she wondered for the first time whether she had got it the wrong way round. She fancied she saw genuine remorse in his eyes.

She was having none of it.

'It is not me to whom you owe the greatest apology,' she said curtly. 'I believe Jana and Mountfort have the strongest cause to seek revenge for your actions that day.'

Sweetclover blinked in surprise. 'Mountfort lives?'

'He does.'

The change that came over Sweetclover was surprising. His posture, his demeanour and bearing all relaxed as if a great burden had been laid down.

'Then I am, after all, not a murderer.' He spoke softly, in seeming disbelief.

'Not for want of trying,' muttered Dora, spitefully. Sweetclover appeared not to hear her.

'But this is wonderful. For me it has been seven years since that day. Seven years I have lived with the belief that I killed a wounded man in cold blood. It . . .' he struggled for the right word. 'It transforms you, killing a person. Makes you think of yourself differently. You wear the mark of Cain and there is nothing in this world or the next that can wipe that stain away. But if what you say is true, then perhaps all is not lost for me. Perhaps my immortal soul may find some peace.'

Unbidden, Dora found herself remembering the look on her brother's face as she slid a length of cold steel between his ribs. There had been a moment of disconnection, as if something inside her crumbled or broke away. She saw again his eyes widening in shock, the thin trickle of blood snaking from his parted lips, the weight of him pulling the sword downwards as his legs crumpled beneath him.

The vision was vivid and encompassing and Dora felt breathless and dizzy for a moment before the rise of bile in her throat pushed her back to reality.

'You argue semantics,' she said. 'You decided to kill an unarmed man, you acted on that decision, and you believed yourself successful. That he survived is no thanks to you. Do not think his continued existence absolves you of anything.'

Sweetclover looked deep into Dora's eyes; an unwavering gaze that made her uncomfortable, even as she held it.

'I see you know what it means to kill a man,' he said.

Dora held his gaze, impassive.

'My wife has explained the reality of her life to me, the inflexibility of time,' he said. 'She called it predestination. She

117

does not believe that anything she does matters, she believes that it contains no moral dimension whatsoever. Anybody she kills in her past, she says, is already dead, so what does it signify? She is simply an instrument of fate, destiny, God – whatever you wish to call the force that guides our lives. But I believed I had killed Mountfort in my own time, within my own life. That action cannot be ascribed to fate or time. I was not fulfilling some preordained plan. I acted freely. And now I live within my own future. My wife inhabits her own past and her actions do not matter, morality has no hold on her until she returns to the moment she left. I have no such protection from God's wrath.'

Dora's mouth was hanging open in amazement, and she closed it quickly, aware that she had temporarily let her mask of cool detachment slip.

'That's what she told you?' she asked. 'That's what she *thinks*?'

Sweetclover nodded. 'Of course. I hope, now that you understand, that you will see my wife for who she really is. You think her actions evil, but they are nothing of the sort. She only acts in the manner time requires of her. She is an instrument of fate, that is all. When she returns to her own time, when her plans reach fruition, then you will see the real woman. The woman I know. The woman I love.'

'I saw her when she slaughtered those soldiers at Sweetclover Hall,' said Dora slowly. 'She was gleeful. She enjoyed it. Even if I believed that any time traveller living in the time before they were born is robbed of all free will and becomes merely fate's puppet – and I most emphatically do not – that would not explain or excuse the delight she takes in the death she brings to those around her. You, my lord, are in denial. You need to look at her with clearer eyes. She is quite, quite mad.'

Sweetclover clenched his jaw. 'What do either of us know

of her world?' he said. 'Of the suffering she endured? How can we even imagine the wrongs she seeks to right in her own time? Had either of us seen the wonders of this time ten years ago, we would have screamed, proclaimed them magic, run in terror. Sometimes I find this future world so confusing, so dense with meaning, that I feel the urge to hide. I do not understand their clothing, their language, their entertainment. I cannot judge their morality, for it is shaped by a world I barely comprehend. It is beyond you and me, Dora, to sit in judgement on a woman as removed from our world as my wife. We must either trust or distrust her, that is all we can do. I look into her eyes and see goodness. You see madness. One of us is wrong, and I say, with respect, that it is not I.'

Dora did not know how to respond to this assertion. But she withdrew her sword. 'And Peyvand? I mean, Kaz's mother? How do you justify her death?'

'As I explained, her particular condition dictates that the rules of society do not apply to my wife,' said Sweetclover. 'The woman was destined to die; my wife only influenced the manner of her death, that is all.'

Dora considered this. 'So when she returns to her own time, when she regains her free will, Quil will no longer kill?'

'She has given me her word that the rules of war will apply,' replied Sweetclover. 'Civilians, such as Kaz's mother, will not be harmed.'

Dora could see that Sweetclover was sincere. He truly believed Quil would begin to act in a more civilised manner when she reached her own time again. Dora doubted it.

'So what happens now, Miss Predennick?' asked Sweetclover. 'Kill me? Capture me?'

Dora stood, sheathed her sword and walked away without a word.

Beirut, Lebanon, 20 March 2010 11:22 A.M. - 49 mins after car bomb detonation

Zbigniew Cecka had been a soldier his entire adult life, but he had seen very little combat. He had fired his weapon in anger only twice, both times warning shots, aimed over the heads of his attackers. He gave thanks every day that on both occasions they had taken the hint and turned tail. In some ways it seemed unnatural to him that he was a soldier who had never even tried to take a life, but he was proud of it.

He had, though, seen more death than anybody should ever see. Mass graves, burial pits, villages filled with smoking ruins and smouldering flesh, machete wounds, severed limbs, death by hanging, stabbing, fire, drowning, starvation even, once, crucifixion. Being a peacekeeper might mean never having to kill, but it also meant confronting the aftermath of every imaginable kind of human evil. He knew that it had changed him.

He looked around the foyer of the hospital – at all the parents crying over their children, the children crying over their parents, the doctors and nurses running from one person to another performing triage, sorting the wounded into dead, dying, saveable with luck, injured but not immediately threatened – and he remained immune to both the panic and the professionalism. To him this was a familiar setting, and he knew the best thing he could do was wait his turn.

He sat in the corner of the foyer, out of everybody's way, with fourteen-year-old Kaz lying across his lap. His son's wounds were mostly superficial, but there was a gash in his leg that would need stitches. Zbigniew had come prepared, knowing what the day would bring. A syringe of sedative, some basic field dressings and antiseptic. After the explosion, immediately he had rounded the corner into the next street, he had turned to Kaz – hysterical, crying, confused, terrified, lost – sedated him, dressed his leg and then, ignoring the sirens and the chaos, carried his senseless child two miles to the hospital.

Zbigniew had not escaped unscathed either. He could feel a bruise blossoming on his left thigh and there was a piece of metal sticking out of his upper left arm. He knew not to pull it out; as long as it remained in place until removed by a professional, he would be fine. He was worried about shock, but was doing his best to keep it at bay with concentration and focus.

The worst part was not knowing what had happened to his wife. As instructed, he had not looked back once she had broken away from him and Kaz, so he had no idea whether she had made it to safety. He had no reason to think otherwise, but he had seen enough plans go wrong at the last moment due to random circumstances that he was unable to take anything for granted.

He sat and stroked his son's hair. Even with his face streaked with blood and oil, Kaz was the most beautiful thing Zbigniew had ever seen. His son should have had a sibling or two, that had always been the plan, but somewhere along the way life had got away from him and Peyvand and now it was too late. He took comfort in knowing that circumstances dictated he would have Kaz with him, even if he knew they would spend most of the next few years at each other's throats.

Wondering who his boy would grow into had obsessed Zbigniew for years. Artist, soldier, bureaucrat, politician, teacher, builder, sportsman – there wasn't a life that Zbigniew hadn't imagined for his son. Except time traveller. That hadn't been on the list.

'Dad?'

Zbigniew looked up in surprise to see his son – the older version – standing over him. He was wearing jeans and a T-shirt, both of which looked brand new. Something in his face made Zbigniew uneasy, and he knew all was not well.

'What went wrong?' he asked urgently.

Older Kaz sank down on to his haunches and looked his father in the eye.

'Quil got to her somehow,' he said. 'I guess she tried to make her betray us, lead her to Jana perhaps. Mum just stood there. I don't know what she was thinking. Maybe she was going to try and warn the people in the market, maybe she was sacrificing herself. Maybe she froze. I tried to get to her, touch her, take her to safety . . .'

As Kaz trailed off into silence, Zbigniew felt a pit open in his stomach.

'Did you . . .' he tried to formulate a question, but he was too scared of the answer to put it into words.

'I don't know,' said Kaz. 'Maybe. I don't remember. I was caught in the explosion. I woke up somewhere else. Alone. The last few moments before the explosion are gone. I remember running towards her, but that is all.'

Zbigniew was distracted as young Kaz stirred briefly,

rolling over on to his back and groaning in his sleep. He moved his son's head into a more comfortable position before looking up into an older version of the eyes that lay closed in his lap.

'If she was not with you when you woke, does that not mean you failed?' he said slowly, thinking it through as he spoke.

'Not necessarily,' replied Kaz. 'Dora pulled away from Jana and me during a time trip once and she arrived somewhere else. But yes, it's possible. That's why I came back here. To tell you that, and to search the bodies. She might be here.'

Zbigniew pointed to a corridor that ran off the foyer. 'They're bringing everyone here, even the dead,' he said. 'They're laying them out in a ward down there.'

As he and Kaz looked down the corridor, a steady stream of trolleys passed that way.

'OK, you stay with, um, me,' said Kaz. 'I'll go check.'

Zbigniew reached into his pocket and pulled out his ID.

'Flash this at the door quickly and say you need to check for a UN staffer who may have been in the explosion,' he said. 'They're unlikely to look at it too closely.'

Kaz took the ID, his face pale.

Zbigniew reached out and squeezed his son's arm. 'You don't have to. You shouldn't have to.'

Kaz looked down at him, solemn. 'Yes, I do,' he said, then he rose and walked away.

Zbigniew watched him go, his chest swelling with pride, his stomach hollow with guilt and fear, his head swimming with delayed shock.

He stroked the hair of his sleeping son with his good arm and waited.

Kaz never returned.

Quantum Bubble - Sweetclover Hall, Cornwall, England, 7 April 2158, 8:22 A.M.

Kaz expected to land in the filing cupboard again, but this time he rejoined the flow of time standing in the undercroft of Sweetclover Hall, directly beneath the timebomb's frozen explosion. His friends and the professor were all huddled around the conference-room table and saw him arrive. He expected them to begin bombarding him with questions, and Dora and Kairos had opened their mouths and begun forming queries, but they both stopped themselves when Jana ran to Kaz and hugged him tightly, without a word. They glowed red as they embraced.

Kaz hugged her back, slightly surprised by her display of emotion. After a moment she let go and stepped back.

'I saw you run into the explosion,' said Jana, teary-eyed.

'You're alone,' said Dora.

Kaz was still holding Jana's gaze, amazed by her tears, when Dora made this observation, and he saw realisation dawn in her eyes – Jana hadn't even thought about his mother, she had just been glad to see him. He knew deep down that he shouldn't be angered by this but he was, even though he couldn't have articulated why.

He looked across at Dora and Kairos.

'I wasn't quick enough,' he said. 'I jumped into time when the bomb went off. It was instinctive, I didn't control it. The last thing I remember is my fingers touching her shoulder, but Mum didn't travel with me.'

'Do you think she . . .' Jana didn't need to finish the sentence.

'I checked the hospital afterwards,' said Kaz. 'There was no sign of her body. I think she jumped into time like you did, Dora, in 1645. My touch must have been enough to begin her journey but I have no way of knowing where or when she was thrown to. Or if she was alive or dead when she got there.'

Kairos spoke up then. 'I shall create an algorithm to search all known historical records for any indication of her at any point in time,' he said eagerly, obviously more motivated by the puzzle he was going to try to solve than the prospect of rescuing Kaz's mother.

'I already did that,' said Kaz, angry now at Kairos too. 'I hired someone. There's no trace of her anywhere. She's just . . . gone.'

After a moment of solemn silence Jana whispered, 'Oh Kaz, I'm so sorry.'

'Wait a minute,' said Dora. 'You hired someone? We came straight back here after Beirut and we've only been back about ten minutes. How long have you been away?'

'About a month,' said Kaz, refusing to be defensive. 'I needed to clear my head. I wasn't even sure I was going to come back here, but I thought I owed you a goodbye.'

'Goodbye?' said Jana, her surprise mixed with a touch of anger. 'What do you mean, goodbye?'

Kaz found his resentment bubbling over. 'What do you mean, what do I mean?' he shouted. 'What do you think I mean? I mean, I'm done. We tried to change history and it didn't work.'

'Actually, we do not know that for certain,' said Kairos. 'It is possible that—'

'Who cares?' shouted Kaz. 'We tried to save my mum and now she's lost, probably dead. There's no way at all of knowing if we changed things or not. Maybe this is how it always happened. Except now . . . now I know for certain that it's my fault. Before, I may have felt guilty but at least I knew I wasn't, not really. The only thing we've changed, as far as I can tell, is that we proved I killed my mother. So yes, I'm done. I have to go and make things right with my father. At least I haven't managed to kill him yet.'

'But what about Mars?' said Dora.

'What about it?' spat Kaz.

'You promised,' said Jana quietly.

But he was already walking away.

'Let me talk to him,' said Jana, once Kaz had left the undercroft.

'I think he wants to be left alone,' said Kairos.

Jana flashed him a withering glance. How could such a clever man be so dumb? 'He can jump away whenever he wants,' she said. 'If he's staying, it's because he wants to talk, even if he won't admit it. Leave him to me.'

Kairos looked embarrassed and Dora shrugged as Jana turned away to follow Kaz.

She found him easily enough – he was throwing things around in one of the rooms below, smashing a metal chair against the wall over and over, bending its legs backwards and chipping concrete from the wall. She stood in the doorway until he dropped the chair, now a mangled tangle of metal tubes, and slumped to the floor with his arms round his knees.

'Leave me alone,' he said, refusing to make eye contact.

Jana walked in and sat beside him, careful to give him just enough space that he didn't feel crowded. It was hard to tell which emotion – anger, guilt or misery – was most in control of him, but whichever it was, Kaz was a mess.

'My family lost someone once, about ten years ago,' Jana said quietly. 'It was a stupid accident. No warning, just quick and pointless. A moment's carelessness, someone not paying attention, and bang. Dead. Just like that. And the funny thing is, I didn't really notice the effect it had on my parents. Not for a long time. It was only later, when I was older and I looked back, when I understood all the facts and could put them in context, that I realised how it had changed them.

'My father . . . he was completely overcome with guilt. His whole personality changed. He didn't start drinking or bursting out crying or anything like that. It was subtler. He just didn't trust himself any more. Personally, I mean. He became all about his work. Long hours, weekends. We hardly saw him. I think it was too painful for him to be around us. He became a stranger.

'My mother, on the other hand, she just got angry. Angry at him, angry at me, angry at everything, all the time. Not shouting, y'know? No chair murders. Just a constant low-level anger that had nowhere to go. Every task was a problem, everyone was a parasite, every day was one long battle against the hatefulness of everything. She became a monster, really.

'Grief just ate them both up, in different ways.'

Jana paused, uncomfortable with sharing so much of her family history. She hadn't confided so much in anyone, ever, and she felt bad that she was doing it now just so she could manipulate Kaz into sticking around. Not really, really bad, not bad enough that she was going to stop, but a little bit bad.

'I already grieved,' said Kaz after a long silence. 'I've been sad and angry for years. I'd learned to live with it. But going through it all again – it's . . .' he trailed off.

Jana leaned sideways towards him and put her hand on his.

'I can imagine,' she said. And she could, but he would not have understood how or why, so she did not try to explain.

Jana felt him begin to shake so, ignoring the borealis glow that enfolded them, she hugged him tight as he sobbed. They sat there with their arms round one another for a long time until Kaz sat back, clenched his jaw, wiped his eyes, took a deep breath and very noticeably pulled himself together. Jana was always slightly amazed at how obvious boys always made it when they were getting a grip. Girls just got on and did it, but boys made such a song and dance of the whole thing.

Again she felt a nagging pang of guilt at her manipulation of him. She was only beginning to admit that she liked him in a way she'd never really liked a boy before. It was an unexpected development and she didn't really know what to do with it, so she filed it away as a problem for later. For now, her job was to get Kaz back on board the Mars express.

'Kaz,' she said softly as he gave the stoic smile that all boys seemed to give when they'd had a good cry, 'I don't presume to know what's best for you, but if I were in your shoes, I'd want revenge on the monster who got my mother killed.'

Ten minutes later she poured Kaz a cup of coffee with lots of sugar, how he liked it, and placed it on the conference table in front of him before nodding to Kairos to begin the briefing. She locked eyes with Dora, who nodded to signal how impressed she was that Jana had brought Kaz back to the table. Jana replied with shrug and a grin that said 'I'm just that good, what can I say?'

'Well,' said Kairos. 'Here is what I can tell you. On April fifth 2158 the leaders of the Godless rebellion and Earth's emergency government convened at the conference centre in Barrettown, Mars's capital city, to talk peace.'

'Godless?' asked Dora.

Kairos nodded. 'That is what the clones call themselves,' he said. 'They do not dream, it is a side-effect of the cloning process, no one understands why. Certain religious leaders argue that any creature which does not dream cannot be possessed of a soul and is thus cast out of God's grace. Hence, Godless. I think it was the Pope who coined the phrase. Scientifically offensive, but it caught on and then the clones co-opted it and started using it to describe themselves. It fit with their manifesto of progress through scientific enquiry, which Quil, their leader, talks about often. We are Godless, she would say, for we reject superstition and embrace the scientific method, that kind of thing.'

Jana found herself, not for the first time, thinking that she quite liked the sound of Quil. First she was a human rights activist, then a crusader for science – everything about her sounded great. So why, how, had she turned into the nutbag they'd met in 1645, and why was she so hell-bent on capturing her? Jana had some nasty suspicions, but she did not think this was the time to voice them, so she bit her lip.

'Anyway,' continued Kairos. 'Quil attended the Barrettown

129

peace talks, along with certain key Godless generals. The President of the Earth Emergency Government did not attend, which surprised many, but the Earth delegation was present and nonetheless filled with elder statesmen and women from many nations.

'Above the planet, Earth had attempted to create a blockade and the Godless fleet had halted its advance. A space blockade is nonsense, of course,' he said, breaking out of his serious recitation of facts. Jana sighed; he was clearly about to launch into another digression. 'I mean, you can just fly above, below or around it. It's not like it's a sea battle or something that takes place in two dimensions. Movement through space is movement in three dimensions, and it's therefore categorically a thousand times harder to prevent all movement, as one might in a two-dimensional battle. Perhaps two thousand times. I must remember to calculate that.' He shook himself. 'In any event, the blockade was propaganda, nothing more, but it looked good on TV.'

'So what went wrong?' asked Dora.

Kairos pursed his lips. 'I have to be very careful what I tell you. I need to balance the benefits of you changing history against the risk of telling you so much that if you do change history you'll create a paradox that risks destroying the thing you just fixed. And everything else. So. I have thought about this a lot and what I can tell you is this:

'I can give you two tasks. First, one or more of you will need to get close to the Godless delegation and keep an eye on them. Second, in Barrettown there is a man called John Smith. Find him and talk to him.'

Jana waited for more information and when none was forthcoming she asked, incredulous, 'Is that it? John Smith? It's good job he doesn't have a common name, or he might be hard to find.'

'That's ridiculous,' scoffed Dora. 'What does Smith do? What happens to the Godless? Is there a bomb, or a hitman or some sort of accident? What?'

'I cannot tell you any more than I already have,' said Kairos. 'If you knew the exact nature of the event you are trying to prevent . . .'

'Paradox,' said Jana.

Kairos nodded. 'And an ever bigger disaster would unfold,' he said.

Jana saw Kaz shaking his head in frustration. 'So we're supposed to prevent something happening to someone, but we don't know who or what, only when,' he said.

Kairos fixed Kaz with a wide-eyed stare and said, 'And if you fail, April fifth 2158 will see the single greatest loss of human life ever recorded in a single day.'

In spite of herself, Jana felt a chill at his cold pronouncement. Dora and Kaz must have felt it too, for they fell silent and exchanged glances of mixed confusion and worry.

After a moment, Jana decided to bring the conversation back to practicalities.

'OK,' she said. 'First question: how do we get to Mars?'

'Well,' said Kairos, apparently pleased to be able to change the tone of the conversation. 'Have you not wondered yet how it is that you are not dead?'

'Eh?' said Jana.

'You are travelling in time, yes,' said Kairos. 'But you are also travelling in space. Not just between here and, say, Beirut. But vast, unimaginable distances.'

'Nope, you've lost me,' said Kaz, looking to Dora and Jana to see if either of them were following the professor. Both girls shook their heads.

'Jana gave me the clue when she told me about the glowing

131

rock she saw in the cavern below this cellar,' explained Kairos. 'I think you were right, Jana – that must have been the warhead of the timebomb.' He pointed out of the room up at the ceiling where the exploding warhead floated like a slow-motion threat. 'It is, was and will be blown back through time at the moment of detonation.

'It weakened the structure of time itself as it burrowed back into the past. Imagine time as a crystal, once flawless but now shot through with fractures caused by the warhead's passage from now to then. It is these fractures that you navigate when you travel. And lucky for you that you do, because the warhead of the bomb, the asteroid itself, is buried deep beneath us and it acts as a lodestone, drawing you back to Earth each time you travel. That is why you arrived in Sweetclover Hall when you first travelled – it drew you here. But without the warhead, you would travel only in time, not space.'

Jana had no idea what he was talking about. He looked at the three young people as if everything should now be clear, but obviously Dora and Kaz's faces were as blank as Jana's because he sighed and continued.

'The Earth is in constant motion around the sun, which in turn is in motion around the galactic centre, which in turn is in motion outwards from the centre of our universe,' said Kairos, drawing in the air with his hand to indicate the motion of the Earth through space. 'We are all passengers on a fast-moving vessel, spaceship Earth. If you were to travel back in time an hour – only in time, mind – you would arrive in space, with the Earth thousands of miles distant, cork-screwing towards you. Man overboard. And that would be that for you. But the warhead acts like a magnet, drawing you towards wherever Earth is in the time period you are arriving in.'

Jana thought about this for a moment and found that it made sense, if not for one problem.

'But we travelled to Mars already,' she said.

'What?' said a startled-looking Kairos.

'Yes,' affirmed Dora. 'We did. We were in a battle and we met our future selves.'

Kairos shook his head firmly. 'No,' he said. 'That cannot have been Mars. It must have been Earth.'

Jana was pretty sure it wasn't. 'The sky was the wrong colour,' she said.

'Pollution,' said Kairos firmly.

Jana looked at him sceptically, but didn't push it.

'For you to get to Mars,' he continued, trying to gloss over the preceding exchange, 'you will need to travel to Earth six months ago. There will be cover identities prepared for you, as well as tickets on the first shuttle to Mars. You have plenty of time to establish your covers and bed yourselves into Barrettown before the big day.

'Jana, you will be a journalist, which will give you access to the press conferences and a good excuse to snoop around. Dora, you will be a staff member at the hotel hosting the Godless delegation. Kaz, you will be the wild card – your job will be to work the streets of the city, try and pick up on anything brewing outside the diplomatic zone.'

'And this is all worked out already?' asked Dora.

'It is,' replied Kairos.

'By whom?' she asked.

Kairos shook his head. 'Can't tell you,' he said. 'After you return here, after Mars, I'll tell you everything.'

'As long as you understand that if you're lying to us – if you're working for Quil, say – I will kill you,' said Jana quietly.

'Or I will,' said Dora.

'Or me,' said Kaz.

Kairos looked between them nervously and smiled an unconvincing smile.

'Yay,' he said weakly.

Interlude:
Pendarn, Cornwall, 1646

'You shouldn't feel guilty,' said Kaz, but Dora was not in the mood to be reassured.

'Of course I should,' she snapped. 'We robbed him of the one thing that's most important – free will.'

Jana took hold of her by the shoulders and looked her in the eyes.

'Your brother was brainwashed,' she said. 'Radicalised by religious fundamentalists. He was a young, lonely, vulnerable boy in a big city for the first time in his life, and they took advantage of him and turned him into a weapon. In my time they have whole teams of people dedicated to rehabilitating victims of that kind of treatment, assuming they don't blow themselves up first like that poor boy in Beirut.'

Dora unclenched her jaw and nodded. She knew Jana was right, of course she did, but it didn't stop her feeling as if she had taken something that wasn't hers to take.

In 1645 her brother, fired with Puritan zeal, had participated in Dora's lynching, denouncing her as a witch and handing her over to the militia with which he rode. Shortly thereafter, in the undercroft of Sweetclover Hall, he had come at their father with a sword, leaving Dora no option but to defend him, running her beloved brother through in the process.

Of all the things Dora had seen and done, it was her brother's eyes staring deep into hers, wide with surprise and disbelief as he stood skewered on her blade, that woke her sweating and wild in the darkest hours of the night.

Through her years of preparation and training, it was her brother's pleading stare that kept her going, calling her back to Sweetclover Hall in the hope that she could rescue him, heal him, make amends. So when she delivered him to Kinshasa, pale, delirious, bleeding out from a horrific gash in his stomach, Dora had cried the whole time, releasing four years of betrayal and guilt even as she broke the bonds of time to fix it.

She had been so focused on saving his life, she had given little thought to what the outcome would be if he survived, which he did, just.

And what happened was awful.

Dora's mother, Elizabeth, when put through a mind-writer to undo the conditioning that Quil had imposed on her, reverted surprisingly quickly to the woman Dora remembered. The reconciliation with Thomas, Dora and James's father, had also come quickly. Dora thought the shared experience of walking the hallways of the impossibly clean, geometric future clinic had brought them back together as they marvelled at a world they could not have imagined. Dora remembered that feeling well.

But James, upon regaining consciousness, raved and spat, swore and cried out against the devil and all his works, the infernal witchcraft of his sister and the hell to which he had been brought.

Dora had thought him unbalanced when she was reunited with him in Pendarn, but now he was utterly insane. The only explanation she could find was his enforced transposition across time and her betrayal of him.

(She knew it wasn't a betrayal, it was absurd to think of it in those terms, she was defending herself and her father, she had no choice – but it felt like a betrayal, deep down, where it mattered, where logic held no sway.)

Kept in restraints, sedated to prevent him hurting himself, James languished in a secure room while Dora and her parents debated what to do with him.

It was Elizabeth who finally suggested they use the mind-writer upon him, and Thomas agreed. As far as they were concerned, if this magical machine could realign the humours within their unbalanced son, then it was a simple and good choice to make.

Dora was both relieved and horrified; thankful that she could see a solution, aghast at the implications of pursuing it. If they tampered with his mind, rewrote it to remove the madness, what would be left? There was no guarantee that the man who remained would be James at all. He would be a construct, a phantom, a virtual personality inhabiting her brother's animated corpse. At least, that is what she thought until she looked through the window of his room and saw him there, foaming at the mouth, writhing and kicking against the straps. Better a future as a happy construct than a life of mania that devoured any remnants of the boy she had grown up with.

So Dora gave the orders to the clinic staff to begin preparing a program for the machine to 'fix' her brother's broken mind, knowing even as she did so that she would never forgive herself for it.

Part of the program involved removing all memories of the clinic, so it was decided that after his mind was altered, he would be kept sedated while Dora returned her family to their bakery in Pendarn in 1645. He would awake, back home, believing himself to have just returned from a failed life in London, seeking safety in the loving bosom of his simple family.

Dora did not stay to see him wake. She could not bear the thought of looking into his eyes again. She left while he slept, lying to her parents as she promised them that she would visit them soon.

After confessing as much to Kaz, he had worked on her, gently but persistently, to return home and visit her family. She resented his interference, but he was kindly and she knew he was right. After their journey through Quil and Jana's lives, Dora found herself with a newborn appreciation of her family, their comparative normality and the value of their unconditional love.

Kaz and Jana were happy to come with her for moral support, although they needed to keep a low profile and not engage with any of the other villagers lest they be bombarded with unanswerable questions about the events that had transpired when the Roundheads came to Pendarn the previous year.

So they arrived at night, in the woods at the edge of the village, and they walked to the back of Dora's home, waiting for the candlelight that would signal Thomas's awakening and the beginning of another day's baking.

But as they stood there patiently in the darkness, Dora found her fear and guilt rising up again and, to her shame, she tried to turn and run away. Kaz, it seemed, was prepared for this, and he blocked her path and calmly assured her that she had nothing to feel guilty for. Jana echoed his sentiments and Dora gradually calmed down.

Before she had a chance to rethink yet again, the glow of a light from behind the windows called her forward.

'I'll go in first, it'll only be my father,' said Dora. 'Mother and James will be abed for an hour or more yet. I'll come to get you shortly.'

Kaz and Jana did not protest, and Dora, nervous and afraid, pushed open the back door of her house and stepped inside.

A figure was hunched over the oven, preparing the fire. He turned in surprise as Dora closed the door behind her and said, gently so as not to alarm him, 'Hello Father.'

But it was not her father.

James stood in mute wonder, staring at Dora, who must have appeared as a vision in the flickering light of the candle. Her hand flew to her mouth and she gave an involuntary yelp.

How quickly her training had deserted her, she thought. Stepping over this threshold had, with an instantaneous rush of uncontrollable sense memory, stripped away all the layers of protection she had built up around the girl who had last stood in this room. Dora had thought that girl vanquished but here she was, and Dora found herself unexpectedly, overwhelmingly glad to be her again. Perhaps it was fear of her, more than of reuniting with her brother, that had kept her away.

'Oh, I am sorry, James,' said Dora, almost stammering. 'I was expecting Father.'

'Sister?' whispered James. 'Can it be you?'

He stepped forward, holding out the candle, searching out her face in its soft light.

'Yes, James, it is I, your sister Dora,' she said, taking a step forward also. She wanted to run and hold him in her arms, but as she moved to take another step she had a sudden flash of his face as it had been when he dragged her from this room. The cruel sneer on his lips, the bruising hand on her upper arm, the cold contempt in his eyes.

He reached out a hand as if to touch her, to reassure himself of her solidity, and she recoiled slightly.

He stopped his advance and retracted his hand.

'Do I alarm you, Dora?' he asked.

Dora squeezed her hands into tight little fists and willed herself to overcome this weakness. She stepped forward and opened her arms to him.

'Not at all, James,' she said. 'The very opposite, in fact. It gives me great joy to see you again.'

'And I you,' he said, stepping into her embrace and returning it, albeit with a tentativeness that bespoke unease. Dora breathed in the smell of him. It had not changed, and it unlocked yet more parts of her buried self – a memory of lying beside him in the grass looking up as the swallows swooped and dived above them; the sound of his laughter as she tickled him in bed on a cold, frosty night; the feeling of being looked after as he picked her up and carried her home after she fell and cut her knee on a stone in the road.

When the embrace ended, somewhat awkwardly, Dora asked, 'Where is Father?'

'He and Mother have travelled to Lostwithiel, where Goodwife Bamford's granddaughter is being wed,' he replied, to Dora's relief; she had been worried that he might have died while she was absent.

'And he leaves the bakery in your care,' said Dora, smiling.

'He does,' said James.

Dora decided to try a little memory test. 'I recall a time when nothing in this world would have distressed you more than to be, how did you put it? Shackled to the ovens that enslaved us.'

James suddenly looked panicked and upset. 'Did I really say that?' he said. 'I suppose I did. I am sorry for it. My misadventures in London taught me the value of a simple trade pursued with diligence. I was a fool to leave and it shames me that I ever spake to Father thus.'

In that moment Dora felt a chill in her bones the likes of which she had never felt because this shamefaced, downcast, supplicant young man had nothing in common with the James she knew. Her brother had been headstrong and cocksure. Yes, his overconfidence had led him into danger, but it lay at the very core of him. Dora could not be sure whether the man she was talking to, who seemed so devoid of these qualities, was a real person. Is this the man her James would have become had he come to his senses, or was this guilty obeisance the result of their interfering with his mind?

How could she ever know for sure?

Aghast at what she might have done, Dora pulled him into a hug again.

'It's all past now,' she said. 'Don't worry about it. You're home, that's all that matters.'

But the words sounded hollow to her, and she knew that she would never forgive herself. Repelled by the shade that she had conspired to create, she stepped back from the hug as gently as she could.

'I must collect my things,' she said, moving towards the door.

'Let me help you,' said James, making to follow.

Dora held up her hand. 'No,' she said. 'You start the fire. I shall not be long.'

'As you wish, sister,' he said with a sad smile.

Did he know she was never coming back, she wondered, as she rejoined Kaz and Jana in the woods?

'We're going,' she said.

Before they could bombard her with questions, she grabbed their hands and pulled them after her, knowing that she could never return to Pendarn again.

Part Two

Beneath a butterscotch sky

BBC - From Our Own Correspondent

Carolyn Geary has spent a month on Mars, covering the preparation for the peace conference.

The air on Mars tastes different.

No, 'taste' is the wrong word. Air swirls around your nose and mouth simultaneously, so your impression of it is neither taste nor smell, but a subtle amalgam of both senses. There is no word to describe the sense of air's composition as experienced by a person, so I will co-opt one — tang.

The tang of the air on Mars is different to the tang of the air on Earth. Even in the most polluted parts of mankind's homeworld the air still has a subtle note of chlorophyll; even in the most pristine, a hint of metal. But the air of Mars — or, more accurately, the air within the dome that encloses the capital city of Barrettown — has a quality of clay, caused by the mixing of regolith with the humidity released by the water treatment plants. It is not unpleasant — it doesn't coat the tongue or clog the nose — but it does take some getting used to. It reminds me of the smell of the art room in my school, where we used to make pots.

There are those who will tell you the tang is a sinister thing, caused by drugs fed into the air supply by the government, a necessary measure to keep the populace docile. I pass a small group of protestors as I walk to the conference centre. They are tall and willowy, the tell-tale sign of Mars-born, raised in gravity less than half that which their genetic heritage designed them to inhabit. They carry placards and banners, which look quaintly old-fashioned beneath the huge advertising screens of the retail district. There is a booming market in air filters — customisable units that you attach to your wall. They claim to 'purify' the air and although their marketing materials make no mention of the spurious claims of the clean-air protestors, they are profiting from the paranoia the protestors foster. Better safe than sorry, seems to be the watchword of most Martians.

If I believed in conspiracies, I might suspect the protestors were funded by the manufacturers, but concluding that one bunch of conspiracy nuts are actually fakes funded by another conspiracy leads down a very deep rabbit hole indeed.

The air is the subtlest of the differences between Mars and Earth. Tourists or short-term visitors are encouraged to wear weighted boots and belts, to simulate Earth gravity. You are scanned when you arrive and then issued with custom weights tailored to your mass, height and weight distribution. But while they make walking easier, they lull you into a false sense of security, leading you to forget when sitting on or rising from a chair that the rules have changed. On my first day I managed to sit easily enough, but upon pushing myself back into a standing position I shot upright at an alarming speed, lost my balance and collided with the table.

Then there is the sky. Mars may look red from Earth, but from its surface the sky is a rich butterscotch that fades into dark caramel as the sun sets, small and distant. It's counterintuitive, but the warm colour of the sky somehow conjures up a feeling of cold; to look up at the heavens, through the diffraction of the dome, is to remind yourself that the rarefied atmosphere outside this bubble of hot air is 60 degrees below.

The city itself, huddled beneath a diamond sky, is beautiful. Likhachyov, who won the commission to plan and design it after a long winnowing process and a public vote, has used the latest organic construction techniques to force-grow a kind of ground-level skytown; despite the low gravity, the dome restricts the height of buildings, preventing the kind of towering forest effect conjured in the newer cities near the equator. The influence of Gaudí is apparent everywhere, his evocation of nature's fluidity in solid structure now recreated with nature itself. When you look out of the dome towards the horizon, all you see is dust, but the city is an oasis of green, rich and verdant in its very bones. The only thing that betrays its nature is the lack of chlorophyll in the tang of the air — these buildings, though grown, are dead now, their development halted at the appropriate moment, freezing them in place, solidifying their beams and buttresses. They still photosynthesise, but their energy is siphoned away to supplement that provided by the nuclear power stations that lie beyond the horizon, their brutal simplicity hidden from the green gaze of the sinuous city.

I cannot speak to the culture of Barrettown. My press pass restricts my movements to the affluent zone at its very centre. Here, where the bureaucrats and politicos rub shoulders with the representatives of those corporations who have a stake in the Mars project, there is little trace of the melting-pot mentality that reigns outside this enclave within an enclave. Like all cities, Barrettown can be roughly broken into districts with their own personalities. But there are areas where the law is more negotiable, and tourists like me would be at risk. At least, that is what the authorities tell me and since they prevent me exploring 'for my own protection', I must take their word for it. I could speculate there are things occurring in the city proper that the authorities do not wish journalists such as myself to witness, but that is another rabbit hole down which I demur to plunge.

So I come and go between my hotel, the conference centre that is preparing to host the peace conference and a collection of briefing rooms and offices. This is the domain of the unimaginative, the bean-counters, the ambitious and the diplomatic. Everything is bland and efficient. The carpets are plush, the seats are all leather, the fruit plates opulent. In the political heart of this city, everything conspires to make you feel like you are back on Earth, safe in the arms of the old order. Everything feels drearily, dispiritingly familiar.

Everything except the tang of the air and the butterscotch sky.

Barrettown, Mars,
4 April 2158, 2:22 P.M. -
19h 48m to the event

Dora finished the article and handed the tablet back to Jana.

'The green gaze of the sinuous city?' she quoted, laughing.

'What? I was trying to be evocative,' replied Jana grumpily, reaching for a slice of kiwi fruit. The fruit plate in front of her was exactly as she had described in her article – opulent to the point of being offensive. There was more fruit piled on it than the three of them could comfortably eat. The hydroponic gardens of Mars were productive and successful, but this was still the kind of conspicuous consumption designed to prove how well-off you were. It offended her, and she was guilt-eating her way through every piece of fruit on the plate as a kind of protest. She felt bloated and uncomfortable, and was worried that the contents of her stomach might actually be fermenting, but she was damned if she was admitting defeat.

'I think you were trying too hard,' said Dora, not unkindly.

'That's what my editor said.'

'So he's not going to run it?'

'No. He told me to stick to the facts.'

'Harsh.'

'I liked it,' said Kaz firmly.

'Thank you,' replied Jana, leaning over to give him a playful kiss on the cheek.

Kaz was sitting beside her on one of the four leather sofas that ringed the low table at the centre of Jana's hotel suite's lounge. The room was square, and it depressed Jana no end. She had been in some of the other hotels, the ones aimed at tourists, and the rooms were beautifully Martian – organic, rounded, hardly a straight line anywhere. But this hotel, the one created for the visiting government officials, was aggressively nonconformist. That is to say, it was the very image of Earth conformity – each room a box, with corners and carpets and square windows and rectangular doors, all right angles. It was very high-end – flock wallpaper, mahogany furniture, cotton sheets – the height of anonymous luxury, but it was the luxury of the old world not the new, as characterless as a roadside motel despite all its airs and graces. Jana had wanted to stay at any hotel but this one, but Quil would be staying here during the negotiations, on the top floor, and this was where Dora worked. So this was where they were stuck. Of course, the BBC's budget had only stretched to a small basement room, but Dora had insisted they use their own resources to upgrade to a suite where they could meet undisturbed. Jana had asked Dora where she'd got the money from, but Dora had told her she didn't want to know.

'I think you're a good writer,' said Kaz, smiling for the first time in days.

'You don't think my sentence structure is archaic, my vocabulary old-fashioned, my style prolix and my observations prosaic?' said Jana archly.

'Is that what he said?' asked Kaz.

'Verbatim.'

'What a jerk.'

'You didn't mention the problem with sleeping,' said Dora.

'What problem?' asked Kaz.

Jana took another bite of kiwi, enjoying the sharp sweetness that was leavened, as everything was on Mars, with a subtle undertone of clay. Her stomach protested as she swallowed. She flashed Dora a look intended to communicate 'Shut up and stop embarrassing me', but which apparently communicated 'Go ahead and blab my bedtime secrets'.

'She is a very restless sleeper,' said Dora, gleefully spilling the beans about her room-mate. 'Last night she turned over in bed so violently that she took off! I woke up because she was screaming, and when I looked over at her bed, she was three feet up in the air, tangled in the sheets, waving her arms around like she was fighting off a swarm of bees.'

Jana glared at Kaz. 'Don't crack a smile,' she warned sternly.

Kaz adopted his most serious face. 'Wouldn't dare,' he said.

'So is this the end for Carolyn Geary, travel writer?' asked Kaz.

'Reckon so,' replied Jana. 'The conference starts tomorrow, so that was probably my only shot at getting an article published before it all kicks off. A month getting my cover in place, then a month spent recycling press releases for the BBC, and not even a crappy travelogue piece to show for it.'

'So, wait,' said Dora. 'Do you really want to be a writer?'

Jana squirmed inwardly. She told herself it was the fruit. 'Um, I dunno,' she said. 'Maybe. Kinda. I mean, look, have you thought about what we're going to do if and when we can stop running from Quil? We're in a completely unique position. We can travel in time, people! Think of the books we could write!'

Kaz looked surprised. Dora looked amused.

'No, seriously, think about it,' Jana continued. 'You could write the most realistic historical epics ever. It would be amazing if I could, say, write a book set in Ancient Rome *while actually living in Ancient Rome*!'

'Huh,' said Kaz.

Jana rounded on him. 'What does that mean?' she snapped.

'I just, um, never pictured you as an author. That's not . . .' he trailed away, quelled by Jana's 'shutupshutupshutup' stare.

'So what are *you* going to do?' she said curtly, folding her arms.

'Win the lottery, buy an island, a Ferrari and a plane, watch a lot of movies and maybe become some kind of spy,' said Kaz.

'A spy?' Jana crammed as much scorn as she could, which was a lot, into her response.

'Yeah,' he said. 'If I needed to get some blueprints or something, I could pop back to before they were put in the supervillain's impregnable safe and take a picture.'

Kaz's face was impassive, so Jana couldn't tell whether he was winding her up or not. She thought about it and decided that she did not believe his answer. This is what he would have told her before Beirut – a boy's dream of being James Bond – but since he had lived through the loss of his mother for a second time there was a weight to him, a seriousness that had not been there before. She didn't call him on it, though; she tutted and muttered 'Boys', before turning to Dora and cocking her head by way of asking the same question.

Dora didn't hesitate. 'I have already been a spy, Kaz, and

it is less fun than you might think. And I have no artistic ambition, Jana. If you had asked me five years ago what I wanted, I would have said a quiet life, a herd of goats, a husband and children. Now . . .' She shrugged. 'I would settle for somewhere safe to live, with no one hunting me, looking after my parents as they grow old.'

Jana could think of no rejoinder to that, so she nodded and reached for a plum.

'Ooh, turn it up!' said Kaz, pointing over Jana's shoulder at the screen that dominated the far wall. Jana waved her hand in the gesture that told the TV to unmute, and the sound kicked in to accompany the news footage.

Jana recognised the arrival hall of the Phobos elevator, the place where people and materials disembarked after travelling down from low orbit in a car tethered to a massive carbon nanotube fibre. Despite the size of the fleet that she commanded, which even now hovered above the planet, Quil had been refused permission to land so much as a shuttle, so the elevator was her only route to the conference.

The arrival hall was immense, the size of a cathedral, with rows of thickly twined wooden columns leading into a canopy of interleaving branches.

On the screen Jana could see the rows of dignitaries lined up to receive Quil's delegation. They stood on both sides of a long carpet – blue, not red – that ran from the huge doors of the elevator carriage. Behind the dignitaries were row upon row of soldiers, standing to attention, weapons holstered but noticeable, dressed in orange and brown camouflage kit designed for combat. The message was clear – we may be diplomats, it said, but we have formidable backup in case it's needed.

Jana did not expect Quil to be intimidated.

The elevator doors slid open and a phalanx of Godless soldiers stepped out, marching in formation, rifles held across their chests. These men and women all wore simple black uniforms and an expressionless dull metal face mask. The masks were customised; each displayed a different design – some painted, some etched, some covered in stickers or slogans. Each was unique to the soldier beneath it, the only indication of individuality amongst the otherwise uniform soldiers. The men were all the same height and build as each other, the women likewise, with only the masks to differentiate between them. They stood in stark contrast to the Earth Force soldiers who lined their pathway, impassive but distinctly diverse in terms of height, colour and facial features.

'I know I'm not supposed to pick sides, but the Godless freak me out,' muttered Kaz.

'Don't use that word,' snapped Jana without looking at him.

He muttered something that she couldn't make out and chose not to query.

'I wonder if they have blue tattoos under their masks,' said Dora.

Jana shook her head. 'No. The goons we met in 1645 and 2014 were Celts, I'm sure of it. They came from the past; Quil's retro-engineered creations. These are the original models.'

Once the first wave of masked soldiers had passed, a smaller group of people emerged from the elevator. Although their clothes were the same as the foot soldiers who had preceded them, they wore stripes on their shoulders to denote rank and were not marching. Despite these differences, they were similarly uniform in physical type – all the men cut from one cloth, the women from another, and all with customised masks. In the middle of them strode Quil, who did not fit the physical pattern of the soldiers she commanded; she was lithe and tall where they were solid and short. Like her underlings, she also wore a mask, decorated with simple swirls of black, like a monochrome version of Van Gogh's *Starry Night*. She was a striking figure amid the conformity of the delegation, literally standing head and shoulders above the rest.

The camera zoomed in on her, picking out the brown eyes that stared from behind the metal, and the tumble of black hair that spilled behind it. Quil did not glance left or right, merely carried on walking, sandwiched in between her cohorts, down the long carpet to the doors, out of the building and into the waiting tram. The Earth delegates seemed unsure how to respond to being blanked by the person they stood in line to greet. After a few moments they broke ranks and began to mill about in muted confusion. The soldiers who had stood behind them remained immobile. The camera caught a tram pulling away, heading for the hotel.

'She's here,' said Jana. 'Now the fun really begins.'

She reached for an apple and took a loud, crunchy bite.

Barrettown, Mars,
4 April 2158, 10:02 P.M. –
12h 6m to the event

Dora greatly disliked her uniform. In keeping with the old-world aesthetic of the hotel, she was required to dress in the manner of a very traditional maid. She had not wanted to be a maid in 1640, and she certainly did not want to be one now, but domestic staff had one thing in common whatever time they lived in – they were practically invisible to the people upon whom they waited. The plain black dress and white pinafore aided anonymity, and she was glad of that. The level of alert in this hotel was as high as it could be, and she didn't want to draw attention to herself.

She had been working in the hotel for a month, and although it was the last thing she wanted to do, she had allowed herself to sink into the rhythm of it. She was good at her job, polite with the guests, did not rise to the outrageous bullying of her line manager and smiled freely and often. She had become the perfect maid – discreet, non-confrontational, patient to a fault, slightly boring but full of goodwill. She was going to be *so* glad when she could drop the mask and start hitting people again.

Since they had arrived on Mars, Dora and her friends had worked tirelessly to find out about Quil, her war and the situation in which they found themselves. Annoyingly, access to information on Mars was tightly controlled. They had a kind of intranet – a Mars-wide network connecting the four major cities and the smaller outposts – but information coming from Earth, or the colonies and ships further out in the solar system, was tightly policed. A shield of satellites surrounded the planet, with only approved communications passing between Mars and the rest of the system. From what they had been able to glean, the opportunity to construct a new internet from scratch here on Mars had allowed the government to build in controls at the most granular level – while Earth's system remained chaotic and decentralised, Mars's was regulated, centralised and entirely transparent to the authorities. Subversive voices were few, so Dora did not completely trust the information they were able to uncover. Nonetheless, after disregarding the most obvious propaganda, the bare outlines of the war were discernible, and they fitted with the facts Kairos had given them, and those she had established herself some years previously.

Quil was the leader of an army of workers from the outer edges of the solar system. Her army was exclusively composed of corporate clones, specially bred to work in the hostile environments of the asteroid belt and the various stations set up on assorted moons and dwarf planets. Cloning was, if you believed the official line, a simple and uncontroversial matter. Men and women were force-bred and quick-grown to work as miners and asteroid jockeys. They were treated fairly and equitably by the corporations who had given them life, but they had no rights as such. Dora recognised legal slavery when she saw it, but the government stance was that the clones were ungrateful and uppity. There were dark hints that maybe there was some inherent mental instability caused by the cloning process, that they were some hideous swarm of Frankenstein's monsters accidentally unleashed and now good for nothing but extermination. They were creations, property, no different to a tool or a spaceship.

The madness of the clones, their design flaw, was the only explanation offered for the onslaught of the clone army, but Dora didn't believe it. It didn't take much imagination to work out the kind of treatment and conditions these non-people must have received at the hands of their owners, far out in space, away from the prying eyes of do-gooders.

In 2156 Dora had seen Quil's videos, read the revelations she had unleashed via the Earth press. But here on Mars, two years later, she could uncover no record of those reports at all. Maybe they had never reached Barrettown, or maybe history was being rewritten.

A revolution of some sort had probably been inevitable, and almost certainly doomed. The corporations would have had strong measures in place to keep the clones quiescent, they weren't stupid, they would have known the risks. Dora guessed Quil was the wild card, the element in the mix that the corporations hadn't seen coming. Somehow she'd persuaded the clones to unify behind her, had provided leadership and tipped the balance. But how, and why?

Quil was an enigma. While all the other soldiers in her army were iterations of the same basic male or female templates, identical in all ways, Quil was not. There was no indication that she was a clone at all, so there was great confusion about why the clones would follow her, and why she would want to lead them. The clones had begun to wear masks, individualised to enable distinction, and Quil had followed suit. There were no pictures of her – at least, none in the public domain. Although she claimed it was a gesture of solidarity with her troops, speculation was rife that she was hiding her face for other reasons. Conspiracy theories abounded – she was a famous master criminal who had been set for execution ten years previously, orchestrator of a miraculous escape, gender-reassigned and out for revenge on the government that had sentenced him; she was an alien, softening up the solar system by inciting civil war preparatory to a full-blown invasion; she was a time traveller from the far future, sent back in time to change the past. Dora kind of liked that one, and briefly wondered if this whole adventure would get so tangled that she or Jana would end up travelling back in time and playing Quil's role to fix some terrible reality-threatening paradox.

Dora hoped not. She was having a hard enough time keeping track of things as it was; she wasn't sure she could cope if things got any more complicated.

The only thing that was certain is that nobody knew who Quil was, where she came from, or why she was leading this army. Her objectives were obscure, her endgame unfathomable. Dora was certain the Earth authorities knew far more than they were telling the populace, but there was no way for her to get to the truth via a screen.

The hundreds of repurposed mining vessels that constituted the Godless fleet had so far been unstoppable. Various colonies had put up a fight, but they had been swiftly and easily overcome. The news told of massacres, spinning lurid tales of hideous atrocities so obscene that Dora again questioned the truth of them – did clones really eat human babies? *Really?* It seemed unlikely to her, but the news insisted it had happened on Charon. As colony after colony had fallen, and the corporations had been forced to shut down all mining activities, the outcry and panic had increased. Determining that the best chance of stopping the clones was to make a single stand, Earth had sent its entire fleet to Mars and had pledged to stop the Godless in their tracks.

According to the news channel, Earth's fleet was overwhelmingly superior to that of the Godless. Ramshackle mining ships stood no real chance against purpose-built warships, footage of which was plastered across the screens almost continuously, showcasing sleek, gleaming battleships bristling with weapons and staffed entirely by crisply uniformed supermodels with really, really white teeth. The coming battle would be over in minutes, apparently, and then everything would return to normal.

Which raised the question – if it was going to be such a pushover, why were Earth bothering to negotiate? Why had they agreed to talk peace with the Godless here on the supposedly neutral territory of Mars? Dora had no idea what was really going on above Mars, but she didn't think for one second that it was as simple as a small fleet of mining ships facing off against a vastly superior force. The news insisted that the Godless had requested the peace conference, implying that they had baulked at the size of the opposition they were facing and were trying to find a way to back down and save face. From what she knew of Quil, Dora doubted that was the case. Kairos had said the blockade was propaganda, and she was inclined to believe him. She didn't think Earth would stand a chance if Quil pushed on.

For all her attempts to find out the truth of things, Dora had way more questions than answers. Maybe beyond the doors of the suite ahead of her, she would finally find some.

As she approached the door to the Godless suite, Dora

tried hard to calm her nerves. She was not accustomed to feeling nervous anymore; it had been one of the primary objectives of her training – eliminate the disadvantage that comes from fear. She had conducted covert operations in far more dangerous situations than this without feeling the tiniest flutter of butterflies, but this was personal – she was too invested in the outcome of this meeting to damp down the uneasy feeling in the pit of her stomach. Once she entered that suite, there would be no going back. This was the day it all began, from Quil's perspective. Whatever actions Dora and her friends would take at this point had, in the original timeline, led to a terrible tragedy and set Quil upon their heels.

She scolded herself and remembered how helpless she had felt in Sweetclover Hall, the day her world had changed for ever. The timidity, the fear, the way she had retreated into herself as shock had taken hold. Since then Dora had distanced herself from that pathetic whimpering child as much as she was able; that version of herself represented everything she had sought to repress, excise, banish from the person she had turned herself into. So every time she felt fear, she turned inwards in a flurry of self-hatred, embarrassed and repulsed by the final unkillable vestiges of the girl she used to be.

Nonetheless, as she pushed the refreshments trolley she kept her face neutral, her pace steady and even, gave no outward sign of her internal struggle. She had no idea what to expect when she stepped beyond those doors.

The two template faces of the Godless were well known, plastered on screens and walls across the city. The material for the male clone had been taken from a Samoan line. His eyes were dark, his skin light brown, his nose flat and wide above a full-lipped mouth. The female clones had Asian echoes, epicanthic folds, button nose, thin lips but a perfectly symmetrical face. If they had taken their masks off, Dora wondered if she'd be able to identify individuals. Tattoos, hairstyles, make-up, piercings, facial hair – all would offer means to distinguish individuality between identical faces. Age would also be a factor, as clones were produced in batches so some would be older, some younger. Maybe environmental factors would have made a difference – scars and injuries, different skin tones depending upon what levels of ultraviolet light they had been exposed to, or which chemicals had been involved in the particular mining process they'd been forced to use. The unquantifiable element would be their mental states; how their individual experiences had shaped their personalities. Would differing amounts of cynicism, trauma and anger have shaped their faces in unique ways?

And then there was the third face of the Godless: Quil. Dora doubted their leader, who had gone to such lengths to preserve her anonymity, would allow her face to be seen by a strange maid but maybe, in an unguarded moment, she might catch a glimpse through a half-open door or a reflection from a conveniently placed mirror.

Dora had a horrible suspicion she would recognise their tormentor. This, more than anything, was the source of her fear.

There were four Godless guards outside the suite's door – two men, two women. One of the men had an entirely blank mask. It was the only one she'd seen undecorated in any fashion, and the dull metal combined with the singularity of it rendered it uniquely threatening, as if there was nothing behind the mask but purpose, no person at all. This one didn't move or speak, but she saw his eyes follow her as she walked forward. If her reconnaissance turned into a fight for any reason, he was the one she'd have to deal with first. The other man had a yin/yang on each cheek of his mask, while the two women had symmetrical patterns of delicate painted leaves; Dora recalled that matching masks denoted marriage or at least couplehood within the Godless. The idea of marrying someone with the same face creeped Dora out. She couldn't decide whether it was more like narcissism or incest.

Yin/yang and one of the women stepped forward and barred her way. Neither spoke, but they made it clear they would take the trolley into the suite.

'I'm sorry, but I'm not supposed to let you do that,' protested Dora. 'It has to be served properly.'

Yin/yang shook his head firmly.

'Please,' Dora wheedled, giving her very best performance of a scared service worker. 'My supervisor will freak out and I'll really cop it.'

Leaf mask shook her head and pointed back to the lift, indicating firmly that Dora should go.

Dora stood there for a moment allowing her lip to tremble. She even mustered a single tear. But the hand stayed pointing and eventually Dora gave in and turned away, leaving the trolley behind.

Seemed things weren't going to be that easy after all.

Twenty minutes later, she was heading to the kitchen to collect another tray for room service, trying to think of strategies to infiltrate Quil's suite, when her manager collared her. Marsborn, and thus tall and thin-boned, he was also comically fat. When he walked his gut would undulate in the low gravity, which, combined with his spindly arms and legs and great height, made him look like a thin man with a balloon full of jelly stuffed up his jumper. He was a pedantic man too, and Dora braced herself for a lecture on following orders and how she shouldn't have let the trolley out of her sight, especially since the guest in question was an evil dictator who could nuke their hotel from orbit if she didn't like the pastries.

'Predennick,' he said, his voice as wobbly as his belly. 'There's some kind of problem in the delegation suite. Can you pop up there and do clean-up for me, there's a good girl.'

Dora decided that scared and patronising was better than annoying and bossy, so she gave him a pass on the sexism, nodded once and ran off to get her clean-up kit.

This time when she approached the doors – still nervous, still trying to tamp it down – Yin/yang stepped to one side and held the door open for her. She smiled her thanks and entered, carrying her bucket, sprays and cloths. She had expected there to be swarms of Godless inside but in fact it was quiet as the grave. She was immediately on high alert, suspecting a trap. There were so many different ways her cover could have been blown, not least by Sweetclover popping forward and dropping her in it, that she couldn't take anything for granted.

When she moved through into the main lounge area she immediately saw the problem. Someone had thrown the fruit plate, splattering grapes, orange slices and all manner of berries across the wall.

Dora was aware that she was not alone. She could hear breathing and faint movements to her right, but she did not look, not wanting to alert whoever it was. She did not get a sense of being stalked, so she pretended she was unaware and tutted loudly before putting down her bucket and pulling on some rubber gloves.

'I'm sorry about the mess,' said a voice behind her. Dora

started, aping surprise, and turned to see Quil sitting on a corner chair, surveying the room from behind her mask.

'Oh, I'm so sorry, ma'am, I didn't realise you were here,' said Dora, giving her best impersonation of a frightened housemaid. 'Shall I come back later?'

'No. Please continue. I imagine it will start to smell if left long enough.' Quil was softly spoken, her body language relaxed. She had no tablet or book and she was sitting with her hands folded in her lap. Dora got a sense that she had been enjoying the quiet.

Quil's voice was different. The barely concealed madness that had seeped out of her in Sweetclover Hall was absent. This woman seemed calm and composed.

'Yes, ma'am,' said Dora, and began wiping the wall clean, using the cloth to gather up the fruit pulp that had stained the already gruesome wallpaper. As she cleaned, she tried to work out how best to start a conversation. Her best-case scenario had been to overhear a meeting, or catch a glimpse of a secret communication on a screen, but here she was apparently alone in the suite with the woman who was the focus of all her efforts. And she had a huge advantage because Dora knew Quil's future – *possible* future. She had been so unprepared for such a stroke of luck, she had no idea how best to exploit it. It turned out she didn't have to – Quil was feeling talkative.

'One of my generals found the food . . . offensive,' volunteered the most feared military leader in the solar system.

'Was the fruit spoiled, ma'am?' asked Dora, sticking to her role.

Quil laughed softly. 'No,' she said. 'Nothing like that. He was a miner on a dwarf planet. Lived his whole life on processed protein bars and algae soup. He finds such largesse inappropriate.'

'Large what, ma'am?' asked Dora.

'Largesse,' said Quil patiently. 'It means luxurious generosity.'

Dora nodded her head and said, 'Oh, I see,' in a manner designed to make Quil think this dim little maid had no clue whatsoever.

'He spent his life starving and now, because he strikes fear into the hearts of his oppressors, they offer him more fruit than he can possibly eat,' explained Quil. 'It angers him – and me – but I have more self-control than he. And I hadn't quite finished the plums. I love plums.'

Dora could hear a smile in Quil's voice. She continued wiping the wall; the sickly sweet smell of fruit juices mingled with the antiseptic odour of the wipes she used to finish the job to create a noxious smell that made her curl her lip in involuntary disgust.

'What is your name?' asked Quil.

'Dora, ma'am.'

'That's a nice name. Pleased to meet you Dora, I am Quil.'

'I . . . I know who you are, ma'am.'

'Of course you do.' Was that a tinge of regret Dora could detect?

'You are not a Martian,' said Quil.

'No, ma'am,' replied Dora. 'Earth-born. Came here with my parents a couple of years ago. My mother got a job with the administration.' Dora parroted her cover story.

'Do you like Mars?' asked Quil.

Dora made a show of considering her answer, but she was mostly masking her surprise at how friendly and chatty Quil was being. 'I like it well enough,' she said. 'But the gravity does not agree with me. I feel like I'm wasting away sometimes.'

Quil nodded. 'That will happen, you lose bone density and muscle tone. That's why they made us Godless. Genetically engineered to thrive in extremely low-gravity environments. Makes them perfectly suited for work out on the edge. My troops are actually finding the gravity here on Mars quite uncomfortable.'

Which raises the question, thought Dora, how they would function if they were required to fight a ground war on Earth? She filed that piece of information away for later consideration.

'Don't think that's privileged information, my dear,' said Quil. 'I would not have told you if I did not think the Earth government knew it already.'

Dora stopped and turned, feigning affront. 'I wouldn't tell a soul, ma'am,' she said. 'I'm not a gossip.'

Quil was silent for a moment and then laughed. 'You are either terribly naive or a very good little spy,' she said. 'Either way, you will be asked to repeat every detail of this conversation to large men in dark suits as soon as you leave this suite.'

Quil waved away Dora's protests. 'It doesn't matter, child,' she said. 'They will not hurt you. It's nice to have someone different to talk to.'

Dora settled for a simple 'ma'am' and continued cleaning on her hands and knees, tracking down errant blueberries.

Quil seemed content to let the silence linger, so after a few minutes Dora decided to take a chance on continuing the conversation.

'Ma'am, you said "us Godless". But you . . . you are not like the others.' She let the question hang, playing the tentative girl, nervously curious rather than cunningly interrogatory.

'No, I am not,' replied Quil. 'I am a clone, but not like them. Not bred for hard labour. I was designed for a very different purpose.'

There was no subtle way to voice the obvious next question, so Dora looked quizzical and hoped Quil would volunteer more information. She did not.

Again Quil let the silence hang for a while, but Dora was conscious that she was being studied.

'You are a very pretty girl,' said Quil.

Dora faked a nervous, embarrassed laugh. 'Thank you, ma'am.' She then made a play of trying to return the compliment and failing, hoping it would restart the conversation. 'I, um, I really like your mask,' she said. 'Nice patterns.'

The eyes behind the whirling black spirals and cold, dull metal sparkled. 'Why thank you, I drew the designs myself. They are mathematical. Fibonacci fractals. They remind me that everything is numbers.'

'Numbers, ma'am?'

'Physics, higher mathematics,' said Quil. 'Trust me, it's all very complicated and you're probably better off knowing nothing about it.'

'If you say so, ma'am. I've never had a head for figures. Is that the only reason you wear it?'

'My reasons are my own,' replied Quil, still kindly but more firm in the face of a direct question.

'Yes ma'am, sorry ma'am, I didn't mean to be impertinent.' Dora resolved to let the silence last this time. She located what she thought was the last of the blueberries beneath one of the sofas, then turned her attention to some pieces of kiwi fruit that had been mashed into the carpet by angry boots.

'Are you scared of me?' asked Quil as Dora used a scraper to get all the little black seeds out of the pile.

Dora considered her answer carefully and decided to be honest. 'You are not what I was expecting,' she said cautiously, keeping her eyes on her work.

Quil seemed amused by this. 'What did you expect?' she asked.

'Someone bossy and shouty, who would threaten me a lot.'

'Get a lot of those, do you?'

'Especially in this suite, ma'am,' said Dora, risking a little bit of cheek.

'I bet you do,' laughed Quil. 'They are your enemy, Dora. Mine too. The people who think they own us, who tell us what to do and punish us if we dare to think our own thoughts, try to live our own lives. Earth tells you that we are your enemy, but that is the biggest lie of this entire war. We should be allies, you and I. The real enemy, our mutual enemy, sits in big houses and luxurious suites like this, never giving a thought to the people who mine the minerals that make their toys, who serve their food, who clean up after them.'

There was passion in Quil's voice now. Not the ranting fervour that Dora had heard in the past, but a balanced, politicised anger, focused and reasoned. She began to get a sense of the path Quil had walked, from righteous indignation to rebellion and eventually to madness. It made a kind of sense. She risked a bit more cheek, gambling that this version of Quil – the rebel who resented authority – would warm to someone who gave a bit of lip.

'That's as may be, ma'am,' she said, concentrating on her work, avoiding eye contact so the challenge was less direct, 'but I don't see you helping me clean up this mess.'

For a second Dora thought she'd made an error. It took Quil a couple of seconds to get over her surprise and bellow a single appreciative 'Ha!' Then she rose from her seat, walked over to Dora, picked a roll of paper towels out of the bucket, got down on her hands and knees and began drying out the damp patches of carpet that Dora had just washed.

Dora was both pleased and disconcerted. Pleased that she'd judged Quil correctly and seemed to have formed a bond of respect so quickly; disconcerted because if she hadn't known what a madwoman Quil was going to become, Dora would said she quite liked her. This was definitely not the Quil she had met, and she wondered how awful the imminent, unspecified tragedy must be to drive her to such extremes.

She considered the best way to capitalise on this opportunity. As she did so, Dora found a plum under an occasional table. She reached out, picked it up and proffered it to Quil.

'You said you like plums,' said Dora, smiling.

It was impossible to see if Quil smiled back, but the eyes wrinkled, so Dora thought she did.

Quil reached out to take the fruit and as she did so, her index finger brushed gently against Dora's little finger.

A little cluster of red sparks arced between their fingers. Quil's laughing eyes suddenly widened in shock and then narrowed in suspicion.

'Wait,' said Dora, 'I can—'

'Guards!' yelled Quil, backing away from Dora as quickly as she could.

The suite doors burst open and the four guards from outside ran into the room, guns drawn.

'Crap,' said Dora.

Barrettown, Mars,
4 April 2158, 10:14 P.M. -
11h 54m to the event

'That was disgusting,' said Jana, shuddering with revulsion and pulling a face. 'Seriously, that might be the most horrible thing I have ever put in my mouth.'

She put her empty shot glass down on the sticky bar top and eyed it suspiciously.

'You get used to it,' muttered Kaz, slamming his empty glass down beside hers and motioning for the barkeep to fill them up again.

'What is it even made of?' Jana asked.

'You don't want to know,' Kaz replied with a faint smile.

The barkeep, a tall willowy Martian girl with long hair dyed shocking pink and eyes to match, refilled their glasses and walked away. Kaz had a tab here. He knew the barkeep's name (Shindra) and she knew his usual drink; he even had a favourite booth. Jana guessed that he'd charmed the regulars into accepting him. The barkeep had given him a warm smile when they'd arrived, but although a couple of the barflies had inclined their heads in subtle greeting, the rest of the clientele ignored him.

This was an engineers' bar, its regulars the men and women who worked to maintain the giant terraforming engines that squatted in the valley beyond the ridge to the west of the domed town. These were people who worked long hours in hot, oily chambers of deafening noise, constant vibration and foul smells. They were heavy drinkers, liked their liquor rough and ready, their entertainment loud and raucous. They were all ages, from young boys to old women, and although they seemed more than eager to fight each other at any opportunity they had shown no sign of wanting to take a chunk out of the newcomers. Jana felt kind of invisible, which surprised her. She'd expected to get at least a few catcalls when she'd walked in, fresh meat. Instead she'd hardly garnered a glance. As she and Kaz walked to his booth she wondered if it was because she was with him.

The bar was dingy and dimly lit. Neon signs, floating screens, pool table. There was music, a weird mix of industrial sounds and stringed instruments that Kaz had told her was something called Nu-Martian. If it wasn't for the sounds, and the clay in the air, this might have been any dive bar in any Earth city. Not that she'd been to any, she'd not had that kind of childhood, but she'd seen movies.

He slid into the booth by the door and Jana slid in opposite him. The bench was bare wood and the table may have been varnished once but it had been worn smooth by the forearms and drinks of customers. Above Kaz's head Jana could see a screen replaying Quil's arrival on a seemingly endless loop.

Shindra brought them another round of drinks but Jana pushed hers away with a grimace. Kaz smiled again, sank his in one gulp, then did the same with hers.

'What's the proof on that stuff and how much have you been drinking?' she asked.

173

'I told you . . .'

'Yeah, I don't want to know,' sighed Jana. 'I get it.'

Kaz smiled and leaned forward, conspiratorial. 'Actually,' he said, 'it's all an act. I can't stand the stuff. I tried it once and it stripped the skin off the roof of my mouth. Shindra gives me coloured water instead, and because I drink so much and don't fall over, the locals think I'm some kind of hard-drinking tough guy.'

Jana gaped in astonishment. 'But . . . but . . . you let me drink one!?'

Kaz grinned. 'Initiation,' he laughed. 'Now you're one of the clientele.'

She slapped his arm. 'You louse,' she said, determined not to let on that she actually found it pretty funny.

'When's he supposed to be getting here?' she asked.

Kaz shook his head. 'He doesn't work like that,' he said. 'He'll get here when he gets here. He doesn't do timetables. Makes it harder for people to track him down, he says.'

'Huh. OK, so we sit and wait for him.'

Kaz nodded.

'On Mars,' said Jana, shaking her head in wonder. 'We're waiting for a criminal in a dive bar on Mars. That sounds like a song or something.'

'Opening line of a book.' He put on a thick American drawl. 'I was waiting for a criminal in a dive bar on Mars when the broad walked in through the door and all heads turned. With legs that went all the way up to her ears, she was Olympus Mons and I wanted to climb her.'

Jana laughed. 'Guaranteed bestseller,' she laughed. 'But really, Mars.'

'Really.'

'Doesn't it worry you?' she asked. 'We found pictures of

us in a battle, in Quil's basement lair, remember? And the sky in those photos looked exactly like the one outside. Not to mention the versions of ourselves that Dora and I met during our first trip.'

Kaz nodded, but held up a finger. 'But that battle might be us winning,' he said. 'It could be that the tragedy we're here to avert is a nuke or something, and a little battle is actually the better result.'

'Or Kairos could be wrong,' countered Jana. 'We could create an alternate timeline. In which case what we do doesn't really matter as long as we stay alive.'

Kaz shrugged. 'Who knows,' he said. 'I'm sticking with Kairos for now. It might be my mother's only chance, so I choose to believe him.'

Jana was shocked that Kaz still thought he could save his mother. She couldn't see any chance for Peyvand but she didn't push Kaz to explain. Whatever plan he was cooking up to save her, she didn't want to discuss it now.

'It's simple, really,' he said, clocking the look on her face and explaining anyway. 'If Quil never gets blown back in time, then she can't kill my mother.'

Jana smiled, nodded curtly and changed the subject.

'So is this what you've been doing while I've been writing copy and Simon and Dora have been cleaning rooms and serving lunch, hanging around in this bar?' she asked.

'You sound resentful,' Kaz replied, teasing. 'Not enjoying your first job?'

'Don't change the subject,' said Jana. 'You had a job to do too – find John Smith.'

'I have done,' he said. 'That's why you're here.'

'But it's taken you a month,' Jana protested. 'Have you honestly been in this bar every day, drinking coloured water and asking anyone who looks dodgy whether they know someone called John Smith?'

'Of course not.'

'Good.'

'There are three other bars I hang out in, too.'

Jana pursed her lips at him, but he broke into a cheeky grin and she found she couldn't really get angry with him.

'Kairos gave me some leads, based on what they found in the investigations conducted after whatever is supposed to happen tomorrow,' explained Kaz. 'There's a guy who arranges false papers for people and they reckoned he had supplied Smith's entry visa for the central zone of the city. He's hard to track down, but Kairos pointed me to one of his competitors – the woman who actually forged the papers that got you out of the central zone this evening – and she told me this was our guy's preferred drinking hole. In fact, he's been on holiday in one of the other domes and only got back two days ago. In return for a modest cash donation she set up this meet. I let her think I was the law, willing to let her slide if she'd point me to the big fish I was really after. She was only too keen to help me take care of her rival.'

'Nice,' said Jana. 'Maybe you will be a spy after all.'

'I'll drink to that,' replied Kaz, taking a fresh fake shot off Shindra's tray and necking it before she'd even had a chance to put it on the table in front of him.

'Chaser?' Shindra asked Kaz as she placed another shot glass in front of Jana.

'Two please, Shin,' said Kaz.

She nodded, and Jana was sure she caught a tiny appraising glance in her direction from the willowy Martian girl as she glided away.

'So you, uh, hitting that?' she asked, as casually as she was able, regretting it as soon as the words left her mouth.

Now it was Kaz's turn to laugh. 'Hitting that? Did you really just ask if I was hitting that? Did those words really come out of your mouth?'

'What?' said Jana, covering her embarrassment with bravado. 'That's what guys in your time say, isn't it. I've seen films and stuff.'

'No, Jana, guys in my time – well, guys like me, anyway – don't call girls "that" and don't use the word hit instead of the more obvious.'

'So I should have said sleeping with her?' Jana asked, confused.

'Oh my God, will you stop!' Kaz was laughing hard. 'What are you doing?'

'Asking a simple question, jeez.' She was suddenly quite self-conscious. It was not a feeling she was accustomed to and she did not like it one bit.

'You don't have brothers, do you?' asked Kaz.

'You know I don't,' said Jana, scowling.

'Any close male friends? Boys you hang with? Anyone you dated?'

Jana thought back to her life before Pendarn. She'd had friends, sure, and some of them were boys but, if she was honest with herself, she saw them more as accessories than people. Toys she could play with to keep boredom at bay. And as for boyfriends, no way. Hector had tried to kiss her once after math, but she punched him so hard his right eye swelled shut. Actually, she felt kind of bad about that now.

'Not really,' she answered. 'I suppose you're my first real boy friend. As in friend who's a boy, not . . .'

'I get it,' Kaz reassured her, still laughing slightly at her awkwardness. 'I suppose groups of boys might speak like that, and ask direct questions like that, among themselves. I don't know really. I moved around so much I was never really a part of any group and I'm honestly not sure I'd have wanted to be. But either way, it's not the kind of thing friends ask each other, at least, not in that way, not in my time. But it's OK, it's fine, really. Keeping track of all the different social conventions and behaviours across different time periods and, hell, planets now, is hard. And to answer your question, no. Shindra has a guy. He's about ten foot tall and twelve foot wide and I'm pretty sure he's sharpened at least two of his teeth to points.'

'I think she's kind of into you, though,' said Jana. 'She gave me a look, like she was sizing up the competition.'

'Really?' Kaz seemed genuinely surprised. 'OK, hadn't picked up on that. Huh. Well, if you're her competition that would make Shark-Teeth mine, and as nice as she is, that's not a game I want to play.'

'Or is it that she's got competition?' Jana asked, teasingly.

'What?'

'Oh come on, Kaz,' she scoffed. 'You spent six months as a pirate. You're not telling me there wasn't a girl in the mix somewhere or somewhen, good-looking lad like you.'

Kaz folded his arms and leaned back against the hard wood of the benchback as Shindra placed large tankards of beer in front of them both. He shook his head in amused amazement.

'Are you jealous, Jana?' he asked, smiling, when the barkeep had retreated again.

Jana scoffed. 'Not likely.' She took a sip of the beer. It was watery and tasteless but it helped wash away the lingering aftertaste of the shot.

'Before he left Kinshasa,' said Kaz, smiling, 'Simon said he thought I should ask you out.'

That stopped Jana dead. It wasn't what he'd said so much as how he'd said it that brought her up short. He was passing it off as jokey, but there was something about the way he'd avoided her eyes as he'd said it that gave the game away. She'd been enjoying the playful banter, a bit of good-natured back and forth, just teasing, no actual charge to it. She wondered if she'd not misjudged the situation completely.

'Simon is not the love god he likes to make out,' she lobbed back. 'He's the last person you want to be taking dating advice from.'

'Oh, I don't know.'

Crap.

She had, she'd completely got the wrong end of the stick. This wasn't friendly piss-taking, this was flirting. How could she possibly have missed that? She made a lot of very good excuses for herself, mostly involving time travel, near-death experiences and travel to alien worlds holding her focus instead of things like hormones and romance and stuff, but the fact remained that she could kind of see, if she squinted hard at her recent behaviour, how Kaz might have interpreted it as romantic interest.

She had to deal with this quickly, otherwise she'd end up losing the only friend she'd ever really had.

'Kaz, listen—'

Before she could continue, he held up a hand to quiet her. He was looking over her shoulder down into the bar.

'He's here,' said Kaz. 'At the bar ordering a drink. Shindra's pointed us out. He's coming over. Be cool.'

Be cool? Jana was kind of offended by that. She was far cooler than he'd ever be. She made a mental note to return to the whole unfortunate romantic misunderstanding thing at the first opportunity and turned her attention to the new arrival.

He was an old man. Really old. Probably the oldest she had ever seen. Small, hunchbacked, his face a thin tracery of spider web lines over deep crevasses. Thick tufts of hair sprouted from his ears and nostrils like some kind of infestation, and his eyebrows curled up so high they met his hairline and kind of merged with his fringe, making him look like he had badger stripes. His teeth varied between dark brown and black, but when he put his glass down on the table his hands were as steady as could be and his eyes, when he turned them upon Jana, were sharp, clear and full of wit.

'Mademoiselle,' he said, imposing a smile on his ruined face. There was nothing lascivious about his gaze, though. He was simply being polite.

'Hello,' she said.

'Mr Brock?' asked Kaz and it was all Jana could do not to slap her forehead. What a perfect name for Mr Badger-stripes; actually, it was probably his pseudonym for that precise reason.

'That's me, young man. How can I be of assistance?' As the old forger spoke he pulled a stool across and perched on it, resting his folded arms on the end of the booth table.

'I need some information, and I can pay handsomely for it.'

Mr Brock's cadaverous smile widened.

'Tell me more,' he said.

Barrettown, Mars, 4 April 2158, 10:22 P.M. - 13h 12m to the event

Dora knew, somewhere at the back of her mind, that fighting the guards was the worst possible thing she could do. If she put up no resistance and explained herself, she could spin any kind of story to explain the sparks. It all depended how much Quil had already figured out about the asteroid she had turned into a bomb. Did Quil know she could travel in time? She'd recognised the sparks, so she must at least have experienced some kind of temporal glitch, but she might not understand what it meant, not entirely. If Dora could avoid a fight, she might perhaps be able to persuade Quil she was an ally, sent from the future to protect her.

But as all of these thoughts were running through her conscious mind, Dora's subconscious training, instinct and muscle memory kicked in.

Yin/yang was first through the door, with the two leaf-pattern women flanking him and Blank-mask bringing up the rear. Quil was to Dora's left, still crabbing backwards from her in alarm.

Dora grabbed the bucket full of pulped fruit mixed with the cleaning fluids that had scrubbed it off the walls and tossed it towards Yin/yang. It caught him full in the face, and although the mask afforded protection from most of it, his eyes were exposed. He howled in pain and staggered backwards as the noxious pulp liquid splashed across his eyeballs. Momentarily down, but definitely not out.

Leaf-pattern one and two kept moving forward, swerving either side of Yin/yang, their weapons raised. Dora flipped backwards, head over heels, landing on all fours on the other side of the low coffee table. She grabbed the edge of the table and flipped it, using it as a shield just in time to deflect their weapons. She heard the buzz of their lasers firing and saw smoke rise from the other side of the table as they burned through it. The wood would only last a second or two, at best. Dora stood and heaved the table at them, throwing it with all her might. It caught them both in the chest, knocking them off their feet.

Blank-mask was the only opponent still active, and he jumped nimbly over the falling women and landed firm on his feet, gun aimed straight at Dora's head. There was nowhere for her to go.

'Don't kill her!' yelled Quil to the guard, giving Dora the opportunity she needed. She jumped forward, kicking Blank-mask square in the chest. He grunted and dropped his gun, but fell back into a fighting pose, clearly well trained. His chest was so solid, Dora's foot was vibrating with the aftershock of the impact. Damn, these clones were built tough. For the first time, her conscious mind realised quite how deeply in trouble she was.

Dora matched Blank-mask's fighting stance. Yin/yang and the two leaf-patterns were still struggling to gather themselves.

If she struck now, she might have a chance of making the stairwell. Dora lunged forwards, raining a flurry of blows down on Blank-mask's rock-hard frame, but he deflected or absorbed every one as if it was the tiniest annoyance. He landed one solid counter-punch, a right hook that made Dora's head ring and caused a deep sharp crunch from her jaw, which spiked with sudden pain as her mouth filled with blood. She lost her balance and went down on one knee, but even as Blank-mask raised his fist to deliver the knockout blow, Dora reached forward and jabbed as hard as she could at his groin. Not all solid then, she thought as he froze in the moment of shock that precedes the pain of being punched hard in the balls.

She took advantage of the brief respite to launch herself forwards, past Blank-mask, punching out both arms at once at Leaf-pattern one and two as they were clambering to their feet, sending both sprawling again, then shoulder-charging Yin/yang, who had ripped his mask off and was rubbing his eyes frantically.

Then she was past them and into the corridor, running hard for the stairwell. She couldn't wait to call a lift, but if she could get through the stairwell door, she had a chance.

'Stop!' That was Quil's voice, calling after her. Dora ignored it and ran on. A sizzling blast of hot light blew past her head and burned through the lift doors ahead of her.

'I don't need to kill you to stop you!' shouted Quil.

Dora eyed the distance to the stairwell door and knew Quil was right. She didn't have a chance of making it.

She stopped running, spat the blood out of her mouth and turned to face the fractal mask of the woman she could have befriended, arms wide and unthreatening.

'I'm not your enemy,' said Dora. 'Think about it. If I'd

183

wanted to kill you, I had plenty of opportunity before we sparked.'

Quil stood in the suite doorway, legs apart, pistol held straight ahead of her aimed at Dora's chest.

'Who are you?' said Quil, breathing fast.

'My name is Dora, as I said. I work here as a maid.'

Dora saw the light lance out from Quil's gun and it seemed like an age before she felt the pain in her hand. Shaking, she held the hand in front of her, marvelling at the small, neat, smoking hole Quil's laser had burned in her palm. Dora could see through it. She felt her head begin to swim as the pain kicked in, but she gritted her teeth and fought it back; she'd endured worse.

'Who are you and why are you here?' repeated Quil. Three of the four guards behind her had regained their feet and were standing beside her, also aiming their weapons at Dora. Blank-mask was still down.

'OK, OK,' said Dora, her jaw shooting with pain every time she spoke. She suspected Blank-mask had fractured it. 'Can I sit down? Can we go back inside and talk about this?'

'If you move an inch I'll bisect you,' growled Quil. 'Talk.'

'I don't know how much you know,' said Dora. 'Those sparks, when we touched – have you seen something like that before?'

Quil nodded.

'When you were experimenting with the asteroid,' continued Dora. 'The one that has the . . . unusual characteristics?'

Quil did not nod this time, unwilling to volunteer any more information, waiting for Dora to continue.

'Are you sure you want your soldiers to hear this?' asked Dora, talking through gritted teeth as her punctured hand throbbed and burned.

'I have no secrets from my personal guard,' replied Quil.

Dora considered her options and decided that a version of the truth was the best choice.

'OK,' she said. 'Those sparks are created when two people who have been exposed to that asteroid come into contact. It's a reaction. It means I'm like you.'

'A time traveller,' whispered Quil.

Dora nodded.

'I knew this day would come,' said Quil softly. 'I've been waiting for you for *years*.'

That was interesting because it strongly implied that Quil had already travelled in time at least once.

'So what are you? Assassin or historian?' asked Quil. 'Have you come back to kill me, change history, prevent my victory? Or are you here to study me, get close to the legend?'

Dora shook her head. 'Neither. I'm not from the future. I'm from the past.' It wasn't the whole truth, but it wasn't a lie – she had come to Mars from the near future, but she was born in the seventeenth century.

Quil cocked her head, confused. 'The past? That doesn't make any sense. Why would someone from the past be interested in me?'

Dora thought fast and came up with the most plausible story she could. 'I'm a kind of researcher. My job is to map out the future, then travel back and pass on what I've learned to the authorities. They use the intelligence I gather to shape events, nudge history towards the outcomes they desire.'

'Fascinating,' said Quil after a moment's thought. 'Maybe I could believe that. Maybe, but I hope you understand that I can't afford to take the chance. I wonder, could you jump off into time faster than the beam of light from this gun could travel from here to there?'

That confirmed to Dora that Quil had travelled in time, otherwise how would she know it was as simple as a thought – somebody unfamiliar with the process would probably assume there was some kind of machine involved.

'I don't know,' said Dora. 'I don't intend to find out.'

A loud chime sounded from inside the suite behind Quil and her guards. 'Someone get that,' barked Quil, keeping her attention firmly focused on Dora. Blank-mask rose to his feet behind Quil and shuffled away.

'I have to assume you're an assassin,' said Quil. 'I think I win this war and you're the last gasp of a dying counter-revolution, sent back in time to kill me and change history.'

'I promise you,' Dora pleaded, 'that's not the case.'

The lift behind Dora pinged and she heard the doors slide open, followed quickly by a sharp intake of breath as whoever had come to talk to Quil found themselves walking into a stand-off.

'What's going on here?' barked a strong male voice from behind Dora. This was a voice accustomed to giving commands and having them obeyed. Dora wondered if the other Godless, the lower ranks, spoke the same way. After all, they had the same vocal cords.

'You have to be the general who threw the fruit,' said Dora, without looking round. 'Am I right?'

'Quil,' he said, 'explain this.'

'There was an attempt on my life, General,' said Quil, her aim not wavering, her eyes remaining fixed on Dora.

'Oh come on, that's a total lie,' protested Dora. 'I never touched you, and you know I could have.'

'Curious timing,' said the general, who had walked out of the lift and was now walking past Dora towards Quil. He stopped to study Dora, but he was careful – he did not block

Quil's line of fire and he never came within arm's reach of Dora.

'She's just a girl,' he said casually.

'What did you mean about timing?' asked Quil.

The general turned away from Dora and continued walking towards the suite doors. 'One of our operatives has warned us of a planned attack on Charon. This peace conference is a sham, as I said all along. They've drawn us here to outflank us. And I don't think it's a coincidence that at the same time they're planning to hit our supply lines, somebody tries to take you out.'

Dora rolled her eyes. 'Look, I've already explained, I wasn't trying to—'

She wasn't able to finish her sentence because she was falling forward. Her brain didn't understand what was happening. All she knew was that there was a flash of bright light and then the floor was rushing up to meet her face. She tried to step forward, regain her balance, but something was terribly wrong with her legs. She threw out her arms to break her fall, and she managed to stop her face slamming into the floor, but as she tried to use her feet to absorb some of the impact, basically falling into a press-up, she again found that they were not responding properly. She hit the ground awkwardly, not at the angle she was expecting, oddly lopsided and feeling the carpet on her thighs rather than through the toes of her shoes.

She saw black spots at the edges of her vision and realised with horror that she was passing out. God, had Quil shot her? Was she dying? She looked up to see a row of masked faces staring down at her. She couldn't tell if they were registering shock, pity or glee. All she could see were unsmiling metal lips and shadowed eyes.

She tried to speak, but the only sound that came out was a kind of strangled groan. As she sank into the carpet, unable to hold herself up, she twisted her head to look back and see what was wrong with her legs.

The last thing she saw before she passed out were her feet, still in their shoes, standing upright behind her, smoking from the stumps where her ankles used to be.

Barrettown, Mars,
4 April 2158, 12:56 A.M. –
9h 12m to the event

The corridor was littered with sacks of uncollected garbage, and stank accordingly. The lights were almost all broken, but one was hanging in there, casting a sickly yellowish glow.

'You bring me to the nicest places,' said Jana.

She cursed inwardly, excruciatingly aware that her every attempt at a quip probably read to Kaz like a veiled come-on.

'Oh yeah, I know how to show a girl a good time,' he replied, smiling.

Jana died a little inside.

'Which one was it again?' she asked.

'Brock said he lived in flat 29,' Kaz replied.

Jana checked the door closest to her. 'This is 20,' she said. 'It must be down the other end of the corridor.'

'Tread carefully,' he warned.

They picked their way through the maze of rubbish, both of their faces wrinkled in disgust at the aroma. At one point Jana accidentally kicked a pile of rubbish and an enormous rat burst out of cover and lolloped away. She was ashamed by the strangled scream she emitted at the sight of its slick oily fur.

'Ugh,' she groaned, pulling her most disgusted face. 'There are rats on Mars? How did that happen?'

Kaz shrugged. 'They get everywhere,' he said. 'We had a whole community of them on the *Hispaniola*.'

'Was that your pirate ship?'

'Arrr.'

'Did you see the size of that thing?' said Jana, shuddering. 'It was like a small dog. And it lolloped! Rats are supposed to scurry. That unholy thing lolloped. Not natural.'

They reached the door without encountering any other giant rodents, and they paused, nervously.

'So what's the plan again?' asked Jana.

Kaz pulled a gun from his pocket and flicked the switch to activate it. 'We improvise. All we have to do is stop this guy going anywhere for the next twenty-four hours. We hold him hostage and then let him go. No need to do anything drastic.'

'And what if he's an assassin?' whispered Jana. 'A trained killer? I'm not sure he's going to be quite the pushover you think.'

Kaz smiled rakishly. 'And I am Sealegs Kaz,' he said. 'Terror of the seven seas, buccaneer of high renown and the best shot with a flintlock this side of Tortuga. I am more than a match for a common killer.'

Jana gaped. 'I don't think that paint-stripper was as watered-down as Shindra told you,' she said, shaking her head.

Kaz winked and knocked on the door. There was no immediate response, so Kaz knocked again.

Jana had a nasty thought and stepped to her left, pulling Kaz after her. 'Hey, don't stand in front of the door,' she warned. 'What if he starts shooting?'

There was a noise behind the door and Kaz nodded to Jana, who fervently wished she had a gun too.

'Who is it?' shouted a man from inside. His voice was high and sharp, and he sounded nervous.

'Mr Smith?' asked Jana.

'Who wants to know?'

Jana thought quickly. 'Environmental services,' she said. 'We're here to deal with reports of an infestation of vermin.'

Kaz looked impressed and gave her a thumbs-up.

'About time,' replied the man inside the flat as Jana heard him undoing a collection of locks. 'One of those damn rats actually tried to take my dinner off me the other . . .' His complaint trailed away as he opened the door and found himself staring into the business end of Kaz's gun. He was holding a baseball bat in his hand, but it was clear he wouldn't be able to raise it before Kaz drilled a hole in him.

Smith reacted quickly, trying to push the door closed again, but Kaz had jammed his foot in the way and forced his way inside. Jana followed and closed the door behind her as Smith backed away from his two unwelcome guests.

'Drop the bat and sit,' said Kaz, indicating a tattered old sofa that was mostly buried under a pile of old clothes. The flat smelled only slightly less disgusting than the corridor outside, and Jana vowed not to leave the living room – if it was this bad, she didn't want to imagine what kind of state the kitchen or bathroom might be in.

'No wonder you have rats,' she said. 'You live like one.'

Smith was a thin-faced Martian, stubble-chinned and beady-eyed. He sat staring at Kaz's gun, eyes darting left and right as if searching for escape or aid.

'Are you alone?' barked Kaz. 'Is anybody else in this flat?'

Smith shook his head vigorously. 'No, no, no, only me. Just me.'

Kaz nodded over at Jana. 'Check would you?' he asked. 'Don't want any surprises.'

'And what am I supposed to do if I find someone lying in wait in the bedroom, huh?' she protested. 'You've got the gun.'

'Use his bat,' said Kaz. 'He dropped it by the door.'

Jana ran over and scooped it up, wincing at the greasy feel of the warm handle. She briefly wondered how baseball would work in lower gravity, but dismissed the thought as a distraction. The front door opened straight into the living room, and only two doors led off from it, one on the right, one on the left.

Holding the bat high, Jana kicked the door on the right open and was hit by a wave of smell that made her gag. Kitchen. She didn't stare too closely at the pile of plates in the sink, and tried hard not to notice the greenish tinge of mould that encrusted it. There was nobody in there, so she turned and repeated the operation. Bathroom. The smell was simply indescribable and it made Jana's eyes water. A fat rat squatted in the sink, staring at her with tiny black eyes. She headed back to the living room.

'All clear,' she said. 'But I am going to have to scrub myself pink raw when we get back to the hotel. And maybe dip myself in bleach.'

Smith was sitting on the sofa, which was so old and saggy that it practically swallowed him up. He cut a pathetic figure, a far cry from the smooth professional killer Jana had half expected.

'I haven't got any money,' he wheedled. 'You can see that. Can't even afford to get the water turned on more than

192

once a day. I've got nothing worth stealing, so you might as well go.'

Having checked the flat, Jana wanted to sit down, but couldn't bring herself to sit on the carpet, which turned her stomach, or the armchair, which she was sure had a thin coating of rat fur on it. She settled for standing next to Kaz and looking menacing.

'Mr Smith,' she said. 'We know that you recently procured an illegal pass for the conference centre. Would you mind telling us why?'

Smith's eyes narrowed. 'Who are you? Secret service? Police?'

'We could tell you,' said Kaz seriously, 'but then we'd have to kill you.'

Jana bit her lip to stop herself smiling. 'Answer the question,' she said, 'and there's a good chance you'll live another day.'

'I knew it was a stupid idea,' muttered Smith, resentfully.

'What was a stupid idea?' asked Kaz.

'Hitting the hotel during the conference.'

Kaz and Jana exchanged puzzled glances. Luckily, Smith did not notice; he was too busy staring at his nails, sulkily spilling his guts.

'They'll all be distracted, he says. Security will be all over the conference area, he says. We can crack the hotel's safe and be home before anybody even notices, he says.'

'Who said?' asked Jana.

'This Earther,' said Smith. 'Like you, all short and stout. Recommended to me by the syndicate. Said he needed a cracksman. Best in the business, me.'

'Yeah, rolling in it, aren't you,' replied Jana.

Smith shrugged. 'Easy come, easy go,' he said. 'Anyway,

193

please don't kill me. I was supposed to meet this guy outside the conference centre at ten tomorrow morning, crack the safe for him, and then get out of there and wait for ten per cent to appear in my account.'

Kaz turned to Jana. 'What do you think?' he asked.

'Mr Smith, you are possibly the filthiest excuse for a human being I have ever met,' said Jana. 'Not only that, you are epically, epically dumb. I mean really spectacularly, depressingly stupid.'

Smith looked hurt. 'No need for that,' he mumbled.

'We need your pass and a full description of this Earther who contacted you,' Jana continued. 'When we've got them, we're going to leave here and forget we ever met you. If you keep your mouth shut and stay out of trouble, we won't have cause to remember. Understand?'

Smith's face was a mixture of resentment and confusion. 'Who *are* you?' he whined.

'Believe it or not,' sighed Jana, 'I think we're the people who just saved your pathetic excuse for a life.'

Kaz and Jana emerged into the corridor a few minutes later.

'Can I have my bat back,' said Smith plaintively, standing in the doorway.

Jana turned and handed it to him. As he took it, she held on for a moment and looked him in the eyes. 'Remember,' she said. 'Stay here for at least the next day. Don't set a foot outside. OK?'

'OK, OK,' he replied. Jana relinquished her grip on the baseball bat and Smith stepped backwards and slammed his front door in their faces, flashing them a spiteful grimace as he did so.

'You've obviously worked something out, so spill,' said

194

Kaz as they gingerly negotiated the garbage bag alley to the exit.

'A heist, in the middle of one of the biggest security operations in history?' replied Jana. 'It's the dumbest thing I've ever heard.'

'Or the cleverest.'

Jana glared at Kaz.

'Yeah, OK, dumbest,' he said.

'Smith isn't an assassin,' said Jana. 'And I don't believe we're here to prevent a heist. There is no heist. Smith's a patsy, an idiot who'll turn up at the wrong moment looking as guilty as it's possible to look. I'll bet you any money he's being set up to take the fall for an assassination attempt.'

'You mean this whole thing's been a wild goose chase?' said Kaz, dismayed.

'Not quite,' replied Jana. 'At least we got a description of the guy who approached Smith about the job. All we can do is search the conference centre for him. That's assuming he's the assassin and not some go-between.'

'You've got an impossible job,' said Kaz.

'Me?'

'I don't have a press pass, remember?' said Kaz. 'I can't get into the peace talks.'

Jana shook her head. 'That hooch is making you as dumb as Smith, Kaz. Which is good, 'cause you're going to have to pass as him.' She handed him Smith's forged entry authorisation and took the gun from his hand in the process.

'Hey,' he protested, but Jana was already firing over his shoulder, back down the corridor. There was a pathetic screech and the smell of burned meat.

'Try lolloping now, you freak,' muttered Jana, pushing open the exit.

Barrettown, Mars,
4 April 2158, 1:40 A.M. -
8h 28m to the event

The centre of the city was in lockdown. Every road was blocked by Earth troops in riot gear, standing in lines, impassive behind mirrored visors, guns ready. Vehicles with heavy weapons mounted on them lined up behind the soldiers, and concrete barriers funnelled all people and traffic into narrow checkpoints where their authorisations could be checked at the point of multiple weapons.

As Kaz climbed off the tram and looked down the boulevard towards the barriers, he was shocked that there were no protestors waving placards, chanting slogans, holding hands. Riot police meant there was a potential riot, didn't they? But in fact the streets were quiet. This was a road of office blocks and functional buildings, no residences or shops, and all business had been suspended for the duration of the talks. It was a ghost town.

The quiet disconcerted Kaz more than the deliberately intimidating security cordon. It spoke of a populace utterly cowed, scared to raise their voices, controlled and monitored and surveilled beyond the point of protest. He remembered something his father had told him after a peacekeeping effort had been besieged by an army of angry citizens demanding their departure. Kaz had asked why they hadn't shot at the people throwing stones and bottles at them, and Zbigniew had told him that his job was to protect the people's right to protest and that if the army ever forgot that, and started telling people what to do, a very dangerous line would have been crossed.

Kaz didn't think the soldiers he was walking towards would have any qualms about crossing any kind of line and he wondered whether Jana was right about the clean-air protestors being tolerated because it improved sales. He toyed with the authorisation card in his pocket, turning it over and over in his fingers nervously. If it tripped an alarm, he had no illusions about what would happen next – he'd vanish into a deep dark hole. He was lucky, he knew he could jump out of a holding cell at any moment, slip away through a crack in time. But he didn't fancy the beating he'd take before he was left alone long enough to make his escape, and once he left it would be no easy feat to return.

'Stay cool,' said Jana, who walked alongside him. 'We're both going in on forged authorisations, but we need to swan through, make eye contact, smile, be relaxed. Don't let your body language give you away.'

'How is this so easy for you?' whispered Kaz. 'It's like lying is your superpower.'

They reached the barrier and handed their cards to a soldier who ran them through a scanner and waved them through.

'Piece of cake,' said Jana once they had passed beyond the cordon.

'OK. Yeah,' said Kaz, sarcastically. 'That's the hard bit over. Now all we have to do is identify and stop a professional assassin – assuming we're right about all this – and prevent a war. Piece of cake.'

Kaz stopped walking as he found Jana's hand on his chest. She looked up at him, not angry but definitely pissed off.

'Listen Kaz,' she said firmly. 'I don't know what's up with you. One minute you're flirting, the next minute you're pretending like you're a secret agent in a cheesy movie, the next you're a petulant boy. You're part of the team, and if we have any chance of pulling this off, it's only with your help. So please just pick an attitude and stick with it, at least that way I'll know which version of you I'm dealing with.'

Kaz looked down at Jana, unsure how to respond. Part of him wanted to fly into a temper and tell her to get lost, another part wanted to grit his teeth, take the criticism and apologise. Unfortunately another part of him entirely won out, and he leaned down to kiss her.

The look of disgust on her face as she realised what he was doing wasn't something he was going to forget in a hurry. She backed away, holding up her hands.

'Jesus, Kaz,' she said.

'But, I thought . . .' Kaz didn't really know what he thought.

'What did you think?' Jana shook her head in astonishment and dismay. 'That I was going to swoon into your arms?'

'Um,' Kaz mumbled. He felt his face going red and he wanted to be anywhere but there.

'Well I'm not,' Jana continued.

Now she was angry, but even through his embarrassment Kaz caught an unexpected tone in her voice, as if she was more angry at herself than at him. This made him even more confused.

Jana put her hands on her hips and stared at him for a moment. 'Kaz. I like you. I really do,' she said. 'I've never liked a boy this way . . .'

Kaz's heart leapt.

'. . . As a friend, I mean,' Jana continued.

Kaz's heart fell.

'I don't have friends,' she said, looking both defensive and slightly scared. 'Not really. Not in my own time.'

'You mean boyfriends?' said Kaz.

Jana shook her head. 'I mean *friends*,' she said firmly. 'Any friends. Real friends. People you trust your secrets with. I can't trust anybody with my secrets so it's always been easier not to have friends. I have acquaintances, buddies even, but not any friends. Not like you.'

She reached out, took his hand and looked up at him imploringly. Kaz felt more confused than he'd ever felt in his entire life. Was she telling him she loved him or what?

'Kaz, I like you,' she said. 'I think maybe you're my first ever true friend. I haven't told you all my secrets yet, but I will. I think. Soon, probably. But . . . but we can't date. We can't be a couple, you and me.'

'Why not?' said Kaz, raising his free hand to her cheek, completely at a loss to understand what the problem was.

'Because I'm gay, you moron,' said Jana, sighing.

'What?' he said, aghast, pulling back his hands sharply.

'I was waiting for the right moment to tell you,' Jana continued, more apologetic than he'd ever seen her.

Kaz suddenly felt like the stupidest person in the history of the world. He was engulfed with embarrassment so profound it made his stomach feel hollow.

'Oh man,' he said softly.

Without even consciously deciding to do so, he closed his eyes and willed himself elsewhen, feeling the sensation creeping up on him, the pull of time itself taking him by the hand and shepherding him out of the real world.

Then he felt a very hard sting on his cheek and his eyes snapped open and he was still on Mars.

Jana's face was an inch from his. 'Don't you dare!' she shouted.

'Did you just slap me?' he asked, stunned.

'Damn straight I did,' she hissed. 'And I'll do much worse if you try to run away again!'

'I wasn't running away,' he protested. 'I was just going to clear my head.'

'Bullshit,' retorted Jana. 'You do this again and again. As soon as things get tricky, as soon as you're not in control, you try and jaunt off to God knows when and take a holiday. Your first instinct is to run away.'

'I came back for you in Pendarn!' Kaz shouted back. 'I came back to the quantum bubble after Beirut.'

'Yeah, you come back and help out until the next time things get difficult and then off you go again, leaving us in the lurch,' she said hotly. 'And you know what, I can't really stop you. You could spend your whole life jumping from time to time, place to place, always excusing yourself from your life every time you get uncomfortable. But it's pathetic, Kaz. What kind of a life is that? You're better than that, smarter than that. We need you. *I* need you.'

'I thought you were gay,' Kaz said, surprised at his spiteful tone. He regretted it even as he said it, so he didn't protest when it earned him another ringing slap.

He didn't get a chance to apologise because Jana turned

200

her back on him and walked away. 'Screw you, Kaz,' she shouted over her shoulder.

Kaz stood there, cheeks on fire, unsure what to do with himself. Jana's revelation, and her contempt at his response, had got to him. He trusted her and liked her, and her good opinion was important to him.

He took a deep breath and watched her walking away. She was gay? He really hadn't seen that coming. Could he have screwed things up more entirely if he'd tried? He ran after her, caught up and walked alongside her. She didn't acknowledge his presence at all as they entered the plaza, which was dominated by the conference centre, a dome of entangled wood at the very centre point of the city, mirroring the dome above it in miniature.

'I'm sorry,' Kaz said eventually.

Jana grunted so Kaz stepped ahead, turned to face her and stopped. She stopped too, folded her arms and stared him down.

'I mean it, I'm sorry,' said Kaz. 'You're right, I do run. And I shouldn't. But . . . it all gets too much and . . . Look. I am your friend. Really. I don't want to let you down, OK? Any of you. I'm here and I'm going to help. I promise I won't run. Everything else can wait, but for now . . . I'm sorry.'

Jana considered him. 'Idiot,' she said, not unkindly.

'Yes I am,' agreed Kaz as he stepped aside and Jana continued walking. He fell into step beside her.

'All business?' he asked.

'All business,' agreed Jana. 'For now. I've been thinking about how we handle this and I can only come up with one plan.'

'I'm listening.'

'I think we split up, take one delegation each and tell them everything we know,' she said. 'We say we're investigative journalists, that we think we've uncovered a plot and they need to respond.'

Kaz was confused. 'Both delegations? Why both, surely we only need to tell the Godless? I mean, the assassin must be working for Earth, right?'

'And if the assassin has been hired by a Godless traitor, someone who wants Quil out of the way?' asked Jana. 'Maybe one of her generals thinks she's being weak by attending the peace talks, wants to push the advantage and carry straight on to Earth. Having her bumped off would remove all obstacles.'

Kaz nodded agreement and mentally kicked himself. He should have realised that without having it pointed out to him.

'So one of us tells the Earthers, one of us tells the Godless,' he asked.

'Yes.'

'You know this means one of us will draw the short straw,' said Kaz. 'One of us is going to basically surrender to the people who called in the hit.'

'Yup,' said Jana. 'Got a better plan?'

Kaz shook his head. 'Nope.'

'So one of us is probably going to get a bit roughed up and thrown in a cell,' said Jana wearily.

'Terrific,' said Kaz. 'Which do you think is the most likely source of the hit, Earth or Godless?'

'Godless,' said Jana after some thought.

'OK, so I'll take them, you take the Earthers.'

Jana looked at him, concerned. 'You sure?'

'Arrr,' he said.

Barrettown, Mars,
4 April 2158, 6:32 A.M. –
3h 36m to the event

Jana stood before her suite's bathroom mirror checking that her chameleon shroud was working. She had opted to be someone else for the duration of her stay on Mars, and the holographic disguise made it easy.

The nose was bigger, as were the ears, the eyes were wonky and the lips were thin to the point of non-existence. Mousey hair, dull grey eyes. She wasn't ugly, just plain. Jana had deliberately selected the kind of face no one would look at twice if they passed her in the corridor. The less attention she drew to herself, the better.

Dora and Kaz had questioned her decision to adopt a disguise on Mars. Neither of them felt it necessary, so why did she? She'd avoided the question until they got tired of asking it. She couldn't tell them the real reason – that she was afraid of what might happen if she were recognised. That might raise too many awkward questions that she wasn't yet ready to answer.

Jana had been conscious of her attractiveness from an

early age, of the way it made her peers act towards her, the way it made adults favour her over her classmates even when there was no logical reason for them to do so, but she never felt she really owned it. The day she realised who she was, what she was, she had stared at herself in the mirror for hours, studying the contours of her face. It didn't feel like she was looking at her own face, more like a painting or a photograph. Her beauty was borrowed, stolen from that first version of herself, the one who died so stupidly, so young. She had become distanced from her own face, resentful of the way she looked. She wanted to mix it up a bit, claim it, stamp her ownership on the face that had been forced upon her.

She was thirteen when she sneaked away from school and got her first tattoo, an intricate laser-burned stark white fractal pattern on her right cheek. Her mother's response had been exactly what Jana had expected and wanted. The fight went on for a week, her mother coldly furious, her father trying to be the peacemaker, seeing both sides, vacillating helplessly between the twin poles of his family, well-meaning but ineffectual. When the week was done, her mother's patience gave out and she ordered her security team to literally drag Jana to a clinic where she was strapped into a chair and drugged so they could pin her head still and remove the offending pattern.

Having made her point, Jana moved on to more subtle forms of modification. She could pop her piercings out during school hours, and whenever she went home her mother never looked at her closely enough to notice the various holes in her nose, ears and lips. It took about a year for Jana to grow tired of this approach. Most of the kids she knew made fun of her increasingly extreme appearance, and she was bored by those who thought she was like them and tried to claim her as part of their tribe. The black-clothes body-mod crowd were as hidebound by convention as their more mainstream classmates, although they wouldn't admit it. So at around fifteen most of the piercings came out, just a nose stud and double earrings, nothing too attention-seeking, and Jana began to consider the advantage her borrowed face gave her, the tool it could be.

She'd been ruthless in the exploitation of her beauty, even after she came to understand that she didn't give a crap what adults thought, and it wasn't boys she wanted to attract. Twisting boys round her little finger was the easiest thing in the world, once she put her mind to it. Sweet ones, dumb ones, jocks and brains, rich and poor, white and black – they were all basically the same in Jana's eyes. If a boy was straight, she learned how to make him pay attention to her. They were useful in all sorts of ways, but mostly for amusement value. She would see how far she could push them, how extreme they'd be willing to go in order to gain her favour. It had become second nature to her.

So as she stood there in the bathroom on Mars, staring at her new face, the one she had chosen for herself, she wondered what her choice of disguise said about her. Could she ever, really, own her own face, feel it was hers and hers alone? Maybe after a lifetime of therapy. Maybe after it had started to show its age, etched into something new by the wrinkles and creases created by experiences she alone had had.

Maybe when somebody truly loved her.

She regretted having given Kaz the wrong impression. She hadn't meant to do it, but it seemed flirting and manipulation had become second nature to her and she knew she'd done damage by encouraging him without even meaning to. She felt her face, her real face, blush with shame as she remembered the way she'd stripped down in front of him in the bakery in Pendarn.

Here on Mars, where she'd been hiding behind a plain face/mask for over a month, he'd obviously still harboured feelings for her, feelings that had continued to grow. She wasn't sure what it meant for him to be attracted to her even when she had denied herself her beauty, but it made her afraid and happy at the same time, even as she knew there could never be anything truly romantic between them. She simply wasn't wired that way.

She flashed her eyes at her reflection, liking the way they looked. She briefly wondered how Dora felt about the new look, then dismissed the thought, irritated with herself. She had things to do, she couldn't afford this self-indulgence.

Her disguise was good enough, she decided. She was ready to face Quil, mask to mask.

Barrettown, Mars,
4 April 2158, 6:51 A.M. -
4h 17m to the event

Dora's head felt heavy and tight but her body was warm and distant. She knew she'd been drugged, but she couldn't recall why or by whom. Thinking was hard, but she tried to marshal her thoughts, concentrate on her breathing and settle herself. After a few seconds – or maybe minutes, or hours – she felt centred enough to try to open her eyes. The light made her wince and it took a few moments for the blur of colour to swim into something like focused shapes.

She was looking into a pair of brown eyes rimmed by metal.

'I'm sorry,' said Quil. She sounded it, thought Dora. She actually sounded sorry.

Dora tried to reply but her tongue was too big, her mouth felt like it was full of sand. After a few tries she managed, 'Wha for?'

'I had to make sure you couldn't run, you see,' said Quil. 'I mean, not literally. Well, actually literally, yes, but also through time.'

Dora couldn't formulate a question, so she just looked quizzical.

'You're like me, aren't you?' asked Quil, her astonishment apparently undiminished. 'You can travel in time. The sparks proved that, the reaction that occurred when we touched. I can't control it, not properly. Not yet, maybe never. But I have to assume you can. I have no idea where or when you really come from. You might be telling the truth, you might be some kind of researcher from the past trying to shape events, but you could also be a killer from the future, or some meddler who wants to change history. Whoever you are, it's not a coincidence, you being here at this moment. These talks are a turning point. The outcome will determine the course of history and I have to assume you're here to affect them. Until I know for sure, I can't risk letting you go. But how do I imprison you? A cell won't hold you, chains either – I bet you can jump off to another time whenever you want. I had to find a way to keep you here, you see. That's why I did it.'

'Di wha?' asked Dora,

'Sliced your feet off.'

Dora felt a surge of panic and fear. She remembered the unimaginable sight of her own feet, cut off at the ankles. She tried to move her head, look down at herself, but her movement was very restricted, though whether by the drugs or by restraints she really couldn't tell.

'You may not know this, but at this point in history it's child's play for us to grow you new ones and attach them,' explained Quil. 'In a week's time you'll be good as new, but until then you're stuck here. You can't risk jumping off through time with no feet, can you? A quick slice of the laser and you were cut and cauterised in an instant. It isn't permanent, but

I get to keep you exactly where I want until we fix you. We're going to have plenty of time to get to know each other, Dora. And I have so many questions.'

Dora tried to look past Quil, to see where she was, but her vision was swimming in and out of focus. All she could really see were those eyes. They were calm and unemotional, but not unsympathetic. There was still no sign of real madness. Dora tried to consider Quil's point and could see the logic of it; cutting her feet off was an extreme course of action but it was expedient, reasonable and had a point. Quil may be calculating and pragmatic, thought Dora, but she still isn't insane. Not yet.

'We gave you a strong anaesthetic,' said Quil. 'You've been under for a few hours. You shouldn't feel any pain now, but you will be uncomfortable for a while. The wounds are clean and dressed but you're in shock and we need to monitor you carefully.'

'Quil, we need you.' This was the general's voice, originating somewhere beyond Quil's eyes, in the great blur. Dora's eyesight was next to useless, but she could hear perfectly.

'Excuse me, my dear,' said Quil. The eyes vanished, replaced by a haze of movement. Dora reckoned Quil had stood up and walked away.

'There's something you need to hear,' said the general. 'This journalist has presented herself and told us someone at the conference wants you dead.'

Dora heard Quil laugh. 'That's hardly news,' she said.

'She has information about a *specific* plot. I think you should hear her out.'

There was silence for a moment. When Dora next heard voices they were more distant, as if coming from another room, perhaps on the other side of a partially open door. She was shocked when she realised who Quil was talking to, but try as she might she couldn't make a cry loud enough to attract Jana's attention.

'We have a description of the person who commissioned Smith, but we don't know if this is the killer or a middleman. I thought you needed to know,' Dora heard Jana say. 'Double security, run some more checks on the venue, that kind of thing.'

'Thank you,' said Quil politely. 'My security staff will debrief you thoroughly.'

Dora lay helpless, caught between triumph and defeat. It sounded as if Kaz and Jana had identified the killer and warned Quil in time. Perhaps their plan was working – perhaps the conversation she'd just overheard would be enough to change history. She was still injured, drugged and captive, though. If she couldn't hold out, if Quil used some kind of interrogation technique that Dora hadn't prepared for, her knowledge could still do irreparable damage to the timeline. What if they were creating a version of the future that was far, far worse than the one they were trying to prevent? Would the information in her head be enough to make that happen? She wasn't sure, but it had to be a risk.

Dora made a decision. If Kaz and Jana had managed to prevent the assassination attempt, then she herself was the biggest risk. Injured or not, she had to take the chance. She was a liability; she had to take herself out of the equation.

Dora closed her eyes and concentrated on the numbers, trying to feel her way towards a time jump. Usually this process was easy for her, but she was drugged, her senses were scrambled. She couldn't grasp them, the equations slipped away from her every time she felt them emerging from the fog. It was hopeless.

'So it seems you are a killer after all.'

Dora opened her eyes to see Quil's boring into her again, harder and colder.

'No,' she managed to splutter.

'Just had a visit from a journalist who seemed to know all about it. The patsy you arranged, the middleman you're working with. What was the plan, hmm? When were you going to do it? I can't understand why you didn't kill me when we were alone earlier. You could have done it and jumped away before anybody knew it had happened.'

'No,' growled Dora again.

'Was it supposed to be a spectacle, is that it?' asked Quil. 'Kill me on camera at the conference itself. Yes, that would have more impact, wouldn't it?'

'No!'

'The question is: why did she hire a time-travelling killer? Actually, never mind why, *how* would someone do that?'

Dora felt helpless and despairing. She didn't think they'd changed history. Quil was jumping to the wrong conclusions, painting Dora as her enemy. This must be how it happened, the beginning of her hatred of them. Damn it, if only she could speak properly, if only she could explain.

'We came here to negotiate in good faith and we've been betrayed,' snarled Quil. 'The people need to know that. We call a press conference right now, in the hotel. We parade our assassin, play the recordings, show everyone how treacherous that monster in the White House has been. Then we head straight for Earth and blow her to hell. I don't know why I ever trusted her. This is exactly what she was always going to do. I should have realised that. It's her nature.'

Dora assumed Quil was talking about the president of Earth's emergency government, but Quil's anger seemed strangely personal. She closed her eyes and tried again to find the maths, to slip away into time, but the drugs were blocking all her senses, not just her eyesight. She was well and truly trapped.

'Let the press know, five minutes in the lobby,' she heard Quil say. 'And get a detail to carry her downstairs. Put her in a chair out of sight. We can bring her out to show the cameras.'

'She's a young maid with her feet chopped off,' replied the general. 'She doesn't really look like an assassin. I don't think showing her off to the cameras is going to help.'

'Do as I say!' shouted Quil, although Dora thought Shouty General was making a lot of sense. 'It'll send a message to the president. She'll see we've got her killer and she'll know we've beaten her. She's the only audience that really matters.'

'As you wish.'

'And message the *Stefan*, tell them to prepare the weapon for deployment.'

'With pleasure.'

Dora heard heavy footsteps and then the world tilted. She was being lifted off whatever bed or sofa she'd been lying on. She tried to struggle but she was rag-doll limp. Imprisoned in her own broken body, powerless to fight, Dora felt deep shame.

Four years ago she'd sworn she'd never need to be rescued again, that henceforth she would be the one doing the rescuing. She'd trained and trained, turned herself into a warrior, extinguished all trace of girlish weakness in pursuit of some kind of perfection – the perfect killer, the perfect spy, the perfect woman of action. But here she was, more completely powerless than she had ever been.

She had failed herself in the most fundamental way, and

for the first time since the day she had made that vow, she couldn't keep it all at bay any more.

Loathing her own weakness, Dora began to cry.

213

Barrettown, Mars, 4 April 2158, 8:20 A.M. – 1h 48m to the event

Kaz nursed his head as he sat on the bare rock floor of a small storeroom in the basement of the Earth delegation's hotel. Apparently the Earthers weren't keen on too many people finding out about the planned attempt on Quil's life. What a surprise. The squaddie who had thrown Kaz down here had taken a liberal view of his superior officer's order not to hurt him, obviously feeling that pistol-whipping didn't fall under the category of 'hurt'.

His fingers came away from the back of his head covered in blood. He was starting to see zigzag lines at the periphery of his vision and it felt like someone was pushing a spike through his brain.

He had been in this kind of room before and knew what came next. Sooner or later some big nasty guy would walk through the door and start *persuading* him to talk.

He rose unsteadily to his feet, his head swimming, and stood for a moment until his dizziness subsided. First task – find out if there's a guard outside. He hammered on the door, wincing as the noise and vibration cracked his brain, and yelled for help. No response. So they'd abandoned him. Maybe they'd thought he'd be unconscious for a lot longer, or maybe – and this thought made him nervous – they'd been distracted by something more pressing.

He was in a store-cupboard with only a broom, a mop and some bottles of cleaning fluid. More in hope than expectation, he looked up in case there was some kind of ventilation duct he could crawl out through, but of course there was nothing. His only hope was rescue – which he knew was not coming – or forcing the door.

Bracing his back against the wall, he brought his knees up and kicked hard against the door. The impact shot up through his legs and made his hip ache. This was going to be a long process. He kicked again and again, his head splitting, his legs aching, and the soles of his feet began to feel like raw steak, despite the trainers he was wearing. But persistence paid off, and after a few splintering noises one mighty kick popped the lock and Kaz limped out into the hotel basement.

Kaz made straight for the service entrance and was outside within a minute. When he reached the plaza shortly thereafter he could see there was something happening at the Godless hotel.

To get from the hotel hosting the Earth delegation to the one hosting the Godless he had to run across the huge plaza that stretched in front of the conference centre. Paved with slabs of cut Mars stone, red and smooth, it formed a semicircle with a massive fountain in the centre. In amongst the cascades of water was a carved replica of the lander that had brought the first humans to Mars. Kaz was surprised by how small it seemed, especially compared to the gleaming military space vessels he saw nightly on the news broadcasts.

The entrance to the Godless delegation's hotel was swarming with clone troops. They had formed a cordon at the entrance and a crowd of journalists and politicians were trying to get through. Their credentials were being checked by a group of Godless soldiers with hand-held scanners while people were being waved through one at a time. The crowd was getting restless at the delay. The conference was supposed to start in an hour, so this was very much not part of the plan for the day. Kaz wondered whether the Godless were responding to Jana's warning. He still had John Smith's bogus access-all-areas pass card, so he figured he'd be able to get inside and see what was happening. He reached the edge of the crowd and asked a man what was going on.

'Press conference,' said the man, a short, fat politician with a florid face and a badly cut suit.

'What about?' asked Kaz.

'Don't know. But it's got to be big if they're tearing up and throwing away the schedule for the day. I don't like the . . . uh-oh.'

The man was looking over Kaz's shoulder back across the plaza. Kaz turned to see what had alarmed him and saw a platoon of Earth troops jogging across the plaza in formation, weapons across their chests. Kaz didn't like the look of this at all. The crowd of people seeking entrance were about to be sandwiched between two opposing groups of armed soldiers, and he couldn't imagine that would end well for anybody. Deciding he had to get inside right now, Kaz abandoned his instinctive politeness and began barging his way through the crowd, desperate to get to the front. He'd managed to penetrate a few feet towards the Godless soldiers when he heard some cries of alarm from behind him and the crowd immediately began surging forward, pushing and crushing him. Kaz belatedly realised that forcing his way into a large crowd of people who were about to get a fright had not been the smartest plan he'd ever come up with. He craned to see what was happening ahead of him. The Godless guards were holding steady, and their weapons were being lowered to point at the crowd. Kaz remembered what had happened in Pendarn, and felt ill at the thought of how quickly and efficiently those weapons could slice the whole crowd in two.

The crowd were beginning to shout now, begging to be let in, yelling warnings about the Earth troops to the Godless, turning in their fear on people they accused of shoving them. Kaz felt an elbow sharp in his ribs and the breath was pushed out of him by the crush of bodies on all sides. Even above the tumult of the crowd Kaz could hear barked orders echoing around the plaza behind him, as the Earth troops took up positions. All it would take was one itchy trigger finger and there'd be a massacre.

There was a sudden sharp pain in the small of his back where someone's bag was pressing into him, and Kaz felt himself being literally lifted off his feet and carried along by the swell of the crowd. Kaz felt the same feeling that had plagued him ever since he realised that Smith had been a wild goose chase, the feeling that events were snowballing, gathering momentum in spite of anything he and his friends were doing. He was beginning to feel powerless, the same sick feeling he'd had when he heard his mother had frozen in the market – that time had its own plans and he was, at best, an irrelevance.

Ahead of him he saw the Godless troops stepping aside, flanking the crowd to the right and left, abandoning their screening process and allowing the people to flood into the hotel while they took up new positions to block the advance of their counterparts from Earth. Kaz found his feet again and managed to begin running as the pressure around him eased slightly. He had no doubt he'd be trampled if he lost his footing, so he concentrated on staying vertical and letting the rush sweep him along.

When the momentum finally eased enough for Kaz to step sideways and out of the flow, he was in the ballroom that sat adjacent to the hotel lobby. At the far end were a row of tables that were obviously the focus of attention. Camera drones hovered in the air around the tables, waiting for the press conference to begin, and the crowd of spectators, all buzzing with curiosity and alarm, were ranged around the tables, standing because the press conference had been called at such short notice there'd been no time to lay out seating. A phalanx of menacing Godless troops stood in a row between the crowd and tables, weapons free and ready for use. They wouldn't be letting anyone get near Quil.

Kaz worked his way to the edge of the room and began pushing forward. If Jana were here, he guessed she'd be up front with the Godless delegation, held prisoner until she'd given her account of events for the cameras. It was imperative he talk to her, or at least get her attention, let her know he was here in case the situation got out of hand and they found themselves in the middle of a gunfight. Kaz tried to think of any way to de-escalate the situation, but the best he could do was to get as close to the front as he could and then turn and scan the faces of the crowd in the hope that he'd be able to pick out the man Smith had described. He knew this was a forlorn hope – the description they had might not even be the killer, and in a time when chameleon shrouds were a thing, anyone could look totally different anyway – but it was all he could come up with while he waited for the event to get under way.

There must be over a thousand people in here, reckoned Kaz. The Mars-born were the easiest to pick out because they stood on average a head taller than their Earth-born cousins. Smith had been specific that the man who'd hired him had not been Mars-born, so Kaz ignored them. He broke the room up roughly into quadrants and began systematically checking faces, feeling increasingly dispirited with every second – if the assassin thought anyone was looking for him, or even if he was just incredibly cautious, he'd be wearing a chameleon shroud anyway.

The noise of the crowd briefly increased, then quietened, so Kaz turned to the front in time to see Quil and a collection of officers walking in through a side door and taking their places behind the tables. They did not sit. Again Kaz was struck by how different she was to the clones that stood alongside her, her slender height so distinctive amongst a group of short, squat semi-siblings. Kaz looked for Jana, but could see her nowhere so he turned away again and resumed his examination of the audience, listening to Quil address the now hushed crowd as he did so.

'Today was supposed to be a day of peace,' said Quil, her voice loud and strong. The crowd produced a short collective intake of breath at this statement and its implications. Kaz could see the fear on the faces he was scanning.

'We have brought our fight for liberty and justice to the heart of the solar system,' Quil continued. 'None of Earth's attempts to halt our advance have met with the slightest success, so do not be fooled when they tell you they are giving us one last chance to think again before they stop us for good. Empty bravado. They are beaten and they know it. They have been outgunned and outmatched at every turn. This peace conference is, in effect, their surrender. We came here to negotiate terms, to see if we could avoid attacking Earth or Mars. I am tired of this war, a war I never wanted. And if there is a chance to stop it now, I thought, I had to take it. My generals advised otherwise. They told me we should press our advantage, cut straight to Earth, solidify our victory and dictate terms to the broken rulers who have abused and oppressed us for so many years. There is no doubt in my mind that we could do so, if we wished. But how many people would die as a result? If there was a chance that this peace conference could save even a single life, I was willing to give it a chance, to give Earth the opportunity to bring this madness to an end. My generals told me I was foolish, that this whole event was a ploy to buy time for Earth to stage some form of counter-attack. One even dared to call me a dangerous fantasist to my face. I demoted him and sent him away. If you're watching this, Kule, on one of the ships in orbit above me, I apologise. You were correct. My wish to avoid further bloodshed made me foolish. It is not a mistake I shall make again.'

Kaz was beginning to go face-blind, as all the fear-etched faces began blending into one amorphous mass. He blinked away the blurring and moved on to the next quadrant of the audience.

'While we prepared for the talks,' continued Quil, 'while we sat in a suite in this very hotel identifying the compromises we were willing to make in the interests of peace, the forces of Earth, under orders from its treacherous president, planned two separate attacks upon us before the conference was even due to begin.'

The feeling of the crowd changed again, this time away

from fear and towards a kind of horror, a realisation that things were about to go horribly wrong.

'Earlier this morning we received intelligence of a planned attack on our base on Charon. Earth plans to break the ceasefire in a matter of hours, to take advantage of our presence here to strike at our supply lines. This news alone would be sufficient for us to abandon the peace talks and continue our attack upon Earth. But at the same time that cowardly attack was being planned, another was under way in this very hotel.'

The crowd gasped and ducked instinctively as the sound of gunfire came from somewhere outside. It was a short burst, the distinctive whine of a heavy laser. The room went silent, everyone waiting for a return of fire. None came. Kaz assumed it had been a warning shot from one side or another. The stand-off on the plaza wasn't going to last much longer. Quil paused only briefly, then continued.

'My staff were contacted earlier today by a brave journalist,' she said. 'An Earth-born whose devotion to justice and truth stands in stark contrast to her president's devotion to treachery and repression. She informed me that she had uncovered a plot to assassinate me during the peace talks. Her evidence was compelling, and will be provided to you all in due course. But it was unnecessary, and in fact confirmed what I already knew. Because the assassin was already among us, had in fact infiltrated this hotel.'

Kaz felt a sick feeling deep in his stomach as he heard Quil say, 'Bring her out!' He turned back to the tables to see Jana pushing a wheelchair in which sat Dora, her eyes wide and staring, her mouth moving but producing no sound. Oh God, what had they done to her? He tried to catch Jana's eye, but she was staring straight at Quil, her face showing no emotion. If she felt even half as sick as he did, she'd be wanting to take a pop at Quil herself. He hoped she didn't have a gun, because if she did he was pretty certain that right now she'd have no qualms about slicing their tormentor in two and jumping straight back into the past.

'Here is the journalist, Carolyn Geary,' said Quil, pointing at Jana. 'She should be an example to all of you. And here is the assassin, a young Earth girl, a hotel maid, brainwashed and trained by the president's secret forces. Do you see her, Madam President?' Quil was no longer addressing the crowd of people in the room, but was looking up into the lens of a camera drone that hovered in front of and above her. 'Do you see your puppet with her strings cut?'

Kaz couldn't work it out. How the hell had Quil come to the conclusion that Dora was an assassin?

Kaz tried to get Jana's attention, standing on his tiptoes and raising his hand as high as he dared, but she remained fixated on Quil, who in turn remained focused on the camera drone, staring into the imagined eyes of her enemy.

Unable to help or intervene, Kaz turned and examined the crowd again, desperate, hoping against hope that he'd get lucky.

'I say this to you, Madam President,' said Quil. 'Your duplicity has cost you your life. I am coming for you. The Godless are coming for you. We will descend and we will swarm and we will ferret you out, no matter how deep you bury yourself, how far you run, we will find you and you will see justice at my hands.'

There! Kaz squinted, focusing in on one face. The hairline was higher than he'd expected but the eyes, the nose, the high cheekbones – surely that was the man Smith had described to them. But there was something else about him, something that made him stand out and made Kaz sure that he was the one – he wasn't looking at Quil. Alone among the crowd, he was staring slightly to the left and above Quil's eyeline. Kaz followed his gaze but it took a few moments before he realised the man was staring at one of the camera drones.

In the instant Kaz realised Quil's assassination was imminent, and that he alone knew it was coming and had any chance of stopping it, he froze. Because why would he want to intervene? If she died now, their troubles would be over. If she died now, she couldn't be blown back in time, spend years recuperating in Sweetclover Hall, assemble her army, devote her time to hunting them down. If he kept his mouth shut and let her die, everything would be fine.

He became aware of movement and he turned to see Jana, who had picked him out of the crowd. She was looking straight at him and, without thinking, he pointed and yelled.

'Jana, the camera!'

Jana looked up at the camera drone in confusion for an instant before she realised what was happening, stepped away from Dora's wheelchair and flung herself at Quil.

'Get down!' cried Jana. 'Get down!'

The Godless soldiers moved towards Jana, raising their weapons, and Quil turned her head to see what was happening.

That saved her life.

A white beam shot out of the camera drone, missing Quil's head by the tiniest of margins. The Godless soldiers, now presented with two targets, switched their focus from Jana to the camera, bringing their weapons to bear. Now unimpeded, Jana made it to Quil in a moment and flung herself at the masked woman, sending her sprawling below Kaz's eyeline in a shower of red sparks. The air lit up with laser beams as the Godless soldiers cut down the camera drones. Some members of the crowd began screaming, some began running for the door, some fought forward to get a better look. It was utter chaos, blinding light, deafening noise. And then Quil's voice cut through it all, booming through the speakers.

'Did that man call you . . . Jana?'

Barrettown, Mars,
4 April 2158, 8:32 A.M. -
1h 36m to the event

'Dora. Dora, can you hear me?'

Jana whispered, afraid that the Godless soldiers would overhear her. She stood with her hands on the back of the floating chair that carried her friend, feeling sick to her stomach and trying not to show it on her face. There was something terribly wrong with Dora. It wasn't only the dilated pupils and vacant stare, the livid bruise on her left cheekbone or the limp way she sat in the chair, like an old rag doll. There was something awfully wrong about the blanket that covered her from the waist down. It didn't sit right. It made Jana nervous, but she didn't dare lift it to look because that would raise the suspicion of her captors.

She stood outside the ballroom waiting for Quil to give the cue for her entrance. She had not wanted to do this, had begged Quil not to parade her before the cameras, but Quil had insisted.

She had been surprised by how easily she had convinced the Godless staff of her story, how quickly they had passed her up the chain of command until she was face to mask with Quil herself. The meeting had been short and sweet; she passed on what she knew and had been handed back to the senior command staff. She'd felt nervous as she was ushered into the suite, but she kept reminding herself that this Quil did not know who she was, had not yet decided to hunt her down. And anyway, she was wearing her chameleon shroud and using a well-established cover. Even if this whole plan went as wrong as she thought likely, there was no way Quil would ever be able to link Carolyn Geary with Jana Patel.

Jana had discovered a very different Quil in that suite. Surrounded by soldiers who deferred to her, standing straighter and taller than the older, isolated, injured version Jana had confronted in Sweetclover Hall. The tone and tenor of Quil's voice was different too, lighter and higher than the low, slightly raspy voice that had emanated from the scorched vocal cords of her future self. The edge of madness was missing, also. The glint in the eyes that peered out from behind her mask, the edge of mania in the way she said things, in the twitchiness of her broken body language – all absent in this younger, calmer version.

The arrogant decisiveness was the same though, Jana recognised that all too well. Quil had ordered her soldiers to keep Jana under guard, despite Jana's strident protests, and she had brooked no resistance, had waved Jana's protests away as if they were the most irrelevant words she had ever been troubled to dismiss. This was a clear antecedent of the woman who had changed so easily from reasonable entreaty to murderous action when Jana had defied her in Pendarn.

Unable to escape, but not openly threatened, Jana had no choice but to play along with Quil's plan, even after she'd been presented with her semi-comatose friend. She'd tried to tell them that she didn't think Dora was part of the plan, that they should be looking for the man whose description Smith had provided, but Quil was convinced Dora was the person they were looking for. Jana was horrified that Dora had messed up so badly; it wasn't like her.

She felt a shove on her shoulder and realised it was time for her entrance. Swallowing hard, she pushed Dora out of the corridor and into the ballroom, blinking at the lights from the camera drones that floated above her. Thank God she'd decided on wearing the chameleon shroud; her face being beamed direct to the president of Earth was probably the only thing that could make this situation even worse.

She did not smile for the cameras, and she was relieved that she was not required to make any kind of statement. Her face had appeared next to her byline a few times and on a couple of vid reports, so she would be recognised as a journalist by the kind of people who would be analysing this broadcast for any scrap of intelligence they could get – that was presumably enough for Quil's purposes; it added credibility to the story she was selling.

As Quil made her speech, Jana wondered about Kaz. Given her experiences with the Godless, it seemed likely that she'd been wrong and the assassin was working for Earth. Kaz was probably languishing in a cell somewhere answering some very awkward questions. She would have felt confident of rescuing him with Dora by her side, but Dora was out of action and needed care.

She looked out at the crowd, squinting past the lights from the cameras, trying to see if there was anyone she recognised. Almost immediately she locked eyes with Kaz and felt a wave of relief.

Through the glare of the lights it took a moment for her

to see that he was pointing frantically to one of the camera drones. She looked up at it then back at Kaz, puzzled.

'Jana,' she heard him yell. 'The camera!'

She looked up at it again and the penny dropped.

'Get down!' she cried, backing away from the wheelchair and moving towards Quil. 'Get down!'

The Godless soldiers turned to her, alarmed. Quil also turned to look just as a beam of intense white light shot from the camera Kaz had been pointing at, barely missing Quil and burning a hole in the ballroom wall.

Laser fire exploded around Jana as she dived into Quil and bundled her to the ground before the bodyguard whose job it really was to take such action had finished firing at the cameras.

She realised her mistake the instant she made contact with Quil and a penumbra of red sparks engulfed them both. Quil hit the floor hard, and her mask was ripped off, rolling away from them. Jana scrambled backwards, knowing her cover was blown and guessing exactly how things could have gone so wrong for Dora. Jana's eye-mods were flashing a tiny red light to let her know that her chameleon shroud had shut down. The discharge of time energy must have fried its circuits. Her disguise had gone.

'Did that man call you . . . Jana?' said Quil, turning to face her.

And there they sat, both their masks ripped away, face to face beneath glowing arcs of laser fire, staring as if into a mirror.

'You're her aren't you?' said Quil, breathless. 'The original.'

She crawled towards Jana, spider-fast, grabbed her shirt and brought her face right up next to Jana's, underlit by the sparks that danced where they were touching.

'You look exactly like I did when I was born,' said Quil.

Jana stared into an older version of her own face, one she realised she had seen before, in a dream.

'Oh my God,' breathed Jana. 'I'm sorry. I'm so sorry.'

Quil looked into her eyes, probing, fascinated, horrified, angry and sad all at once.

'You will be,' she said.

Barrettown, Mars,
4 April 2158, 8:42 A.M. -
1hr 26m to the event

The crowd in the ballroom was out of control.

With gunfire ahead of them, they had all turned and were trying to force their way back towards the closest exit – two sets of swing doors halfway down the room, or the larger set of main doors in the middle of the far wall. Kaz tried to push his way against the tide. He had to get to the front, see what was happening, but the mass of frightened people surged around him and he couldn't make any headway. The gunfire began to peter out as the last of the camera drones was shot out of the air, spiralling down into the crowd trailing flame and landing just ahead of Kaz. He heard a particularly loud scream as it dropped out of sight. Realising that he was wasting his time fighting the crowd, he concentrated on standing his ground and letting the people flow around him. It took all his effort not to be swept off his feet and trampled, but after a long minute the crowd thinned and he found himself standing alone facing the tables where Quil had been making her speech.

The scene before him was a mess. The tables had been knocked over, there were bags and wrecked camera drones littering the floor. In the smoke from the burning hardware, Kaz could see a few scattered bodies; whether shot, trampled or felled by falling cameras, he couldn't say. His first instinct was to run and help them, but he was more concerned about Jana and Dora, neither of whom were anywhere to be seen. All of Quil's party had gone.

Where would they be heading, he wondered? He thought it most likely they'd try to head back up to rendezvous with the fleet in low orbit. Assuming Dora and Jana were able to make physical contact, they could both escape at any time. Even if they weren't, there was nothing to stop Dora jumping away on her own. But as Kaz ran after Quil's party, one thing was nagging at him – why hadn't Dora jumped away before? She had let herself be paraded in front of the press conference in a wheelchair, which didn't seem right to Kaz at all. Dora was too strong-willed to let herself be used like that. Had she been drugged, perhaps? That might prevent her jumping away. And if she was stuck here, so was Jana.

Pushing through the door into the corridor behind the ballroom, Kaz realised he might be their only hope of jumping away safely, which raised the question of how he was supposed to get close enough to touch either one of them when they were being held captive by a fast-moving team of heavily armed soldiers.

The corridor was empty, but there was still a lot of noise coming from the direction of the lobby – shouts, screams, gunfire. If that was where the action was, Quil's team had probably ushered her out the back way. They wouldn't want to cross the plaza, not with the ongoing confrontation taking place there. The best route for them was to head straight from the hotel into the conference centre and then exit out the back. If the Earth troops remained preoccupied with the fight in the plaza, there was a chance Quil's party could make their escape unhindered.

The atrium that connected the hotel to the conference centre was only a short distance away, so Kaz didn't break stride. He burst through a large door and emerged underneath an intricate lattice of what looked like ivy created a canopy through which dappled light formed pools of orange glow on the polished wood floor. At the edges of the atrium the wood curved upwards into rising beams that formed the structure from which the ivy sprouted, like canvas spanning the distance between tent poles. It was elegant and beautiful, but Kaz didn't spare it a second glance.

At the far side of the atrium he saw a knot of Godless soldiers moving quickly away from him before a beam of white light shot by his head forcing him to fling himself to the ground, scrabbling to hide behind the wooden pedestal of an enormous fish tank within which turtles and tropical fish floated, unconcerned by the chaos around them.

Kaz peered around the side of the pedestal hoping to catch sight of his quarry. He saw the soldiers disappearing into the conference centre through an arch of intertwined ivy boughs, and broke cover immediately, sprinting in pursuit. The characteristic flash and fizz of gunfire came from ahead of him and not for the first time he wondered why it was, for someone accused of running away all the time, he so often hurried towards things most people fled.

Pausing at the archway, he leaned round to get a better look at what was happening up ahead. He was looking into a reception area where a row of tables had been set up covered in badges, snacks, jugs of water and lots of cups for tea and coffee. Service staff – cleaners, caterers, the people who had been here preparing for the first round of talks, which had been due to start in about an hour – were beginning to emerge gingerly from cover. Kaz could see no soldiers or casualties, so the shooting must have been warning fire designed to clear a path.

'Which way?' he shouted as he ran into the reception area. A scared cleaner pointed to a corridor. Kaz saw Quil's party grouped together at the far end by a pair of glass doors. One of the soldiers at the rear turned towards him and Kaz dived into the nearest room just before the warning shot lanced past. He guessed that the far doors led outside and that Quil's party were going to make a break for it.

He heard a clattering sound from outside and risked leaning his head out to see. The corridor was empty, so he resumed his pursuit.

When he reached the glass doors he saw the Godless in the boulevard, forcing passengers off a tram at gunpoint. Access to this part of the city was tightly controlled even when there wasn't a peace conference about to start, so the people disembarking were functionaries and support staff, all of whom were running for their lives; no have-a-go heroes in that bunch. Kaz did a double-take when he saw Jana because he had been looking for the face she had been wearing since they travelled to this time period. Something must have gone wrong with her chameleon shroud, because she was wearing her own face. The remaining Godless, including Quil, were all still masked. Kaz watched as Dora was lifted from the wheelchair by one of the Godless and lifted into the tram; he gasped as he saw the dressings on her ankle stumps. Now he knew why she hadn't jumped away, but it was such an unexpected development that it took him a moment to process its obvious implications – Quil must know Dora was a time traveller.

Kaz roared in frustration. First his mum, now this. Kairos had got it all wrong. They weren't changing a damn thing.

Outside, the tram began to pull away and Kaz knew he had no hope of keeping up with it. His only chance lay in working out where they were going and making his own way there. Quil and her party had two options – the elevator or the spaceport. After a moment he dismissed the elevator; it was controlled from the surface so it was too risky. They could get halfway up only to be brought back down again. No, if they were trying to get off the planet they'd need to do it old school. A rocket or shuttle or something.

Kaz's train of thought was derailed by an explosion outside. Without waiting to see what had caused it, he pushed through the doors. About two hundred metres down the boulevard, he saw the tram Quil had commandeered lying on its side wreathed in smoke illuminated by flashes of gunfire.

Godless soldiers emerged from the confusion and took up positions, firing away from the tram in the direction they had been travelling, where Kaz assumed Earth forces must have blocked the road. Beams of return fire lanced through the smoke. Kaz saw one Godless sliced in half from head to crotch, the two halves flopping away from each other.

This might be Jana's best chance to slip away in the confusion, and he reckoned it likely that the Godless would just abandon Dora, not wanting to carry the dead weight as they fought their way through the town.

Then an especially bright beam of laser fire cut through the smoke and Kaz blinked away the flash blindness to see an armoured gun platform hovering above the ground a long distance beyond the upturned tram. It didn't have caterpillar tracks but it was undeniably a tank, its impressive array of weaponry trained on the Godless soldiers. A thick white beam of energy lanced from its huge main gun and sliced the tram in half. Above the almost deafening buzz of the gun Kaz heard screams from inside the vehicle.

Barrettown, Mars, 4 April 2158, 8:42 A.M. – 1hr 26m to the event

Jana stared into Quil's familiar face and realised she'd known ever since a vision of her older self had appeared to her as she recuperated in Kinshasa. She'd written it off as a drug-induced hallucination and in the absence of proof she'd refused to believe it, suppressing the truth as if her life depended on it.

The voice had given her away. The Quil she had met at Sweetclover Hall had been badly burned, her vocal cords damaged, so she spoke in a kind of hoarse rasp. The version she'd met in Kinshasa – and she was now certain that it had been Quil, not a dream of any kind – had not suffered such damage and although her accent was different from Jana's, she had the same voice. So when Jana met Quil in the suite to pass on the warning about the assassin, she had recognised the voice, even from behind the mask. She had realised who was behind it, and with that understanding, the reason for Quil's mask became obvious. She was wearing it for the same reason Jana was – she didn't want to be recognised. Jana imagined she'd remove the mask at the moment best calculated for impact, probably on camera, with the president kneeling before her in defeat. That's what Jana would do.

The screams and the gunfire, the trampling feet and the crashing camera drones, made it impossible to hear or be heard. Quil, unmasked by Jana's rescue, scrabbled on the floor and retrieved her mask, snapping it back across her face.

'Fall back, and bring the prisoners!' yelled Quil as one of her guards handed her a gun. There was no return fire, and the crowd were all running in the opposite direction, so they were safe for now but the peace talks were over before they'd begun, that much was clear. Jana cursed Kairos and his insistence on giving them so little information. The assassination attempt had happened and it seemed unlikely that Jana and Kaz had changed anything. In fact, it looked like their presence here, and Dora's carelessness, had created exactly the situation they had been sent here to avoid. It was Beirut all over again. Jana felt trapped by the implacable inevitability of time itself.

She needed to jump away, get out of here as soon as possible. There was nothing to be gained by staying around. The sooner she got back to the quantum bubble the better. She rose to her feet and was immediately grabbed by two Godless soldiers and hurried through the ballroom doors into a leafy atrium. Quil was ahead of her, leading the way with her personal guards, who scanned through 360 degrees as they ran, alert for snipers or threats of any kind. Jana turned to look behind her and saw Dora was no longer in the wheelchair; a soldier had thrown her over his shoulder and was carrying her with little effort. All Jana could see were Dora's foreshortened legs dangling over the soldier's chest. She did a double-take and realised that Dora's feet were missing. She barely had time to process her horror and disgust before the realisation hit her – the only way to get off Mars was if all three of them were together.

'Gunfire in the plaza,' shouted one of the Godless. 'Earth forces trying to storm the building.'

'Tell them to hold the line as long as possible,' yelled Quil, still running. 'We need them to cover our escape.'

There was a bright flash ahead of her and a laser beam lanced past Jana's head. She turned to see who the Godless were firing at and fancied she caught a glimpse of Kaz diving behind a fish tank, but it was hard to be sure.

Quil led them out through the atrium into the conference centre, hurrying past the tables laid out to welcome delegates and journalists, down a corridor and through the rear doors into a wide boulevard. A tram was approaching.

'Secure that!' shouted Quil, and her soldiers moved to block the rails, weapons raised. As the vehicle ground to a halt and frightened passengers disembarked, Quil turned to Jana.

'I don't get it,' she spat. 'You warn me about Dora and then save my life back there. But you're a time traveller, like your footless lady-friend. What's the play? What's she planning? Why are you here?'

'There is no play,' said Jana, pleadingly. 'Honestly, we came to try and save your life. It was Earth that was trying to kill you, not us.'

Quil stepped forward, her mask inches from Jana's face. 'Then why is it you? Of all people, why you? You must be working for her; it's the only thing that makes sense. Who better to anticipate my actions, to identify my weaknesses? I should have realised.'

'I promise, I'm not your enemy,' said Jana. 'I'm not working for her. I've got just as many reasons to hate her as you do.'

'What do you know about my reasons?' hissed Quil.

'More than you'd think.'

'Clear!' a Godless soldier shouted from the tram and the group hurried aboard, Jana being dragged, Dora being carried. The driver sat in the cabin at the front, terrified, with a gun to his head.

'Does your route take you by the spaceport?' Quil asked him. He nodded. 'Then take us there as fast as you can.'

The tram began moving as Jana was forced down into a seat by her escort, who sat next to her with his gun jammed in her belly. She turned to look for Dora, but the soldier grabbed her head and forced it forward. Quil remained up front, crouched beside the driver.

'Update!' she yelled over her shoulder.

'Forces in the plaza are falling back into the hotel and fortifying their positions,' yelled a soldier. 'Earth forces appear to be concentrating there, doesn't look like they know we've left yet.'

'They know all right,' replied Quil ruefully. 'There must have been five separate security cameras watching us take this vehicle. They'll be deciding where to put the roadblock already. I don't think—'

Quil didn't get to finish her sentence. The tram had hardly travelled 100 metres, but there was already a tank ahead of them. Jana saw it in the distance, hovering above the ground, weapons pointed straight at them. She felt a chill as she recognised the war machine – it was the same one she'd seen on her first jump through time. She was catching up with herself. Which meant any moment now she was going to get a nasty gash across her head.

'We need to get out of here!' she yelled, but she was too late.

239

A thick white beam of light lanced out of the tank, slicing into the tram. The heat was intense, the light blinding, the noise overwhelming. Jana lost all sense of up and down, left or right. The world became a senseless jumble, and she felt herself falling slowly towards the ground, objects smashing into her as she fell, something heavy catching her across the forehead. She felt herself land, felt something land on top of her and gradually, as she lay there, her senses returned one by one. She was lying in the twisted wreckage of the tram, the air smelled of burned metal and cooking flesh, her vision was blurred but gradually she was able to make out shapes. As her eyesight cleared she could see a face, close to hers. She gasped as she realised it was Dora. Her face was covered in blood, her eyes were closed, and she was pinned to the ground by a heap of assorted metalwork. Jana tried to reach for her – if only she could make contact, she might be able to jump them away. But it was hopeless; there was too much debris in the way. Knowing that this might be her only chance to escape, Jana gritted her teeth and pushed as hard as she could, trying to rise from the ground and topple the wreckage off herself. She screamed with the effort, felt things popping in her back and her chest, where it felt like the wound she'd sustained from the knife at Pendarn was ripping itself back open. She gave thanks for Mars's lower gravity as she felt herself rising free; she didn't think she'd have been able to escape so easily on Earth. Wreckage tumbled off her with a crash and she made to rescue Dora, but directly in front of her another pile of debris shifted and one of the Godless soldiers began to rise to her feet, blocking Jana's route. Jana saw two guns lying discarded beside her, so she grabbed them. She had no choice but to run, so that's exactly what she would do.

Taking to her heels, Jana fled the smoking ruin of the tram, running at right angles to the tracks, heading for a side street where she could shelter.

She heard cries and screams from behind her, but did not turn to see.

She just ran.

Barrettown, Mars, 4 April 2158, 9:14 A.M. - 54m to the event

Kaz saw Jana make a break from the burning tram and hared after her.

The boulevard stretched out either side of him, curving away in the distance. The boulevards of the city formed a series of concentric circles widening out from the conference centre like ripples on water. Straight roads also radiated out from the plaza, like the spokes in a giant wheel, cutting across the circles as they ran to the edge of the dome. Jana was running for the nearest spoke road, limping and awkward in the light gravity. Kaz ran more easily, and they met at the junction. It sounded like the tank was firing again, and he could hear the buzz of small arms returning fire. There were more distant explosions too, coming from the hotel and conference centre.

Kaz skidded to a halt beside Jana and they crouched in a doorway. She had a nasty gash across her forehead and blood was dripping down into her eyes. She wiped it away with her sleeve, wincing, then handed a gun to Kaz.

'Where's Dora?' asked Kaz, all business.

'In the tram,' said Jana. 'Couldn't get to her. Unconscious.'

'We need to get her out of there,' said Kaz. Without waiting for a reply, he scurried out into the street and back to the corner, craning his head around to see what was going on. The wreckage of the tram was on fire, and a group of Godless soldiers were exchanging fire with the tank as their comrades struggled to free someone from the wreckage. He figured it was Quil. There was no sign of Dora.

He hurried back to Jana. 'I would say that we have to regroup,' he said. 'Jump away, take some time, strategise, return with a plan. But I don't think you'd go for that somehow.'

'Damn straight,' Jana replied with a grim smile. 'We can't risk it. We need to grab Dora first. We can't leave her here.'

A huge explosion rocked the ground.

'That came from the conference centre,' said Kaz. He rose to his feet again and hurried back to the junction. Godless troops were backing out of the conference centre on to the boulevard, firing back into the building as they did so. There were multiple explosions inside the building and Kaz could see flames licking at the wooden structure of the atrium that linked the centre to the hotel.

He was about to turn and run back again when a bright flash of red caught his eye. He squinted through the smoke and for a second, through the haze, he saw a familiar figure sprawling on a fresh pile of rubble – was that Dora? He squinted. Yes, it was, but younger, as she'd been when he first met her.

He sprinted out of cover. With gunfire to his right and ahead of him, he was behind two lines of Godless, both firing away from him. If he was quick, and kept low, he might be able to pull this off. He ran into the smoke and was instantly blind. Making a best guess of where he'd seen Dora, he ran on until he literally stumbled across her. She was flailing and screaming, utterly beside herself with fear and confusion. He grabbed her shoulders and pulled her towards him, trying to turn her so he could look her in the eyes and reassure her. He briefly wondered why she was soaking wet. Dora screamed even louder when he touched her and lurched forward, away from him, crawling away. He grabbed her feet and pulled her back to him, ignoring the kicks. In one smooth movement he hoisted her up and over his shoulder, marvelling at how light she seemed. He turned and ran with her, still kicking and screaming, punching his back and crying out, back to where Jana was waiting. She had relinquished their doorway and was now sheltering behind a small wall outside a restaurant on the junction of the boulevard.

With laser beams whizzing all around him, Kaz concentrated on running straight and not falling over. After what seemed like a lifetime, but was probably only a few seconds, he dumped Dora at Jana's feet and took shelter behind the wall himself.

He stared in amazement at the young girl, hyperventilating, face a mask of terror, dressed in simple seventeenth-century clothes that were soaking wet and plastered to her thin frame. Kaz reached towards her and put his hands on either side of Dora's head, holding it steady so she was looking up at him.

'Calm down, Dora, breathe,' said Kaz. 'It's OK. You're all right. It's a lot to handle first time. I remember. But you need to concentrate, you'll only be here for a moment. I need you to listen, yes?'

Dora nodded and Kaz let her head go.

'Don't,' he heard Jana yelling behind him. 'You mustn't tell her—'

A series of small explosions blossomed across the street as the Earth forces within the conference centre tossed grenades at the Godless.

'There is one thing you need to know,' Kaz said, leaning forward to whisper in Dora's ear, but then there came the familiar red flash and she was gone, jumping away back through time on her maiden voyage.

'What the hell was that, Kaz?' yelled Jana. 'Were you seriously about to tell Dora her future?'

'For all we know she's lying dead in that bloody tram right now,' Kaz yelled back. 'Of course I was trying to warn her!'

Jana lowered her head for a moment, then looked up at him. 'You're probably right,' she said. 'Now, assuming she's still alive, how do we get to our Dora?'

They peered over the wall. The Godless soldiers had formed a defensive knot at the junction of the adjacent street. It looked like a small group were holding position, which probably meant that the larger group were falling back down the street that ran roughly parallel to theirs. The Earth troops had taken up position in a number of places – including behind the wreckage of the tram – and were streaming gunfire at the clones. The tank was level with the tram now, rotating slowly to bring its main gun to bear on the barricade. Meanwhile, the Godless fire was concentrated on the soldiers behind the tram, the smoking carcass of which was being sliced and diced a hundred ways.

'If Dora's still in there, she's dead,' said Kaz bluntly. 'We have to hope the Godless have still got her.'

'You're right, come on,' agreed Jana, turning and running down the street away from the fighting. Kaz followed.

Jana stopped at the next junction, where another wide circular boulevard cut across the road. This road, which was mostly lined with three- or four-storey residential blocks, still had civilians on it. People were evacuating their homes carrying their most prized possessions, many dragging or carrying crying children. All of them were running away from the explosions and gunfire that echoed up the street.

'Those soldiers back there can't be the only Earth troops in the city,' said Kaz breathlessly. 'They're going to cut Quil off sooner or later.'

'There!' Jana pointed down to the next junction. The Godless came running fast out on to the boulevard, firing back over their shoulders down the street.

Kaz watched them intently. 'There's Quil,' he said, pointing her out; she was easy to spot because of her height.

'And there's Dora,' said Jana, pointing to a Godless soldier who had their friend slung across his shoulder.

'Thank God,' breathed Kaz.

'They're not safe yet, look!' yelled Jana.

Kaz looked where she was pointing. A tank was floating round the curve of the boulevard ahead of them. Before the Godless party could make it fully across, the tank's main gun fired into the blocks they were running towards, slicing into them and bringing them tumbling down in a cacophony of screaming wood. The structures of the organic residences caught light, while the bricks that had formed some of the internal structure spilled out on to the street. Kaz looked on, appalled, as he saw burning bodies tumbling from rooms suddenly exposed to the open air. The Earth tank had blocked the Godless escape, but only by knowingly killing civilians. The pragmatic ruthlessness was breathtaking.

A similar sound began building behind them and Kaz looked across to see clouds of dust and smoke billowing upwards from the street the Godless had just run down.

'They're boxing them in,' said Kaz in disbelief. 'Literally demolishing the city around them to make a cage.'

'And we're going to be trapped in it too,' said Jana.

'But that means . . .' Kaz turned to look down the boulevard in the other direction. Sure enough, he could see another tank rounding the curve in the road.

'We are so screwed,' he said.

Barrettown, Mars, 4 April 2158, 9:34 A.M. – 34m to the event

Jana stared at the approaching tank and experienced a moment of déjà vu.

'Uh, Kaz, I think . . .' but before she could say it, she saw the tell-tale red flash of a time traveller's arrival about forty metres away and she knew what she had to do.

She broke cover and ran towards the flash. Nobody was firing in this direction – the Godless hadn't yet realised there was another tank outflanking them. She heard Kaz yell in alarm as she ran, but she ignored him. The tank fired as she ran, slicing through the row of buildings to her right. Dust and smoke bloomed into the street, shards of rock, brick, metal and burning wood rained down on her, but she kept running. A laser beam zinged past her shoulder – the Godless had noticed the tank.

Keeping low, Jana hurried on and nearly tripped over the terrified girl lying in the street, looking away from her towards the approaching tank.

Jana reached out and grabbed the girl's shoulder, turning

her round so she could look into the eyes of her younger self. The fear and confusion in them made her heart ache. Did she really look like that? She always pictured herself as strong and capable, in control at all times, and meeting Quil had done nothing to dispel that self-image. But this younger version of her – and not that much younger, only a few weeks – looked out of her depth, scared and desperate.

'You'll be all right,' said Jana, instinctively trying to re-assure. 'I can't tell you how or why, but you'll be all right. I promise.' Her younger self stared up at her in amazement. 'Oh, and—'

Her vision flared with red and the world around her dissolved, spun and then resolved itself into a familiar pattern of brick.

She was back in the quantum bubble.

'Shit!' she muttered. And then louder, 'Shit! Shit! SHIT!'

How could she have been so stupid? In all the confusion, the noise, the flashes of light, the crashing and screaming, she'd somehow not realised that her hand was still on her younger self's shoulder and the red fire was building between them. She'd inadvertently jumped through time, abandoning Kaz. She stood alone, furious at herself, feeling freaked out and anticlimactic – thirty seconds ago she'd been in the middle of a firefight and now she was full of adrenalin that she had to burn off. It only took a second to come up with a way of doing that. She spun on her heels and ran to the stairs, clattering down them and hurrying between all the rooms of this odd subterranean maze until she found Kairos, humming to himself, drawing equations on a screenboard.

She took a deep breath and began to yell at him.

Barrettown, Mars,
4 April 2158, 9:58 A.M. -
10m to the event

Kaz, alone and annoyed at being so, peered round the corner.

Quil and her group of fleeing Godless had evaded the Earther's trap and made good their escape down a side street, and the tanks both ahead of and behind them were hovering away up parallel streets in pursuit. The Earth troops broke cover, pursuing the Godless down the side street. After such commotion the boulevard seemed shockingly empty and quiet as the noise of battle moved away to their left.

Seeing no choice but to follow, Kaz gave chase. There were bodies strewn across the road; soldiers of both persuasion, and many civilians also.

Reaching the junction of the street down which the fighting had progressed, Kaz took cover behind some rubble. It took a moment for him to make sense of what he was seeing.

The Earth soldiers were gunning down everyone on the street. Civilians who had left their homes to flee the fighting were being cut down as they fled.

Kaz couldn't begin to imagine why they were doing such

a thing, but he knew full well he wasn't just going to sit by and let it happen. He raised his weapon and sliced without hesitation through first one then another soldier.

There was some return fire, but not much, and none of the soldiers bothered to turn round and fight a rear-guard action; their orders were obviously to pursue Quil at all costs. Behind them, hovering in the air above the corpses, flew drone cameras, recording the carnage. Kaz shot a few of those down too, disgusted by their ghoulishness, before resuming his pursuit, scanning the massacre victims for Dora, zeroing in on bodies in Godless uniforms, looking for the soldiers who had been carrying her.

The firing ahead of him stopped, but Kaz nonetheless approached the next junction cautiously. Peering round the corner into the boulevard, he saw no soldiers at all. People were milling around in panic, most running, but the Earth soldiers had stopped firing upon civilians and seemed to have vanished into the crowd. Had they cut across to intercept Quil?

Kaz grunted in frustration and turned to look back at the road he'd just run down, and found himself staring straight at Dora. He cried out in alarm and ran back to her. She was lying spreadeagled on the ground, unconscious, by the body of a Godless soldier. There was blood all over her face, but it wasn't until he glanced down towards her legs that he felt properly sick. When he saw her missing feet his bile rose and, unable to help himself, he turned away and threw up.

When he had gathered his wits he checked her pulse. It was weak, but she was still alive. He checked her body for injuries but, besides the obvious, there seemed to be no major damage.

Pulling her tight to him, Kaz willed himself elsewhere and the street full of bodies faded away.

Just as he left Mars behind he fancied he saw the sky blotted out by a curtain of descending flame . . .

Quantum Bubble

'You are Godless,' that's what she'd said. 'You don't dream.'

When Jana was lying in the clinic in Kinshasa, out of her mind on painkillers, recovering from major surgery, she had a vision.

She saw her older self, lying in the bed next to her, and she talked to her. The memory was of that encounter, hazy and insubstantial, like a half-remembered dream. Jana had dismissed it, ascribed it to the drugs, but she had still asked Dora whether she was the only person in that wing of the clinic, studying Dora's face as she answered, trying, but failing, to ferret out a lie.

Yet even as she'd tried to deny the reality of her memory, she'd known, deep down, that it hadn't been a hallucination. Especially when Dora had revealed that Quil's army called themselves Godless. It was a word Jana had heard only once before, from the older version of herself she couldn't quite believe had been a mirage.

So when she'd watched the footage of Quil arriving on Mars, had seen her body language as she'd walked imperiously past the waiting dignitaries, Jana had felt a thrill of recognition and fear. Could it be . . .?

Unable to access any of Quil's video speeches through the

Mars net, she had been unable to hear the clone leader's voice. She knew it wouldn't sound like the Quil she had met in 1645 – by that point in her timeline, Quil's vocal cords had been burned to a crisp and she spoke with a wheezing rasp – but she thought she would know, when she heard Quil's voice, if her suspicion was correct.

So when she stood before her in the suite and told her about John Smith and the likelihood of an assassination attempt, Jana hung on every word that emerged from behind Quil's inscrutable fractal face mask.

As Quil spoke, the certainty hardened in Jana's stomach and she felt a fear unlike anything she'd ever known. Could Quil really be her? Some mad, driven future version of herself? She couldn't make sense of it. Not least because Sweetclover was never, ever going to be Jana's type. It didn't add up. What could possibly happen to turn her into this monster?

Of course, there was another possibility . . .

She had wanted to run then, just like Kaz. To close her eyes and magic herself away. But she had to help Dora, and she couldn't very well take off after berating Kaz the way she had. As she'd walked out in front of that crowd, pushing Dora's wheelchair, she'd known that somehow everything was about to come to a head, but she hadn't expected to find herself face to face with Quil, both their disguises ripped away.

'You're her, aren't you?' Quil had said. 'The original.'

Which answered a lot of questions, but raised a whole lot more.

Chief of which – how had Quil ended up in the bed beside her in Kinshasa? In a wing that Dora said was hers and hers alone?

As she ran through the war-torn streets of Barrettown,

Jana puzzled on this, trying to fit the pieces together. So when she arrived, earlier than planned, back in the quantum bubble, frozen in time beneath Sweetclover Hall at 8.22 a.m. on the seventh of April 2158, she had one thing, and one thing only, that she wanted to shout at Professor Kairos, who stood before a screenboard writing equations on it and humming to himself.

'Where is she?'

Kairos jumped in alarm, and dropped his pen. 'Oh, you're back,' he said, clapping his hands excitedly. 'What happened? Where are the others?'

But Jana was out of patience. She walked up to the professor, grabbed the lapels of his lab coat and pulled him right in close.

'Where is she?'

Kairos looked confused but not intimidated, which annoyed Jana even more, so she pulled him so close that the tips of their noses touched, and she growled.

'Um, who . . . who do you mean?' he asked, finally having the good grace to look a little uncertain of his footing.

'Me,' snapped Jana impatiently. 'Old me. Quil.'

'Oh, right, um, I think she's in the gym' said Kairos. 'Doing some rehab exercises.'

'We don't have a gym.'

'Yes, we do,' Kairos spluttered. 'There are a set of rooms we blocked off, on the floor below, so she could stay here and not interact with any of you until after Mars. Apart from her time recuperating at the clinic in Kinshasa, she's been sequestered there.'

'Show me.'

Jana pushed him away towards the door. He didn't need telling twice; he led her back to the stairs.

'Jana, please,' he pleaded as they descended. 'What happened on Mars? Where are the others?'

She pushed him ahead of her with a grunt and he nearly tumbled forward down the stairs. He took the hint, and didn't speak again until they reached a locked door at the end of a corridor to which Jana had never paid the slightest heed. He typed in the key code and the door clicked open.

'Stay here,' said Jana, pushing past him and through the door into the room beyond. It was a large bare-walled room, probably originally used for storage, but made homely by the addition of a bed and a desk on which some books were piled.

Jana heard noises from an adjoining room, strode over and looked inside to see Quil doing stretches. She walked straight in without a word. Quil became aware of her and stood up straight to greet her, but before she could get a syllable out Jana punched her in the face as hard as she possibly could. She put her whole weight into the right hook, pushing from her shoulder. It felt good as her fist made contact. It felt justified and righteous.

Quil's face flared red, with sparks and blood.

She staggered back, taken completely by surprise, but quickly regained her composure.

'What the . . .'

Jana raised her gun and aimed it squarely between Quil's eyes. The older woman wisely decided to let her protest go unfinished.

'Have you been to the 1640s yet?' barked Jana.

Quil narrowed her eyes, surprised at the question, then shook her head. 'No,' she said. 'For me it was only fifteen days ago that we met on Mars, and I've been here or in the clinic ever since. The person you met in the past . . .'

Jana stepped closer until the barrel of the gun was pressing into Quil's forehead.

'Good,' she snapped. 'Then I kill you now and all my problems disappear. I've been saying all along that we should just shoot you. You die before you hit the past and time resets itself.'

Quil stared deep into Jana's eyes, holding her gaze. She didn't say a word. She made no attempt to call her bluff, made no pleas for mercy.

Jana wanted to. She squeezed the trigger slightly, biting her lip. Come on, for God's sake, she told herself. This woman stabbed you without hesitation, and you're *her*, kind of, so you must be capable of this. This is within your abilities. Squeeze the trigger. Kill her.

She stood there for at least a minute, wrestling with herself. Eventually she yelled in frustration, stepped back and lowered the weapon.

'You should have told me!' Jana shouted.

Quil stood still for a moment, then very deliberately used her sleeve to wipe the blood off her upper lip. She seemed to consider her response very carefully.

'I couldn't,' said Quil. 'Kairos has explained the rules to you. You had to go to Mars blind.'

'In the clinic, when you spoke to me – what was that?'

'An accident,' said Quil, shrugging. 'One of the orderlies misheard an instruction and stashed us in the same recovery room. Dora was furious.'

So was Jana. What other secrets was Dora keeping from her and Kaz?

'I wondered if maybe, after we talked . . .'

'What?' snapped Jana.

'I wondered if you'd perhaps question what happened in

Barrettown,' said Quil. 'I hoped you'd figure out the way I was behaving didn't fit with the woman you'd already met. I hoped you'd work out what was happening.'

'Work what out? What was happening?' shouted Jana. 'After the tram, after I escaped. What happened to you? What happened to Dora?'

'I don't know, not exactly,' Quil said.

Jana raised the gun again, knowing even as she did so that it was an empty threat. 'If she died there, it was your fault,' she said.

Quil inclined her head in acknowledgment. 'You're right. But you don't have all the facts. Things on Mars weren't quite what they seemed to be.'

Jana sneered. 'Here it comes. The excuses, the lies, the cover story. Go on, then. Make it good. Explain to me how it wasn't you that chopped her feet off. That it wasn't you who decided we were assassins based on nothing except your paranoia.'

Quil sighed and spoke through gritted teeth, her patience beginning to fray. 'Jana,' she said deliberately. 'I was poisoned.'

Jana's mouth dropped open in disbelief. She started to laugh, but was interrupted by Kairos, his voice echoing in from the corridor outside.

'She's telling the truth, you know,' he said. 'Can I come in?'

He didn't wait for Jana's permission, but he looked quite nervous as he entered the room.

'In Kinshasa, after Quil was shot, when the doctor had her on the operating table,' continued the professor, 'he obviously had to do all sorts of tests. Blood tests, genetic profile, that sort of thing. She was brimful of a drug designed to induce psychosis. It was custom made, bespoke, targeted specifically to her DNA.'

'The doctor said it was one of the cleverest things he'd ever seen,' said Quil, taking up the story. 'It took him two days of analysis to work out what it was. Took him another three to create an antidote. But as you can see, I'm all better now.' She smiled and held out her hands.

Jana's mouth was still hanging open. 'I don't understand,' she said finally, lowering her gun and dropping to sit on the floor. Her adrenalised fury had burned away and now all that was left was confusion and fatigue.

Quil sank on to her haunches and looked into Jana's eyes.

'I do,' she said. 'It was in the food at the hotel. I was stupid and naive. I focused so much effort on selecting my personal guard, ensuring my physical security, I didn't consider more subtle forms of attack.'

Jana shook her head. 'But why didn't she kill you?'

Quil shook her head, smiling ruefully. 'And create a martyr? No. The plan was to drug me, erode my judgement, make me paranoid and aggressive. I was supposed to go mad during the peace talks, start making unreasonable demands, reject all sensible compromises. Either I'd lose the support of my generals and be unseated by a coup that she could turn to her advantage, or I'd get so paranoid about being unseated that I'd bump them all off myself and try to run the whole army alone. Either way, it would have created a huge opportunity for her.'

'Huh,' said Jana. 'That's actually quite clever.'

'Yes, it is,' agreed Quil. 'And manipulative and evil.'

'That too,' agreed Jana. 'But she was ever thus.'

'The thing was,' said Quil, sinking down to sit properly opposite Jana, 'I didn't know what was happening to me. It all seemed perfectly logical in my head. As soon as I realised Dora was a time traveller, I immediately concluded she'd been sent to kill me. It was the only thing that made sense to me. So of course when you turned up trying to warn me about an assassin, it only reinforced my paranoid certainty.'

'And when you saw my face . . .'

'Yes.' Quil nodded. 'That clinched it. I assumed she'd sent you.'

Jana sat silently for a moment, letting this information sink in. 'So if that's true, there's one thing I don't understand.'

'Who was the assassin working for?' Quil pre-empted.

Jana nodded. 'Exactly. It wasn't in her best interests to kill you. Her plan, which was working beautifully, relied on you going bananas.'

'The assassin was *supposed* to miss,' said Quil. 'There was evidence planted to implicate one of my own generals in the plot. She was trying to seed discord. In the event, things spiralled out of control much more quickly than she anticipated and she had to improvise.'

'She told you this?'

Quil nodded. 'She spent quite some time gloating after I was captured.'

Jana sat opposite Quil and let the silence hang for a moment. There was a lot for her to process.

Another thought occurred to her and she looked up at Quil. 'You know, if the drug was specifically designed for you, that means she knew who you were. Beneath the mask, I mean.'

Quil nodded solemnly. 'That was my biggest mistake,' she said. 'I was sure she didn't know.'

'I have a question,' said Kairos.

Jana sighed. 'Go on,' she said wearily.

'You keep saying "she",' he said. 'She drugged you, she knew this, she did that. Who are you talking about?'

Jana exchanged a quick glance with Quil, then addressed Kairos as if he were asking a stupid question. 'The president, who else,' she said.

'Oh, yes, of course,' said Kairos, but he was looking at Jana curiously, head cocked to one side.

Jana held his stare and waited for him to work it out. It took a moment; she could almost see the cogs whirring behind his eyes until they widened in recognition and understanding.

'Oh,' he breathed slowly. 'Oh, how did I not see this before?'

'You take a moment, Prof,' she said and then turned to Quil. 'OK, so let's backtrack. When you got to Mars, were you serious about the peace talks?'

Quil winced. 'Yes and no,' she said. 'I didn't think they'd work. I expected betrayal and subterfuge, but I was willing to negotiate in good faith. I had demands and conditions, which I knew were unlikely to be met, but I was willing to try.'

Jana believed her. 'So you arrive, in good faith,' she said. 'You get poisoned, go a bit nutty. How did you get on to Dora?'

'We accidentally touched,' replied Quil. 'There were sparks.'

'So you know about time travel? Can you . . .?'

'I have done, but I can't control it. Can you?'

Jana shrugged. 'A bit,' she said. 'Dora and Kaz can do it better than me, but they've been doing it longer. I'm told my skills will improve. Look, we can talk this out later, but for now let's concentrate on Mars. You realise Dora's a time traveller, I turn up and appear to confirm she's a hitwoman. You call a press conference, someone tries to kill you, all hell breaks loose, both our masks come off and we both get a shock. We all make a run for it, but the tram gets shot up. I

261

escape from you. You carry on on foot, with Dora. You make it to the next road then get pinned down. That's when I get pulled back here. So when I left, you were trapped, with Dora, and my friend Kaz was going to try and rescue her from you. So what happened next?'

Quil looked at the floor, unable to meet Jana's eyes, which made Jana nervous. She looked up at the professor, who was still studying her face intently.

'Professor,' said Jana. 'You sent us to Mars with only one piece of information – that someone called John Smith was going to try and kill Quil. How did you know that?'

'Guesswork, mostly,' he admitted. 'Forensic examination of data from the day indicated that a very good fake pass was used to enter the restricted area shortly before. We knew there was an assassin, so we assumed that was him.'

Jana shook her head. 'No, Prof,' she groaned. 'That was Kaz. The only reason he had that pass was 'cause you sent us to the guy who had it.'

Kairos went pale. 'Predestination.'

'If you say so,' muttered Jana. 'You refused to tell us much because you didn't want to risk creating a paradox. Now I'm back and it looks to me like the events played out exactly as they did first time round. We didn't manage to stop the assassination attempt, so I don't know if we changed anything or not. You have to tell me now. In the original timeline, what happened next?'

Kairos and Quil looked at each other seriously, then Quil nodded gently. 'We'd better show her,' she said.

The way she said it made Jana terribly nervous. Quil rose to her feet and reached out a hand to help her up.

'Sparks, remember,' Jana said caustically as she rose under her own steam.

Kairos and Quil led Jana back up the stairs to the conference area in the old undercroft. They sat round the big table and Kairos called up a screen.

'The events you lived through on Mars took place only three days before we rescued Quil from Earth interrogation and created the quantum bubble,' he said. 'So for me, what you are about to see is very recent history.'

'You have to understand,' added Quil, 'that all broadcasts from Mars are strictly controlled. The only version of events made public was officially approved. You'll see what I mean.'

Kairos waved his hand and the screen came to life.

Over an opening shot of the city, filmed long-distance so it looked small and fragile huddled beneath its dome on a vast plain, a male voice intoned:

'This morning, the Mars peace conference was due to begin with a public ceremony, but events took a dramatic turn before talks could get under way.'

Shaky footage of the city plaza, shot from above, so probably a drone camera. Godless troops lined up across the entrance of the hotel, blocking entrance and exit.

'At around 9 a.m. Mars time, Godless troops cordoned off the hotel where they had been staying, taking hundreds of journalists and hotel staff hostage and delivering a stark message.'

Close-up of Quil's mask, and her voice saying, 'The Godless are coming for you. We will descend and we will swarm and we will ferret you out, no matter how deep you bury yourself, how far you run. We will find you and you will see justice.'

It occurred to Jana that being unable to see Quil's lips move was a great advantage to the Earth propaganda machine – they could film her mask and edit her voice to say whatever they wanted, although in this instance they hadn't needed to make too many changes.

Cut back to the plaza and footage of the battle raging outside the hotel.

'Earth forces attempted to negotiate with the terrorists, but it was hopeless, and the massacre of the hostages began.'

The picture then cut to inside the hotel ballroom, showing people running for the exits in panic. The picture floated above the crowd zooming in on Godless troops firing. The way it had been edited made it look as if they were firing into the crowd rather than at the camera drones. A flash, and the picture went blank. The screen stayed black for a moment as the voiceover continued ominously.

'The Godless were forced to retreat, but when Earth soldiers entered the hotel they found no survivors.'

Now the report cut to the bridge of the Earth flagship, the one that had featured so prominently in the news reports in the days before. The scene was utter chaos, with explosions and smoke, the captain's face lit by flame as he bellowed orders.

'Earth's flagship, the *Redoubtable*, in geostationary orbit above the city, had no warning of the cowardly surprise attack, launched simultaneously with the Godless attack in the city below. Overwhelmed, she took heavy damage and the captain was lost in the first volley.'

The next shot, filmed through the dome from high above the city, picked out a bright bloom of flame in the sky above before panning down to show the streets around the plaza and the conference centre. Jana could see the tanks, but they were not firing. People scurried everywhere – soldiers and civilians, fleeing and fighting.

'In the city, the Godless pressed their advantage by attacking local residents in their homes.'

A close shot of a housing block crumbling – crucially,

there was no footage of the tank's laser, which had cut through it the moment before the film began.

'Faced with such indiscriminate slaughter, our tanks had no choice but to open fire in the hope of saving lives.'

A spectacular shot of the tram being sliced in half. Then the screen abruptly cut to a studio and the news anchor, looking solemnly into the camera.

'But despite all the efforts of our heroic soldiers to save the innocent residents of the city, it was not to be. The Godless monsters cut a bloody, merciless swathe through the fleeing civilian population.'

Bodies in the street. Hundreds of them lying like fallen dominoes, in layers like scythed corn.

'Dear God,' whispered Jana.

'Not us,' said Quil. 'By the time these people died, we were three streets away. They were killed for the cameras.'

Jana felt sick and turned away.

'No,' said Quil angrily. 'You've got to see this.'

Jana looked back at the screen as the voiceover continued.

'The *Redoubtable*, mortally wounded by a cowardly attack, could no longer maintain orbit,' said the anchor solemnly.

And now, without voiceover, a shot of a bright streak racing through the skies of Mars, burning a blinding trail through the upper atmosphere. A massive sonic boom and the camera shook. Debris fell from the dome itself, shaken loose by the force of the blast, raining down diamond shards and steel on to the buildings below. But that was irrelevant in the end, as the fireball raced closer and closer. Jana gasped as she realised it was going to smash straight into the city.

The picture became a single huge ball of flame and then cut to black.

Kairos waved his hand and the screen vanished. Jana sat there in shock at what she'd seen.

'How many?' she whispered after a moment's silence.

'Everyone,' said Quil. 'Everyone who was still in the city when the ship hit. Over half a million souls.'

'We hoped you would be able to save them,' said Kairos quietly. 'But after this, and Beirut, I think we have our answer about time. We can't change the past unless we deliberately create a paradox, and the risks inherent in that are too great. I have to conclude that to all intents and purposes time is a single line, fixed, unchanging and unchangeable. It's self-correcting and we're powerless in the face of it.'

'I don't give a damn about time, Professor,' said Jana, coldly furious at his analytical detachment. 'I give a damn about my friends. About Dora and Kaz.'

Jana turned to Quil. 'How did you escape?' she asked. 'You obviously weren't there when the ship hit. How did you get out?'

'The report was edited, full of lies, you saw that,' explained Quil. 'They conflated time. A lot happened between the tram being shot and the ship crashing, it was over an hour.'

'So tell me.'

Barrettown, Mars, 4 April 2158, 9:58 A.M. - 10m to the event

Quil was having trouble keeping it together.

The war had been raging for a decade, so this was not her first taste of action. She'd been under fire before, pinned down, outnumbered and outgunned, desperately hunting for a way to beat the odds and turn the tide of battle. All those times she'd remained calm and collected, even the first time. The manner of her birth had inured her to fear and horror from the very start. She had survived that, she could survive anything.

So why now, in yet another firefight on yet another planet, was she finding her pulse racing, her thoughts misting, her panic threatening to overwhelm the calm focus that lent authority to her command?

It was almost as if there was something wrong with her head. It felt indefinably wrong, like she was suffering from concussion or a migraine. Her hands flew to her hair in momentary panic – had she been hit by something and not noticed? She could detect no bruises or wounds.

Maybe she was finally losing her nerve.

'There's another one,' shouted her lieutenant, pointing back down the boulevard. She followed his gaze and saw a second tank open fire on one of the residential blocks behind them, sending debris across the street, blocking their retreat.

'If we don't move now, we'll be trapped!' he yelled.

Quil knew he was right. She had to make a decision quickly, even though her thoughts felt as jumbled as the debris she was staring at. She couldn't work out how this situation had gone south so quickly and completely.

When she had agreed to the peace talks, she'd done so from a position of strength. Her forces were so overwhelmingly superior that she'd felt reasonably safe coming to Mars with a small security force. The government knew that if they tried anything, the retaliation would be swift and decisive. She would be exposed, but what would be the point in trying to kill or capture her? It would only hasten their defeat. None of what was happening made sense to her.

She forced herself to speak.

'You, you and you,' she said, picking out three soldiers. 'Stay here and lay down covering fire. The rest of us will make for that cross-street.' She pointed to the entrance to one of the spoke roads that led to the dome's edge. The buildings on the corner had been demolished by the tank ahead of them, but now the dust had cleared somewhat she could see it was passable, albeit with a bit of climbing that would leave them briefly exposed. There was no other option, though.

'Once we're safe, join us,' she said, knowing that the three soldiers covering her escape would not be joining her at all.

'Yes, ma'am,' they chorused, unquestioning.

'Bring the girl,' she added. Her lieutenant nodded and hoisted Dora, still unconscious, across his shoulder again.

'On three. One, two—' A massive burst of laser fire cut

across them from the junction of the road they'd recently exited, cutting down one of the soldiers.

'GO!' screamed Quil and she led the retreat as all but three of the Godless broke cover and ran for the debris. Laser fire burned the air around them as they ran. They only had to run the length of a street and scramble over a pile of rubble; at most it took twenty seconds, but they felt like the longest seconds of her life. She reckoned she had about thirty soldiers when they broke cover; by the time they made it to the other side of the rubble and were running down the street, no longer under fire, she counted eighteen. Her lieutenant, and Dora, were not among them. She cursed inwardly at the loss of the mysterious time traveller, but there was nothing she could do. Their only chance was to make it to the spaceport, commandeer a vessel and break for the fleet. She glanced up, wondering if news of the situation down here had reached the ships. A bright flash in the sky, like a star flaring so bright it could be seen in the daytime, gave her the answer. She had little concern for her ships – the Godless vessels massively outnumbered the Earth fleet. The enemy's ships may be impressive, but they were few. The best they could hope for would be to delay the advance for a while.

They were not alone on the street. Slow-moving civilians, or those who had stopped to gather possessions from their houses rather than just running, were still struggling down the road away from the fight. All had their backs to Quil and her group, so it was only as they drew level or overtook them that the civilians realised they were there. Most screamed and ran sideways into buildings, some turned and ran back towards their homes in total unreasoning panic. One young man actually ran at them wielding a baseball bat, but her lieutenant cut him down.

On they ran, to the end of this street and straight across the next circular boulevard. The crowds of civilians were thicker here so they had to push and shove their way through panicked people who didn't know where to run. Their progress slowed, especially when one group of men decided to have a go and charged at them. They managed to bring down two of her soldiers and were kicking and stamping them when a single sweep from her gun-beam put a sudden stop to the violence. After that the crowd peeled away from the Godless and their speed increased again. Behind them, towards the centre, they could still hear explosions and gunfire, which made no sense to Quil. Who were the Earth forces shooting at?

The crowds gradually thinned. It seemed those people who were running were mostly heading in the opposite direction, towards the elevator. The civilian population here, where the fighting still seemed a few streets away, were not yet pouring out of their homes in panic. They passed trams stopped dead in the street; the system must have been shut down to prevent them hijacking another vehicle.

'Half a mile, ma'am,' grunted a soldier running beside her.

'There'll be resistance,' replied Quil breathlessly. She pointed to one of the ubiquitous security cameras that hung from the lampposts. 'They know where we're heading.'

Their progress was unimpeded, and though their presence provoked extremes of fear or anger, all they had to contend with were jeers or screams from bystanders until they reached the outermost circular boulevard, the one that ran inside the rim of the dome.

The spaceport buildings, a huge complex of warehouses used to store materials for both import and export, were two streets to their left, about a hundred metres, built into the edge of the dome itself. Outside the dome, on the other side of the diamond sheets that composed the city's skin, were a series of runways and landing pads designed to receive all kinds of vessels. Quil zoomed in on the craft currently in dock and quickly identified the best suited for a quick clean escape – a nimble, rugged little mining craft that sat among rows of large, slow haulage vehicles.

She counted her soldiers. They were down to sixteen.

'Can anyone see fortifications, checkpoints, any kind of barricade?' asked Quil urgently.

Nobody could, which made Quil deeply uneasy. She was sure there were soldiers lying in wait everywhere. She felt a deep fear, a kind of overwhelming paranoia about the silence and stillness ahead of her, but she fought it down and turned to her soldiers.

'All right, listen,' she said, projecting calm resolve but unable to hide a slight, uncharacteristic tremble in her voice. 'This is almost certainly a trap. They know where we are, they've had time to prepare. But we have no choice but to carry on. So, see that mining vessel there?' She pointed to the ship she had picked out, still connected to the dome by the airlock tunnel used for passage to and fro. 'Everyone make for that. The first person inside, prep for take-off. And understand – the person at the controls is in charge. They get to decide when they cut their losses and take off. If you're all aboard and I'm stuck behind, don't come get me. That's an order.'

The soldiers nodded.

'Fan out as soon as we break cover and run for your lives. Good luck to us all.' Quil crouched, ready to run. 'On my mark. Mark!'

She took off like a sprinter from the starting blocks, her loyal guards at her side, and she ran as fast as she ever had.

She had been half expecting a volley of fire the moment they broke cover, but when they'd covered half the distance in a few seconds, she began to think they would make it.

Almost the instant she had registered that thought, there was a blinding flash of light and a deafening hum. Unable to see or hear, her fear overwhelmed her and she froze in the middle of the street, blinking away the blindness, shaking. Even in the midst of what she was beginning to think was a panic attack, she was still questioning her responses, unable to accept that her reactions were natural, so out of character were they.

As her vision returned she turned through 360 degrees, looking for her soldiers, hoping against hope that some of them had made it.

All sixteen of them lay around her in various pieces.

She was the only one still standing, and that didn't last long for she fell to her knees and screamed her fury at the sky as she noticed the snipers on the rooftops all standing, no longer hiding their presence, all their weapons trained on her.

'Do it then!' she bellowed, crying. 'What are you waiting for?'

A single Earth soldier strolled casually out of the nearest port warehouse. An officer, tall and confident, he did not seem bothered at all by the carnage that surrounded him.

He walked up to Quil and looked down at her.

'Get up,' he ordered contemptuously.

He was right, realised Quil. What the hell was she doing on her knees? She wasn't going to be taken like this. She took a deep breath and rose to her feet as elegantly as she could, but her knees were shaking and her bottom lip was trembling. She faced down the officer with all the defiance she could muster.

He sneered and held out a tablet.

'Take it,' he said.

She did so, and looked at the screen to see the face of the president looking out at her. The desk and the window were familiar – she was calling from the Oval Office.

'Take off the mask,' said the president.

Slowly, Quil reached her free hand up and undid the clasp at the side, holding the edge of the mask between her fingers and pulling it away. Hot, dry air caressed her face. She stared through the screen into the eyes of the president, in direct contact, in full sight for the first time. They had exchanged messages through intermediaries and diplomatic channels, traded propaganda videos and speeches, even talked briefly on an audio channel once the peace talks had been finalised.

But they'd never looked each other in the eyes, even on screen.

Quil had been waiting for this moment all her life. She had dreamed of it, fantasised about how she would unmask herself, the shock and surprise of it, the delicious pleasure of seeing realisation dawn in the eyes of her vanquished enemy.

This was not how she had imagined it at all.

The president looked out at her calmly from the glass tablet screen, and Quil realised that she had already known. Somehow, despite all Quil's precautions, the president had learned her identity long before today.

Which left only one thing for Quil to say.

'Hello, Mother.'

Interlude:
Beirut, Lebanon, 20 March 2010 10:48 A.M. – 15 mins after car bomb detonation

Henry Sweetclover felt light-headed and nauseated.

The stump at the end of his right arm throbbed angrily, but the anaesthetic Dora had administered was blocking the worst of the pain. That didn't stop the world swirling around him as the shock took hold, though. The Beirut sky seemed to swoop and twirl above him while the roof beneath him undulated like a boat in choppy waters.

The noise from the blast site in the street below was frenzied and disorientating – shouts and screams and sirens.

He could not understand why Dora had walked away from him. She had every justification for killing him, and even if she'd not felt it was right, it was certainly the safest course of action for her to take. Her mercy – no, it was worse than that – her indifference disturbed him.

He needed to get back home, so he closed his eyes and

willed himself there. But before he felt the tug of transition he opened his eyes again, alarmed at what he felt.

Fear.

But not fear of death, or time travel or anything as mundane as a sword. He realised, to his dismay, that bubbling up in him unbidden was fear of his wife and her reaction to his failure.

He turned his head and retched, vomiting until his stomach was empty and he was dry-heaving a thin trickle of bile. Reflexively, he wiped his lips on his sleeve, nauseating himself even more as he realised he'd just wiped vomit on the fresh white bandage protecting his severed wrist.

Grimacing, he closed his eyes again, told himself not to be weak and slipped away in a flurry of fire.

When he opened his eyes again he was sitting in the driveway of Io Scientific in the dead of night. He cursed his lack of precision – right place, wrong time. But was he off by only a few hours, or more?

Using his left hand, he clumsily pulled his mobile out of his pocket and waited for it to register a signal. When the 4G icon lit up he dialled his wife. He just had the strength to tell her where he was before he passed out.

Henry woke some hours later, in bed, in the converted church he and his wife called home.

(How she'd laughed when she'd realised she could buy and live in a church.

'Deconsecrated ground? So appropriate for a Godless,' she'd chuckled.)

He was connected to a drip, which made sense – Quil would have wanted to avoid the attention a hospital admission would have brought. When he turned his head he saw her, asleep in a chair beside his bed. Dressed in a fitted black suit, she looked every inch the powerful tech executive, except for her slumped head and the book open on her lap; they made her look vulnerable.

He smiled to see her, remembering the long years he had spent sitting beside her bed in the undercroft of his house, reading to her as her burns healed. Now she was repaying the favour, keeping vigil for him.

He found himself ashamed that he had allowed fear of her to enter his heart for even a second.

'Darling,' he said softly.

She jerked awake, momentarily disorientated, but her face filled with concern when her eyes met those of her injured husband. She sat beside him on the bed and took his remaining hand in hers, kissed his fingers, then his lips, and rested her forehead against his.

'I should have sent more backup,' she said. It took a moment for Henry to realise that she was apologising. She didn't normally do apologies.

'I don't think it would have made any difference, my dear,' he replied. 'Dora is formidable indeed. She dispatched the local mercenaries and sliced off my hand before we even knew she was there. I do not believe a larger force would have taxed her much.'

'That's as may be,' said Quil. 'But if you had been properly supported . . .'

Henry shrugged, an awkward, clumsy gesture for a man lying down with his wife holding his only hand.

'I've underestimated them at every turn,' she said ruefully. 'Her especially, your scullery maid. Was *she* there – the other me?'

Henry nodded. 'I had her,' he said, 'until Dora intervened. She made good her escape.'

Quil sat upright and released Henry's hand.

'That's it, then,' she said, as if coming to a decision.

'It?'

'No more messing about,' said Quil. 'We tried to change things, but it didn't work. I tried to get answers, but it didn't work. Enough. It's a sideshow, and it's distracted us long enough. Henceforth we have one priority and one only – we prepare our assault on the future. Our work in this time period is almost complete. I don't think we need another staging post. We can wrap things here and jump straight to 2158. I've waited long enough.'

She squeezed his hand excitedly.

'But first,' she said with a disarming, girlish smile. 'You and I need to take a holiday!'

Henry laughed. 'A holiday? Are you serious?'

Quil nodded. 'Absolutely, darling,' she said, smiling. 'We can get you a new hand and take in the biggest and best show in the history of the planet.'

Henry blinked in surprise. 'A new hand?'

'Of course,' said Quil. 'Child's play to replace an appendage in my time. I sliced Dora's feet off once, but you don't see her hobbling around on crutches, do you!'

Henry felt a rush of relief. It had not occurred to him that his injury was reversible. Quil noticed his joy and gave a feline smile.

'I need a husband with two hands,' she said, her eyes hooded and twinkling.

After a lingering kiss, Henry asked, 'I thought you couldn't go back to your era, at least before the attack, for fear of being recognised.'

Quil waved away his objection airily. 'I shall wear a chameleon shroud. We can explore the Paris Expo undetected.'

'The Paris Expo?'

'The greatest exhibition in the history of the world, if you believe the hype,' said Quil, in a tone of voice that implied she really, really didn't. 'A gaudy show to distract Earth's population from the clone fleet bearing down on their fragile little planet. But I expect it will amuse us for a few days. Shall we go?'

Henry nodded.

'Good, sleep now,' said Quil as she kissed his forehead. Then she returned to her seat, opened her book and began to read to him as he closed his eyes and was lulled to sleep by her voice.

Part Three

Plan B

20 March 2010, 10:32 A.M. - 30s to car bomb detonation

Peyvand saw her husband and son walking away from her and felt her feet turn to lead. What was she doing? How could she run and leave everyone here to die? But how could she betray her son and his friends, either? Her brain froze, she couldn't move, couldn't decide, couldn't think. Some deeply rational part of her insisted that the last twenty-four hours had been nothing but a dream. Time travel? That was insane.

Maybe that was it – maybe she was going mad.

She saw the black car moving through the market with its windows blacked out but it didn't register as a threat. She just stared at it numbly.

She heard her name. No, not her name; someone was calling her Mum. Was that Kaz? How could he be behind her when she was watching him walk away in the opposite direction? She opened her mouth to reply and turned towards the sound and then—

A touch on her shoulder, a blinding flare of red fire, deafening noise, a wave of hot air and then a strange feeling of weightlessness, as if she was falling fast through solid ground.

A part of her recognised the sensation as time travel and she was shocked back into herself, her shock-fuelled fugue state shattering as she fell.

She had no sense of anyone else travelling with her, not like last time, and she had time to wonder where Kaz was before the darkness began to lift and an object slowly faded into existence in front of her.

As Peyvand re-entered consecutive time, she found herself standing in the undercroft of Sweetclover Hall, staring down the barrel of a gun.

Kinshasa, Democratic Republic of Congo, 23 May 2120 – 38 years to timebomb impact

'We need a Plan B,' said Dora, firmly.

Kaz didn't know whether he was impressed or dismayed by her declaration.

The hospital room was flooded with morning sunlight, streaming in through the picture window. Dora lay in bed, her stump-end legs hidden beneath the sheets. Her replacement feet were nearly finished growing in a tank somewhere, and the surgery to attach them would take place either tomorrow or the day after. A week's rehab would be all that was required and then she'd be good as new, but inactivity did not sit well with Dora. She coped less well than Jana had after the operation to sew up her knife wound; at least she had been willing to read some books to pass the time. Dora mostly lay there brooding.

Kaz was glad of the respite. He had been wanting to find some time to get his head clear again, and overseeing Dora's recuperation was the perfect excuse. Dora wanted him to go back to the bubble and update Kairos and Jana, but Kaz didn't see the point of splitting up and had resisted, couching it as a selfless act – which it was, kind of.

Kaz spent his days walking in the city park that surrounded the clinic. He didn't venture into town; he didn't want to be around people. Balmy weather, quiet, time to think – it was perfect. He kept replaying his final moments on Mars, seeing the sky turn red with fire. He had no idea what could have caused it – a bomb, perhaps? Maybe one of the Godless ships in orbit had targeted the nuclear reactors? Whatever it had been, he thought he now knew what the tragedy Kairos had hoped to avoid was – Barrettown had been destroyed, he was sure of it.

When Dora first regained consciousness she explained how things had gone wrong – the accidental brush of a finger was all it had taken. For days she sat and stared at the wall, refusing to speak further. Kaz became worried about her mental health. He knew the signs of depression and in his judgement Dora would have stayed in bed even if she could walk. She seemed paralysed, physically and mentally, by her failure. It was as if she had never even considered the possibility of screwing up. He spent a day being resentful of the fact that she seemed to have taken this failure so hard when she'd basically shrugged off his mother's death, but he couldn't sustain his anger in the face of her melancholy.

He'd sat and asked about her family, her training with Garcia, her plans for the future, but he'd only received one-word answers. Eventually he gave up and just sat with her in companionable silence, being there in case she needed him, letting her know by his presence that she was not alone, but not imposing himself in any way. Whatever peace she needed to make, she would have to negotiate it with herself.

All the while, in a laboratory, her flesh, muscle and tendons grew around a framework of force-grown bone as her new feet took shape.

Kaz had timed their arrival in Kinshasa perfectly. They'd slipped into being only moments after their younger selves had departed for the quantum bubble. If this surprised or alarmed the staff, they gave no sign of it. Kaz wondered what else went on at this clinic, in the other wings.

Kaz sat and thought about his mother, about how knowing she was dead had been easier than not knowing whether she was alive.

He thought about his father, about how he had endured the post-Beirut years of Kaz's anger and pain, had tried his best to be a role model, a carer and a confidant to his sullen son, even though he knew he was going to fail. Returning to Poland and making things right with him seemed ever more urgent.

He thought about Jana. Weird, manipulative, clever, funny, stroppy Jana, the girl he'd started to fall for but who he now realised was not a future partner at all, but a present friend, a friend who didn't *do* friendship and seemed to have been as surprised by her feelings for him as he was by their lack of romantic intent. He felt a surge of affection for her when he remembered how crestfallen she'd looked when she'd told him she was gay, and a flush of embarrassment when he recalled his clumsy, knee-jerk reaction. He had to make things right with her, too. Even as he took advantage of this hiatus in excitement he could hear her lightly mocking voice upbraiding him for running away yet again.

Why did he feel such loyalty to Dora and Jana anyway? They were just some random girls who'd literally dropped into his life. He didn't owe them anything. He was his own man, he could go when and wherever he wanted. What was stopping him jumping away right now? Dora's hospital bills were paid and she'd be able to go her own way as soon as she was fit. But even as he thought this, he dismissed it as unworthy of himself. He couldn't pinpoint when it had happened, but Dora and Jana were as much his family as his parents, that was all there was to it.

On the tenth day of Dora's bed rest, Kaz's reverie was interrupted when she spoke her first words in days: 'We need a Plan B.'

It took Kaz a few moments to focus on what she'd said and formulate a response to such an unexpected outburst.

'Seriously?' he eventually replied, deliberately responding as if a paused conversation had just started again, not making a big deal of her days of silence. 'What would be the point? Mars was a disaster. Literally, a disaster. Aren't we done? Why do we need to seek Quil out again? Why can't we just get on with our lives? What makes her our problem? I know you and Jana agreed that if we failed on Mars we'd go back to 2014 and kill her. And I know I signed up to that. But . . .' he shrugged and shook his head, unable to articulate the pointlessness of such an action.

'Only a week or so ago you told me you still wanted to keep trying,' Dora said, agitated and annoyed. 'You said, and you were right, that if we could stop Quil being blown back into the past somehow, maybe we could still prevent your mother dying. That's what you said.'

Kaz lowered his head, ashamed.

'Yes. Yes I did,' he admitted. 'And the next day I wised up. I want to get you well, hook up with Jana in the bubble, if that's where she went, then leave all of this behind. I owe my dad a visit and an apology. Then I think we should turn our backs on Quil and everything to do with her.'

Dora tutted and turned her face away. 'You mean hide,' she said. 'Find some backwater in time and be anonymous.'

'Yes,' agreed Kaz. 'That's exactly what I mean. Let's get on with the business of living actual lives. Find a home, settle there, build something normal. We're not soldiers, we're just normal people.'

'Speak for yourself,' said Dora darkly.

Kaz bit his lip and thought carefully before speaking again. She'd come out of her fugue in combative mood and he didn't want to make it worse, but at the same time, now she was engaging again, he wanted to try to understand what was going on with her beneath the alternate silence and aggression.

'Dora,' he said gently. 'You're not a soldier. You never were. You're a girl whose world fell apart in the most horrible way. Some people would have cried for a year, some would have eaten all the cake in England, some would have been able to let it all just roll off their backs. But you decided to turn yourself into a ninja. Someone invisible and silent.'

'And lethal,' said Dora, not making eye contact.

'That too,' agreed Kaz. 'But faceless, anonymous. I liked the Dora I met when she was fourteen. She was a good kid. Out of her depth, but brave. She had no secrets. I could look at her face and know instantly what she was thinking. She was a person, Dora. Courageous and scared and funny and angry and full of love for her family. You are none of these things. You pretend them sometimes, when we're all together, in between crises. But your smile is not real, your laugh is not real, your anger is not real.'

'I made myself what I needed to be,' said Dora quietly.

'You don't need to be anything, Dora,' said Kaz. 'You need to be a person. You lost yourself. I hoped all the time you were spending back in 1645, with your family, would help you come to terms with things. But—'

'I didn't go back,' Dora whispered, staring fixedly at the bedspread.

'What?' asked Kaz.

'To Pendarn,' said Dora. 'I haven't been back there, not since I dropped them off. I left and I haven't been back.'

'In God's name, why?' asked Kaz, astonished. 'Where were you going all those times you left this clinic when Jana was recuperating?'

'Nowhere special,' said Dora, finally looking up at Kaz. 'A few days here, a few days there. I went to the theatre a lot. Did a lot of training. Found this great nightclub, Studio 54. Did a lot of dancing.'

Kaz felt overwhelming sympathy for Dora. She had been just as lost as he had, maintaining a facade for the people around her, ignoring the emptiness beneath.

'I thought, by becoming this soldier, this warrior, I would become a new person,' said Dora. 'That's what I wanted, more than anything else. To not be me anymore. Maybe I was too successful.'

She lapsed back into silence, and Kaz resumed his patient vigil.

Sweetclover Hall, Cornwall, England, 2014 – 144 years to timebomb impact

It was a bittersweet experience for Henry, coming home to Sweetclover Hall. He still owned it, or rather, Io Scientific did, but it was no longer his home. He pushed through the old front doors, kicking up dust and brushing away cobwebs. He knew his wife and some employees had already come this way and were at work deep beneath his feet, but apart from a few footprints in the dust, the house could have been empty for a hundred years.

He paused in the entrance hall, looking towards the drawing room where Quil had proposed to him, down on one knee with her arms spread wide, laughing and twinkle-eyed at all the seventeenth-century taboos she was breaking.

The main staircase stood before him. A few steps had rotted away and fallen through, so he was not able to climb to his old bedroom, or revisit the room where his father had died.

He walked to the cellar door and stood looking down at the old stone steps where he had first seen his wife, lying broken and fading, so long ago. Even now, the undercroft gave him a chill of remembered childhood fear as he descended the steps and made his way along the brick corridor that led to the main chamber.

He passed the door that led to the icehouse passage, built on a whim of his father's but abandoned to spiders and rust almost immediately, and then entered the main chamber. All trace of the technology that Quil had plundered from the future and brought back to the 1640s was gone. It was now just a big empty space. He stood there for a long while, remembering happier, simpler times before, with a reluctant sigh, heading for the lift that would take him down even further.

Henry did not like visiting the cavern beneath his house. It was cold and dark and wet. Sounds echoed eerily whenever anyone moved or spoke. And it was lined with thousands of cocoons, each holding a perfect monster.

Quil had explained the cavern's origin to him when she first brought him down here. In 2158 the warhead of the timebomb blew a huge crater in the ground where his house was (would be) and then it had travelled back in time, blown back thousands of years until it arrived, exactly where it had landed; which was, of course, at that point in time deep underground. The final discharge of energy from the asteroid had burned a perfectly spherical void in the rock. The warhead had lain there ever since, travelling forward in time in its cavern home. Eventually it would meet its younger self and be obliterated.

'That's why the explosion was so much more devastating than I expected,' she told him. 'Because the warhead crashed into its older self, waiting patiently beneath the house. The energy released was exponentially higher than I calculated, and the effects much more dramatic.'

Henry did not entirely grasp her explanation, so she drew him a diagram. This did not help, and he still did not understand it, but he pretended he did so that she would stop explaining.

As he stepped out of the lift into the cavern, he shivered. To his left stood the cold fusion generators, installed centuries ago and still running perfectly. Ahead, almost lost in the gloom, the softly glowing warhead of the timebomb sat waiting. The glow had faded since the 1640s, as if it were a battery slowly running down. And around the walls, rising up ten rows high and circling the entire circumference of the cavern, were the cocoons.

'Hank!'

His wife had seen him and was beckoning him to join her and a group of technicians beyond the reactors, at the cocoon that marked the beginning of the series.

'We're nearly done,' she said as he walked over to her.

A series of gas canisters were lined up in a row, a daisy chain of hoses connecting them to the first cocoon. He looked over his shoulder and saw a similar set-up at the cocoon, which marked the last in the series.

'And this is the last treatment?' he asked.

Quil nodded eagerly. 'This is the last one. After this, we seal the lift shaft, brick up the entrance and they can sleep undisturbed till their alarm clock goes off at exactly 8:15 a.m. on the seventh of April 2158. Just time to get out of bed before the real wake-up call hits.'

Henry nodded, happy at her happiness, but apprehensive as the final piece of her plan fell into place.

'And what will this modification do?' he asked.

Quil smiled devilishly. 'You'll see,' she said.

'All set, ma'am,' said one of the technicians.

'Then what are we waiting for?' she replied, indicating that he should proceed.

The technicians pressed some buttons on the portable console that controlled the outflow of the gas bottles and a light blue haze began to fill the nearest vertical line of cocoons. The figures within, already misshapen and nightmarish seen through the old, mottled glass of their encasements, vanished in the blue fog as it migrated around the room, filling each of the pods before seeping through into the next in sequence.

The silence was broken suddenly by a loud bang somewhere in the distance, and Henry thought he caught a glimpse of blue gas seeping into the air as he heard the tinkle of glass falling onto rock and a horrible wet slapping sound.

'Sealing off container twenty-five slash three and re-routing flow,' said a technician as his fingers flew over the console's buttons.

'What was that?' asked Henry.

'Some of the subjects might experience a side-effect of the process,' Quil said as another loud bang sounded from even further away and she pulled a comical grimace. 'An explosive side-effect.'

'Sealing off container thirty-two slash eight and re-routing flow,' intoned the technician.

Henry jumped nearly out of his skin as a hand slammed up against the glass of a cocoon near to him, and he caught disturbing half glimpses of a figure moving within the smoke.

Quil walked over to the cocoon and placed her hand upon the glass. 'Shhh,' she whispered. 'It'll all be over soon.'

Then there was another crack, and another, and one by one the figures within the smoke-filled prisons began to squirm and writhe, fingers scratching helplessly against the glass,

292

tortured faces pressed up against it offering him short, phantasmagoric visions of suffering and insanity.

His stomach churned and he turned away.

'I'll see you back at Io,' he said as he walked towards the lift as quickly as he could.

If his wife replied, he did not hear her above the rising susurration of whispery groans echoing around the cavern.

Henry Sweetclover punched the button on the lift, willing the doors to close quickly. As he rose through the earth he could not avoid feeling that he was leaving a place of evil. A place of evil ruled over by his wife.

As he stepped out of the Hall's front door he was certain that it was the last time he would cross this threshold.

He had not expected to be so happy about saying goodbye to his home, but he turned his steps towards his car with relief, and drove away without looking back.

Quantum Bubble

Kaz took Dora's hand and surrendered himself to her control.

'It's all about numbers,' she said as the red glow built around them. 'See if you can sense the equations as we go.'

As they slipped away from Kinshasa he was aware of the finesse of her movement through time, the fine detail of her course corrections, the confidence and ability she possessed. He envied her, and looked forward to the day he would have such facility. And yes, he did have a sense, a strange, half-formed inkling of numbers swirling around them. Was this something to do with how they travelled?

The undercroft of Sweetclover Hall melted into existence around them.

'Thank God,' said Jana, who was sitting at the conference table beside the spot where they materialised. She burst out of her chair and flung her arms round Kaz, hugging him tight in spite of the sparks. It took all of Kaz's concentration to stop them spiralling off into time.

'I was so sure you'd been killed,' she breathed into his ear. 'I'm so happy to see you, you've no idea.'

Kaz returned the hug gladly.

'What happened to you?' he asked, gently extricating himself from her embrace.

'I touched myself,' said Jana.

'Excuse me?' said Dora giving Jana the side-eye.

Jana slapped her playfully on the arm and pulled her into a hug, though not, Kaz noted, as emphatically as she'd hugged him, and it was far less welcome on Dora's part.

'What happened to the innocent village girl?' laughed Jana. 'I meant I met me, from when I first jumped through time. I put my hand on my shoulder to calm myself, which I remembered my older self doing. And I was so focused on reassuring myself that I jumped off into time by accident.'

Kaz squinted with the effort of trying to decipher her meaning.

'There were far too many reflexive pronouns in that sentence,' said Kairos, rising from the table to greet the new arrivals with smiles and handshakes.

'Oh my God,' exclaimed Jana, her hand flying to her mouth as she looked down at Dora's shoes. 'I forgot about your feet. How are you standing?'

'We went back to the clinic in Kinshasa,' said Kaz. 'They grew her new ones.'

'They what?' said Jana, disbelieving.

'They can clone whole people,' said Dora. 'Why not feet?'

Jana nodded. 'I s'pose. How do they feel?'

'Same as they did before,' said Dora. 'You'd never know they were spare parts.'

Kairos indicated that they should sit, and they did so, gathering round the table as they had done twice before. Kaz ended up sitting between the two girls.

'Look at me,' he said, smiling. 'A rose between two thorns.'

They both jabbed him with their elbows and scowled at him, which made him stupidly content.

Then they went through the now-routine protocol of checking their relative timelines – Jana had been back for about a day, Dora and Kaz had stayed in Kinshasa for three weeks before returning. Next they recounted their separate stories of their final day on Mars and asked Kairos to fill them in on what had happened after they'd left.

'As far as I can see,' he said, 'you were unable to change the outcome of events.'

'And what was that outcome?' asked Kaz, even though he was certain he already knew.

'Once things went wrong on the surface, the Godless fleet opened fire on the Earth ships,' said Kairos solemnly. 'The Earth flagship, *Redoubtable*, crashed into Barrettown, completely wiping it out.'

Kaz nodded sadly. He had shared his suspicion with Dora, so her reaction was similarly muted. But Jana showed no reaction at all. He presumed Kairos must have told her before he and Dora had arrived, but there was something about the studied way she was showing no emotion on her face that aroused Kaz's suspicions.

'And Quil?' he asked. 'What happened to her?'

Kairos glanced at Jana, just for an instant, a micro-expression that confirmed to Kaz that there was something he was not being told. Again.

He had been planning on making his pitch again, his argument that they should turn their back on all of this and find somewhere safe to build new lives, but that intention crumbled when faced with Jana and her secrets.

As Kairos opened his mouth to answer, Kaz cut him off, turning to Jana and saying, 'We agreed that after Mars there would be no more secrets. Kairos was going to tell us everything he knew. That was the deal.'

Jana met his gaze, and he could tell she was nervous about something, though he couldn't say what.

'Then let him tell us, Kaz,' said Jana in mock exasperation. But Kaz wasn't buying it.

'Everything Jana,' he said. 'The whole truth. How this bubble got set up. Why. Who by. What the plan is now.'

'He was about to tell us about Quil,' said Jana, pantomiming puzzlement.

'Yes, he was,' said Kaz. 'But why do I think that she's got more to do with Kairos than he's telling us? And why do I think you know about it too?'

'I don't—' Kairos began to protest, but Kaz interrupted him again.

'You told us this was a top-secret government black site, yes?' he asked.

Kairos nodded, apprehensive.

Kaz pointed out of the room towards the ceiling, where the timebomb hung in a frozen explosion. 'So why,' he asked, 'was that bomb fired at this location by Quil's forces after the Mars disaster?'

Kairos shrugged, but it was unconvincing. Kaz had had plenty of time in Kinshasa to ponder all the unanswered questions that plagued him, and he was keen to find out whether his suppositions were correct.

'I'll tell you why, shall I?' said Kaz, managing to be confrontational without aggression, a skill he'd been trying to master for a long time and felt like he was starting to finally get the hang of. 'It's because Quil was being held here, probably tortured, and they wanted to silence her before she could give away their military secrets.'

It was a guess, but Kairos did not have a poker face. The truth of Kaz's assertion was writ large there.

'So I think you should—' Kaz began.

This time it was Kaz who was interrupted, by Dora, who

297

uttered a loud 'Ha!', grabbed Kaz's arm, turned him to face her, then leaned forward until her nose was an inch from his.

'You know what this place is, don't you?' she said smugly.

'What?' he said, slightly annoyed at being upstaged.

'This place. The bubble. Kairos. All of *this*.' She waved her arms around expansively, brimful of excitement. '*This* is my Plan B.'

Dora looked across at Jana. 'Is she here?' she asked. 'Is Quil here somewhere? Because if I'm right, if this is my Plan B, she's got to be here. She's been here all along, hasn't she? This bubble is a rescue attempt, isn't it! She was going to be thrown back in time by the bomb and we intervened to stop it. That's what the bubble is.'

Jana and Kairos exchanged another glance, then Jana turned to Dora and nodded.

'Yes,' she said reluctantly. 'We recruited – will recruit – the professor, rescued Quil from interrogation, and created this safe environment for our younger selves to operate from.'

Dora clapped her hands in glee. 'I knew it. Damn, I'm good,' she said, beaming, as she folded her arms. 'So, bring her out, let's talk to the psycho, get this mess sorted.'

Kaz was just as concerned by the current, enthusiastic Dora as he had been about the morose one. She seemed to have swung from way too sad to way too happy, way too quickly. He would have to keep an eye on her, because he was worried she'd get herself, or all of them, into trouble.

Jana pursed her lips and shook her head. 'Sorry Dora, we can't do that quite yet,' she said. 'The prof here insists that before we speak to Quil, we need to travel back and make this place happen.'

Kairos interrupted. 'Otherwise this bubble would become a logical impossibility, you see, and it might collapse,' he said.

Dora rolled her eyes and huffed.

'Really?' said Kaz, still not entirely trusting Jana and Kairos. 'Can't we talk to her now and tidy up loose ends later?'

'Far too dangerous,' said the professor emphatically. 'You must create the loop before you close it.'

Kaz studied Kairos, uncertain whether he was being completely truthful. Jana's eyes were pleading with Kaz to just go along with things, but he decided he'd had enough of working in the dark.

'Listen, all of you,' he said. 'I'm here, OK? I'm in. I'm part of this and I promise you I'll see it through to the end. But I've had enough of lies and half-truths and I can tell there's information you're not sharing with us.'

'Kaz,' said Jana. 'Please, trust me. We need to do what Kairos says.'

She looked sincere, desperate for him to agree. He knew she wouldn't withhold anything that could harm him or Dora, he trusted her that much. But that wasn't enough. He was no longer prepared to let anybody else, especially Jana, decide what he could and couldn't know.

'No,' he said, shaking his head. 'If Quil is here, we all need to talk to her before we do another thing. There's something you're not telling us, and I won't help until I know what it is.'

'But—' began Kairos.

'And that's final,' said Kaz.

Jana looked at the tabletop for a minute, then looked up at Kaz, resigned. 'All right,' she said. 'If you insist.'

So saying, she rose to her feet and walked out of the room, heading for the stairs.

Kairos laughed nervously as Kaz scowled at him.

'I told you we needed a Plan B, didn't I Kaz?' said Dora breathlessly. 'This is a great plan, don't you think?'

All trace of the reserved facade she had worn ever since she'd rescued him and Jana in New York was gone. It was almost as if, having decided to try to be more like her old self, she was trying too hard and tipping into mania.

'I'll let you know when this is over,' said Kaz.

They sat in silence for a few moments more, although Dora paced to and fro restlessly. Eventually the stairwell door opened and Jana walked back to the conference room. Walking beside her was a woman Kaz immediately recognised, by her body language, as Quil. It took a little longer for her face to become visible, her dark skin hiding the detail in the half-light until she was in the doorway of the conference room.

'Hello, everybody,' said Quil with a hint of timidity. 'Dora.'

She nodded at Dora, who stood ready to fight.

'I . . .' Kaz said, mouth agape, unsure what to say. 'What I mean is . . .' He breathed out heavily and shook his head. 'No, I've got nothing.'

'Kaz, Dora,' said Jana in a measured voice. 'I'd like you to meet my clone. She calls herself Quil.'

Kaz was glad he was sitting down; he could feel his knees weaken beneath the table. His mind had gone completely blank.

'Guys,' said Jana, moving to sit down, followed by her older mirror image. 'Quil and I really, really need your help.'

Kaz sat staring at Quil in amazement. She was Jana, but ten or fifteen years older. Much younger than he had expected Quil to be – he'd imagined a woman in her forties, not her early thirties. There were subtle lines by her eyes and mouth; it was not an old face, but it was definitely older than Jana's, harder in the jaw, more tense around the eyes.

'Your clone?' said Dora, still standing.

'I am, yes,' said Quil. 'Jana never returned – will never return, from your perspective – to New York after the day she jumped from the roof. I was custom built, commissioned by our parents as a replacement for the daughter they lost. Force-grown to the same age, given all the memories they had stored from her chip. It was going to be a seamless transition. No one would ever know. Not even me. But things . . .' She took a deep breath and sighed, closing her eyes. 'Things did not go smoothly.'

Kaz literally shook his head to help clear away the confusion and return himself to some semblance of sense. He looked up at Dora, who looked down at him, wide-eyed. He couldn't tell whether she was going to kill Quil or burst into tears. Possibly, she was still deciding.

'OK,' he said after gathering his thoughts. The implications of this revelation raced around his mind like a tangled line of toppling dominoes. 'This changes everything. It explains a lot of things. But it makes other things way too confusing to wrap my head around.'

'Actually, it is quite . . .' Kairos trailed into silence under the force of Kaz's hard stare.

Kaz looked into Jana's eyes. His Jana, not the freaky carbon copy sitting beside her, held his gaze. She had never looked so vulnerable, so dependent upon him. He guessed that she had wanted to keep Quil's identity a secret not because it was dangerous to the timeline, or for any of the other reasons Kairos would have offered. He thought it was because it struck too close to home, that it made her the crux of events in a way that she had never wanted. Her eyes sought re-assurance from Kaz. Tell me I'm the important one, they seemed to beg him. Tell me I'm not a supporting character in someone else's story.

'So here's what I need,' said Kaz after smiling at Jana in the most reassuring manner he could, then turning to Quil. 'I need you to tell us everything. Your whole life, from . . .' he was going to say birth but stumbled on the thought of her emerging from a vat in a lab somewhere. 'From start to now. All of it. No secrets, full disclosure. If we're going to save you from becoming the woman we encountered in the past, we need to know who we're helping, and why.'

'We'd be helping Jana, Kaz,' said Dora. 'She's Jana. That's what a clone is, a copy. Whatever she's done, it's exactly what Jana would have done in the same circumstances.'

'That's not necessarily true,' she said. 'There are some fundamental differences between Quil and me.'

'Such as?' asked Dora.

Jana flashed Kaz a 'help me' look that he did not at first understand. Then he remembered Quil's husband and his face must have registered his surprise and confusion because Jana rolled her eyes, a brief moment of her old sarcastic manner breaking through her uncertainty.

'We have been comparing our memories. They are not consistent,' said Quil.

'How's that possible?' asked Kaz.

Quil looked to Jana as if asking an unspoken question. Jana nodded.

'We think it would be best if we showed you,' said Jana. 'Quil has offered to take us with her on a kind of sightseeing tour.'

'Call it my life in ten time jumps,' said Quil, smiling. Kaz was taken aback to realise this was the first time he had ever seen Quil's smile. It was more feral than Jana's, but it seemed honest enough.

'First Jana will take us through her youth – there are some

things she feels I should see,' continued Quil. 'Then I will pick up the tale and show you what happened to me between 2141 and today.'

'We think that when we return here, we will all have a clear understanding of what's happening, and maybe, please God, some idea about how to fix it all,' added Jana.

Kaz considered. 'What do you think, Dora?' he asked.

'Count me in,' she said, her voice low with menace. 'But Quil, if you try anything underhand I will kill you without hesitation. What you did, what you will do, might do, to my family demands punishment. So do not test me.'

Quil nodded. 'Understood,' she said. 'And Dora, I am sorry about shooting you. I was not entirely in my right mind at the time. You will understand once you know my story and I hope you will be able to forgive me, both for what I have done and for the things I might do in some possible future.'

Dora grunted non-committally, then nodded to Kaz.

'But listen,' said Kairos urgently. 'No matter what you discover, you must go back in time and set up this place, recruit me, rescue Quil – if you don't, the consequences could be—'

'Yeah yeah, we know,' said Kaz, rising from his seat. 'OK, how do we do this?'

Quil and Jana stood too and walked round the table to Kaz and Dora.

'If we all join hands,' said Jana, 'I think I'll be able to steer us to the first stop.'

'I'll just wait here shall I?' said Kairos, still seated. Everybody ignored him as they linked fingers and the quartet formed a ring of red fire and stepped out of time.

Kairos didn't even have time to sip his tea before they popped back into existence exactly where they'd left. They looked tired and drawn. Their clothes were different and Quil staggered once she'd solidified and had to be held up by Jana, who helped her to a chair.

'Right Professor,' said Dora, stern-faced and visibly angry. 'Tell me what we have to do to get this place set up. We've got work to do.'

Paris, France,
21 January 2158 –
81 days to timebomb impact

Henry flexed the fingers of his new right hand, amazed at how they felt. Supple and sensitive, they were completely of a piece with his arm. If the hand hadn't been missing a couple of scars and a few wrinkles, he'd never have known it wasn't the original.

He reached for his wife and took her hand in his. It felt good there.

Paris was like a dream to him. Until Quil had brought him here, 2014 was the furthest forward he had travelled. That was miraculous enough, but the Paris of 2158 would have driven him insane had he not had time to adjust to 2014 first. Everything was so alien to him. Vehicles that flew, buildings that grew, implausibly tall people who Quil told him came from another world. It was dizzying and wonderful and he never wanted this holiday to end.

It was not completely flawless, though. His wife was different here. There was a tension in her that confused him. On the surface she was enjoying herself, and he could tell not all of it was for show. Freed from the endless preparations for the attack, she showed signs of a lightness that reminded him of the woman he had first met in 1640. As their time together had passed, and her responsibilities had weighed more heavily upon her, she had lost some of the frivolous capacity for fun that seemed to have returned, briefly, during their sojourn here.

But there was anger too, hidden but unshakeable, that he had not known in her before. Being in this place, amongst these people at this time, fostered a cold, hard nub of hatred deep within her. This was only a few months away from the intended date of her attack. This was the world, and these were the people who would feel her vengeance.

Despite this, and he suspected for his sake, she had thrown herself into enjoying the Expo. He had experienced zero gravity for the first time, and while he had clumsily crashed into everything and everyone he could, he had wondered at how comfortable she was when weightless – balletic and graceful, controlled and precise, she was like a fish in water.

They had immersed themselves in simulated environments, exploring asteroids and planets far out in space, unable to discern any detail that hinted at the unreality of it. He would take the beauty of Pluto's icy mountains to his grave.

They had enjoyed music, theatre and dance so far removed from that which he had known as a child that he would not have known them as these things had he not been told. He would only have known that they were beautiful and they stirred his soul to joy.

They ate fine foods, drank fine wines, stayed in the finest suite of the finest hotel in town and lived like royalty for two weeks.

And then, in an instant, it was over.

'I am bored with my mask,' said Quil, out of the blue, as they walked hand in hand along the Seine by Notre Dame. With a flick of her wrist she switched off her chameleon shroud, and the face she had been wearing vanished, her true face revealed.

'What are you doing?' asked Henry, suddenly panicked, looking around and seeing two surveillance cameras covering the place where they stood. 'I thought you were afraid to be recognised? We're on camera!'

'Oh come here, you lunk,' said Quil, pulling him into a passionate kiss to which he wholly surrendered – kissing her shroud-face had always felt oddly like being unfaithful. When they separated, she took his arm and firmly led him on with their walk.

'It is only a short distance to the hotel,' she said. 'We shall collect our things and pop back to 2014 to make our final preparations.'

Henry's mind was racing to keep up. This lightning change in her demeanour was startling. Could their interlude be over so suddenly?

'Why have you removed your mask?' he said again.

Quil sighed, playing the coquette. 'You see, darling, when I was being interrogated by that awful little man I told you about . . .'

'In my house in the future, I remember,' said Henry.

'Well, he showed me some pictures,' she said. 'Pictures of me in Paris with a mysterious, tall, dark stranger. At first I thought they were fakes, but then I realised they must be photos of my personal future. So here we are. Closing the circle. Posing for the cameras. Call it a statement of intent.'

Henry walked alongside his wife, struggling to process this sudden and unexpected development.

'So you knew we were going to come here?' he asked, unsure whether to be amused or surprised, so completely was his understanding of events being rewritten.

'Uh huh,' agreed Quil.

'Since . . .?'

Quil gave him her biggest smile. 'Since the day I arrived at Sweetclover Hall, all deep-fried and broken, and saw your face. It was destiny, hot stuff.'

Henry felt a cold chill wash over him and a sudden twinge of the fear he had felt in Beirut. She had known so much more than him at every step of their relationship. She had known from the start that they would become lovers, that they would travel to this time and place – more, that they *had* to travel here to keep time on track.

Every certainty that he relied upon was suddenly called into question. Did she really love him, or was he just a means to an end? Had their entire marriage been one long manipulation designed to bring him to this moment? Once they returned to 2014 would he be . . . disposable? Worst of all – she had always sworn that she had not used the mind-writer on him, but could he now trust this? Were his own feelings for her manufactured by machine? Never mind whether he could still trust her love for him, could he trust his love for her?

One simple admission was all it had taken to make him question the very core of his life. His paranoia threatened to run away with him. He forced himself to be logical, keeping step with his suddenly suspect wife as they strolled by the Seine, making a show for the cameras. But logic was no help.

His heart told him that she could not have faked her love. His heart told him that no machine could have conjured his passion from the air.

But logic told him that she could, and that he could not trust his own mind. All the time he had known her, the one defining characteristic of Quil had been her single-minded determination to return to her own time at the head of an army. Anything that stood in the way of that was swept aside. Anything that could aid her cause was ruthlessly pursued. He had thought himself her ally and equal. Now he had to wonder whether he was really only a pawn.

Logic had failed him, so he concentrated on the one thing that had carried him this far.

The feel of her hand in his, of their fingers intertwined, the certainty, calm and happiness it gave him. In the face of such strength of feeling, all logic crumbled.

And if a tiny voice at the back of his mind reminded him that he might not have been in control of his own thoughts, that his free will might have been an illusion, he ignored it.

Kielce, Poland, 2 December 2013 – 145 years to timebomb impact

Dora wasn't talking. She sat at the cafe table staring out at the street, nursing her coffee without a word. Kaz had tried to winkle an explanation out of her. All she would say was that James was fine but he would not, as she had hoped, be joining them on their mission to rescue Quil from Sweetclover Hall and create the quantum bubble. Dora had only been in her parents' bakery for five minutes, but it was clear that whatever happened in there had shaken her deeply. He wasn't sure whether she was distracted by it, or whether it had hardened her resolve. He tried to match her eyeline – was she keeping watch with extra focus, or just staring into space?

He exchanged a glance with Jana who shrugged; she had no idea either. The smell of fresh coffee and pastries swirled around the trio as Kaz dipped a croissant in his coffee and bit off the soggy end.

The two women who worked here had been surprised to find three young people waiting patiently for them to open. At this time of year, when the ice was thick and the mornings dark, early birds were few and far between. One of the women – Kaz couldn't remember her name – had stared at him quite openly, confused and trying to place his face. He had caught her a couple of times since, stealing glances at him, puzzled. He smiled back and she looked away, embarrassed. Had he changed so much in just over a year?

He checked the clock on the wall.

'Any minute now,' he said.

He looked out across the street to the apartment block opposite. Unlike the tall, solid concrete monoliths that ringed the old city centre, this was a refurbished pre-war building, clean and bright. The lights in a few apartments had come on while they had been watching, as people pulled themselves out of bed and prepared for work. The window of Zbigniew and Kaz's apartment remained dark, however. Kaz remembered sneaking around, using the light from his mobile to illuminate his way to the door, carrying his backpack over one shoulder, holding his new boots in his free hand, walking on stockinged feet lest he wake his father. At the time he had thought he was being stealthy, but now he knew that Zbigniew, far from being asleep and oblivious, was probably sitting in his room listening to his son steal away, knowing that he had to let him go.

The double doors at the front of the building cracked open and Kaz saw a hunched figure exit into the cold, pull a backpack over his other shoulder so it was seated properly, and then take off walking confidently towards the railway station. His younger self did not look back at the home he was leaving, did not spare his father a second thought.

Kaz remembered feeling only relief and excitement as he made his break with the past and set out on what he was determined would be a new life lived on his own terms. Now he felt angry with his younger self's uncaring selfishness.

'You want me to go warn him?' asked Jana, as if reading his mind.

Kaz shook his head. 'He wouldn't listen,' he said, watching himself being swallowed by the gloom. He looked up and saw the lights come on in his apartment. So his father *had* been waiting for him to leave.

He felt a hollow ache at the thought.

'I think you're up,' said Jana.

Kaz nodded, drained his coffee and rose from the table.

'Good luck,' said Jana as he walked to the cafe door. Dora remained silent, still staring.

The bitter air was a sharp contrast to the steamy warmth of the cafe, and Kaz pulled his coat tight around him as he picked his way across the street, careful not to slip on the ice. He paused when he reached the blue door to the apartment block. He remembered thinking that he would never set foot in this place again – in fact he was thinking this even now, half a mile down the road. How strange that he should be walking back through the door both five minutes and thirteen months later.

He had purposefully left his key behind on the dining-room table as a statement of intent, so he had to press the button to buzz his apartment. The door clicked open without a challenge, and Kaz climbed the stairs to the third floor where the apartment door was open a crack.

Taking a deep breath, he pushed through and stepped into his old life.

His father was sitting at the table, staring at the front door key. He did not acknowledge Kaz.

Kaz closed the door gently behind him, then walked over and took a seat beside Zbigniew. They sat silently for some minutes, Kaz waiting for his father to speak first, his father just staring at the key.

'I tried so hard,' he said eventually, looking up at Kaz, who was startled to see tears in his father's eyes. 'I'm sorry.'

Kaz didn't know how to respond. He had never seen his father show a moment's weakness in his whole life. Even when his wife was killed (or was lost, or whatever had happened to her), Zbigniew had been stoic and controlled. He was not a man for emotion unless it was anger, and those times when it burst free were few and short-lived. Practical, undemonstrative, even cold on occasion, he was not a man who cried.

So taken aback was Kaz that he couldn't bring himself to reach out a comforting hand, let alone attempt a hug. He felt sorry for him, but he did not think his pity would be welcomed. More than anything, Kaz felt embarrassed for his father, aware that he would later feel ashamed by this show of weakness.

'It's OK,' he said. 'I'll make some coffee.'

Leaving his father to compose his thoughts, Kaz calmed himself by mechanically filling the moka pot and putting it on the stove, a task he'd performed for his father countless times before. He boiled the milk, frothed it, layered it on top of the coffee to make a leaf pattern and laid it before his father, who was now sitting watching him, dry-eyed.

'Thank you,' said Zbigniew quietly.

He took a few sips and then, seeming to take strength from the drink, he looked up at Kaz, who could see his father was more himself, his brief moment of vulnerability quickly banished.

Kaz had been fixated on returning here and making it right with his father for so long, but now he was here, he couldn't think of what to say.

'I – my younger self – owes some money,' said Kaz, nervously. 'To Jacek's mob.'

His father rolled his eyes and scoffed. 'Idiot,' he muttered.

313

Kaz pulled an envelope of money from inside his jacket and pushed it across the table to his father.

'That will cover it,' he said.

Zbigniew left the money where it was, not rejecting it, but not accepting it either.

'Your mother?' he asked, staring into his coffee.

'No,' said Kaz.

Zbigniew grunted and sipped his coffee.

This is intolerable, thought Kaz. And so, falling back on the tried and trusted techniques he had seen his mother deploy over and over again, he decided to give his father a task to perform; he was always happy when he had something to do.

'Dad,' said Kaz. 'I think I need your help. As a soldier.'

Zbigniew looked up at Kaz then, and Kaz fancied he saw a glimmer of life return to the cold eyes of his broken dad.

'Tell me,' he said.

Cornwall, England, 7 April 2158, 7:45 A.M. – 36 mins to timebomb impact

The sky was clear but there was no moon, so the night was cold and dark, which suited Kaz. Dawn was a couple of hours away, so even the birds were silent.

Kaz lay on his stomach on the damp grass and looked down at Sweetclover Hall. Strange to think that the stately house was now over 500 years old; it had still been in its thirties when he'd first set foot inside. It wore its age well. The stone had weathered, there was more ivy clinging to the walls, the clock tower was no longer there and the garden was lively and well kept, but aside from that it was recognisably Dora's old place of employment. There were, however, a thousand new security measures – motion sensors, pressure traps, guards, dogs, fences, drones – not to mention the sub-terranean extensions and all the work done inside to turn this house into a fortress.

Even given that they could materialise inside the house, thus bypassing all the external security, this was still going to be a dangerous and challenging infiltration.

'Everybody ready?' asked Dora.

'Yes,' said Kaz.

'Yup,' said Jana.

'Against my better judgement,' said Professor Kairos.

'And mine,' said Zbigniew.

'Remember the plan,' said Dora, calmly. 'If we all remember our parts and stick to what we rehearsed, this should go smoothly.'

Dora could draw the original floor plan from memory, but none of them had any idea how much of the original layout remained inside the building's shell. It was possible it had been completely gutted and rebuilt from within.

Quil had given them as much information as she could about the room she had been held in and its relative position, but if they tried to arrive in the main body of the house they would essentially be going in blind. The solution Dora had suggested was simple – they would arrive in the area they knew best, the basement beneath the undercroft. They would then have to work their way up to rescue Quil as quickly and quietly as possible.

They knew that during the first attempt their timetable had slipped and they had only managed to activate the quantum bubble at the last possible second. Despite Kaz's protestations that this was impossible to change – hadn't everything they'd been through proved that to her yet? – Dora was intent on trying to secure a better outcome than the one that had left the frozen timebomb hanging ominously over their heads.

Kaz was not happy about this at all, but he had been overruled.

'All right,' said Dora. 'Check your shrouds.'

Unlike their infiltration of the UN building in Beirut, when

Kaz and Jana had sheltered within the dampening field of Dora's shroud in order to hide themselves from cameras and surveillance devices, this mission required each of them to carry their own device. One by one the team stated their devices were working.

'Weapons check,' said Zbigniew.

Everyone except Kairos checked their guns' power packs and switched off the safeties. Kaz noticed that Dora did not need to check her weapons – she always kept her swords sharp.

'Professor, is the device ready?' asked Jana.

Kairos tapped his rucksack and nodded. Creating the quantum generator had taken him three years of highly focused research and development, all funded by Dora's financial sleight of hand. He looked pale as a ghost, but Kaz knew him well enough by now to know that he was probably more nervous about using the device in the field for the first time than infiltrating a secret government torture camp. For him, getting shot would be bad, but failing in his scientific endeavours would be mortifying.

'Let's go then,' said Dora, holding out both hands. Kaz and the others stepped forward and all five of them joined hands in a circle, which crackled and sparked as the time energy within them flowed from person to person.

'I stepped into a burning ring of fire,' sang Kaz, as Dora took control and steered them forward in time a minute, aiming for the filing cupboard at the very bottom of Sweetclover Hall's new subterranean extension.

They arrived safely in the little room and immediately had to shuffle and squeeze to accommodate everyone.

'Whose idea was this again?' muttered Jana as she removed Kairos's elbow from her face.

Unlike last time, they were prepared for the door to be locked – Kaz had brought a copy of the key with him. Within moments they had spilled out into the corridor. It was dark and cold, with the faint smell of damp and a number of other doors leading off into rooms that didn't interest them. At the far end was the metal staircase that led up three levels to the original undercroft. There was nobody around, so their initial objective had been achieved – they were in and undetected.

Dora led the way, sword drawn, with Kaz behind her, Kairos in the middle, then Jana and Zbigniew bringing up the rear. The metal stairs were noisy, so they were all wearing linen-swathed slippers to ensure they made as little noise as possible. Nonetheless, Dora went first, ascending to the first landing and checking for guards or staff down the corridor that led off it. She could be totally silent, so it made sense for her to take point. Happy that there was no one around, she signalled for the others to follow her. Kaz indicated for the others to follow as he proceeded up the stairs. Kairos might as well have been a herd of rhinos. How anybody could manage to make so much sound in linen-swathed slippers was beyond Kaz, but there was nothing to be done.

Zbigniew remained at the bottom, keeping an eye on the lower corridor.

When everyone had assembled on the landing, Dora moved up to the next one. When she signalled the all-clear, Kaz, Jana and Kairos moved up to join her and Zbigniew ascended to the first landing, still covering the rear.

This was also clear, so the progression was repeated. On the next landing, Dora again signalled the all-clear, but when Kaz joined her he heard the unmistakeable sound of someone crying.

It was a man, and the crying was pitiful. Kaz held up her

hand to halt his friends' ascent and crept down the corridor to establish where it was coming from, despite Dora's whispered insistence that he should leave it.

He drew level with the farthest door and listened closely.

Someone was being beaten in there. He could hear the fists and feet landing, and the helpless crying of the victim, but the torturer wasn't saying a word. He listened long enough to establish that it was unlikely the man's ordeal would be ending soon, and crept back to the stairs and ushered everyone up to join him and Dora.

When Jana joined them on the landing she heard the crying immediately and looked at Dora quizzically.

'None of our business,' whispered Dora, beginning her climb to the next landing.

Kaz looked at Jana. He shrugged. She shrugged. Then together they turned and walked down the corridor towards the room where the man was being tortured.

They both drew their weapons and Kaz was about to knock on the door when Dora appeared at his shoulder.

'We can save him after we've set up the bubble,' hissed Dora. 'He'll be in inside it anyway.'

'He could be dead by then,' spat Kaz in response.

Dora rolled her eyes, as if she couldn't believe they were arguing about this. 'This is exactly what we said we wouldn't do,' she said in her normal voice as she walked past them impatiently. Before Kaz could react, she kicked open the door, sliced a startled heavyset man's right arm off as he turned towards her, and barked 'Stay here, we'll be back for you,' to the quivering bloody mess of a man cowering in the corner.

'Now come on!' growled Dora as she stalked past them back towards the stairs.

Kaz shared another glance with Jana, gave another shrug and ran after Dora.

They all now hurried up the stairs, all pretence of stealth abandoned until they reached the swing doors that opened into the undercroft. Dora slipped through them and returned a moment later, indicating that the undercroft was all clear.

Kaz followed close behind Dora as she led them up one more flight, to the first floor where they knew Quil was being kept. They had lost precious seconds dealing with the prisoner, but Kaz was confident they were still within their timeframe. Ahead of him, Dora took a deep breath and cracked the door open ever so slightly. Kaz could hear no noise beyond her.

The corridor was deserted.

This was actually going to work.

Dora pushed through into the corridor, sword drawn, and Kaz followed behind her.

He heard the door click shut behind his father as they walked towards the room Quil was being held in.

He also heard the door lock once it was closed.

He spun and looked back in alarm to see an inner metal door slide down across it, barring their exit.

'They know we're here,' he said.

The room Quil was being held in was straight ahead of them, and as soon as he had spoken, Dora turned and ran to it. She tried the handle but it was locked, so she knocked.

Site 2A (formerly Sweetclover Hall), 7 April 2158, 8.17 A.M. - 5 mins to timebomb impact

In a small nondescript room on the ground floor of a building that did not officially exist, Quil was being interrogated. In the three days since her capture on Mars, she had been kept in total isolation. She had no idea what had happened after her capture, how the battles in Barrettown and above it had played out.

What they intended to do with her.

Quil had been expecting something more dramatic than this bland sequestering. She had expected to be shipped to the White House and a confrontation with the president, the woman who had commissioned her creation seventeen years previously. But it seemed her 'mother' was not going to give her the satisfaction of a face-to-face confrontation.

After spending two days in solitary, being shunted from ship to ship, she had finally ended up in this room, with this bland interrogator, and she was enjoying stringing him along, trying to prise information from him.

So far she had established that someone within her own

army had betrayed her, and that she had been photographed in Paris some weeks previously with a man she had never met. Since she had never been to Paris, she concluded that these photos had been taken at some point in her personal future, when her ability to travel in time had matured enough for her to control it. With that revelation, her fear evaporated. This idiot inquisitor had shown her proof of her own survival and eventual liberty. There was nothing he could threaten her with now. All she had to do was wait for her chance . . .

'So, let me get this straight,' said the interrogator, leaning back in disbelief. 'You're saying . . . what? That at some point in the future you will travel back in time?'

'Looks that way from where I'm sitting,' said Quil, smugly.

'That is your explanation? Time travel?'

'Hey, don't knock it till you've tried it.'

'But—'

He was interrupted by a frantic knocking. The interrogator leaped out of his seat and hurried to open the door.

Quil could not see who had knocked on the door, but she did see the point of a sword burst from the interrogator's back, hear the sigh as his last breath left him, see the sword retract through his torso, see his body topple sideways, lifeless, to the floor.

For a long, stunned moment she stared into the eyes of the person with the sword who stood in the doorway. And the eyes were all she could see, for above the black clothing was a balaclava with a single slit for the eyes.

Quil rose to her feet. She had not been expecting her fortunes to reverse so quickly, but she wasn't going to protest. 'Who the hell are you, and how the hell do we get out of here?' she asked.

The black-clad figure stepped wordlessly into the room

and then to one side. Four people, all dressed the same as the first, hurried in. One of them bolted the door once they were all inside. Another threw the table over to clear the centre space. Ignoring Quil, four of the newcomers ran to the four corners of the room. Each laid a small grey chip on the floor and then ran back to the centre of the room. All five of them formed a circle around Quil, joining hands to enclose her in a protective ring.

'You know, I think we've done it in plenty of time,' muttered one of them, a woman by her voice.

The charges went off and the floor dropped away beneath them.

They fell a short distance and landed flat inside a dark echoing space. Quil's ears rang with a high-pitched whine, stunned by the force of the explosion.

She heard a faint muffled cry of 'Scatter' from one of her rescuers, and she was dragged away from the wrecked floor. She looked up and saw a square of light above her – the room they had just blown their way out of.

Another of the team yelled something as he crouched in the middle of the recently fallen floor. Quil thought she made out the word 'quantum', but that was all. The team had a piece of apparatus in their hands, a tangle of metal and wires that looked like nothing Quil had ever seen.

The persistent ringing of a distant alarm began to penetrate the whine. She supposed it was coming from the room above, as the people in the facility realised they had been infiltrated.

There was a brilliant flash of light from the centre of the dark space and an image of a massive room, divided into rooms by glass walls, with doors leading off in many directions, seared itself on to her retina before the flash faded to be replaced by a steady glow from the apparatus.

The hands that had dragged her clear of the rubble now spun her, and Quil found herself face to face with one of her rescuers; the one with the sword.

'Who are you?' she shouted.

Her rescuer pulled the balaclava off, and Quil gasped as she realised it was Dora, the maid/assassin/time traveller whose subterfuge had been the catalyst for the disastrous end to the venture on Mars.

Dora held Quil's head firmly between her hands, stared into her eyes and mumbled something that she couldn't quite make out above the sirens and the fading ring of the explosion in her ears.

Then everything went horribly, horribly wrong.

Quil had seen plenty of combat and was accustomed to the sensation of time slowing down, of moments elongating endlessly as the moment of crisis approaches.

But this felt nothing like that.

This felt as if time was literally slowing down. And only for her.

The five rescuers stood frozen like statues as Quil surveyed the scene before her.

The wreckage of the interrogation-room floor lying in a square of light cast from above.

The body of the interrogator, broken and bloodied, sprawled half on the floor of the room he had died in, half on the floor that lay beneath it.

The strange apparatus that glowed, and the bubble of coruscating light that was expanding from it so very slowly, swallowing up the rescuers one by one.

Dora's face, frozen in mid-sentence.

The shadowed outline of the huge subterranean room they now stood in the centre of.

And then a slow, deep rumble from above. Quil looked up and saw, to her complete horror, the ceiling of the interrogation room begin to split apart in a slow billowing cloud of concrete dust. She thought she glimpsed, within the chaos of debris, a shiny metal point, descending towards them. To Quil, in her crazy slowed-down state, it seemed as if a missile was pushing its way through the solid building almost gently.

It was directly above her. In less than a second it would smash into them, obliterating them entirely.

The edge of the bubble of light had reached her. All the others were now ensconced within it.

She turned and moved towards them, entering the light, presuming that it offered some kind of protection, that this apparatus was part of some complex rescue plan and the light represented a shield to protect them from the fate that literally hung over them.

She was halfway into the bubble, the line that marked its limit bisecting her lengthways, when time resumed its normal speed.

Quil staggered through the wall of light as it flew past her, like the surface of a bubble expanding.

Her senses were scrambled and she felt as if she was surrounded by a swirling fog of numbers and symbols, a haze of mathematics and equations.

'Oh no you don't!' cried Dora, and Quil felt a hand grab her arm. She steadied herself, closed her eyes and willed the room to stop spinning. Gradually she felt herself slipping back into sync with her surroundings, planted on the solid floor, anchored by the hand on her arm.

The moment passed, her senses cleared, and Quil remembered where she was and who was holding her in place. She opened her eyes and stepped forward, wrenching her arm free of Dora's grasp and turning to face her rescuers.

The four other people who had burst into her interrogation room and blown their way through the floor into the cellars beneath the building had all removed their balaclava masks and were busying themselves in different ways.

The tall, fat Asian man was fussing over the machine in the centre of the floor, aided by a young dark-skinned man with short hair who was shouting out readings from a tablet device. The two others – a tall white man who carried himself like a soldier and a young woman who had not yet removed her balaclava – were circling the still-expanding perimeter of the bubble, weapons drawn, ready for trouble.

And in front of her stood Dora, but different to how she'd last seen her – now she was confident, haughty, intimidating and heavily armed.

Quil considered her words carefully before opening her mouth.

'Last time we met, you tried to kill me,' she said. 'Today you're trying to rescue me. Why?'

'I told you then and I'm telling you now,' replied Dora. 'I was not trying to kill you. Exactly the opposite, actually.'

'And I told you then and I'm telling you now, I don't believe you.'

Dora shrugged. 'Honestly, I don't care,' she said as she turned her back. 'Is it stable?' she shouted.

'Well . . .' replied the Asian man, seemingly too focused on his work to elaborate further.

The expanding edges of the light-bubble had passed beyond the walls of the chamber now, and the two guys were securing the doors; it was a huge old cellar, so they were going to be some time. The chamber, stone-floored and brick-lined, was broken into rooms by thick glass walls. But the big old room was not the most amazing sight – that was above her head.

Quil stood and looked up at the timebomb, gasping in wonder as it hung, suspended as if in amber, above them all.

'How is this possible?' she whispered.

'I have a pet professor,' said Dora, indicating the older man. 'He's clever with time.'

Quil peered closer, realisation dawning. 'Oh my God, that's Kairos isn't it? Yasunori Kairos.'

Dora nodded. 'The one and only.'

'If you knew how long I've wanted to talk to him,' said Quil, stepping forward. Dora blocked her way.

'Later,' she said. 'Let him work. If the quantum bubble bursts . . .' She pointed upwards at the timebomb.

'Quantum bubble?' said Quil, her brain kicking into high gear as she analysed all she had learned in her long years of temporal experimentation.

Kairos let out a cry of triumph. 'Stable!'

Quil followed Dora over to the ecstatic scientist, who was jigging around the strange machine that pulsed and glowed atop the pile of rubble that had once been the floor of the room above.

Dora patted Kairos's back and smiled. 'I never doubted you for a moment, Professor.'

'I bloody did,' muttered the dark-skinned young man.

Dora scowled playfully at him. 'Kaz,' she said, 'you are too much the pessimist. How's the perimeter? We don't want any surprises.'

'Going as fast as we can,' said the older man.

'There were two of me,' said Quil slowly. 'When you switched the quantum bubble on I was right at the edge of the field.

It kind of cut me in two. I was looking out at myself – one of me in the bubble, one of me outside the bubble. And then the version of me outside vanished.'

Kairos looked across at her, his eyes widening. 'What did you say?' he asked breathlessly.

But Quil never had a chance to repeat herself. A door as yet unsecured, in the far corner of the chamber, burst open and a young woman in army uniform came running into the room, screaming at the top of her lungs and spraying the room with gunfire.

Quil felt an impact, like a punch in her stomach, knocking the wind out of her. She recognised the feeling; it wasn't the first time she'd been shot. She tried to fling herself sideways, to duck and cover. But her legs would not respond. The room spun and she found herself toppling backwards, like a felled tree, powerless to stop herself.

Her head hit the stone floor hard, and she blacked out.

Quantum bubble

Kaz felled the soldier with a single shot.

'Go!' he yelled at Dora, who did not need telling. She leaned over Quil, grabbed her hand and together they vanished in a red flash, heading for Kinshasa two years in the past where a crash team was waiting for them. If all went according to plan, they would be back shortly and Quil would recuperate here in the bubble.

Zbigniew ran to the wounded soldier and knelt beside her, pushing her gun away and assessing her injuries.

'How is she?' asked Kaz, appearing above him.

'Not good,' muttered Zbigniew. The soldier had a hard face but it was full of panic and fear as she gasped for breath, her eyes wide and staring. 'She took it in the chest. I think her lung's collapsed.'

Jana joined them, eased Zbigniew aside and leaned over the dying soldier. 'I'll take care of it,' she said, then she grabbed the woman's hand and together they vanished just as Dora and Quil had done.

Zbigniew leaned back on his haunches and looked up at Kaz, who met his gaze. Kaz wondered what was going through his father's mind.

Was he shocked by the efficiency Kaz had shown?

Was he angry at the ruthlessness?

Was he proud?

Zbigniew broke the gaze, his face a mask unyielding of answers. He rose to his feet. 'Kaz, with me,' he shouted. 'Let's make sure there are no other surprises waiting for us down here.'

'Coming,' said Kaz, removing his balaclava.

Kaz and his father explored all the lower levels of the facility – the original undercroft and the extra floors that had been added beneath it – and found nobody besides the prisoner they had rescued. Kaz whisked him off to Kinshasa as well.

When he returned to the undercroft, Dora had already returned with Quil and a doctor. They were carrying Quil on a stretcher towards the stairs, heading for the room where she would recuperate.

'That took a week,' said Dora as she passed him, shaking her head wearily.

As they disappeared downstairs there was another flash and Jana appeared. She looked straight into Kaz's eyes and shook her head, his face a mask of regret. Kaz felt a hollow ache that he could not name. He did not know how to respond other than with a curt nod of acknowledgment.

The next day Dora jumped away with Kairos to sabotage the bomb in Quil's lair in 1645 so that it was a dud before she even began the countdown.

During their search of the subterranean facility, Kaz and Zbigniew hunted exhaustively for any means of access to the cavern that they knew lay deep beneath them. The lift shaft that Quil had used in 1645 had been filled with concrete and covered in flagstones a long time ago, and there was no evidence anywhere that the people who had expanded the undercroft had any knowledge of the army of genetically altered soldiers that slept below them. It made Kaz nervous to know they were setting up shop directly above an unknown force, but try as he might, he could imagine no way in which they would be a threat.

After a couple of days, they convened in the conference room.

'OK,' said Dora, taking the lead as she had done since the debacle on Mars. 'I think we're done. Quil is safe downstairs. I think it's time for us to jump forward. I can't think of anything we've missed.'

'I stay here, yes?' asked the professor.

Dora nodded. 'Yeah, you're here for the duration. Zbigniew, do you want to come with us or are you heading home?'

'I will return to my home, I think,' said Zbigniew after a moment's thought. He did not meet his son's gaze, and Kaz again found himself frustrated by his father's stoic refusal to let slip any clue to his emotional state.

There was an awkward silence until Kaz realised the others were waiting for him to volunteer to ferry his father home.

'Let me,' he muttered, unable to hide his resentment as he reached out, grasped his father's hand and whisked them both back to Poland in 2014.

They arrived in a patch of parkland in Kielce, hidden from prying eyes by a blizzard.

Kaz let go of his father's hand and stood awkwardly, not knowing what to say. All he wanted to do was jump back to the future, but he felt that he had to say something, anything, before he left.

'OK,' he said eventually. 'I'll just—'

He was taken completely by surprise when his father cut

him off mid-sentence by pulling him into a clumsy embrace. Kaz stood awkwardly for a moment, then returned it.

When Zbigniew let him go and stepped back he simply said, 'Take care, son,' and walked away into the snow.

Kaz waited until his father was lost in the whiteout, then took a deep breath and flung himself forward in time.

Kinshasa, Democratic Republic of Congo, 3 May 2120 - 38 years to timebomb impact

There was something different about her head, Quil decided.

Her body was a mess of anaesthetic, scar tissue and patching; it felt distant from her, as if it was something in another room to which she was only tangentially connected. That's what happened, she supposed, when you were patched up after taking a bullet.

(Why did the soldier's gun use bullets? Would a laser weapon have interfered with the Hall's security grid somehow? She should be grateful, she supposed, because in the time it took for her to take a bullet, she could easily have been sliced in two.)

As she lay in bed, floating gently on a cloud of drugs, she knew that there was something different about her head. Something had changed between before and after. An edge had gone, a fury and a fear. She wondered if perhaps she'd suffered brain damage, some kind of surgical accident, loss of oxygen to the brain. But no, that didn't feel right. It was more subtle than that.

She heard a soft rustling to her left and rolled her head.

There was another bed beside hers, containing a young woman, fast asleep. Quil wondered who she was and why she was here, in the recovery room with her. As she was pondering her room-mate, the young woman turned in bed, so Quil could see . . . her own face. A memory surfaced through her surprise, of a chameleon shroud blurring to reveal the same face, a face that horrified and astounded her. But now, through the haze of drugs, with her intangibly different brain, Quil couldn't place the memory. Was it possible that it was a dream? Clones don't dream, she told herself. But if they did, wouldn't it be like this? Blurry, indistinct but vivid at the same time, surreal and hallucinatory.

She was not even sure the younger version of herself in the opposite bed was real. Was she dreaming now? She couldn't be sure.

With some effort, she propped herself up on the pillows so she could sit upright and look down at her doppelgänger and study her. She was beautiful, she decided, not sure whether she was seeing herself as she truly was, but wanting to believe in the beauty of her younger, more innocent self.

After a few minutes of half-aware reverie, Quil spoke to her room-mate.

'Your breathing has changed,' she said, her voice sounding muffled in her own ears, as if she was hearing herself through a tube or a closed door. 'I can tell you're awake.'

There was no response for at least a minute, but then the prone figure said, 'I am not awake,' in the slurred voice of a drunk.

'The only alternative is that I am a dream,' said Quil, meaning the girl she was talking to. Which of the speakers was she again? Was she the one sitting up or lying down? She didn't feel quite sure.

'Do you feel like a dream?' asked the dream.

Quil considered the question. 'You are Godless,' she told herself. 'You don't dream. So I must be real. I feel solid, but I am floating.'

'Me too,' said her younger dream self, which was stating the obvious because they were the same person. Weren't they?

'They have good drugs here,' said Quil. 'You were stabbed. I was shot.'

She did not know how she knew this. Had she overheard someone talking while she was half awake? It was an odd detail for her to have made up.

'Sucks to be us,' she said, lying down.

'Sucks to be me,' she said, sitting up.

'And me.'

'That's what I said.'

Quil was more confused than ever, trying to pin down her identity through a miasma of anaesthetic and brain fuzz. Was it possible she was just lying in a room talking to herself?

Her imaginary (?) younger self opened her eyes then, and raised herself up on her elbows.

'Do I know you?' she asked.

'Kind of,' replied Quil.

'Are you . . .'

'You?' said Quil. She nodded, which made her head swim. 'Kind of.'

'What do you mean, kind of?' her younger self said, seemingly irritated. 'Actually, forget it. You were right the first time. You're a dream. Hallucination. All you are is very good drugs.'

As the dream girl lay back down and closed her eyes, Quil struggled to understand why she was so annoyed. She knew she was a dream. Hadn't she already said as much? She was dreaming this child. That was all there was to it.

'Keep telling yourself that, kid,' she said to herself. 'Sleep now. But when you wake up, you and I have so much to talk about. So very, very much.'

Glad she had made a note to have a good hard talk with herself, Quil lay back down and surrendered to sleep once again.

As she was drifting off she thought she heard a door open, and someone complaining, demanding to know why Quil had been put in a room with someone else. But that couldn't be right, could it?

There was nobody here but her.

Quantum Bubble

Kaz put his feet up on the conference table and swigged his coffee.

Jana sat next to him, sipping her drink and casting disparaging side-eye at his feet.

'Are we finished?' she asked.

Kaz nodded. 'I think so,' he said. 'We rescued Quil from the government, eliminated the poison that was driving her mad, fixed her up and let her recuperate here. We've all met her now, we know her story, she knows who we are, where we came from, why everything happened the way it did. She doesn't think we're government agents, she knows that the Mars disaster wasn't our fault.'

'So we have changed history?' asked Dora.

'Looks that way,' said Kaz, smiling. 'I can't see any way for her to become the woman who hunted us in 1614, or the woman who arranged Mum's death in 2010.'

'But I remember your mother standing there, unable to move because of what Quil did to her,' said Jana.

'Kairos is vague on the details – nothing new there – but he thinks that when we travel back to any time before this bubble we'll find history altered,' explained Kaz. 'He thinks there's a possibility our memories might be rewritten and we'll never know any of this happened.'

'If Kairos is right, it didn't,' said Dora, who sat opposite them, staring into her tea. 'My mum was never brainwashed. And neither was my brother.'

'You say it like it's a good thing,' said Jana, who sat beside her, munching her way through a bag of plums.

'I think it is,' said Dora firmly. 'He will remain a dangerous zealot but at least he will be himself. He will have control of his own destiny, it will not be stolen from him.'

Kaz didn't think that was much of a victory at all, but he could understand how it might look that way, seen through the prism of Dora's new obsession with free will.

'Where is Kairos?' asked Jana, keen to change the subject.

'He dragged Quil off into his little study downstairs and slammed the door in my face,' said Kaz.

There was a long pause.

'You don't think . . .' said Jana, eyes widening theatrically.

'Euw, no,' said Kaz, laughing.

As if on cue, the undercroft doors swung open to admit Quil and Kairos, who walked towards the conference room with focused intent. When Kaz saw the set of their faces he felt a rush of fear.

No, not again. Not when they were so close . . .

Kairos and Quil entered and took seats next to Jana and Dora. Kairos was pale as a ghost and looked almost as if he were in shock. Everyone was staring at them, wondering why they were so solemn but not wanting to ask. Nobody wanted to break the mood.

'I am afraid we have bad news,' said Quil.

'The . . . the quantum generator . . .' Kairos trailed off

into silence, seemingly unable to complete his thought. He looked across at Quil helplessly.

'The quantum generator malfunctioned when it was switched on,' she said.

'Malfunctioned how?' asked Jana.

'It did not malfunction,' whispered Kairos. 'It just created an unexpected phenomenon.'

'I was caught on the edge of the bubble as it was created,' said Quil slowly. 'You were all inside the initial circumference, remember? I was furthest away from the device.'

'I remember you said there were . . .' Dora also trailed off, and Kaz could see realisation dawning in her eyes.

'What?' he asked, taking his feet down off the table and leaning across it urgently. 'Quil, what did you say?'

'Two of me,' said Quil, meeting his gaze. 'I said there were two of me. For a moment, just a second, when the generator was switched on, I saw a reflection of myself, outside the bubble, looking in at me. But the image vanished as the bubble expanded. I thought it was an illusion. An echo. I don't know what I thought.'

'I spent most of my time the last few weeks playing with calculations, trying to explain the quantum echo, as I called it,' said Kairos, staring at his hands. 'It was a diverting puzzle for me. A weird side-effect of the quantum generator, nothing more.'

'So what has changed?' asked Kaz.

'The mathematics led me to a conclusion,' said Kairos. 'An inescapable truth. I did the calculations over and over, trying to prove myself wrong. But I could not.'

'The Professor tells me he explained Schrödinger's Cat to you,' said Quil. 'Do you remember?'

Kaz, who had been embarrassed by his ignorance first

time round, had made an effort to memorise this to avoid future humiliation. 'Something that exists in a state of quantum uncertainty can be both dead and alive until it is observed by a third party,' he said confidently. He had hoped for an acknowledgment of his cleverness from Jana, but she was staring in horror at Quil and Kairos.

'Not just alive and dead, Kaz,' said Jana, still staring fixedly at Quil. 'But in one of any two states – up and down, left and right, here and not here. It's called a superposition.'

'When I was caught in the quantum field, just for a moment, I existed in that state,' said Quil. 'I was both inside and outside the bubble. During that instant, everybody was looking at Kairos. Nobody was looking at me. And the version of me that was outside the bubble was pulled off into time before the superposition collapsed.'

There was a long silence. Kaz could see that Dora and Jana were devastated but try as he might, he couldn't quite wrap his head around what he was being told.

'Sorry,' he said. 'What are you saying? That . . . that we split you in two somehow and the other version of you is the Quil we met in the past?'

'Oh God,' said Jana, burying her head in her hands. 'We thought we'd finally done it. We thought we'd actually changed history. But we didn't. We just created our own pasts. Again.'

'You're Schrödinger's time traveller,' breathed Kaz.

Dora leaned forward and clasped her hands together, addressing Kaz. 'We tried to alter the course of events, to prevent us arriving at this point. We failed utterly. Our response to that failure has been to take exactly the opposite approach – to dabble in time, creating closed loops and buttressing this timeline. We have manipulated and coerced our past selves into arriving in this moment. I cannot help but feel that we have betrayed ourselves. Made ourselves the kind of puppets to fate that the mad version of Quil believes us all to be. Have we at any point really, truly exercised free will? Because I am not sure that we have. I think we have stolen it from ourselves.'

'Yes,' said Kairos, looking up at last, shamefaced. 'That's certainly one way of looking at it. If time is, as I now suspect, unalterable and fixed, then only people moving forward through time one day after another, or perhaps, moving forward and *only* forward through time in jumps, can truly have agency. Anyone travelling into the past, no matter how much they may perceive their actions to be chosen freely in the heat of the moment, is in fact destined to act in the ways they always did. They make a trap for themselves.'

'Which would mean she is right,' said Dora, 'this other version of Quil who's living in the past. That it doesn't matter how many people she kills, what decisions she makes, no matter how obscene. She has no choice but to act that way.'

'The ultimate get-out-of-jail-free card,' said Jana.

'So does that make her less of a psychopath?' said Kaz. 'This is a pointless discussion. She chooses to behave in a certain way, her actions have consequences.'

'Don't forget the poison,' said Quil, mildly. 'She still has that crap in her system, making her paranoid. Add to that the trauma you say she suffered on her trip back through time – the burning, the pain, the years of convalescence.'

'You're making excuses for her,' said Kaz, unable to mask his disgust.

'I am her,' replied Quil. 'Quite literally.'

Kairos shook his head. 'You are missing the point, Kaz,' he said. 'I do not believe, and apparently neither does the other version of Quil, that she has a choice at all. Her actions are predestined. By surrendering to that you could argue that she is absolved of all responsibility for what she does. From her perspective, and from that of the model of time that we are discussing, she only regains her free will when she returns to the moment she left and resumes her journey into her own future.'

'And the same holds for us,' said Jana. 'Every time we jump into our own past, no matter what we do, we only end up creating the exact events we are there to prevent.'

'Yes,' said Kairos. 'Your whole lives up until this point may in fact have been predetermined by your older selves. In fact, there is nothing to say that we are not still slaves to destiny, being manipulated even now by our older selves for some purpose we cannot imagine yet.'

Nobody replied to this and silence hung there for a minute as they all absorbed the implications of Kairos's theories.

'So we make a deal,' said Dora. 'Here and now, we all swear that, no matter what, we will never, ever try to influence past events again. From this moment we only travel forward.'

Everyone at the table nodded their agreement.

'You're forgetting Steve,' said Kaz, looking at Dora.

'Who?' asked Kairos.

'Someone from our future,' explained Kaz. 'They wore a disguise, refused to tell us who they were. They intervened after we first met, rescued us from Quil and Sweetclover in 2014.'

'I'm not forgetting,' said Dora.

'But you rescued him or her from 2014,' said Kaz. 'Brought them to Kinshasa, got the doctors there to fix them up and then let them leave. And you've not told us who he or she was. Is it one of us, breaking the promise we just made? Is it you?'

Dora bit her lip. 'It's not me, I promise. I can't tell you who it is. They told me some elements of the future. Only some. But I can't tell you who they are. Not yet.'

Jana hit the table hard in frustration. 'So we're still stuck,' she shouted. 'We're still being toyed with by someone from the future, possibly one of us. We're still time's playthings.'

'I promise,' said Kaz, 'that if it turns out to be me, I will give myself a big slap the moment I realise. Promise.'

Jana laughed at this, and most of the group cracked grins. The tension eased slightly.

'I wish you'd tell us, Dora,' said Quil softly.

Dora shook her head. 'Sorry. I swore an oath.'

'So it's not going to be as simple as just promising to go forward only,' said Jana, her frustration plain on her face. 'There are more loops to close.'

Dora nodded. 'A few, yes,' she said.

'So,' said Kaz.

'So,' said Jana.

They all turned to Quil.

'So,' she said. 'We have to work out what we do now.'

'Quil – the other Quil – has no idea the bubble exists,' said Kaz. 'She doesn't know we're waiting for her. As far as she's concerned she's coming here to wake up her army and finish the war. So why don't we just sit here and wait for your evil twin to arrive?'

'Because when she does, you will see two of me for a millionth of a second, and then the superposition will collapse,' said Quil, rolling her eyes to show just how stupid she thought the question was. 'One of us of us will wink out of existence. I'd prefer not to take the chance that it will be me.'

'Yeah, but it might not be,' said Kaz. 'It's a fifty-fifty shot. And if she vanishes, problem solved. You've been purged of the poison that made you go nuts, you know we're not your enemies. If the superposition collapses and cancels her out, leaving you, it's all sorted. We switch off the quantum bubble, you go back to your war, we go back to wherever and whenever we want to be. End of story.'

'But what about Steve?' said Jana. 'Don't you think his interference implies that it's not that simple? I think it means that there is still some issue left to resolve.'

'Which makes you think that I'm going to go "poof" when my other half arrives,' said Quil solemnly.

Dora nodded. 'I think so,' she said. 'We have to assume that when mad Quil arrives here, friendly Quil will vanish. And we'll be back to dealing with a psychopath who wants to kill us.'

There was a solemn silence as they digested that fact.

'We need to get you out of here,' said Kaz curtly. 'Am I right, Professor, to think that if they cannot be seen together by anybody, the superposition will not collapse?'

Kairos shrugged despondently. 'I think so,' he said, 'but who knows?'

'So if we make sure you and she never meet, then you both continue to exist,' said Jana with hope in her voice.

'It's worth a try,' said Quil. 'But . . .'

'But what?' said Jana.

'But you'll still be at risk from her,' said Quil.

'Um,' said Kaz nervously as he noticed that Quil was starting to glow red. 'Guys!'

Quil looked down at herself and stood up from her chair in alarm.

'What's happening?' asked Dora.

'I think we talked too much,' said Kaz, drawing his gun and pointing it at Quil.

'Hey!' yelled Jana indignantly.

'No, he's right,' shouted Quil as the glow around her intensified. 'I could—'

She never finished her sentence. Everyone winced and covered their eyes as Quil was engulfed in a blinding penumbra of red light. As Sweetclover appeared beside her, the woman they had been speaking to seemed to shimmer and burn, writhing and screaming as the superposition that had split her in two collapsed, the quantum state resolved itself and the universe chose which Quil would remain.

Sweetclover solidified and immediately backed away from the pillar of fire that was his wife. Violent winds whipped around her as if she was the eye of her own personal tornado, and there was a sound that mingled with her screams, a sort of tearing, rending noise as if reality itself were being shredded.

'What have you done?' screamed Sweetclover, holding his hands up over his eyes and falling to his knees. 'What have you done to her?'

The wind whipped faster, the noise increased, the fire burned brighter until there was a loud explosion and a flash of sun-bright white. Then silence and stillness and the slow returning of their vision as their eyes readjusted to the comparative gloom of the undercroft.

Dora was quick off the mark. She leaped forward and grabbed Sweetclover by the scruff of the neck, dragging him away from Quil. She knelt beside him and held a sword to his throat.

Kaz and Jana both had guns trained on the blank spot in their vision where the light had blinded them, waiting for their eyesight to recover. Which version of Quil would be standing before them? And what should they do if it was the wrong one?

Quil had fallen to the floor after the explosion and now she slowly rose to her feet. She was smoking and glowing, like metal fresh from the furnace. Her clothes had burned away, but her flesh was unharmed, so she stood naked. It was impossible to tell which version had been extinguished and which now stood before them. 'That . . . hurt . . .' she said as her eyes rolled back in her head and she collapsed to the floor again, unconscious.

Henry Sweetclover was frantic.

'What have you done?' he cried over and over. Anger, horror and sadness mixed in together as he looked at her body lying motionless. 'What have you done?'

'Calm down, Henry,' said a voice close to his ear. Dora. 'We didn't *do* anything.'

Henry didn't – couldn't – believe her. He and Quil had walked into some kind of trap and they'd killed her. If there was a tiny measure of relief inside his grief, he did not acknowledge it to himself as he wept.

'She's alive,' he heard Kaz say. 'Too hot to touch, but her chest is moving, she's definitely breathing.'

Henry exhaled and groaned in relief.

'Which one is she?' asked another voice urgently. Jana.

'Can't tell,' replied Kaz. 'She looks the same, I think.'

'Not burned?' asked Jana.

'No,' replied Kaz, who was swimming into focus.

Suddenly Jana's face was right in front of his, and Henry's disorientation momentarily increased as he was confronted by an angry younger version of his wife.

'Did she have her face fixed?' demanded Jana.

'What?' mumbled Henry.

'Your wife, did she have her burns sorted out,' shouted Jana. 'Plastic surgery, you know?'

'Uh, yes,' he replied, stammering. 'Yes, yes she did.'

Jana turned away from him. 'So it could be either of them,' she said.

'Or an amalgam of the two, perhaps,' offered a tall older man who was nervously shifting from one foot to another at the end of what Henry could now see was a huge table.

'What?' said Jana, angrily.

'I don't know,' the tall man protested in a whine. 'This is all uncharted territory.'

'We should make her comfortable,' said Dora, still close in by Henry's ear, although the sword had been removed. 'Get her downstairs into a bed. Keep her safe, but guard her. In case.'

'Where are we?' asked Henry, blinking up at the brick ceiling, feeling as if he should know the answer to his question.

Kaz reached down, grabbed Henry by his lapels and hauled him to his feet, bringing their faces close together and saying, through gritted teeth, 'You're home, you bastard.'

Henry gasped as the room swam into focus. Beyond the tables and chairs was a glass wall through which he could clearly see the undercroft of Sweetclover Hall.

'My God, what's that?' he asked as he saw a huge ball of flame hanging, frozen, above the centre of the room.

'Where were you going?' asked Kaz.

Henry forced his attention back to Kaz, who was still holding him tight by the lapels of his jacket.

'2158,' he said. 'Ten minutes after the timebomb detonated.'

'That explains that,' said Jana.

Henry didn't think it explained anything. 'Does it?' he asked.

'Anyone trying to travel to any point in time that lies past

347

this moment gets pulled in here,' said Dora. 'It's not a trap. Not exactly.'

She laid her hands on Kaz's as she spoke, gently getting him to release Henry. He did so, and stepped back, but the aggressive sneer remained on his face.

Henry looked around the cellar of his home. 'I hoped I'd seen this place for the last time,' he said. 'I was expecting to arrive on the ridge, looking down into a smoking crater where my house had been.'

Jana and the older man were carrying his wife out through the glass door. He wanted to run to her, but he glanced at Dora first, tacitly asking permission – he did not want to feel her blade again.

Dora nodded and Henry ran to his wife. As he took the place of Jana, holding his wife by the shoulders, there was a loud bang and a flash of light from the centre of the undercroft. The man holding Quil's feet looked up in panic and shouted to Henry to put Quil down.

Henry did so, confused and angry, as the man ran to a piece of mechanical apparatus that sat in the middle of the undercroft floor. It was fizzing and sparking.

'Oh no, oh no!' cried the man, as he leaned over the device and pressed buttons.

Dora, Kaz and Jana came running out and joined him.

'What's the matter, Prof?' said Jana.

'The bubble, it's destabilising,' babbled the man. 'The collapse of the superposition has thrown all the readings off, blown something in the machine. I don't think it can hold. We have to get out of here. NOW! Or we'll all be vaporised!'

'Look!' cried Kaz, pointing to the frozen explosion that hung above them.

At first Henry could not make out what he was supposed

to be looking at, then he saw it. The fire and smoke were moving, almost imperceptibly – the ceiling was exploding very, very slowly.

'It could go completely at any moment,' said the professor.

The machine gave another loud bang and, as Henry watched, the explosion sped up slightly.

The bang also had an effect on his wife, who jerked suddenly and violently on the floor, as if going into a fit. Henry knelt beside her and held her hand, frantic with worry.

She thrashed about with her arms and he was forced to let go of her hand. Instead he reached out and grabbed her head, turning it to face his, hoping the sight of him might calm her. The panic and fear in her eyes made his blood run cold – did she not recognise him? What had they done to her?

'My love,' he said, stroking her cheek. 'It is I, your husband. It's Hank, sweetheart.'

Gradually her vision seemed to clear and he saw the recognition in her eyes.

'Hank?' she whispered. 'What happened?'

He helped her to her feet and then removed his jacket and draped it around her naked shoulders, pulling it tight and zipping it up for her.

'I don't know,' he said, studying her face. It seemed younger to him. The faint blemishes and barely perceptible unnatural creases caused by her surgery had gone. Was this truly his wife?

'Step away from her, Henry,' said Dora from behind him.

Henry turned and was amazed to see Jana, Dora and Kaz all standing in a line, all holding guns aimed at his wife.

He turned to face them and pulled Quil behind him, shielding her with his body.

'What are you doing?' he asked, so very confused.

'Yes,' yelled the professor from over by the smoking machine. 'What are you doing? We need to get out of here!'

But the three young people facing Henry did not react to this entreaty. They stayed steady, guns aimed.

'Quil!' yelled Jana, her face inexplicably screwed up in grief. 'Do you recognise this man?'

'Of course I do,' spat his wife from behind him. 'He's my husband. What is this place? What have you done to me?'

Jana bowed her head and Henry realised, to his amazement, that she was crying, even as she kept her gun levelled straight at him and his wife.

'We can end this right now,' said Kaz.

'I agree,' said Jana, looking up, her tear-streaked face a mask of fury.

There was a beat, but Dora did not chime in as they had obviously expected her to.

'Dora?' said Jana.

'I don't know,' said Dora. 'This isn't what I expected.'

'What did you expect?' yelled Jana. 'What haven't you told us?'

Dora held Henry's gaze for a moment, and he could see that there was a question in her eyes that he couldn't answer. After a moment, she nodded.

'Very well,' she said.

'Please, no,' said Henry, as it dawned on him that he and Quil were standing in front of a firing squad. But he saw no pity or mercy in their eyes.

He turned and clasped Quil tight in his arms, burying his face in her neck and squeezing his eyes closed as he waited for death.

All the hatred that burned in Kaz's chest felt like a tight ball of fire as he aimed his gun at Henry Sweetclover's head. All he needed to do was squeeze the trigger and the people who had conspired to murder him, his friends and his mother would be gone for good.

He began to squeeze the trigger, slowly, gently – if asked, he would have been unable to tell you whether he was hesitating out of reluctance to commit cold-blooded murder, or a desire to extend the moment of sweet revenge as long as possible.

And then his mother burned into existence right in front of him, staring down the barrel of his gun.

She was literally smoking, her clothes in tatters, hair wild, face streaked with soot. The smell of the Beirut car bomb washed over Kaz once more, triggering an overwhelming rush of traumatic memories that froze him, just for a second, in stunned disbelief.

A second was all Sweetclover needed.

He stepped forward and smoothly wrapped his arms round Peyvand, bracing one hand against her temple and the other against her neck, before stepping back to keep his wife sheltered behind him.

'Where am I?' screamed Peyvand. 'Who is that? Kaz? Kaz?'

Kaz realised that she could not see, her eyes still blinded by the flash of the car bomb explosion.

She struggled in Sweetclover's grip, but he was too strong.

'Yes, Mum, it's me,' said Kaz, lowering his gun as calmly as he was able and waving for the others to do the same.

'Peyvand, stop struggling,' said Dora as she lowered his weapon, her voice full of firm authority.

Kaz's mother did as she was bid, but her breathing was ragged, her eyes stared madly and she was visibly shaking.

Another small explosion sounded through the doors.

'We have to go. Now,' pleaded Kairos. 'The bubble is about to burst, that warhead will impact and this whole house will be destroyed.'

Jana deposited her gun on the floor and stood upright. Kaz could see Dora doing likewise, but somehow he couldn't bring himself to lower his weapon.

'Kaz,' said Dora, his name a warning. 'Kaz, drop the gun.'

Kaz held his aim, breathing hard, so angry that he was shaking with it. Sweetclover met Kaz's gaze and there was a resolve in his eyes that Kaz did not doubt. He lowered his gun but, unlike his friends, he put his in his pocket. He would get his chance, sooner or later.

Quil stepped out from behind her husband as soon as Kaz's hand was empty.

'Kick your guns to me,' she said briskly.

Jana and Dora did so.

'Good,' said Quil, bending down and picking one up. 'Now finally, perhaps I can be free of you.'

She raised her gun and pointed it to the left of Dora, who stood at the far left of the group. She pulled the trigger and a white-hot beam shot out. She swept it sideways, towards her husband's one-time servant.

Quil was intending to kill them all.

'No,' cried Kaz, scrabbling in his pocket for his gun.

Perhaps it was the threat to her son, perhaps she simply regained her composure, but Peyvand screamed in rage, grabbed Sweetclover's arm and pushed it upwards, throwing off his grip, turning towards her captor and head-butting him.

He staggered sideways, knocking into Quil and throwing her aim off.

The upward curve of the beam sliced through Dora's hair but missed her flesh. She moved forward to intervene, as did Kaz, but before they could take a step, the struggle was over.

Sweetclover staggered backwards away from Peyvand, his nose spraying blood . . .

. . . Quil, unbalanced by him, lurched sideways, her gun arm going wild, trigger still depressed, beam still lancing out wildly . . .

. . . cutting straight into Peyvand's shoulder with a terrible hiss.

It took only a millionth of a second for the beam to slice from her clavicle through her ribs and spine and burn free through her hip.

Peyvand gave a terrible scream that strangled off into silence as her top half slid stickily sideways and fell to the floor.

Sweetclover was still falling backwards when Quil grabbed him and together they vanished into time with a flash of red fire.

There was no time to react, to scream, to cry, to run. No time for anything. Time stopped.

Literally.

Kaz felt time slow around him as if he was an insect stuck within air that was thickening like sap into amber.

A glow, fierce and terrible, emanated from outside the room, from the place above the bubble where the warhead of the timebomb pushed against their thin protection. The very fabric of reality seemed to warp and fold, coruscating waves of light burst across them, but their sightless eyes registered nothing.

Then there was only noise and light and heat as the quantum bubble collapsed, the warhead slammed into the ground and Sweetclover Hall, and everything in it, was vaporised.

Epilogue: Cornwall, England, 7 April 2158, 8:21 A.M. – 1 min to timebomb impact

The morning air was cool and crisp. The sky was blue and it buzzed with insects and birdsong as Quil and Sweetclover appeared in a flash of flame on a high ridge that looked down into a familiar valley.

Both dressed in combat gear, carrying weapons, they looked out of place in such a rural idyll.

'There,' said Quil, pointing down at the old house that lay about a mile away and at least a hundred metres below.

'It has hardly changed,' said Sweetclover, holding binoculars to his eyes. 'How old is my home now?'

Quil closed her eyes as she did the calculation. 'Five hundred and thirty-nine years.'

'Incredible,' he breathed.

'Up!' said Quil urgently, and Sweetclover lowered his binoculars and looked up into the sky. It took a moment to find what she was pointing out, but then he picked out the missile. It seemed to hang there silently, growing larger at an almost leisurely pace until suddenly there was a huge flash and it began to arc down from heaven trailing fire and smoke, screaming towards the house his father had built. The sonic boom hit them just as the missile impacted, knocking them off their feet.

Sweetclover had been expecting an explosion, flame and fire and smoke. But there was none of that. In fact there was only silence once the sonic shockwave of the missile's descent had passed over them. He sat up warily, looking down into the valley.

Where his house had stood for so many centuries there was now only a crater, deep and round, with glass-smooth edges.

'Come on,' said Quil, and she began to walk down to the site of the impact.

It only took ten minutes to reach the crater. As they stood on the lip, Sweetclover heard a cracking sound from within it and peered into its depths.

The smooth glass surface at the very bottom of the crater cracked and fell away into an even greater depth. And out of the hole crawled something that had once been a man. Then another, then another. Within a minute, the creatures of Quil's new army were streaming up from the depths, climbing the walls of the crater in their black outfits, weapons strapped across their backs. Without a word being spoken they began to fall into ranks, forming up square, at attention, facing Quil, who stood before them, arms behind her back, the very embodiment of military authority.

'It worked, my love,' said Sweetclover. 'All your enemies have been vanquished, all obstacles overcome. All your plans have led to this. You have regained your free will.'

Quil turned to him and smiled. She reached out, grabbed his chin and pulled him forward into a passionate kiss.

When they broke, she turned to the army, the members of which continued to pour from the ground like a horde of hungry golems.

She took a deep breath and gave the order she had waited decades to give.

'Kill *everything*!'

Acknowledgements

This was a toughie, and it wouldn't be in your hands if my editor, Anne Perry, hadn't gone *way* above and beyond in her efforts to help me beat it into shape. My agent, Oli Munson, also helped enormously by ensuring I didn't have to worry about any of that complicated business stuff.

There have been many people whose support has been invaluable, including but not exclusively, Sophia MacDougall, Justin Rowles and Jason Arnopp, as well as all my colleagues at the 9–5 job I had while this book was being written – Graham, Hannah, Andrzej, Lizzy and Michael.

Last but not least I owe endless thanks to my wife, without whom I'd be a shambling, half-dressed, muttering mess with feral children.

And now, back to the flowcharts to wrap this saga up!

Enjoyed this book?
Want more?

Head over to

CHAPteR 5

for extra author content,
exclusives, competitions – and lots
and lots of book talk!

Our motto is
'Proud to be bookish',

because, well, we are ☺

See you there . . .

f Chapter5Books 🐦 @Chapter5Books